Alexander Macrae

History of the Clan Macrae

With genealogies - With plates, including facsimiles and a map.

Alexander Macrae

History of the Clan Macrae
With genealogies - With plates, including facsimiles and a map.

ISBN/EAN: 9783337390310

Printed in Europe, USA, Canada, Australia, Japan

Cover: Foto ©Andreas Hilbeck / pixelio.de

More available books at **www.hansebooks.com**

HISTORY

OF THE

CLAN MACRAE

WITH GENEALOGIES

BY

THE REV. ALEXANDER MACRAE, B.A.,

CURATE OF ST HELEN'S, BISHOPGATE, LONDON.

"Seallaibh ris a' charraig o'n do ghearradh a mach sibh."
"Look unto the rock whence ye are hewn."

DINGWALL: A. M. ROSS & COMPANY.
1899.

PREFACE.

——:o:——

THE preparation of this History has been prompted by a desire to put on record, before it is too late, the fast diminishing oral and traditional information with which it is still possible, in some degree, to supplement such meagre written records of the Clan Macrae as we happen to possess, and, though it probably contains little which can be of interest to the general reader, yet my purpose will be fulfilled, and my labour amply rewarded, if it proves of interest to the members and connections of the Clan itself.

The work of collecting information was first begun as a recreation during a brief visit to Kintail in August, 1890, when I had the good fortune to make the acquaintance of an excellent folk-lorist and genealogist, the late Mr Alexander Macmillan, Dornie, from whom I received much of the traditional and oral information recorded in this book. By 1893, I had succeeded in collecting sufficient matter for a series of " Notes on the Clan Macrae," which appeared in *The North Star* at intervals between July, 1893, and June, 1896, when the writing of this volume was commenced.

The difficulty of the work was greatly increased by the fact that it was possible to carry it on, only at long intervals during occasional periods of freedom from the labours of an exceptionally busy life. Another great disadvantage was the fact that a large part of the information received from the Country of the Macraes had to be collected by correspondence. I am, therefore, well aware that, though the greatest care has been taken to obtain correct information, and to verify every statement, yet there are undoubtedly many blemishes and defects in the book which might have been avoided if the work had been of a more continuous nature, and if it had been possible for me to have direct oral communication, more freely, with the genealogists and folk-lorists of the Macrae Country.

The genealogical portion of the book, up to page 224, is based mainly upon the MS. History of the Clan, written by the Rev. John Macrae, of Dingwall, about two hundred years ago, including the additions made to it by various transcribers down to about the year 1820. In the case of several families the genealogy is continued down to the present time, from family Bibles, family letters, registers, and other sources of information, and where there are continuations from oral sources great care has been taken in selecting the names and particulars to be included, and much matter has been left out because it could not be sufficiently authenticated and confirmed to warrant its publication. The result is that a great many families are incomplete, but there are very few genealogies of which this cannot be said.

In any case, omissions are a less evil than mistakes,
and my endeavour throughout the book has been,
as far as possible, to be correct in my information,
however meagre it might be.

The Roman numerals up to page 234 represent
in every case the number of generations from Fionnla
Dubh Mac Gillechriosd, the reputed founder of the
Clan Macrae of Kintail, and it is hoped that the
genealogical portions of the book are otherwise
arranged clearly enough to be easily followed.

A controversy has recently arisen as to which
family contains the lineal representation of Fionnla
Dubh Mac Gillechriosd. Such controversies are far
from uncommon in old families, even when for many
generations they have possessed estates and titles to
which the lineal succession has always been recorded
with greater care than was ever done in the case of
any family of the Macraes. The lineal succession of
Fionnla Dubh Mac Gillechriosd is usually held to
be in the Inverinate family, and that is the opinion
of the Kintail genealogists whom I have had the
opportunity of consulting.

At the same time, the lineal representation of
the founder of the Clan is claimed by two other
families. The Macraes of Conchra claim, on the
strength of family traditions and old family letters,
that the founder of their branch of the Clan, the
Rev. John Macrae of Dingwall (page 142), and not
Alexander of Inverinate (page 69), was the eldest
son of the Rev. Farquhar Macrae of Kintail.

The Torlysich family, again, claim that their
progenitor, Farquhar (page 186), was the eldest son

of Christopher (IV.), Constable of Ellandonan (page 24), and that the reason why John of Killin refused to give Farquhar the post of Constable (page 28) was, that the appointment of the eldest son to a post formerly held by his father might lead the Macraes to regard the office of Constable as hereditary in their own family, and that they might thus become inconveniently powerful for the Mackenzie family, which at that time was small and comparatively unimportant.

In all the copies of the Rev. John Macrae's history that I have seen, Duncan, the first of the family who settled at Inverinate (page 30), is stated to have been older than his brother Farquhar, and Alexander of Inverinate is stated to have been the eldest son of the Rev. Farquhar Macrae of Kintail; and as the Rev. John Macrae's MS. history formed the chief written authority at my disposal, I have felt justified in continuing the genealogy of the Inverinate family as the direct lineal representatives of Fionnla Dubh Mac Gillechriosd.

It might seem hardly worth while recording some of the lists of names given, without dates or any other particulars, in the genealogical portions of the book, but no such list has been given without satisfactory reasons for believing it to be correct, as far as it goes. Some of those lists will probably be recognised, as their own families, by readers in the Colonies and also in the United States, where the descendants of Macrae emigrants from Kintail are both numerous and prosperous, and the interest taken by some of them in the preparation of this

book shows that they have not yet lost the traditions
of their Clan or forgotten the home of their fathers.

It is hoped the Appendices will add somewhat
to the interest of the book.   Very much more might
have been written about Kintail did space permit,
and for the same reason the collection of poetry is
much smaller than was originally intended.   The
Royal descents in Appendix F are given on the
authority of Burke's genealogical publications, and
various Mackenzie genealogies.   It has not been
found possible to identify all the place names in
Appendices H and M, probably because of the way
they are spelled, but though the spelling of the
original documents has been in almost every case
retained, most of the names will be easily recognised.

It is needless to say that this book could not have
been written without the help of many generous
friends, some of whom are no longer within reach of
this expression of my gratitude—among them Sir
William Alexander Mackinnon, K.C.B., Captain
Archibald Macra Chisholm, Mr Alexander Mackenzie,
the Clan Historian, and Mr Alexander Matheson,
shipowner, Dornie, one of the best read and most
intelligent of Highland seannachies, whose acquaintance it was my misfortune not to have made until only
a few weeks before his death, which occurred on the
14th of October, 1897.   In addition to the help
acknowledged from time to time throughout the book,
I am specially indebted to Mrs Mackenzie of Abbotsford Park, Edinburgh (now of Portobello), for much
information and help, and for many interesting recol-
lections of more than one Kintail family ; to Mrs

Alister MacLellan (of Ardintoul); to Mrs Farquhar
Finlayson, Rothesay; to Major John MacRae-Gilstrap
of Ballimore, who was one of the first to take an
interest in this work, and who, in addition to old
family papers, placed also at my disposal a large
quantity of material collected at his own expense in
the Register House, Edinburgh; to Sir James Dixon
Mackenzie of Findon, Bart., for the use of old and
interesting documents in his possession; to Mr
William Mackay of Craigmonie, Inverness, for much
help, given on many occasions, with a readiness and
kindness, which to me will always form a pleasant
recollection; to Mr Horatio Ross Macrae of Clunes
for the fac-simile of signatures to the Macrae-Campbell
Bond of Friendship, as well as for the use of documents bearing on the history of the Inverinate
family; to the Rev. Donald Macrae, B.D., minister
of Lairg, for much help and many valuable suggestions; to Professor Donald Mackinnon, M.A.,
Edinburgh, for information about the Fernaig MS.,
and for valuable suggestions about the extracts from
it in Appendix J; to Mr Charles Fraser-Mackintosh,
LL.D., of Drummond, for the Kintail Rent Roll of
1756 in Appendix H; to Mr John H. Dixon of
Inveran for Appendix K; to Mr P. J. Anderson,
librarian of Aberdeen University, for Appendix L;
to Mr Alexander Macbain, M.A., Inverness, for the
fac-simile page of the Fernaig MS.; to Mr Farquhar
Macrae, Dornie; to Dr Donald Macrae, Beckenham;
to Major Frederick Bradford McCrea, London; to
Lieutenant-Colonel J. H. Carteret Carey of Castle
Carey, Guernsey; to Mr Farquhar Matheson, Dornie,

who prepared the map, which is interesting as recording some old Kintail place-names now no longer in use; to my brother, Mr John Macrae, for help in the transcription of old documents; to my mother for help in the translations given in Appendix J; and to the publisher, Mr A. M. Ross, and his foreman, Mr John Gray, not only for putting up with inconveniences and delays caused by the fact that, in almost every case, the proofs were sent for revision to some members of the families whose histories are here recorded, but more especially for the never-failing courtesy and kindness which have made the passing of the book through the press a work of interest and pleasure.

ALEXANDER MACRAE.

WANDSWORTH COMMON, LONDON,
15th March, 1899.

SUBSCRIBERS.

——:o:——

Anderson, Provost John N., Stornoway.
Bain, James, Public Library, Toronto, Canada.
Bignold, Arthur, of Lochrosque.
Burns, T. H. S., solicitor, Dingwall.
Burns, William, of Drummondhill, Inverness.
Cameron, J., accountant, National Bank, Dingwall.
Campbell, A. D., sen., J.P., Cape Colony.
Carey, Lieutenant-Colonel J. H. Carteret, Castle Carey, Guernsey.
Chisholm, George S., Dingwall.
Chisholm, Mrs Maria F., of Glassburn.
Cole, Mrs George Ward, St Ninian's, Bay Street, Melbourne,
    Australia.
Colquhoun, Sir James, of Luss, Bart.
Cran, John, Bunchrew.
Davidson, Major N., of Cantray.
Douglas, Hugh Beaton, Montana, U.S.A.
Ferguson, R. C. Munro, of Novar, Raith, Kirkcaldy.
Finlayson, Mrs F., Achamore Park, Rothesay, Bute.
Fletcher, J. Douglas, Roschaugh House.
Fraser, Alexander, solicitor, Inverness.
Fraser, George, Rondebosch, Strathpeffer.
Fraser-Mackintosh, C., LL.D., of Drummond, Inverness.
Hawes, Mrs, 2 Victoria Mansions, Western Parade, Southsea.
Hood, George, Corporation Buildings, Glasgow.
Kennedy, Miss Adelaide, 71 Great King Street, Edinburgh.
Largo, Count de Serra, of Tarlogie.
Macbain, Alexander, M.A., Raining School, Inverness.
Macdonald, H. L., of Dunach.
Macdonald, Lachlan, of Skeabost.
Macdonald, Peter, Carlton Place, Glasgow.

Macgregor, Duncan, "Glengyle," Victoria, Australia.

Macintyre, Malcolm, Imperial Hotel, Stornoway.

Mackay, John, 9 Blythswood Drive, Glasgow.

Mackay, William, Craigmonie, Inverness.

Mackenzie, Andrew, of Dalmore, Alness.

Mackenzie, Æneas, Stornoway.

Mackenzie, Duncan, Royal Hotel, Stornoway.

Mackenzie, George, Scaforth Lodge, Ballifeary, Inverness.

Mackenzie, Mrs Isabella, 2 East Brighton Crescent, Portobello.

Mackenzie, Sir James D., of Findon, Bart., 15 Redcliffe Square, London, S.W.

Mackenzie, William, Crofters Commission, 6 Parliament Square, Edinburgh.

Mackenzie, W. D., of Farr, Inverness.

Mackinnon, Duncan, London.

Maclellan, Mrs Alister, Ellensdale, Craigmore, Rothesay.

Maclennan, A., Lienassie, Stromeferry.

Maclennan, Alexander, Craig, Auchnashellach.

Maclennan, The Hon. Justice, Canada.

Macrae, Alexander, Applecross.

Macrae, Alexander, Belfast.

Macrae, Alexander, Bristol.

Macrae, Alexander, Edinburgh.

Macrae, Alexander, Inshegra School, Kinlochbervie, Lairg.

Macrae, Alexander, Ledgown, Achnasheen.

Macrae, Alexander, 46 Lady Menzies' Place, Edinburgh.

Macrae, Alexander, 1 Leopold Place, Dingwall.

Macrae, Alexander, London.

Macrae, Alexander, Napier, New Zealand.

Macrae, Alexander A., Winton, Southland, New Zealand.

Macrae, Alexander Fraser, Gelantipy, Victoria, Australia.

Macrae, A. H., Macrae, Georgia, U.S.A.

Macrae, Bailie John, Dingwall.

Macrae, Captain Alexander Gordon, 4th Argyle and Sutherland Highlanders (late 93rd).

Macrae, Charles Colin, M.A., Barrister-at-Law, London.

Macrae, Christina, Melbourne.

Macrae, Christopher, Carr, Kintail.

Macrae, Colin George (of Inverinate), W.S., Edinburgh. (5 Copies.)

Macrae, Donald, Gelantipy, Victoria, Australia.

Macrae, Donald, Anderston, Glasgow.

Macrae, Donald, Wilmington, North Carolina, U.S.A.

Macrae, Donald, M.D., Council Bluffs, Iowa, U.S.A.

Macrae, Donald, Violet Villa, Tewkesbury Road, Cheltenham.

Macrae, Douglas Gordon, London.

Macrae, Dr Charles M., Stornoway.

Macrae, Dr Donald, J.P., The Firs, Beckenham, Kent.

Macrae, Dr Farquhar, Alness.

Macrae, Dr John Farquhar, Portland House, Charleville Road, West Kensington, London, W.

Macrae, Duncan, Belfast.

Macrae, Duncan, Brockton, Massachussetts, U.S.A.

Macrae, Duncan, J.P., Ardintoul, Stromeferry.

Macrae, Duncan, J.P., D.L. (of Conchra), Kames Castle, Bute.

Macrae, Duncan, J.P., of Strathgarve, Queensland.

Macrae, Duncan, Salen Hotel, Salen, Aros, Mull.

Macrae, Duncan, Taranaki, New Zealand.

Macrae, E. Farquhar, Macon, Georgia, U.S.A.

Macrae, Farquhar, Hawke Bay, New Zealand.

Macrae, Finlay, Montana, U.S.A.

Macrae, Finlay A., London.

Macrae, G., G.P.O., Inverness.

Macrae, G. A., 1 Johnhouse Buildings, Lothbury, London, S.E.

Macrae, George Hay, Saint Paul, Minnesota, U.S.A.

Macrae, George P., 425 West Baltimore Street, Baltimore, U.S.A.

Macrae, Horatio Ross, W.S., of Clunes.

Macrae, Hugh, Edinburgh.

Macrae, Hugh, 27 Lansdowne Crescent, Glasgow.

Macrae, Hugh, Wilmington, North Carolina, U.S.A.

Macrae, J., Berwickshire County Council, Dunse.

Macrae, J., Salen, Aros, Mull.

Macrae, J. F., Fernaig, Lochalsh.

Macrae, James, Lewis Street, Stornoway.

Macrae, James, London.

Macrae, James, M.A., M.D., C.M., Huntly.

Macrae, James, of Ure & Macrae, 81 Bath Street, Glasgow.

Macrae, James, 242 Westgate Road, Newcastle.

Macrae, James Davidson, J.P., Killin.

Macrae, John Alexander, Niagara Falls, Canada.

Macrae, John, Beaverton, Ontario, Canada.

Macrae, John, Edinburgh.

Macrae, John, Ellangowan, Chambers Crescent, Edinburgh.

Macrae, John, Suffolk County, U.S.A.

Macrae, John, Glennaig, Auchnashellach.

Macrae, Kenneth, C.E., Oban.

Macrae, Kenneth, Fairview, Ravenhill Road, Belfast.

Macrae, Kenneth, Portree.

Macrae, Kenneth F., Dayville Grant Coy., Oregon, U.S.A.

Macrae, Kenneth Stuart (Conchra), Newark-on-Trent.

Macrae, Lieutenant Colin William (Conchra), The Black Watch.

Macrae, Lieutenant J. H., Fort Snelling, Minnesota, U.S.A.

Macrae, Lieutenant-Colonel Roderick, Dacca, Bengal, India.
     (2 Copies.)

Macrae, Max. L., Macrae, Felfair County, Georgia, U.S.A.

Macrae, Milton A., Cincinnatti, U.S.A.

Macrae, Mrs M. W., Edinburgh.

Macrae, Murdo, of Kinbeachie, Conon.

Macrae, Murdoch, Gairloch.

Macrae, Peter, Dundonnell.

Macrae, Rev. Alexander, F.C. Manse, Clachan, Kintyre.

Macrae, Rev. David, Morag, Maxwell Park, Glasgow.

Macrae, Rev. Donald, B.D., The Manse, Lairg.

Macrae, Rev. Duncan, Wood Green, London.

Macrae, Rev. Godfrey W. B., Cross, Stornoway.

Macrae, Rev. James Duncan, Manse of Contin.

Macrae, Rev. Roderick, Carloway, Lews.

Macrae, Roderick, Gladstone House, Beauly.

Macrae, Roderick, Gelantipy, Victoria, Australia.

Macrae, Roderick John, Wandsworth Common, London.

Macrae, Stewart, Victoria, Australia.

Macrae, Stewart (of Conchra), Newark-on-Trent.

Macrae, Thomas G., Prescott, Arkansas, U.S.A.

MacRae-Gilstrap, Major John (Conchra), of Ballimore, Argyleshire
     (late 1st Batt. Black Watch).   (12 Copies.)

MacRae-Gilstrap, John Duncan George, younger of Ballimore.

McCrae, George Gordon, Anchorfield, Lower Hawthorn, Melbourne,
     Australia.

McCrae, Boyd M., Dundee.

McCrae, John, Beechwood, Glasgow.

McCrae, John Morison, Perth, West Australia.

McCrae, Kenneth, London.

McCrae, Lieutenant-Colonel David, Guelph, Canada.

McCrae, William, Berkeley Road, Dublin.

McCrea, B. H. E., M.B., London.

McCrea, Harriet M. (widow of Major-General R. B. McCrea, R.A.), Guernsey.

McCrea, Major Frederick Bradford, London (late 8th "The King's" Regiment).   (4 Copies.)

Maine, Mrs N., Melbourne, Australia.

Matheson, Dr Farquhar, J.P., Soho Square, London, W.

Matheson, Farquhar, Dornie.

Matheson, John, M.A., M.D., 14 Gibson Square, London, N.

Matheson, Kenneth, Gledfield, Ardgay.

Mavor, Mrs Ivan, Wandsworth Common, London.

Middleton, W. R. T., solicitor, Dingwall.

Mitchell Library, Glasgow.

Munro, Rev. D., F.C. Manse, Ferintosh.

Nicol, Thomas, Dingwall.

Public Library, Inverness.

Rea, C. F., King Edward's School, Totnes, S. Devon.

Ross, John M., Kelvinside, Glasgow.

Russell, Mrs Madeline, 2 Albert Terrace, Morningside, Edinburgh. (2 Copies.)

Scott, Roderick, solicitor, Inverness.

Stewart, Captain William, of Ensay (91st Highlanders).

Strachan, Sheriff R. M., Glasgow.

Watson, James F., 81 Robertson Street, Greenock.

Yule, Amy Francis, Tarradale House, Muir of Ord.

ADDENDA ET CORRIGENDA: P.113.

line:- {for Kenneth ~~brooks~~ read Kenneth Mackenzie

    1.7. after Jessie, add (See p.116; 1.4.) and
        vice versa.
     12. Before George; add William. And alter
        Sheriff to Sheriff-Substitute.
     13. After John, insert:- Charles Kenneth.(B.
        1889.)
     14. For grandson read Great-nephew.
     16. For Wellington read Washington.
     18. After Troutbeck insert with issue.
        After Kenneth read Alexander; and
     19. Delete"in India." and add "married Rose
        J.Lea, with issue.
     20. After ¯ervice, insert "married Vere ~~Irwin~~
        Irving, with issue. For ¯lmslie read Elm-
        sley.
     21. For David read David Douglas.
     25. For Biera,read Buenos Ayres; formerly at
        Biera. Married and has issue.
     30. After Archibald add May.
PAGE114.
      5. After Miss add Annas S.Broadfoot, niece
        of his sister's husband, Dr A.B.Douglas.

CONTENTS.

—:o:—

CHAPTER I.

CHAPTER II.

CHAPTER III.

CHAPTER IV.

CHAPTER V.

CHAPTER VI.

CHAPTER VII.

CHAPTER VIII.

CHAPTER XIV.

CHAPTER XX.

CHAPTER XXI.

CHAPTER XXII.

APPENDICES.

ADDENDA.

ILLUSTRATIONS.

FORTITUDINE

Macrae.

The Badge of the Macraes was the Fir Club-Moss *(Lycopodium Selago)*;
Gaelic—Garbhag an t-sleibh.

THE HISTORY OF THE CLAN MACRAE.

CHAPTER I.

Country of the Macraes.—Meaning and Probable Origin of the
Name.— Its First Appearance as a Surname.— Traditional
Origin of the Clan Macrae.— Macraes in the Districts of
Clunes and Glenurquhart.—Migration to Kintail.—Campbells
of Craignish said to be of Macrae Origin.—The Connection
of the Macraes with the House of Kintail.—Also with the
House of Gairloch. — The Macraes were Episcopalians and
Jacobites.—Macraes in the Seaforth Regiments.—The Rev.
John Macrae's MS. History of the Clan.

THE Macraes were a small but important clan in the
district of Kintail, in the south-west of the county
of Ross, where they are said to have settled in the
fourteenth century, under the chieftainship of the
Barons Mackenzie of Kintail.

According to the most competent authorities,
the name Macrae or Macrath, as it is written in
Gaelic, means "son of Grace or Luck,"[1] and, so far
as at present known, it occurs first in *The Annals of
the Kingdom of Ireland by the Four Masters*, under

[1] Macbain's Gaelic Dictionary.

A

the year of our Lord 448, a certain "Macraith[1] the
Wise" being mentioned in that year as a member of
the household of St Patrick.   We meet with it
occasionally in Ireland from that date onwards, and
in the eleventh and twelfth centuries it was frequently used in that country as the personal name
of lords, poets, and more especially ecclesiastics.

The name first appears in Scotland at a somewhat later date.   In a Gaelic manuscript of the
eleventh century, called *The Prophecy of Saint
Berchan*, we find the term Macrath applied to one of
the successors of Kenneth Macalpin,—King Gregory
who reigned at Scone during the last quarter of the
ninth century, and was one of the greatest of the
early Scottish Kings.   This seems to be the first
instance of the name Macrae or Macrath in Scotland.
Gregory the Macrath was not only prosperous in
worldly affairs and in his wars against his enemies,
but was also a sincere supporter and benefactor of
the Scottish Church, which he delivered from the
oppression of the Picts, and favoured with his
support and protection.[2]   Considering the meaning
of the name, and the connection in which it first
appears both in Ireland and in Scotland, it is not
unreasonable to suppose that it may have been first
given as a distinguishing personal name to men who
were supposed to be endowed with more than an
ordinary measure of sanctity and grace.   The name
Macrae had thus in all probability an ecclesiastical
origin.

[1] Raith in Macraith is the old genitive form of Rath.

[2] Appendix B.

In a genealogy of the Mackenzies contained in *The Black Book of Clanranald*, we find it stated that Gilleoin of the Aird, from whom the old Earls Gillanders of Ross and the Mackenzies of Kintail are traced, was the son of Macrath (McRrath).[1] Supposing the genealogy to be correct, this Macrath would have lived not earlier than the tenth century. By that time Christianity was fairly established in the Highlands of Scotland, and as the name Gilleoin means the servant of St John, it is not at all unlikely that Macrath also may have been so named from some family connection with the early Church in the Highlands.[2]

The name Macrae (McRaa) occurs also in *The Dean of Lismore's Book* under circumstances which might well have entitled the bearer of it to be called, if not a son of grace, at all events a son of luck.[3]

In those times there were no family or hereditary surnames in this country. Family surnames appear in England about the twelfth century, but it was not until much later that they became common in the Highlands of Scotland. For instance, the surname Mackenzie, which is a comparatively old one, arose in the early part of the fourteenth century. The use of Macrae as a surname is probably of an earlier date than the surname Mackenzie, and that

---

[1] *Reliquiae Celticae*, Vol. II., page 300.

[2] In a Gaelic MS. of 1450, containing genealogies of several Highland families, and published with an English translation in The Transactions of the Iona Club, an ancestor of the Macleans is also mentioned as Gilleoin, son of Macrath (Gilleain mc Icrait). This helps to confirm the tradition mentioned below, that the Macraes, Mackenzies, and Macleans were of the same ancestry, but it is not easy to make anything satisfactory out of those old genealogies.

[3] Appendix B.

it grew in the first instance out of a personal name is evident from the fact that in Gaelic the Macraes are always spoken of as " Clann Mhicrath," that is the " descendants of Macrath."

So far as at present known, the name Macrae is first mentioned as a surname in the year 1386, in an agreement made, at Inverness, between the Bishop of Moray and Alexander Stewart, Earl of Buchan, better known as the Wolf of Badenoch, with regard to some land in Rothiemurchus, in Inverness-shire, which was formerly occupied by a certain Cristinus M'Crath (Christopher Macrae), who was then dead.[1] From that date onwards the name is frequently met with as a surname in various parts of Scotland, not only in the Highlands, but also in Ayrshire and in the south of Perthshire.

Tradition relates that the Macraes came originally from Ireland, and were of common ancestry with the Mackenzies and the Macleans, and it is said that a company of them fought at the battle of Largs in 1263, under the leadership of Colin Fitzgerald, the reputed progenitor of the Mackenzies of Kintail. The Fitzgerald origin of the Mackenzies is now discredited by Scotch historians; but, whatever their origin may have been, it is extremely probable that the Macraes were in some way connected with the same stock, as a strong friendship and alliance existed between the two clans from early traditional times, and continued without intermission so long as the Mackenzies held the ancestral lands of Kintail. The Macraes who settled in Kintail are said to have

---

[1] *Registrum Episcopatus Moraviensis* (Bannatyne Club), page 196.

lived originally at Clunes, on the Lordship of Lovat, near the southern shore of the Beauly Firth, where the site on which stood the house of their chief is still pointed out.[1] So far as the date to which these traditions refer can be fixed, this would be about the middle of the thirteenth century. It is also said that the name was known in Glenurquhart[2] in the twelfth century, which is an earlier date than can well be assigned to any traditions that have come down to us with regard to the settlement at Clunes, but there appear to be no existing traditions connecting the origin of the Macraes of Kintail with the district of Glenurquhart. There are, however, many traditions connecting them with the district of Clunes, and explaining the cause of the migration to Kintail.[3]

According to the Rev. John Macrae, the most probable cause of the migration of the Macraes to Kintail, or, at all events, of that branch of them which afterwards became the most important, was that, though they do not appear to have been very numerous, they were becoming too crowded in the old home at Clunes. At the same time Lovat's own kindred and friends were becoming so numerous that the country could not accommodate them all,

[1] The site of Macrae's house (Larach tigh Mhicrath) is on the southern slope of the Hill of Clunes, and is marked by a number of large stones, which are supposed to have formed the foundations of the house. Tradition says that the house was originally built in the course of one night by supernatural agencies, and the place has always been regarded as a favourite haunt of the fairies.

[2] Mackay's Urquhart and Glenmoriston, p. 12 ; and also the Rev. John Macrae's Account of the Origin of the Macraes, Appendix A.

[3] See chapter on legends and traditions of the clan, and Appendix A.

and this was an additional reason for the Macraes
to move to other places, as favourable opportunities
arose.   Three of the sons of Macrae of Clunes are
said to have left home in this way, but the old man
himself remained in Clunes all his days, enjoying
the esteem and confidence of the Lords of Lovat,
four of whom were fostered in his house.   Of these
three brothers, one settled at Brahan, near Dingwall,
where there was a piece of land in the time of the
Rev. John Macrae, called Cnoc Mhicrath (Macrae's
Hill), and the well which supplied Brahan Castle
with water at that time was called Tobair Mhicrath
(Macrae's Well).   The descendants of this man were
then to be found in Strathgarve, Strathbran,
Strathconon, Ardmeanach, and one of them, John
Macrae, was at that time a merchant at Inverness.

Another son went to Argyleshire, where he
married the heiress of Craignish. His successors afterwards adopted the name Campbell, and maintained a
friendly intercourse with the Macraes of Kintail for
many generations.   A contract of friendship, drawn
up between the Campbells of Craignish and the
Macraes of Kintail about two hundred years ago,
has been kept in the family of Macrae of Inverinate
ever since, and is now in the possession of Horatio
Ross Macrae, Esq. of Clunes.[1]

Another of the sons of Macrae of Clunes is said
to have gone to Kintail.   This was probably during
the first half of the fourteenth century, before the
family of Mackenzie was very firmly established
there.   He might have been attracted to Kintail,

[1]Appendix C.

perhaps by family connections, but quite as likely by the fact that, as the Chief of Kintail was still struggling to establish his family there, the circumstances of the country might afford opportunities of distinction and advancement for a man of enterprise. It is a singular fact that each of the first five Barons of Kintail had only one lawful son to succeed him. Mackenzie being thus without any male kindred of his own blood, earnestly urged Macrae to remain with him in Kintail. Mackenzie's proposals were accepted, and Macrae settled in Kintail, where he married one Macbeolan or Gillanders, a kinswoman of the Earls of Ross, by whom Kintail was held before it came into the possession of the Mackenzies. As the Macraes and Mackenzies were said to be of common ancestry, the Baron of Kintail expected loyal and faithful support from his newly arrived kinsman, and he was not disappointed. The Macraes were ever foremost in the cause of the chiefs of Kintail, and by their prowess in battle, their industry in the arts of peace, and in many instances by their scholarly culture and refinement, they were mainly instrumental in raising the Barony of Kintail, afterwards the Earldom of Seaforth, to the important position it occupies in the annals of Scottish history.

There do not appear to have been any Macraes settled in Kintail as landholders before this, but it is more than probable that several of them had already been in the service of Mackenzie. It is said that Ellandonan Castle was garrisoned by Macraes and Maclennans during the latter part of the thirteenth century, when it was first taken possession

of by Kenneth, the founder of the House of Kintail.[1]
The newly arrived Macrae of Clunes, however, took
precedence of the others, and he and his family
gradually assumed a position of great importance in
the affairs of Kintail. So loyal were the Macraes
in the service of Kintail that they became known as
Mackenzie's "shirt of mail." This term was generally
applied to the chosen body who attended a chief in
war and fought around him. It would thus appear
that the bodyguard of the Barons of Kintail was
usually composed of Macraes. But in addition to
the important services they rendered as mere
retainers of the House of Kintail, the Macraes were
for many generations Chamberlains of Kintail, Con-
stables of Ellandonan Castle, and sometimes Vicars
of Kintail, so that the leading members of the Clan
may be said to have taken, from time to time, a
much more prominent part in the affairs of Kintail
than the Barons themselves did. This continued to
be the case until Kintail passed out of the possession
of the Mackenzies in the early part of the present
century.

It was always the privilege of the Macraes to
bear the dead bodies of the Barons of Kintail to
burial. At the funeral, in 1862, of the Honourable
Mrs Stewart Mackenzie, daughter and representative of the last Lord Seaforth, the coffin was
borne out of Brahan Castle by Macraes only.[2] The
scene was not without a pathetic and historic

---

[1] Appendix E.

[2] On this occasion the coffin was first lifted by Donald John Macrae of
Inversheil, Donald Macrae of Achnagart, Peter Macrae of Morvich, and
Ewen Macrae of Leachachan.

interest. This lady was the last of Seaforth's race, who was a Mackenzie by birth, and it is a remarkable fact that at the funeral, in 1881, of her son, Colonel Keith William Stewart Mackenzie, in whose case the name Mackenzie was only an adopted one, the Macraes, although they claimed their old privilege, did not muster a sufficient number to bear the coffin, and the vacant places had to be supplied by the Brahan tenantry. With the funeral of Mrs Stewart Mackenzie, then, may be said to have ended for ever the intimate and loyal connection which existed for five centuries between the Macraes and the house of Kintail and Seaforth.

But the loyal and valiant support which the Macraes gave the Mackenzies was not limited to the house of Kintail. They were mainly instrumental also in establishing the family of Gairloch. About 1480 Allan Macleod, laird of Gairloch, with his two young sons, was barbarously murdered by his own two brothers. His wife was a daughter of Alexander Ionraic (Alexander the Just), sixth Baron of Kintail, who died about 1490, and sister of Hector Roy Mackenzie, a younger son, who became progenitor of the lairds of Gairloch. Hector Roy took up the cause of his sister, and obtained from the King a commission of fire and sword for the destruction of the Macleods of Gairloch. In this task, which proved by no means easy, Hector received his main support from the Macraes, one of whom had meanwhile encountered the two murderers and killed them both single-handed in fair fight at a spot in Gairloch, which is still pointed

out.[1] In 1494 Hector Roy received a grant of
Gairloch by charter from the Crown, but it was
not until the time of his grandson, John Roy
(1566-1628) that the Macleods were finally expelled, and the supremacy of the Mackenzies fully
established.

It was in Gairloch that the Mackenzies obtained
their first important footing outside of Kintail. At
that time they were only a small clan, and the
struggle which led to the conquest of Gairloch
taxed all their strength, and was both fierce and
prolonged. Hence the great number of legends and
traditions connected with it. After the conquest of
Gairloch their power and influence rapidly increased,
and the other lands which they afterwards held
in the counties of Ross and Cromarty came into
their possession by easier and more peaceful means.
Consequently there are no such stirring traditions
in connection with the acquisition of those other
lands as we find in the case of Gairloch, but
wherever the Mackenzies settled some Macraes
accompanied them, and some of the descendants
of these Macraes are still to be found on all the
old Mackenzie estates. It is in Gairloch, however,
next to Kintail and Lochalsh, that we find the
best and most interesting Macrae traditions and
legends, and it may be mentioned that one of the
Gairloch Macraes, called Domhnull Odhar[2] (Sallow
Donald), who was a contemporary of John Roy, is
represented as the crest of the Gairloch coat-of-arms.
The Macraes were also very renowned archers, and

1 J. H. Dixon's Gairloch, p. 26.   2 Appendix K.

the scene and range of some of their famous shots are still pointed out, both in Gairloch and Kintail.[1]

During the long period of religious and civil warfare which preceded and followed the Revolution of 1688, the Macraes supported the Episcopal Church and the House of Stuart, and as a result they suffered much, not only in property, but also in life and limb. In the Rising of 1715 a great many of them fell at the battle af Sheriffmuir, and tradition relates, as a proof of the loss they then sustained, that in the parish of Kintail alone fifty-eight women were made widows on that fatal day. In 1745, notwithstanding the fact that Seaforth[2] remained loyal to the House of Hanover, a number of young and resolute Macraes left Kintail to join the army of Prince Charles, and it is said that many more would have followed if they had not been restrained by force. Of those who went no one ever again returned, and thus ended for ever their connection as a Clan with the fortunes of the ancient Scottish House of Stuart.

During the closing decades of the last century, when the Highland regiments were raised, the Macraes entered loyally and readily into the military service of their country. Two regiments (in all four battalions) of Highlanders were raised on

---

[1] Appendix K.

[2] William, 5th Earl of Seaforth, having joined the Rising of 1715, his estates were forfeited, and his title passed under attainder. The estates were bought from the Crown in 1741 for the benefit of his son, Kenneth, who was known by the courtesy title of Lord Fortrose, which was the subordinate title of the Earls of Seaforth. Lord Fortrose was the "Seaforth" of the time of Prince Charles, but, notwithstanding his well-known Jacobite sympathies, he considered it more prudent to remain loyal to the House of Hanover.

the Seaforth estates between 1778 and 1804,[1] and the Macraes were numerous in both. Many of them served also as officers, and frequently with distinction, in other Highland regiments, and during the Indian wars of that period, and the great European wars which followed the French Revolution, the Macraes, like so many of the other Highland Clans, added their full share of lustre to the honour of British Arms.

The chief written authority for the early history of the Macraes is the MS. genealogy of the Clan, which was written towards the close of the seventeenth century by the last Episcopalian minister of Dingwall, the Rev. John Macrae, who died in 1704. The original MS., which appears to be now lost, is believed, without any apparent evidence, however, to have been at one time in the possession of the late Dr W. F. Skene. A copy of it, with additions, was made by Farquhar Macrae of Inverinate in 1786. This transcript copy appears to have been taken to India by Farquhar's son, Surgeon John Macrae, where a copy of it, which is now in the possession of Captain John MacRae Gilstrap of Ballimore, was made by Colonel Sir John Macra of Ardintoul about 1816. Several copies of Sir John's transcript appear to have been made from time to time in Kintail and Lochalsh, and are still occasionally met with. A copy of it was printed at Camden, South Carolina, in 1874; and another copy, which belonged to the late Miss Flora Macra of Ardintoul, was published in *The Scottish Highlander* in 1887. The additions made

[1] Appendix D.

by Farquhar of Inverinate appear to have been
limited to his own family, and there is some reason
to believe that the valuable additions now found in
some copies of this MS., with regard to other
families, were made by one of the Ardintoul family.
At all events, Archibald of Ardintoul says, in a
letter written in 1817 to his son, Sir John, then
in India, that he will endeavour to add to the
genealogy down to his own day. The oldest copy
now known to exist is in the possession of Horatio
Ross Macrae, Esq. of Clunes, and bears on the fly-
leaf of it the date 1760, but this is probably the
transcript which was made by Farquhar of Inverinate, and which, though said to have been finished
only in 1786, may have been commenced much
earlier. It is certainly not the original copy. The
style of the MS., though somewhat quaint, is clear
and forcible, showing considerable literary power
and a perfect mastery of the English language, and
there is about it a sobriety of tone which gives an
impression that the writer was thoroughly acquainted with his facts, and that his statements
may be accepted with confidence.

CHAPTER II.

I. FIONNLA DUBH MAC GILLECHRIOSD.

According to the Rev. John Macrae, the founder of
the Clan Macrae of Kintail was Fionnla Dubh Mac
Gillechriosd (Black Finlay, the son of Christopher),
who was removed by two or three generations from
the man who came from Clunes. Finlay Dubh was
a contemporary of Murdo Mackenzie, fifth chief of
Kintail, who died in 1416, leaving an only child to
succeed him. This child's name was Alexander, and
is known as Alister Ionraic (Alexander the Upright).
Alexander being a minor at the time of his father's
death, was sent as a ward of the King to the High

School in Perth, probably after the Parliament which
was held at Inverness by James I. in 1427. During
his absence at school, the Constable of Ellandonan
Castle, whose name was Macaulay, appears to have
been left in charge of affairs, but through the
misconduct and oppression of certain illegitimate
relatives of the young chief, serious troubles arose
in Kintail. The Constable's position becoming now
somewhat difficult, he became anxious for the return
of his young master, and as he was himself unable
to leave his post he proposed Finlay Dubh as the
most suitable person to go to Perth to bring the
young chief home, " who was then there with the
rest of the King's ward children." This choice was
approved by the people. Finlay accordingly went
to Perth, and prevailed upon Alexander to escape
from school without the consent or knowledge of the
master. To avoid pursuit they went to Macdougal
of Lorn instead of going straight home. Macdougal
received them kindly, and Alexander made the
acquaintance of his daughter, and afterwards married
her. In due time they arrived in Kintail, and by
Finlay's counsel and help, the oppressors of the
people were soon brought under subjection, and
order established throughout Mackenzie's land. The
good counsel and judicious guidance of Finlay Dubh
was not lost upon Alexander, who became a good,
just, and prosperous ruler, and greatly increased the
power and the influence of the House of Kintail.
Finlay Dubh had two sons—

    1. CHRISTOPHER, of whom below.

    2. JOHN, who was educated at Beauly Priory,

took holy orders, and became priest of Kintail,[1] in Sutherlandshire. He married, as priests in the Highlands often did in those days, and had a daughter Margaret, who was lady-in-waiting to the Countess of Sutherland, and who appears to have married John Gordon of Drummoy, son of Adam Gordon, Dean of Caithness, son of Alexander, 1st Earl of Huntly.[2] From this marriage descended the Gordons of Embo, and for that reason we are told that "there was of old great friendship and correspondence betwixt the Gordons of Sutherland, come of this family, and the Macraes of Kintail."

II. CHRISTOPHER, eldest son of Finlay Dubh, of whom very little is known, had four sons—

1. FINLAY, of whom below.

2. DONALD, whose descendants lived at Fortrose, where one of them, Alexander Macrae, was a well-known writer whose name appears frequently in legal documents from 1629 to 1673.

3. DUNCAN, who was the most noted of Christopher's sons, is known in the traditions of Kintail as Donnacha Mor na Tuagh (Big Duncan of the Battle-axe). He was a man of great valour and personal strength, and many legends have been preserved of the brave deeds he performed in the

---

1 Kintail was the old name of a district in the north-west of Sutherlandshire, which was divided, about the middle of the last century, into the parishes of Tongue and Durness. The name Kintail—Gaelic, *Cintaillc*, or *Ceanntaile*—is said to mean the head of the two seas—a description which applies to the Sutherland Kintail as well as to the Ross-shire one.

2 Reference is made at some length to this Margaret in The Earls of Sutherland by Sir Robert Gordon, who speaks of her in the highest terms. The Rev. John Macrae's account of the marriage does not agree with Sir Robert's in every point, but there is no doubt that Margaret was related to the Macraes of Kintail.

contests of the Mackenzies and the Macraes with
their common enemies. He greatly distinguished
himself with his battle-axe at the Battle of Park,
which was fought at Strathpeffer between the Macdonalds and the Mackenzies shortly before the death
of Alexander Ionraic, which took place in 1488.[1]
The circumstances which led to this famous fight
were the following :—Coinneach à Bhlair (Kenneth
of the Battle), the son and heir of Alexander Ionraic,
had married Margaret, daughter of John Macdonald
of Islay, who laid claim to the lordship of the Isles
and the earldom of Ross.   One Christmas eve
Kenneth was insulted by Alexander Macdonald of
Lochalsh, the nephew and heir of John of Islay.
In revenge for the insult Kenneth sent his wife
back to her father. The lady, who was blind of
one eye, was sent away mounted on a one-eyed
horse, attended by a one-eyed servant, and followed
by a one-eyed dog. John of Islay and Alexander
of Lochalsh, roused to fury by this outrageous
insult, mustered all their followers, to the number
of more than fifteen hundred warriors, and set out
on an expedition to punish the Mackenzies. The
Macdonalds, plundering and destroying as they
went, directed their march to Kinellan, in Strathpeffer, where the Baron of Kintail was then residing.
They arrived at Contin one Sunday morning and
burned the church, together with the priest and a

---

[1] The exact date of the Battle of Park does not appear to be known, the
official records relating to the Highlands at this time being exceedingly
meagre. Sir Robert Gordon, in his History of the Earls of Sutherland, a book
written about the close of the sixteenth century, says it was fought shortly
after 1476.

large congregation of aged men, women, and children, who were worshipping in it at the time.

Meantime, on the approach of the enemy, Kenneth and his two brothers, Duncan and Hector Roy, sent their aged father for safety to the Raven's Rock, a prominent and precipitous hill overhanging the Dingwall and Skye Railway between Strathpeffer and Garve. They then led their followers, who numbered only six hundred men, against the Macdonalds, and the battle was fought on the moor which is still known as Blar-na-Pairc, a well-known spot about a mile west of the Strathpeffer wells. The Mackenzies were led by Kenneth himself, and Alexander of Lochalsh seems to have acted as leader of the Macdonalds, while their chief warrior was Lachlan Maclean of Lochbuy, called Lachlan Mac Thearlaich (Lachlan, son of Charles). Duncan Mor, who was one of the personal attendants of Kenneth, thinking that he had been somewhat slighted in the arrangements made for the battle, showed unmistakable signs of sulkiness. He was persuaded, however, by Hector Roy to take up a battle-axe and join in the fight. With his battle-axe he did so much havoc that the Macdonalds began to give way before him. Lachlan Mac Thearlaich, seeing this, put himself in Duncan's way in order to check his murderous career. The two champions met in deadly combat. Lachlan being a powerful man, clad in mail and well trained in the use of arms, seemed at first to be having the best of the fight, but, in an unguarded moment, he exposed himself to his opponent's battle-axe, which at one deadly stroke severed his head from his body.

The superior strategy of Kenneth was already telling
severely against the much larger army of the enemy,
and the Macdonalds, seeing their champion killed,
gave up the struggle as lost, and fled.   Duncan Mor
took a foremost part in the pursuit, which was continued on the following day as far as Strathconon,
until most of the Macdonalds were either slain or
taken prisoners.   Both John of Islay and his nephew,
Alexander of Lochalsh, were among the prisoners,
but within six months they were both magnanimously
released.   This victory, to which Duncan Mor had
so greatly contributed, "put Kenneth in great respect
throughout the North," and he was afterwards
knighted by James IV. "for being highly instrumental in reducing his fierce countrymen to the
blessings of a civilised life."

Duncan Mor afterwards took a very prominent
and active part in the great feud between Hector
Roy and the Macleods of Gairloch.   We are told
that "Duncan, with his son Dougal, who was a
strong, prudent, and courageous man, with ten or
twelve other Kintail men, were always, upon the
least notice, ready to go and assist Hector whenever,
wherever, and in whatever he had to do, for which
cause there was a friendly correspondence between
the family of Gairloch and the Macraes of Kintail."
The greatest defeat that Hector Roy inflicted on the
Macleods was at the battle of Bealach Glasleathaid
near Kintail.   Both Duncan and his son Dougal took
part in this fight, in the course of which Dougal was
attacked by four men at once.   On being informed
that his son was in great danger, Duncan calmly

replied, "Leave him alone, if he is my son there is no-
fear of him," and so it turned out, for Dougal killed
the four Macleods without receiving any serious hurt
himself.   At the battle of Druim a Chait[1] (the
Cat's Back), which was fought on a subsequent
occasion at the place so called on the west side
of Knockfarrel, in Strathpeffer, between the Mackenzies under Hector Roy, and the Munros, Ding-
walls, and Maccullochs, under Sir William Munro of
Foulis, Duncan once more distinguished himself
and largely contributed to the defeat of the Munros
and their allies, which was so complete that few of
them escaped alive.   "It is said of this Duncan that
he was in many conflicts and combats, and always
came off victorious, but never without a wound.
He was a facetious and yet a bloody man."

Duncan Mor na Tuagh is sometimes spoken of
as Mackenzie's ploughman, but it is not at all likely
that a member of what appears at this time to have
been the leading family in Kintail next to the Baron
himself should occupy such a position.   The Gaelic
term *Scallag*, which in this case has been translated
ploughman, formerly meant any servant or retainer.
In the MS. history of the Mackenzies, which was
written by Rev. John Macrae, author of the Macrae
Genealogy, it is stated that Duncan Mor happened
accidentally to be present the day of the Battle
of Park, on some other business, and that he was the

---

[1] This battle is sometimes called the Battle of Tobair-nan-Ceann (the well
of heads).   It is said that Hector and his men, being armed with battle-axes
and two-edged swords, did so much execution among their enemies that no fewer
than nineteen heads rolled down into a well in a hollow below a spot where
they overtook a party of the enemy during the pursuit—hence the name
Tobair-nan-Ceann.

principal officer of Kintail. Comparing the various traditional and MS. accounts of this remarkable man, perhaps the most natural conclusion to arrive at is that at this time he may have been young and untried; that he first gave proof of his valour and prowess at the Battle of Park, and that he afterwards became either the factor of Kintail or perhaps the principal officer of the Baron's fighting men. It is not at all unlikely that Duncan Mor began his career as a page or personal servant, that is as the *scallag* of Mackenzie, probably of Sir Kenneth à Bhlair, but whatever the commencement of his career may have been, it is quite certain that a man around whose memory so many legends and traditions of a heroic kind have gathered must have been, in spite of possible eccentricities, an important and leading man among his own countrymen.[1]

The male succession of Duncan Mor na Tuagh failed in the person of Duncan Roy Macrae, who died at Conchraig of Tollie in 1679.

4. MAURICE, married and left issue.

III. FINLAY, eldest son of Christopher, was the contemporary and chief counsellor of John of Killin, ninth Baron of Kintail, who fought at Flodden in 1513, and at Pinkie in 1547. John of Killin was a minor at the time of the death of his father, Sir Kenneth à Bhlair, in 1491. He was still a minor when, in consequence of the death of his eldest brother, Kenneth Og (Kenneth the younger), in 1497, he became Baron of Kintail. Kenneth Og

---

1 For a more detailed account of the exploits of Duncan Mor na Tuagh, see chapter on legends and traditions of the clan.

was the only child of Kenneth à Bhlair's first wife, Lady Margaret Macdonald, of whom her husband disposed in the ignominious manner already described.   A few days after sending Lady Margaret away, Kenneth, at the head of a large body of his followers, went to Lord Lovat to demand his daughter, Agnes Fraser, in marriage.   Lord Lovat, having no friendly feeling towards the Macdonalds at that time, delivered his daughter over to Kenneth, and they lived together ever after as husband and wife.   John of Killin was the first issue of this irregular marriage, and although the marriage is said to have been legitimised by the Pope, Hector Roy declared his nephew, John of Killin, illegitimate, and seized the estates for himself.   Hector being a well known and a very popular man, appears to have received all but the unanimous support of the people of Kintail, and one of the Clann Ian Charrich Macraes, called Malcolm, was made Constable of Ellandonan Castle.   Finlay, however, took up the cause of John of Killin, between whose supporters and those of Hector Roy there arose a feud which lasted for some years.

In course of time, however, John of Killin, young as he was, proved quite a match for his uncle, Hector Roy, whom he surprised one night at Fairburn, by a clever stratagem, and took prisoner. It was agreed between them that night that Hector should hold the estates until John attained the age of twenty-one, after which Hector promised to restore the estates, and to acknowledge John ever afterwards as his chief.   John's supporters insisted that Ellandonan Castle, being the principal residence of the family, should be given up to him at once. As Malcolm Mac Ian Charrich refused, however, to surrender the Castle, John's supporters laid siege to it, and had Malcolm's cattle brought down to the seaside and there slaughtered to feed the besiegers. Malcolm, however, would not surrender without Hector's consent, and even when this was obtained, Malcolm still refused to surrender until compensated for the loss of his cattle.   Hector eventually persuaded Malcolm to yield, whereupon John of Killin dismissed him from the Constableship, to which he appointed Finlay's son, Christopher.   It is said that the Clann Ian Charrich family of Macraes did not afterwards assume much importance in Kintail.

Finlay is said to have had four sons.

1. CHRISTOPHER, of whom below.

2. JOHN, called Ian Mor nan Cas (Big John of the feet), a name which he is said to have received under the following circumstances: Roderick,[1] brother of John of Killin, being charged with manslaughter, King James V. ordered him to be given up to justice. John of Killin accordingly set out with a party of men to apprehend him in Kintail, but Roderick, being a very powerful man, "and unwilling to be brought as a prisoner, while the party were struggling to bring him, and could not, this John took him by the feet, and so got him down, when each man having a leg, an arm, or some other hold of him, they carried him along until he consented to walk on his feet with them to the presence

1 This Roderick was progenitor of the Mackenzies, Achilty, Fairburn, &c.

of his injured brother." John Mor nan Cas left sons, and his descendants appear to have settled in Lochcarron and Kishorn, where several of them are said to have been living in 1786.

3. GILPATRICK is also said to have left issue.

4. MILES or *Maolmuire* was killed at Kinloch-ewe shortly before 1539 by the followers of Donald Gorm Macdonald, of Sleat. Part of a monument erected on the spot where Miles was killed is said to have been standing about 1700. Miles left numerous issue, some of whom appear to have lived in Gairloch, and others in Tain.

IV. CHRISTOPHER, eldest son of Finlay, was appointed Constable of Ellandonan Castle, as already stated, probably about 1511. Very little is known about him except that he held the office with trustworthiness and success, until shortly before Donald Gorm's invasion of Kintail in 1539. His sons were—

1. CHRISTOPHER, called Christopher Beg (Little Christopher), whose male succession terminated in 1685.

2. DUNCAN, of whom below.

3. FARQUHAR, progenitor of the Torlysich family, of whom hereafter. The descendants of this Farquhar were called the *Black Macraes*, as dis-tinguished from the descendants of his brother Duncan, who were called the *Fair Macraes*.

4. FINLAY, called Finlay Dubh. He married Isabel, daughter of Sir Dougal Mackenzie, Priest of Kintail, who is spoken of as a very beautiful woman, but of doubtful character. Finlay lived

at Aryugan, near Ardintoul.   While his brother
Duncan, who married Sir Dougal's widow, was
living in Strathglass, as mentioned below, Finlay
went to see him, and his wife went along with him
to see her mother.   During this visit Finlay's wife
made the acquaintance of a man called Alister
Dubh, a son of Chisholm of Comer.   Alister Dubh
afterwards followed her to Kintail, and, taking
advantage one day of Finlay's absence from home,
eloped with her to Strathglass.   She had a
young boy called Christopher, whom she took with
her.   This Christopher settled in Strathglass, where
he became a man of importance and means, and
from him the Macraes of Strathglass were
descended.   Finlay, believing that his wife had
encouraged Alister Dubh's plot, did not attempt to
bring her back, and disowned her henceforth.

5. JOHN.

6. DONALD.

V. DUNCAN, second son of Christopher IV.,
was called Donnacha Mac Gillechriosd.   He was in
his own day a prominent man in the affairs of
Kintail, and gained great renown for himself by
killing Donald Gorm Macdonald, of Sleat, at the
siege of Ellandonan Castle, in 1539.[1]   The circumstances which led to that event were the following :
Some time before this, Donald Gorm, having
devastated the lands of Macleod of Dunvegan, who

---

[1] There seems to be some doubt as to the date of this siege. 1539 is the
date usually given, but 1537 is also mentioned. As the feud appears to have
continued for some time, and as Donald Gorm made more than one raid into
Kintail, it is possible that 1537 may have been the date of the first raid, and
1539 the date of the one which resulted in his death.

was an ally of John of Killin, passed over to the
mainland, laid waste the district of Kinlochewe, and
killed, among others, Miles, son of Finlay Macrae,.
as already mentioned.   John of Killin, naturally
exasperated by this unprovoked invasion of his.
own territory, as well as by the raid against his.
friend and ally, Macleod of Dunvegan, sent his son
Kenneth to Sleat with a large body of followers to
retaliate on the Macdonalds.   Thereupon Donald
Gorm invaded Kintail with a strong party, carried
off a great deal of booty, and aggravated matters.
further still by killing Sir Dougal Mackenzie,[1]
Priest of Kintail, who was then living at Achyuran,
in Glensheil.   It would appear that both parties
made more than one raid into each other's territories, and that the feud continued for some time.

At all events, on a subsequent occasion, Donald
Gorm, hearing that Ellandonan Castle was but very
weakly garrisoned, made a sudden raid upon it with
a number of birlins or galleys, full of his.
followers, in the hope of being able to take it
by surprise.   The Constable of the Castle at this
time was John Dubh Matheson, of Fernaig, who
had married Sir Dougal Mackenzie's widow,

---

1 Sir Dougal Mackenzie appears to have been a member of the House of
Kintail. A certain Sir Dougal Mackenzie is said to have been one of the
Commissioners sent to the Pope in 1491 to procure the legitimisation of
Kenneth à Bhlair's marriage with Agnes Fraser of Lovat. It is not impossible
that this may have been the man who was killed by Donald Gorm nearly
fifty years afterwards, even though he left a young and marriageable widow.
The Sir Dougal who went to Rome is said to have been made a " Knight to
the boot of Pope Clement VIII."   The title Sir, however, as formerly applied
to the Clergy, did not imply any superiority of rank. It simply meant that
the bearer of it had taken only the degree of Bachelor of Arts, whereas the
title Mr indicated the higher degree of Master of Arts.

and had recently been appointed to the Constableship in succession to Christopher Macrae.   The
rumour that reached Donald Gorm with regard to
the unprotected state of Ellandonan was only too
true, for John Dubh and the watchman were the
only two in the Castle.   The advance of the
boats was noticed by the watchman, who gave
the alarm; but there was no time to gather
men from the mainland before the enemy arrived.
It so happened, however, that Duncan Mac Gillechriosd was passing by on his way from Lochalsh,
and, hearing the cry of alarm, he made for
the Castle with all speed.   He arrived there before
the enemy, and thirsting for revenge against the
Macdonalds for having lately killed his uncle Miles
at Kinlochewe, he took his stand at the postern
gate of the tower and killed several of the crew of
the first galley as they were landing.   As the
enemy crowded upon him in increasing numbers,
he made his way into the tower, and barricad-
ing the gate behind him, joined the Constable and
the watchman in defending the Castle.

Donald Gorm immediately began a furious
battering of the gate, but the dauntless three had
so strongly secured it with iron bars on the inside,
and they harassed the besiegers so much by throw-
ing stones among them from within, that he was
obliged to withdraw his men.   Both sides now
began to use their bows and arrows.   The Macdonalds, who were suffering heavily themselves,
aimed at the embrasures, and in this way they
unfortunately succeeded in killing the Constable.

Duncan was now left alone with the watchman and his last arrow to defend the fort. This arrow he resolved to save until a favourable opportunity occurred for making effective use of it. The opportunity soon arrived, for at this stage Donald Gorm had the masts of some of his galleys taken down for the purpose of trying to make a breach in the wall or to mount it, and as he moved round the Castle to discover the weakest and most suitable point of attack, Duncan, thinking the opportunity a favourable one, took aim with his last arrow, and struck him on the foot. The arrow was a barbed one, and in pulling it out of the wound an artery was severed. Every possible effort was made to stop the bleeding, but without avail. The wounded chief was then conveyed by his men some distance away from the Castle to a reef, which is still called *Larach tigh Mhic Dhomhnuill*, or the site of Macdonald's house, where he died.

For this service against the Macdonalds, James V. gave John of Killin considerable additions of land in the county of Ross, and the Macraes were thus once more instrumental in increasing the substance and the honours of the House of Kintail.

Duncan now thought, with some reason, that he had a good claim to succeed John Dubh Matheson as Constable of Ellandonan, but John of Killin thought him too rash and passionate for the post. He then put in a claim for his brother Farquhar, but, to avoid quarrels and bitterness between the Macraes and the Maclennans, who were also claimants for the post, it was decided to give it to John MacMhurchaidh Dhuibh (John, the son of Black Murdoch), priest of Kintail. Duncan was so much offended at the treatment he received in return for the excellent service he had rendered that he left Kintail in disgust, and went to the country of Lord Lovat, by whom he was kindly and hospitably received. Lord Lovat gave him the lands of Culigeran, in Strathglass, but Duncan killed so many deer in the neighbouring forest of Ben Vachart that Lovat was soon obliged to move him some miles away to a place called Crochel, where he lived for several years. While living at Crochel the Baron of Kintail paid him several visits, and frequently invited him to return to Kintail. Duncan, who had all along retained an affection for his native place, at last decided to accept Kintail's offers.[1] Lord Lovat, however, being anxious to retain him, offered him for a small feu-duty the lands of Clunes which Duncan's predecessors formerly held. Duncan agreed to this proposal, and Lord Lovat being about to proceed to the south, promised him to have the necessary legal documents drawn up there before his return. When Lovat departed

---

1 The year 1557 was probably the date of Duncan's return to Kintail. It was not until after the siege of Ellandonan Castle in 1539 that Duncan left Kintail, and the first Lord Lovat, who died after that date, was Hugh, who was killed at the battle of Blar-na-leine near Loch Lochy in 1544. The news of his tragic end in such a famous battle could hardly have circulated as a rumour that he died at Braemar. Hugh's successor, Alexander, the fifth Lord Lovat, died at Aigas Island, in the Beauly River, in 1557. For some months previous to his death he had been travelling for his health, and it is quite possible that rumours of his death may have circulated during his travels, and may have influenced Duncan's decision to remain in Kintail.

for the south, Duncan went to Kintail to inform his friends of the offer he had received and his intention of accepting it ; but while on this visit a rumour reached him that Lord Lovat had died at Braemar, and doubting whether Lovat's successor would be willing to confirm the agreement, he finally resolved to return to Kintail, where he received the quarter land of Inverinate and Doris-duan.   At Inverinate, a romantic spot on the north shore of Loch Duich, he lived for the rest of his days, as did also his descendants after him for more than two centuries.   Duncan married the widow of John Dubh Matheson, Constable of Ellan-donan.   She was a daughter of Duncan Ban of Glenmoriston, and was first married to Sir Dougal Mackenzie, as already stated.   By her Duncan had two sons and a daughter, who was carried away from her father's sheiling in Affric, by John Macin-taggart from Strathglass, who married her, and by whom he had several sons and daughters. Duncan lived to a good old age.   His sons were—

(1). CHRISTOPHER, of whom below.

(2). JOHN, who was "a resolute and warlike man," and took a very active part in the great feud which raged at this time between the Macdonalds of Glengarry and the Mackenzies of Kintail.   It is said that "few parties were sent out on desperate attempts to infest or annoy the enemy but John was commander, and he seldom or never returned without bloodshed.   He might be called an Hazael for speed of foot."   His brother Christopher used to tell him that his cruelty and bloodshed would

bring judgment upon himself or upon his family ;
and it is stated that, although he had three sons
who lived to old age, their progeny were of no great
consequence.   His sons were—

a. Christopher.

b. Duncan, who was also a warrior like his
father, was an old man in 1654, when General
Monk visited Kintail.   It is said that, some time
before this, Duncan consulted a local seer as to the
manner in which he should end his days, and was
informed that he would die by the sword.   This
appeared so improbable in the case of an old warrior
who had taken part in so many bloody frays, and
invariably escaped unhurt, that the question was
referred to "Coinneach Odhar,"[1] the Brahan Seer,
who confirmed the first seer's prediction.   Duncan,
however, gave the matter no credit, but one day,
while Monk and his army were in Kintail, the old
man left his house in Glensheil, and went up
among the hills, where he was met by some soldiers
who were wandering about in search of plunder,
and who spoke roughly to him in English, which he

---

1 Kenneth Mackenzie, better known as Coinneach Odhar (Dun Kenneth),
or the Brahan Seer, was one of those prophets of former times whose mystic
utterances have so frequently puzzled and startled people by their literal
fulfilment.   He is said to have been born in Lews about the commencement of
the seventeenth century, and to have subsequently moved to the neighbourhood of Brahan, where he worked on a farm as a common labourer.   Having
brought upon himself, by certain unguarded utterances, the resentment of
Lady Seaforth, he was by her orders apprehended, brought to trial as a
wizard, and sentenced by the ecclesiastical authority to be burnt to death at
Fortrose.   This is said to have happened while he was still a young man.
(For an interesting collection of the prophecies ascribed to him by the
traditions of Ross-shire, see *The Prophecies of the Brahan Seer*, by Alexander
Mackenzie, Inverness.)

did not understand.   Unable to brook such an
insult the old man drew his sword, but was
immediately overpowered and killed by the soldiers.
This, we are told, was all the bloodshed committed
by General Monk and his soldiers in Kintail.

    c. Finlay.

G. W. Wilson & Co.]

RUINS OF ELLANDONAN CASTLE.

[Aberdeen

CHAPTER III.

VI. Christopher.—Constable of Ellandonan Castle.—Origin of Feud
    between Kintail and Glengarry. — Kenneth, Lord Kintail,
    obtains Crown Charter for Glengarry's Possessions in Loch-
    carron and Lochalsh.—Christopher and his Family contributed
    to Kintail's success. — Christopher an enterprising Cattle
    Dealer.—His Convivial Habits. — His Friendship with Sir
    Donald Macdonald of Sleat. — Christopher's Marriage and
    Family.—Duncan called Donnacha Mac Gillechriosd.—One of
    the Biggest Men in the Highlands.—Ian Mor a Chasteil.—
    Duncan and a Companion take part in the Fight of Leac na
    Falla, in Skye.—Angus Og of Glengarry invades Lochcarron.
    —Lady Mackenzie and the Kintail Men prepare to intercept
    Angus Og on his return.—Fight at the Cailleach Rock.—Death
    of Angus Og.—His Burial at Kilduich.—Duncan robbed at
    Elycht Fair.—The Rev. John, son of Christopher VI.—Tutor
    or Governor to Colin, Earl Seaforth.—Other Descendants of
    Christopher VI. — The Rev. Finlay Macrae of Lochalsh.—
    Jacobite and Episcopalian.—Supports Rising of 1715.—De-
    prived of his Living.—His Marriage.—His Descendants.—
    Maurice, son of Christopher VI.—Christopher Og.—Domhnul
    na Smurich, and Donald Beg.

VI. CHRISTOPHER, eldest son of Duncan V., was
for some time Constable of Ellandonan Castle. He
is said to have been "prudent and solid in counsel
and advice, bold, forward and daring when need
required, yet remarkably merciful during the bloody
wars 'twixt Mackenzie and Glengarry." The circumstances which led to the great feud between Kintail

and Glengarry[1] appear to have been somewhat as follows : — Donald Macdonald, who was Chief of Glengarry about 1580, when the feud broke out, inherited parts of Lochalsh, Lochcarron, and Lochbroom from his grandmother, Margaret, one of the sisters and co-heiresses of Sir Donald Macdonald of Lochalsh, while Mackenzie of Kintail acquired the portion of the other co-heiress, by purchase, in 1554. With the territories of two such rival clans as the Mackenzies and the Macdonalds, not only closely adjoining, but in some instances mixed up together, as those territories now were, trouble was bound to arise. Men were constantly coming and going between Lochcarron and Glengarry, and it appears that in passing through Mackenzie's territories they frequently committed acts of violence against the people. In such circumstances it was not difficult to find an excuse for a quarrel, and an incident soon occurred which brought matters to a crisis. One of Glengarry's men, having found it necessary for some reason to leave his old home, settled, with his family and cattle, in Glenaffric. Being a great hunter, he frequently resorted to the neighbouring deer forest of Glasletter, which then belonged to Mackenzie of Gairloch. One day, while hunting there, accompanied by a servant, he was surprised by Gairloch's forester, who called upon him to surrender. The forester was a Macrae called Fionnla Dubh Mac Ian Mhic Dhomh'uill Mhoir, or Fionla Dubh nam Fiadh

---

[1] For an exhaustive account of this feud, see Mackenzie's History of the Mackenzies, new edition, chapters on Colin Cam and Kenneth, first Lord Kintail.

(Black Finlay of the Deer),[1] and he also was accompanied by a gillie or servant. The hunter refused to surrender, whereupon Finlay Dubh and his companion killed both the hunter and his servant, and buried them under a bank. As soon as the murdered men were missed, suspicion fell upon the forester and his gillie, both of whom were brought to trial by Mackenzie of Kintail, but nothing could be proved against them. Shortly afterwards, however, the bodies of the murdered men were found by their friends, and, very little doubt being now left as to who were the perpetrators of the dark deed, a party of the Macdonalds set out to take vengeance. Arriving at Glenstrathfarrar, which then belonged to Mackenzie of Redcastle, they plundered the place and killed a brother of Finlay Dubh, the forester, called Duncan Mac Ian Mhic Dhomh'uill Mhoir, whom they found ploughing in his own field. When tidings of this outrage reached Roderick Mor, who was then the Laird of Redcastle, and who had old grievances of a similar kind against the Macdonalds, he resolved at whatever cost, and in spite of the advice of more cautious friends, to take up the quarrel. Such, then, was the commencement of this feud, which lasted, with little intermission, for more than a quarter of a century, and which ended in favour of Mackenzie, who obtained a Crown charter for Glengarry's possessions in Lochcarron and Lochalsh in 1607, and the superiority of all his other possessions. To this result, which added still further

---

[1] For the Kintail tradition of Fionnla Dubh nam Fiadh and his exploits on this occasion, see chapter on the legends and traditions of the clan.

to the power and influence of the House of Kintail, Christopher and his family greatly contributed, and we read that Kenneth, Lord Kintail, " did always ask his advice in any matter of consequence he had to do in the Highlands."

Not only was Christopher a bold and stout warrior, he was likewise an enterprising man of business. He was the first man in that part of the country who sent cattle to the markets of the South. For that purpose he bought cattle yearly from the neighbouring estates, and made so much money in his cattle-dealing that " if he was as frugal in keeping as he was industrious in acquiring, he had proven a very rich man in his own country." But he appears to have been a man of decidedly convivial habits, and to have spent his money very freely, for when he went to Inverness, or to Fortrose, which was then a very important place and much frequented, " the first thing he did was to call his landlord the vintner, and with him pitched upon and agreed for the hogshead of wine that pleased him best, resolving to drink it all with his acquaintances before he left the town." He was on very friendly terms with Sir Donald Macdonald of Sleat, commonly called Donald Gorm Mor, grandson of Donald Gorm, who was killed by Christopher's father at the siege of Ellandonan Castle in 1539. This Sir Donald was married to a sister of Kenneth, Lord Kintail, and being on one occasion in the South, along with his lady, he was detained there much longer than he expected, with the result that he ran short of money. There were no banking transactions in those days, and the credit of Highland Chiefs, at all event in the South, was not always good. In consequence of all this, Sir Donald was obliged to go home for more money in order to enable his lady to travel in a manner suitable to her rank, and meantime she remained behind in Perth, to await the return of her husband. It so happened, however, that Christopher was at this time in the South with cattle, and hearing that Lady Macdonald, the sister of his own Chief, was in Perth, he went to pay her his respects. On learning the cause of her delay, he told her that he had with him money and men enough to meet all expenses, and to escort her safely and suitably to her home, if she would do him the honour of accepting his services. Christopher's offer was gladly accepted, and starting immediately for the North, they arrived at Sleat the next day after Sir Donald himself. Sir Donald, who was greatly surprised and much delighted, persuaded Christopher to remain with him for some days, with the result that a fast friendship was established between the two families, notwithstanding the fact that on one occasion during the visit, while the cups were circulating far too freely, Christopher made an ill-timed reference to the death of Donald Gorm, and so greatly roused the resentment of some of the Macdonalds who were present, that they would probably have killed him but for the interference and protection of his host. Christopher was afterwards greatly ashamed of what he said, and Sir Donald and he continued to be very fast friends.

Christopher married a daughter of the Rev. Murdoch Murchison,[1] Priest of Kintail, and Constable of Ellandonan Castle, who died in 1618, and by her he had seven sons, all of whom were prosperously settled before the death of their father.

1. DUNCAN, called Donnacha Mac Gillechriosd, is said to have been one of the biggest and strongest men in the Highlands. "He was equal in height and bulk of body" to John Grant, the contemporary Laird of Glenmoriston, commonly called Ian Mor a Chasteil (Big John of the Castle).[2] We are told that Duncan could pass through the doorway of the Church at Kintail only by turning sideways, and it appears, from what the clan historian relates of him, that he was no less remarkable for his prowess and force of character than for his bodily size. "He was a stout, forward, and bloody man, and delighted much in arms."

The following incident, which is related of Duncan, not only shows the pleasure which he himself found in fighting, but the light-heartedness and delight with which the Highlanders of those days joined in any affray, whether they were concerned in the quarrel or not. On a certain occasion Duncan and another Kintail man, called Ian Ug Mac Fhionnla Dhuibh (Young John, the son of Black Finlay), were in the Isle of Skye buying horses. On their way home, by the Coolin Hills, they observed bands of Macleods and Macdonalds,

---

[1] See Footnote, page 56.

[2] For an interesting account of Ian Mor a Chasteil, who was Laird of Glenmoriston from 1581 to 1637, see Mackay's Urquhart and Glenmoriston — page 125.

between whom there was a feud at the time, gathering together and making preparations for battle. Neither Duncan nor John was in any way concerned in the quarrel, but Duncan thought that such an opportunity of exercising themselves in the art of war was too good to be thrown away, and he easily persuaded his companion to join in the fight. In order to avoid every appearance of injustice or partiality they resolved to take sides. John joined the Macleods, because his mother was of that clan, while Duncan joined the Macdonalds,. and was no doubt very glad to do so because of the friendship which had been established between his father and their Chief. Duncan had the support of a powerful servant, who managed to get possession of a pass across a rough stream for which both parties were contending. This position he held against the Macleods until the Macdonalds came up in full force, with the result that the Macleods were defeated with great slaughter. Tradition relates that this was a very fierce and deadly struggle, and a large flag-stone, which was covered with blood at the close of the fight, is still pointed out and known as Leac na falla[1] (the flag-stone of blood). As soon as the victory was decided, Duncan, who received the hearty thanks of the Macdonalds, went in search of his companion, John Og, and, when he found him, they resumed and continued their homeward journey as if nothing had hap-

[1] The fight at Leac na falla has been powerfully depicted on canvas by the well-known Highland artist, Mr Lockhart Bogle.

pened. Both had the good fortune to escape without hurt or wound. Such were the stern amusements in which our bold Highland forefathers took most delight.

In his youth Duncan took a prominent part in the great Glengarry feud. On one occasion, during the temporary absence of Kenneth, Lord Kintail, in Mull, Angus Og, son and heir of Macdonald of Glengarry, and one of the bravest and most daring of all his warriors, made a raid on Lochcarron in November, about 1602, and put to death as many of Kintail's supporters—men, women, and children —as he could lay hold of, seized the cattle and drove them to Slumbay on the north coast of Lochcarron, where his followers had left their boats. Meantime news of the raid reached Kintail, and a number of men immediately set out for Lochcarron, but before they arrived Angus Og had already put out to sea, and was beyond reach even of their arrows. The Kintail men now returned to Ellandonan, but a few of the swiftest runners among them took the shortest cut to Inverinate, where they launched a newly-built twelve-oared galley belonging to Duncan's father, and proceeded with all speed to Ellandonan, their plan being, if possible, to intercept Angus Og before he could pass through Kylerea. At Ellandonan they found Kintail's lady superintending preparations for the expedition. The galley was quickly manned by eighteen of the best and the bravest men available, besides the rowers, and placed under the command of Duncan. They had also a small boat to attend on them, and on board the galley they had two small brass cannons and some ammunition, which the lady served out with her own hands, and before they started she gave them an eloquent exhortation to play their part bravely, and to maintain the honour of their clan and their absent Chief like good and true men. She then mounted the Castle wall and watched them as they sailed away under cover of the fast gathering shades of the winter night.

They had not gone far when they met a boat coming to tell them that the Macdonalds were at Kyleakin, apparently waiting for the turn of the tide to help them through Kylerea, where the tidal current is usually so strong that a boat can make little headway against it. Shortly afterwards there passed by the Kintail men, without observing them, a small boat which they concluded to have been sent on by the Macdonalds to see whether Kylerea was clear. They allowed this boat to pass unchallenged lest any alarm should be raised. It was a calm moonlight night, with a covering of snow on the ground, which added to the light and made it easy to sail about even in narrow waters. The Kintail men, therefore, decided to direct their course at once towards the fleet of the Macdonalds, and having filled their row-locks with seaweed to prevent the pulsing noise of their oars, they steered towards Kyleakin. As they approached the Cailleach Rock, which lies off the coast of Skye, and not far from the Lochalsh end of Kylerea, they observed the first of Macdonald's galleys drawing near. They soon discovered that this was Angus Og's great thirty-two oared galley, sailing some distance ahead of the rest of his fleet with "his best men and gentlemen" on board.   Upon observing the Kintail galley, which was quickly approaching him, Angus challenged it two or three times, but the only answer he received was a broadside from the brass cannon, which, breaking some of the oars, disabled his galley and threw it on the Cailleach Rock. His men, think-ing they were driven ashore, crowded on to the rock. When they discovered their mistake, and found a stretch of water lying between them and the main-land, they became completely confused and fell easy victims to their assailants.   Some of them at-tempted to escape by swimming, but they no sooner reached the shore than they were dispatched by men whom Duncan landed by the little boat for that purpose.   Angus had about sixty men on board his galley, every one of whom was either killed or drowned.   He himself was taken on board the Kintail boat alive, but was mortally wounded in the head and in the body, and died before the morning.   The remainder of his fleet, to the number of about twenty galleys, hearing the sudden uproar and firing at the Cailleach Rock, turned back in confusion, and landing on the coast of Skye they made their way to Sleat, and thence crossed to the Mainland. "At this skirmish or little sea fight," says the Rev. John Macrae in his history of the Mackenzies, " not one drop of blood was shed of the Kintail men's, except of one called John Gauld Mac Fhionnla Dhuibh (John the Stranger, son of Black Finlay), whose dirk, being slippery with blood, ran through his fist and cut his four fingers. Certainly their skill and dexterity in that expedition and their unexpected victory and success ought not to be ascribed to them, but to God, whose vengeance justly followed those persons for their bloody murders of men, women, and children, and who can make any instrument prove powerful and effectual to bring His own purpose to pass."

Meantime Lady Mackenzie was anxiously waiting at Ellandonan for the result of the expedition. She heard the firing of the cannon in the night, and from this she concluded that an engagement had taken place. At daybreak she saw her protectors returning, leading Angus Og's great galley along with them. She rushed down to the shore to salute them, and when she inquired if everything had gone well with them, Duncan replied, "Yes, madam, and we have brought you, without the loss of a single man, a new guest whom we hope is welcome to you." On looking into the galley she at once recognised the body of Angus Og of Glengarry, and immediately gave orders that it should be properly attended to. On the following day Angus Og was buried in a manner suitable to his rank at Kilduich, in the same grave as some of Lady Mackenzie's own children. The common tradition in Kintail used to be that he was buried in the doorway of the church at Kilduich, but in a MS. history of the Mackenzies, written about the middle of the seventeenth century,[1] and which may be regarded as

1 This MS., which is frequently quoted in Mackenzie's History of the Mackenzies as the "Ancient MS.," together with Rev. John Macrae's History

conclusive on this point, the writer tells us that to say he was buried in the church door is a "malicious lie," because he himself had seen "the head raised out of the same grave and returned again, wherein there were too small cuts, noways deep."

Duncan, like his father, appears to have engaged in cattle dealing, and from the record of a meeting of the Privy Council held in Edinburgh on the 11th December, 1600, it appears that at the Fair of Elcyht (Alyth?), on the 1st of November, 1599, he was robbed by a certain Oliver Ogilvy and others of twenty-six cows and four hundred silver marks. Duncan died without male issue, but left several daughters.

2. THE REV. FARQUHAR, second son of Christopher, will be mentioned hereafter.

3. THE REV. JOHN, third son of Christopher VI., was "a man of an able and strong body, a sharp and sagacious mind, and somewhat more curious in his learning than his elder brother, Mr Farquhar." Mr John was governor or tutor to Colin Mackenzie, first Earl of Seaforth, at the University of Edinburgh, and appears to have gained a great influence over his pupil, whose "early and unexpected death (in 1633) did so dispirit him that he afterwards lived in the Highlands more obscurely than was expected of him." He also studied medicine, and left behind him a great reputation among his

of the Mackenzies, which, is known as the Ardintoul MS., form the chief authorities for this account of the death of Angus Og.

own countrymen for his skill as a physician.   He was married to a daughter of Dugald Matheson of Balmacarra, and lived to a great age.   He left three sons—Christopher, Donald, and Duncan.   The following extract, from the Rev. John Macrae's history, is interesting as showing what an expensive luxury tobacco was in the days of Mr John :— " I remember that after Mr John's death, when his friends were examining his papers, there was among them a letter directed to him at Edinburgh from Alexander Mackenzie, the first of the family of Kilcoy, and son of Colin Cam, XI. of Kintail, telling he had received the pound of tobacco sent him, and blaming Mr John for not sending him more of it, as he got it so cheap as twenty pounds Scots the pound," that is £1 13s 4d sterling.   It need hardly be added that this sum meant much more then than it does now.

4. FINLAY, fourth son of Christopher VI., and VII. from Finlay Dubh Mac Gille Chriosd, is said to have been a handsome man, and of good ability according to the education he received.   He was frugal and industrious, and left considerable means to his children.   He did not live long, but left four sons, the eldest of whom was

(VIII.) DONALD, called Domhnull Dubh.   He is spoken of as an able, strong man, of good sense, and well to live.   He had five sons and three daughters—

(1.) CHRISTOPHER, "a well-humoured, free-hearted gentleman," died young and without issue.

(2.) DONALD, mentioned below.

(3.) FINLAY.

(4.) DUNCAN.

(5.) FARQUHAR.

(6.) A daughter, who married Alexander Macrae of Achyark, son of Alexander of Inverinate.

(7.) MARGARET, who married Farquhar, son of Alexander of Inverinate.

(8.) A daughter, who married Alexander, brother-german of Murdoch Mackenzie of Fairburn.

(IX.) DONALD, son of Donald Dubh, was called Donald Og (Donald the Younger). He is said to have been well known in the North, and in many parts of the South, for an "affable, generous gentle-man." He was endowed with great natural parts and ready wit, and though he got little education, he was Chamberlain of Kintail for several years, and discharged the duties of the post with exact-ness and success. He married, first, Anne, daughter of Alexander Macrae of Inverinate, who died within a year of her marriage, without issue. He married, secondly, Isabel, daughter of John Grant of Corri-mony, by whom he had several sons and daughters, though the names of only three are recorded—

(1.) ALEXANDER, for whom he made liberal pro-visions.

(2.) THE REV. FINLAY, mentioned below.

(3.) THE REV. DUNCAN, who was a youth of great promise, and an eloquent preacher. He was edu-cated at Aberdeen, and was tutor in the family of Mackenzie of Findon, where he died in November, 1690. He was buried in Dingwall.

(X.) THE REV. FINLAY, second son of Donald Og,

was educated at St Leonard's College, St Andrews, and obtained his degree on the 24th July, 1679. He officiated for a time in the Island of Cumbray, in the Firth of Clyde, which he left at the time of the Revolution in 1688. He was afterwards presented to the parish of Lochalsh by Frances, Countess of Seaforth, in 1695. Being a strong Jacobite and Episcopalian, he refused to conform to Presbytery, or to take the prescribed oaths, and was consequently looked upon as an intruder by the Presbyterians. In 1715 he strongly urged his parishioners to take up arms on behalf of the House of Stuart, under William, Earl of Seaforth, and it was, no doubt, to some extent owing to his influence that so many of the men of Lochalsh joined in that rising. His sympathy with the House of Stuart cost him his parish, of which he was deprived on the 21st September, 1716. The Rev. Finlay is said to have been "a great philosopher and divine, a clear preacher, of ministerial and dignified appearance, and much given to hospitality and charity." He married Margaret, daughter of Duncan Macrae of Inverinate, with issue, and died not later than 1728, as his son, John, was served heir on the 15th October of that year. So far as it can now be traced, the succession of the Rev. Finlay is as follows—

(1.) JOHN, mentioned below.

(2.) HECTOR, who was tacksman of Ardelve, and was alive in 1761, as he is said to have been tutor or guardian to the family of John Macrae of Conchra, who died in that year.

(3.) DONALD, called Donald Bane, married Barbara Macrae, widow of John, son of the Rev. Donald Macrae of Kintail, with issue—

(a.) Finlay, called Finlay Fadoch, a well-known schoolmaster in Fadoch, and afterwards in Ardelve, about the close of the last and beginning of the present century. He afterwards went, when a very old man, to America. He married a daughter of John Macrae (Ian Mac Mhurachaidh), the Kintail poet, and had issue—(*a*1) Duncan, born 1803 ; (*a*2) Anne, who married Duncan Macrae, Drudaig, and went to America ; (*a*3) Barbara, who married Kenneth Mackenzie, Lochcarron, with issue—Kenneth, Malcolm, and Thomas.

(b.) Jane, who married Murdoch Macrae, who had a son, Malcolm, who married Janet Macrae and had a son, John, now living at Dornie, and a daughter, Isabella, married to Roderick Matheson at Totaig Ferry.

(4.) MARION, daughter of the Rev. Finlay, married John Matheson, and had, with other issue, a son,

(a.) Alexander, who was for some years tenant of Reraig, in Lochalsh, and afterwards merchant and schoolmaster at Dornie. He married Catherine Matheson of the Bennetsfield family, and had with other issue—

(*a*1.) John, who married Isabella, daughter of Donald Macrae, and had a large family, of whom are Alexander Matheson, shipowner, and Betsie Matheson, shopkeeper, both living at Dornie.

(*a*2.) Farquhar, who married Isabella, daughter of Kenneth Mackenzie, Kishorn, of the Applecross family, and had a large family, one of whom is Kenneth Matheson, merchant, Salen, in Argyllshire, who is married, with issue. Another is the well-known Dr Farquhar Matheson, of London. After studying at the Universities of Glasgow and Aberdeen, and graduating in medicine, Dr Farquhar Matheson went as a young man to London, where he has risen to eminence in his profession, and is particularly recognised as an experienced and skilful specialist in diseases of the ear, nose, and throat. He is one of the surgeons to the Royal Ear and Throat Hospital, London. For many years he has been one of the best known and most influential Highlanders in London, and is at the present time (1896) President of the Gaelic Society of London, Joint Secretary of the Highland Society, Governor and Surgeon to the Royal Scottish Hospital, a Justice of the Peace for the County of London, and a Fellow of several learned and scientific Societies. Dr Matheson is married and has issue, two daughters, Isabel and Barbara, and a son, Farquhar, at present a student of Cambridge University.

(a3). Margaret married Farquhar Matheson, and had, with other issue, a daughter, Margaret, who married Duncan Matheson, innkeeper, Dornie, and had issue :—Donald, now living in Glasgow, married Christina Macpherson, with issue ; Farquhar, now living at Dornie, married Jane Macrae (Auchtertyre family); Mary married Andrew Ross ; Margaret married Farquhar Macrae now living at Inversheil.[1]

This statement of the descendants of Marion, daughter of the Rev. Finlay Macrae, is taken from a full and interesting account of her descendants, given to the author by the above-mentioned Miss Betsie Matheson of Dornie, in August, 1896.

D

(5). ISABEL, who married Duncan, son of Alexander Macrae of Conchra, with issue.

(XI). JOHN, eldest son of the Rev. Finlay, was served heir on the 15th October, 1728. Tradition says he was one of the best swordsmen of his time in the Highlands,[1] and he appears to have been a man of mark in his own country.. He had a son—

(1). ALEXANDER, who married, as his first wife, Isabella Macrae, and had issue,

(a). Hector married Anne Macrae, with issue ; Alexander, now a blacksmith at Bundalloch, married with issue; and John, who died about 1890, leaving issue.

(b). Isabella.

Alexander, son of John, son of the Rev. Finlay, married, as his second wife, Kate Macrae, and had issue.

(c). Duncan, who married Flora, daughter of John Macrae by his wife, Catherine, daughter of John Og, son of the Rev. Donald Macrae of Kintail, and by her had issue—(c1) John, married with issue, in America ; (c2) Alexander, who died unmarried ; (c3) Donald, now living at Fadoch, married a daughter of the late Alexander Macrae, commonly known as Alister Mor na Pait (Big Alexander of Patt), and has issue :—Duncan, Helen, Alexander, John, now living in London, and by whom this statement of the descendants of his grandfather, Duncan, was given to the author in November, 1896. Catherine, Duncan, Farquhar, James, Donald, Flora ; (c4) Anne, married with issue, in America ;

---

[1] See chapter on legends and traditions of the clan.

(c5) Isabella ; (c6) Flora ; (c7) Helen, married in Strathglass ; (c8) Catherine, married Donald Macdonald, with issue—

(d). John; (e). Farquhar, married with issue, and went to America ; (f). Mary ; (g). Catherine ; (h). Rebecca.

5. MAURICE, fifth son of Christopher VI., is said to have been a strong and industrious man, who loved Kintail better than any other place. He had advantageous offers from Earl Colin to go to Kinlochewe ; but he would not go, and the Earl, appreciating his devotion to his native place, gave him his choice of a tack in it. He was a man of means, and gave money to the Laird of Chisholm, for which he and his successors had grazing in Glen Affric till the principal was paid. Maurice was drowned in Strathglass on his way home from Inverness, and was buried in Kintail. He left issue.

6. CHRISTOPHER, sixth son of Christopher VI., was called Christopher Og. He left sons and daughters.

7. DONALD, seventh son of Christopher VI., was called Domhnull na Smurich,[1] or Domhnull Beg. He was of short stature, " but so remarkable for strength and nimbleness that few would venture to compete with him, since all that did were worsted in such exercises as required strength and dexterity. He was a great drover, lived well but not long, and left no male issue."

[1] Smurich, genitive of smurach, which means dross or dust.

CHAPTER IV.

VII.—THE REV. FARQUHAR MACRAE, second
son of Christopher (VI.), was born at Ellandonan
Castle in 1580. He was a delicate child, but grew
up to be a man of good physique and great bodily
strength. His father, perceiving that he possessed
good ability and a talent for learning, sent him to
school at Perth, where he remained for four or five
years, and became very proficient in Latin. Some

of his exercises and discourses in that language are mentioned as being still preserved in the year 1704. From Perth he proceeded to the University of Edinburgh, where he studied under James Reid, one of the Regents or Professors of the University, and soon surpassed all his fellow students in the study both of classics and of philosophy. His repute for learning and scholarship was so great at the University that he was unanimously chosen in 1603 to succeed James Reid as Regent, but Kenneth, Lord Kintail, who was in Edinburgh at the time, earnestly opposed the appointment, as he was anxious to secure Mr Farquhar's services for his own people in the Highlands. Mr Farquhar himself was not anxious to accept the appointment either, as his great desire was to become a preacher of the Gospel, and with a view to that calling he had already studied divinity at the University. He therefore fell in readily with Lord Kintail's proposal, and about this time left the University to fill the post of headmaster of the Fortrose Grammar School, which then enjoyed a great reputation in the North, and where he remained for about fifteen months. He appears to have passed his "trials" or examinations for the Church while he was at Fortrose, and having been admitted to Holy Orders he very soon acquired celebrity as a "sound, learned, eloquent, and grave preacher."

About this time some ironworks[1] were commenced at Letterewe, on Loch Maree, in the parish of Gair-

[1] For an interesting account of the historic ironworks, not only in Gairloch but in other parts of the Highlands, see J. H. Dixon's Gairloch, page 75, &c.

loch, by Sir George Hay, who afterwards figured prominently in Scottish history as the Earl of Kinnoull and High Chancellor of Scotland. Sir George introduced a colony of Englishmen to carry on the works. It therefore became necessary to provide for that parish a clergyman who could preach well in English, and Bishop David Lindesay, who then held the diocese of Ross, selected the young Mr Farquhar as the most suitable man at his disposal. He was accordingly appointed Vicar of Gairloch in 1608, and continued to hold that office until 1618. We read, however, that another Vicar, the Rev. Farquhar Mackenzie, was admitted to the parish of Gairloch about the year 1614. The probability is that the two clergymen shared the work of the extensive parish between them, and that the Rev. Farquhar Macrae restricted his ministrations to the English-speaking ironworkers, and to the part of the parish which lies to the north of Loch Maree, and which was then regarded as part of the parish of Lochbroom. Mr Farquhar's ministrations gave great satisfaction, not only to the native people of Gairloch, but also to the ironworkers, and more especially to Sir George Hay himself, who found great pleasure in his society, and became much attached to him. Sir George was a learned lawyer and a man of science, and probably did not find the contemporary Laird of Gairloch—John Roy Mackenzie[1]—such congenial company as the scholarly and cultured Vicar. John Roy does not appear to

1 John Roy Mackenzie was Laird of Gairloch from 1566 to 1628. He was a warrior of renown, and among his bravest followers were some of the Macraes of Kintail. See chapter on the legends and traditions of the clan.

have been a very loyal supporter of the Church, for in 1612 we find Mr Farquhar raising an action against him for payment of the teinds or tithes. The action went on for several years, and was won by Mr Farquhar, who, in 1616, let the tithes of Gairloch to Alexander Mackenzie, Fiar of Gairloch, for the yearly sum of £80 Scots.[1] Mr Farquhar lived at Ardlair, which is only about four miles from Letterewe,[2] where Sir George lived, and as there were probably very few men of scholarly and scientific tastes in Gairloch in those days, Sir George and Mr Farquhar were, no doubt, a good deal in one another's company. There is a large and prominent rock of a peculiar shape at Ardlair called the "Minister's stone," which is still pointed out as one of the places where Mr Farquhar used to preach, both in Gaelic and in English.[3]

About 1616 Sir George Hay left Letterewe for the south, in 1622 he was appointed High Chancellor of Scotland, and was afterwards created Earl of Kinnoull. His subsequent career was one of great distinction and usefulness until his death in 1634, at the age of sixty-two. So much was Sir George attached to Mr Farquhar, that when he was leaving Letterewe he strongly urged him to leave Gairloch and seek a wider field for his talents in the south. Sir George offered him a choice of several parishes which were in his own patronage. He also promised

[1] Mackenzie's History of the Mackenzies, New Edition, pages 415-416.
[2] Both Ardlair and Letterewe are situated on the North-East Coast of Loch Maree.
[3] There is an illustration of this stone in Mr J. H. Dixon's book on Gairloch (page 81), which also contains several interesting and appreciative references to Mr Farquhar.

him a yearly pension, and undertook to get him ecclesiastical promotion. Mr Farquhar decided to accept this liberal offer, and to accompany Sir George to the south, and considering his own ability and the great influence of his patron, it is quite possible that if he had done so his career in the Church would have been a very successful and distinguished one. But Colin, Lord Kintail, or more probably his uncle Roderick, the celebrated "Tutor of Kintail"—for Colin was then a minor—interposed, as Lord Kenneth had done in Edinburgh, being resolved at whatever cost to retain Mr Farquhar's services for his own people, and promising him the vicarage of Kintail in succession to the occupying incumbent, the Rev. Murdoch Murchison, Mr Farquhar's uncle,[1] who at this time must have been well advanced in years. Mr Farquhar once more sacrificed bright and promising prospects out of a sense of loyalty to the House of Kintail, and remained in Gairloch.

It was during Mr Farquhar's incumbency of Gairloch that Kenneth, Lord Kintail, finally brought the island of Lews under his rule. In 1610 his lordship

---

[1] It would appear from *Fasti Ecclesiæ Scoticanæ* that Mr Farquhar succeeded his grandfather as Constable of Ellandonan and Vicar of Kintail, as it is there stated that Christopher Macrae, that is Mr Farquhar's father, married a daughter of Murdoch Murchison, Constable of Ellandonan and Vicar of Kintail, Mr Farquhar's predecessor, who would thus be also his grandfather; but according to the Rev. John Macrae, Mr Farquhar succeeded his uncle in the Vicarage of Kintail. There are three men of the name Murchison mentioned in connection with Kintail during this period :—(1) John Murchison, called John Mac Mhurchaidh Dhuibh (John, the son of Black Murdoch), Priest of Kintail, who was made Constable of Ellandonan, in succession to John Dubh Matheson, who was killed by Donald Gorm in 1539 ; (2) John Murchison, who was Reader of Kintail from 1574 to 1614 (the Reader was a man appointed to read the Scriptures and the new Protestant Service Book of this period) ; (3) Murdoch Murchison, who was Vicar of

visited the island, and with a view to revive the
religious life of the people, which was then at a very
low ebb, he took Mr Farquhar along with him.   The
state of matters in Lews may be imagined from the
fact that for forty years previous to Mr Farquhar's
visit no one appears to have been baptised or married
in the island.   The people had practically lapsed into
heathenism, but Mr Farquhar's visit worked a change
and his mission proved thoroughly successful.   Large
numbers of the people were baptised,[1] some of them
being fifty years of age, and many men and women
were married who had already lived together for
years.   The success of this mission went far to re-
concile the inhabitants of Lews to Lord Kintail's
rule, to which they all the more cheerfully and
readily submitted upon his promising that he would
provide for the permanent settling among them of
such another man as Mr Farquhar.   Having succeeded in establishing good order and contentment
in the island, no doubt largely by the aid of Mr
Farquhar, who appears to have remained there for
some time, his lordship, who was seized by sudden
illness, returned to Fortrose, where he died shortly

Lochalsh from 1582 to 1614, when he became Vicar of Kintail, until his death
in 1618. These men were undoubtedly members of the same family, but it is
not clear what their relationship was to one another. From an examination of
the dates it would seem probable that the last two were brothers, and the sons
of the first. In that case, if Murdoch was Mr Farquhar's uncle, as he almost
certainly was, Mr Farquhar's mother would be a daughter, not of the Rev.
Murdoch Murchison, as stated on page 38 of this book, but of John Murchison,
Priest of Kintail, who was made Constable of Ellandonan in 1539.

1 According to one of the traditions of Kintail, the number that came to
be baptised by Mr Farquhar was so great that, being unable to take them
individually, he was obliged to sprinkle the water at random on the crowd with
a heather besom.

afterwards, in 1611, and was succeeded by his son
Colin, who was subsequently created first Earl of
Seaforth.

In 1618 the vicarage of Kintail became vacant
by the death of the Rev. Murdoch Murchison, who
was also Constable of Ellandonan Castle, and Mr
Farquhar was appointed to fill both offices. The
deed by which those appointments were conferred
upon him was drawn up at Fortrose in that year.[1]
At Ellandonan Castle he lived for many years in
"an opulent and flourishing condition, much given
to hospitality and charity." Colin, Earl of Seaforth,
lived most of his time at Fortrose, but made period-
ical visits to Ellandonan in "great state and very
magnificently," Referring to these visits, the Rev.
John Macrae, of Dingwall, grandson of Mr Farquhar,
says—"I have heard my grandfather say that Earl
Colin never came to his house with less than three
and sometimes with five hundred men. The Constable (of Ellandonan) was bound to furnish them
victuals for the first two meals, till my lord's officers
were acquainted to bring in his own customs."
When Earl Colin visited his West Coast estates the
lairds and gentlemen of the neighbourhood and of
the Isles, including Maclean, Clanranald, Raasay,
and Mackinnon, used to come to pay him their
respects at Ellandonan Castle, where they feasted in
great state, and consumed "the wine and other
liquors" that were brought from Fortrose in the
Earl's train. When these lairds and gentlemen left
the castle Earl Colin called together all the principal

[1] The Rev. John Macrae's history of the Macraes.

men of Kintail, Lochalsh, and Lochcarron, who went
with him to the forest of Monar, where they had a
great hunt, and from Monar he used to return to
Fortrose.

Earl Colin died at Fortrose in 1633, and was
succeeded by his brother, Earl George, who confirmed Mr Farquhar in his various appointments
and offices, and renewed his wadset rights to the
lands of Dornie, Inig, Aryugan, Drumbuie, and other
places in Kintail. Not only did Mr Farquhar secure
these rights during his own lifetime, but on payment
of a certain sum of money to the Earl he received
an extension of them for some years in favour of his
son, the Rev. John Macrae, of Dingwall, while the
wadset rights of Inverinate, Dorisduan, and Let-
terimmer, which appear to have been already in the
family for some generations, were confirmed in favour
of his son Alexander on payment of a sum of six
thousand merks Scots.

When Earl George's son and heir, Kenneth, who
was born at Brahan Castle in 1635, was about six
years of age his father placed him under the care of
Mr Farquhar of Ellandonan, where the sons of
neighbouring gentlemen were brought to keep him
company. Here the young heir remained for several
years without suffering any disadvantage, for we
read that under the wholesome rather than delicate
diet prescribed by Mr Farquhar, he began to have
a "healthy complexion," and grew up so strong that
he was able to endure much labour and fatigue,
and so great in stature that he became known as
Coinneach Mor—big Kenneth. He also became so

thoroughly acquainted with the language and circumstances of the people, that he was considered,
in his own time, to be the best chief in the Highlands and Islands of Scotland. Nor was his book
learning neglected, for when he was taken from
Ellandonan to be placed in a public school, he gave
every evidence, not only of ability, but of good
training also. He entered King's College, Aberdeen,
in 1651, but the troubles of the Civil War prevented
him from finishing his course, which, as far as it
went, did full credit to Mr Farquhar's tuition.

But the influence and prosperity of Mr Farquhar
excited the envy and jealousy of some of his neighbours, who made complaint to Patrick Lindesay,
Bishop of Ross, that he was becoming too worldly
and was neglecting his ministerial duties. Upon receiving these complaints the Bishop called upon Mr
Farquhar to preach before the next provincial
Assembly of the Diocese or Synod. The Bishop himself preached on the first day from the text, "Ye are
the salt of the earth." It was Mr Farquhar's turn
to preach the second day, and he had unfortunately
chosen the same text as the Bishop. Mr Farquhar
told some of his brother clergymen of this fact, and
it eventually came to the ears of the Bishop, who
sent for Mr Farquhar and told him on no account to
change his text. Mr Farquhar acquitted himself on
this occasion with such eloquence and ability that it
was "a question among his hearers whether the Highland salt or Lowland salt savoured best," and the
Bishop himself was so impressed with the sermon
that he not only dismissed the complaints as ground-

less but received Mr. Farquhar into special favour.
This must have occurred comparatively early in Mr
Farquhar's incumbency of Kintail, as Bishop Patrick
Lindesay's rule of the Diocese of Ross terminated in
1633, and it was probably some time before that
date, as we are told that he was "held in esteem by
the Bishop ever after"—a phrase which would seem
to imply that the Bishop's personal acquaintance
with him extended over several years.   Bishop
Patrick Lindesay was succeeded by Bishop John
Maxwell, who invited Mr Farquhar on more occasions
than one to preach before him.   His brother clergymen were always greatly pleased with his performances in the pulpit, and on one occasion when the
Bishop himself was asked for his opinion, he declared
Mr Farquhar to be "a man of great gifts, but unfortunately lost in the Highlands, and pity it were
his lot had been there."   Had Mr Farquhar chosen
to carry his services to the more tempting fields of
work afforded by the large towns of the South, no
doubt his career might have been very much greater
and more distinguished from a worldly point of view,
but the memories which he left behind him in Gairloch, and more especially in Lochalsh and Kintail,
where his name is still remembered with affection
and pride, clearly proves that his talents were not
lost even in the Highlands, and that his work among
the people bore rich fruit.

In 1651, Mr Farquhar left Ellandonan Castle,
after a residence of thirty-three years, under circumstances described as follows by the Rev. John
Macrae in his history of the Mackenzies :—After

the defeat of the supporters of King Charles II. at
Dunbar, on the 3rd September, 1650, and while Earl
George was absent in Holland, we find his son,
Kenneth, then a lad of about sixteen, raising men in
Kintail for the Royalist service. He was accom-
panied by his two uncles, Thomas Mackenzie of
Pluscardine and Simon Mackenzie of Lochslin,[1]
Roderick Mackenzie of Dochmaluag, and others.
For some reason or other, not explained, Mr
Farquhar incurred the displeasure of Lochslin, who
was acting as leader, and who would not march off
with the men until Mr Farquhar was removed from
Ellandonan Castle. Mr Farquhar, however, "refused
to go without violence, lest his going voluntarily
might be interpreted as an abdication of his right,
a yielding to the reason pretended against him, and
when all the gentlemen of my lord's friends there
refused to put hands on him, and the young laird
(Kenneth), his foster, refused to lay his commands
on them to remove him, Young Tarbat,[2] being vexed
for delaying the march of the men for the King's
service, and Lochslin himself, led him to the gates
of the Castle, and then Mr Farquhar told them he
would go without further trouble to them, for he
was well pleased to be rid of the Island, because it
was a bad habitation for a man of his age and
corpulency." It is said, also, that he found it too

1 Simon Mackenzie of Lochslin was the father of Sir George Mackenzie
of Rosehaugh, Lord-Advocate of Scotland, a well-known historian and lawyer,
and who, in consequence of his severe administration of the law against the
Covenanters, has sometimes been called the "Bloody Mackenzie."

2 Young Tarbat was George Mackenzie, afterwards first Earl of Cromartie,
and at this time about twenty years of age.

cold for his old age, which is not unlikely, considering the exposed nature of the site on which the
castle stood, nor is it unlikely either that the duties
of Constable were becoming too heavy for a man
of his advanced years.   The question of Mr
Farquhar's expulsion from Ellandonan Castle came
before the Presbytery of Dingwall on the 5th July,
1651,[1] when a letter was read from Mr Farquhar,
who excused himself from attending, " being unable
to travel so far"; while Simon of Lochslin excused
his absence from the same meeting on the ground
that he was employed in the " present expedition "
—that is the expedition which ended in the defeat
of the Royalist Army at Worcester on the 3rd
September, 1651.   The collapse of the Royalist
party at Worcester led to fresh ecclesiastical
developments in the Presbytery of Dingwall, and
this case does not appear to have come under
consideration again.   On leaving the castle Mr
Farquhar took up his residence at a sheltered spot
in the neighbourhood, called Inchchruter, " where
he lived very plentifully for eleven years, some
of his grandchildren, after his wife's death,
alternately ruling his house, to which there was
a great resort of all sorts of people, he being very
generous, charitable, and free-hearted."   When
General Monk's army visited Kintail in 1654,[2] they
took away three hundred and sixty of Mr Farquhar's cattle, for which his friends strongly urged
him to put in a claim for compensation when King

[1] Inverness and Dingwall Presbytery Records, edited by William Mackay.
[2] For an account of General Monk's visit to Kintail, see Appendix E.

Charles II. was restored in 1660, but the old man refused to do so, being so loyal to the House of Stuart that he considered the successful restoration of the King sufficient compensation for any loss he might have suffered in the Royalist cause.

In 1656 Mr Farquhar, who was then seventy-six years of age, is described as "being now aged and infirm, and so unable to do duty as formerly, or as is necessary to embrace or exercise the office and function of the ministry at the said kirk (of Kintail) as their lawful and actual minister." Accordingly the Presbytery of Dingwall, at a meeting held on the 14th February in that year,[1] granted an Act of Transportation to Kintail on behalf of Mr Donald Macrae of Urray (Mr Farquhar's son), who had received a call from the congregation of Kintail with the consent of Mr Farquhar himself and the approval of the Earl of Seaforth. Mr Donald was admitted to Kintail as fellow-labourer and "conjunct" minister with his father, on the 20th July following, by the Rev. Alexander Mackenzie of Lochcarron. A lengthy document, drawn up on the 24th June by the Presbytery, after "long and mature deliberation," and setting forth in great detail the conditions of this "conjunct ministrie," is preserved in the Records of the Presbytery of Dingwall. Notwithstanding the care with which this document was drawn up, difficulties arose between the father and the son with regard to the possession of the vicarage, and the matter was discussed, privately, by Mr Donald's request, at a

---

[1] Inverness and Dingwall Presbytery Records, edited by William Mackay.

meeting of the Presbytery of Dingwall, held on the 29th of December, 1657, when Mr Donald promised to abide by the decision of the Presbytery. The Presbytery gave its decision in favour of Mr Farquhar, who appears to have spent the remainder of his days in peace.

It is so frequently the custom to speak only of what was wild and unsettled in the Highlands of two or three centuries ago that, to anyone interested in the social history of that part of the country, it must be very pleasant to contemplate the life-long work of such a man as Mr Farquhar in a parish so Highland and so outlying as Kintail; but there were many such men in those days—men whose scholarly and cultured refinement was a source of sweetness and light to the community among whom their lot was cast; and though the memory of many of them may have passed away in the great social changes which the Highlands have been undergoing for the last century and a half, yet they were the salt of the earth to their own generation, and the silent and hidden influence of their lives and their labours may still be seen in the politeness and culture which is sometimes to be found even in the humble cottage of the Highland crofter. In the days of Mr Farquhar, Kintail was well peopled, and, being the ancestral home of one of the most powerful noblemen in Scotland, it was a place of considerable importance. The principal men of the district came into very frequent personal contact with the Earl himself, with the natural result that they also became keenly interested in the great religious and political

E

movements with which the Chiefs of Kintail were
in various ways so intimately associated.   Consequently we find among the people of Kintail, in a
very marked degree, the high political and religious
tension which so frequently marks a period of civil
and revolutionary warfare.   Perhaps in no other
district of the Highlands was the religious and
political feeling of the people more pronounced
at this time than in Kintail and the neighbourhood.   This fact is fully borne out by the
tone of the *Fernaig Manuscript*, which is a
collection of Kintail poems of this period, and to
which reference is made elsewhere in this book.
Such, then, were the circumstances of the Highland
community of which Mr Farquhar was for nearly
half-a-century the central figure, and the chief guide
not only in spiritual things, but in things temporal
as well.   Though the sphere of his work and
activity was limited to a remote Highland parish,
his long life was thus a very eventful and anxious
one, and covered one of the most stirring periods of
Scottish history.   It was during his University
career that James VI. succeeded to the throne of
England, and the Royal House of Scotland rose to
the zenith of its ill-starred greatness.   Then, in the
course of time there came the Covenanter movement
and the Civil War, which ended in the execution of
Charles I. and the exile of his family.   Mr Farquhar
himself was a staunch Royalist and an Episcopalian,
so that he belonged to the losing cause of what, so
far as Scotland as a whole was concerned, was
only the minority; but though the army of the

enemy overran his country and plundered his
property, he held stoutly to his principles like a good
man and true. Those principles were doomed in
course of time to be all but totally renounced
and rejected by the people of the Highlands, and
this is not the place to discuss whether in doing so
they did rightly or wrongly, but the steadfastness
with which Mr Farquhar and his family supported
the Scottish Episcopal Church and the Scottish
Royal Family must call forth the admiration of all
who appreciate what is loyal and true in human
nature. He lived for two years after the restoration
of King Charles II., and thus had the satisfaction
in his old age of seeing the Royal House of Stuart
enjoying a fitful return of power and popularity, and
then he died before the true character of the restored King had time to become generally apparent.
And so his end was peace. He died in the midst
of a prosperous grown-up family, regretted and
mourned by all his countrymen, and leaving behind
him memories of goodness and worth which the
lapse of more than two centuries have not effaced.

Mr Farquhar married on the 1st December, 1611,
Christina, eldest daughter of Macculloch of Park,
Strathpeffer, and by her, who died before him, he
had eight sons and two daughters, viz.:--Alexander,
John, Donald, Miles, Murdoch, John, Christopher,
Thomas, Isabel, and Helen. He died in January,
1662, at the age of eighty-two, and was buried
with his ancestors at Kilduich, in Kintail.

CHRISTOPHER and THOMAS died apparently without issue, as their nephew, Finlay, son of John, is

mentioned as their heir on the 28th July, 1696.[1]
The other sons of the Rev. Farquhar Macrae will
be mentioned hereafter.

ISABEL, eldest daughter of Mr Farquhar, married
Malcolm Macrae, son of Ian Og Mac Fhionla Dhuibh,
"a pretty, young gentleman, bred at school and
college," who was killed at the battle of Auldearn
in 1645. After his death, she married William, son
of the Rev. John Mackenzie, of the Dochmaluag
family.

HELEN, second daughter of Mr Farquhar, married
John, younger son of John Bayne of Knockbain.

---

[1] Register of Retours.

CHAPTER V.

VIII. ALEXANDER, son of the Rev. Farquhar
VII., is commonly known as Alexander of Inverinate.   His father procured for him a wadset of the
lands of Inverinate, Dorisduan, and Letterinimmer,
for the sum of six thousand marks, and he is mentioned in the Valuation Roll of the County of Ross
in 1644, as possessed of lands in the parish of Kintail
of the yearly value of £266 13s 4d Scots.   He was
Chamberlain of Kintail under Kenneth Mor, third
Earl of Seaforth, who, as already stated, received

his early education at Ellandonan Castle, from Alexander's father, and by whom Alexander himself was much esteemed.   It is stated in the Rev. John Macrae's History of the Mackenzies, that when General Middleton and Lord Balcarres were in the Highlands raising an army to support Charles II. against Cromwell, probably about 1651, they paid a visit to Seaforth, who welcomed Balcarres in a special manner, and sent Alexander of Inverinate to bring Lady Balcarres, who was a daughter of Colin, first Earl of Seaforth, to Kintail, which, "with some hazard and difficulty, Alexander performed," bringing the lady safe to Ellandonan Castle, where she lived for some time with her husband.   Alexander married, as his first wife, Margaret, daughter of Murdoch Mackenzie, second laird of Redcastle, by whom he had two sons, Duncan and John, and two daughters, Catherine (or Christina) and Mary.   He married, as his second wife, Mary, daughter of Alexander Mackenzie, fourth laird of Dochmaluag, by whom he had seven sons, Alexander, Donald, Christopher, Farquhar, Murdoch, Allan, and Hugh, and at least two daughters, Isabel and Margaret.   The descent of both his wives can be traced to the Royal Houses of Stuart and Plantagenet.[1]

1. DUNCAN, eldest son of Alexander by his first wife, Margaret Mackenzie of Redcastle, will be mentioned hereafter.

2. THE REV. JOHN, second son of Alexander by his first wife, was educated at Aberdeen University, and was laureated, that is, took his degree, on the

---

[1] See Royal Pedigrees. Appendix F.

12th July, 1660.   When the first school was opened
in Dingwall he was appointed master of it.   This
was before the 21st July, 1663, as he is mentioned
on that date as schoolmaster of Dingwall and Clerk
to the Session. He was ordained in 1667 to the parish
of Kilmorack, and was translated in 1674 to the
parish of Dingwall, where he lived and laboured for
thirty years, and of which he was the last Episcopalian minister.   He is mentioned in various documents of the period as Treasurer of Ross.   He is
said to have been a great favourite in the family of
the Earl of Seaforth, who gave him a wadset of the
lands of Dornie, Dronaig, Aryugan, &c., in Kintail,
for the sum of seven thousand five hundred marks.
His influence in Dingwall and the neighbourhood
appears to have been very great, and so loyal was
the feeling of the people, both to his memory and to
the Church to which he belonged, that on his death
they so persistently opposed the introduction of
Presbyterianism among them, that, in spite of
repeated attempts, it was found impossible to settle
a Presbyterian minister in Dingwall until 1716,
twenty-eight years after the Revolution, and this
settlement was made not by patronage or by a
"call" from the people, but by the Presbytery
acting under warrant from the Privy Council.[1]

1 From the record of a meeting of the Privy Council of Scotland, on
the 25th April, 1704, and under the heading "The Agent for the Kirk against
Macraes and others," we learn something of the first attempts made to introduce
Presbyterianism into the Royal burgh of Dingwall after the death of the Rev.
John Macrae. The Rev. William Stewart of Kiltearn, having been delegated by
the "United Presbyteries of Ross and Sutherland" to supply the vacancy, repaired
to Dingwall accordingly, on Sunday, the 16th January. Finding the aspect of
affairs on his arrival rather threatening, he decided to appeal to the magistrates

The Rev. John Macrae was the author of an important History of the Mackenzies, to which frequent reference is made in this book. The clan historian, Alexander Mackenzie, frequently refers to it also, in his History of the Mackenzies, as the Ardintoul MS. He was also the author of a History and Genealogy of the Macraes, which has already been described in the first chapter of this book.

The Rev. John married, before the 21st July, 1673, Janet Bayne, of Knockbain. There is a sasine of that date to Mr John Macrae, Treasurer of Ross, and Janet Bayne, his spouse. By her he had issue as below. He died in January, 1704.

a. Alexander, eldest son of the Rev. John, was educated for the Church, but, as the Episcopal Church was proscribed in Scotland after the Revolution of 1688, he threw in his lot with the Roman Catholics rather than become a Presbyterian. For many years he discharged the duties of a Roman Catholic priest between Brahan and Strathglass,

for protection. The magistrates, however, could not be found, and meantime the ringleaders of the mob surrounded the house in which the minister was, and made the outer door fast with nails. The minister then made a strong appeal to the people from the window of the house, and eventually succeeded, by the help of Sir Robert Munro of Foulis and others from Kiltearn, in regaining his liberty and effecting an entrance into the church. But when the "worship was begun and almost finished," there arrived a company of armed men from the country, among whom the chief ringleaders were John Macrae vic Alister Oig, Hugh Macrae, father (it ought to be brother) to the said deceased Mr John Macrae, late incumbent at Dingwall ; Kenneth Macrae, brother german to Farquhar Macrae of Inverinate ; and —— Macrae, son to Christopher, brother german to the said deceased Mr John Macrae, all in the parish of Kintail. These men having entered the church "upon pretence that they were coming to attend the worship," the said John Macrae vic Alister went up to the door of the pulpit and "presented a pistol to the

and was probably the last who said mass in Brahan
Castle.   He was the first Macrae who became a
Roman Catholic after the Reformation, and was the
founder of the mission which that Church still
carries on in Kintail.   His first converts were his
own cousins, Alexander Macra of Ardintoul and
John Og, son of the Rev. Donald Macrae, last Episcopalian minister of Kintail, and another man called
Ian Buidhe Mac Dhonnachaidh (Yellow John, the
son of Duncan).   In his old age he retired to the
Scotch Roman Catholic College at Douai, in France,
and there died.   The Kintail Mission was well supported by the Macraes, and was afterwards carried
on by the Rev. John Farquharson, a celebrated
priest of Strathglass, the Rev. Norman Macleod, and
others.

   b. John, who married Margaret, daughter of the
Rev. Roderick Mackenzie, minister and Laird of
Avoch.   He is also said to have married, as her
second husband, Anne, daughter of Alexander
Mackenzie, third Laird of Applecross, who survived

minister, threatening to kill him until stopped by the hearers, whereupon the
rest of the armed men approached nearer, and scrambling over the seats to
the pulpit with menacing countenances and arms in their hands, they commanded Mr Stewart to come down and begone, which constrained him to
retire."   The disturbance continued as he passed out through the churchyard,
until at last " the minister, finding himself like to faint through the violence
he had suffered, prayed some gentlemen, his friends, to carry him off any way,
which was done."   Nor did Sir Robert Munro and his friends escape without
blows, and " further, these rabblers cried loudly and frequently King Willie is
now dead and their King is alive."   The ringleaders were summoned by the
Privy Council, but failed to compear, whereupon they were declared rebels,
and their goods and gear forfeited to the Crown.   Various other unsuccessful
attempts were made to introduce Presbyterianism into Dingwall, and though
the Rev. Daniel Bayne was appointed to the living in 1708, it was not until
1716 that he was able to enter upon possession of it.

him, and afterwards married, as her third husband, Colin Mackenzie of Inverness.[1]

*b*1. Alexander, who was served heir to his grandfather, the Rev. John Macrae, minister of Dingwall and Treasurer of Ross, on the 24th of June, 1741. Having afterwards recovered from Seaforth the money for certain wadsets which he held in Kintail, and sold some property which he held about Dingwall, he went into business in Bristol, where he became a prosperous and wealthy merchant, and died without issue in April, 1781. He left a sum of fifty thousand marks[2] to the King's College, Aberdeen, for educating boys of the name Macrae who could be traced in the male line from his great-grandfather, Alexander of Inverinate, " in preference to all others."[3] Several students of the name Macrae held this bursary in past times.

*b*2. Margaret, who married John Matheson, Durinish.[4]

*b*3. Mary, married to James, son of Alexander Matheson of Bennetsfield,[4] and had, with other issue, Catherine, who married Alexander Matheson, some

---

[1] Only the first marriage is mentioned in the MS. history of the Macraes, but both are mentioned in Sir James Dixon Mackenzie's Genealogical Tables of the Mackenzies. The probability is that he was twice married, and that his family was by the first wife.

[2] Fifty thousand merks Scots mortified by the late Alexander Macrae, of Dornie, and left under the management of the King's College of Aberdeen, for educating the children of the nearest descendants from Alexander Macrae, son of Mr Farquhar Macrae, the first Protestant minister in the parish of Kintail. —*Old Statistical Account.*

[3] Appendix L.

[4] For the descendants of this marriage, see Mackenzie's History of the Mathesons.

time schoolmaster, Dornie, who has been already mentioned on page 48.

    c. Christopher, baptised at Dingwall in November, 1682.

    d. Roderick, baptised at Dingwall, 18th August, 1692, and mentioned, in 1763, as the deceased Mr Roderick Macrae in the will of his nephew, Alexander Macrae, some time of Bristol. He married a daughter of Alexander Mackenzie, Chamberlain of Ferintosh, and had issue—

    *d*1. John.

    *d*2. Duncan, who went to Maryland in America, was a lieutenant in the "Provincials" during the American War of Independence, and was killed in the expedition under General Forbes against Fort Duquesne in 1757.

    *d*3. Helen, married to Thomas Maclean, a schoolmaster at Ord.

    *d*4. Janet.

    e. Mary, who married Roderick Dingwall of Ussie. There is a sasine on disposition by Roderick Dingwall of Ussie in favour of Mary Macrae, relict of the said Roderick, in liferent of the lands of Wester Ussie and Bogachro, &c., in the parish of Fodderty, 6th January, 1745. They had issue, at least one son, called John.

    f. Janet, baptised at Dingwall, 8th October, 1693, married John Tuach of Logereit.

    A daughter of the Rev. John Macrae, last Episcopalian minister of Dingwall, was married to John Og, son of John Mackenzie, second laird of Applecross, and had issue.[1] This John Og was one

[1] Sir James Dixon Mackenzie's Genealogical Tables of the Mackenzies.

of the famous "Four Johns of Scotland" who were killed at Sheriffmuir in 1715.

3. ALEXANDER, eldest son of Alexander of Inverinate by his second wife, Mary Mackenzie of Dochmaluag, was called Alister Og, and lived at Achyark, in Kintail. He married a daughter of Donald, son of Finlay, son of Christopher VI., and had issue—

a. John, who was a well educated man and was one of the Seaforth Captains at Sheriffmuir. He was probably the John Macrae vic Alister Oig who took part as ringleader in the riot at Dingwall church in 1704, which has been already referred to. He married and had a son John, who had a daughter Isabel, who married William Morrison, farmer of Baloagie, on the Fairburn estate.

4. THE REV. DONALD, second son of Alexander of Inverinate by his second wife, Mary Mackenzie of Dochmaluag, and IX. in descent from Finlay Dubh Macgillechriosd, was for some time schoolmaster at Fortrose, and became Vicar of Kintail in 1681. He was an ardent Jacobite and Episcopalian, and at the revolution of 1688 he refused to conform to Presbytery, so that Kintail remained Episcopalian for at least another quarter of a century. His name is mentioned in a list of "Episcopal Ministers who enjoy Churches or Benefices in Scotland" in March, 1710, and of whom it is said; "Some of them pray for the Pretender; others do not refuse to pray for the Queen (Anne), and some pray only for their sovereign without naming anybody, but it is generally thought they mean the Pretender."[1]   The

----

[1] The Case of Mr Greenshields—printed in 1710.

Rev. Donald and his family took a prominent part in the Rebellion of 1715, and he had two sons and a son-in-law killed at Sheriffmuir. He appears also to have been involved in the attempt which was made to revive the cause of the Stuarts in Kintail in 1719, and which ended in the defeat of the Jacobite party at the battle of Glenshiel, on the 10th of June in that year, for we read that his church was destroyed by the crew of one of the ships of war that sailed into Loch Duich at that time.[1] He died shortly afterwards, and with him ended the Episcopal Church in Kintail. The Episcopal form of worship in the Highlands at this time differed very little, if any, from the Presbyterian form, as there appears to have been no prayer book used, so that the Rev. Donald would conduct his services after the abolition of Episcopacy and the establishment of Presbyterianism exactly as he did before. This no doubt explains to a great extent the apparent readiness with which the common people of those times seem to have passed from the one form of worship to the other. The leading men of Kintail, however, were not to be satisfied with the mere outward appearance of things. Many of them looked at the underlying principles of their religion as well. The heavy loss sustained at Sheriffmuir, and the treatment to which they had so recently been subjected at the time of the Battle of Glenshiel, had produced among them a particular dislike of the Whig party, with which Presbyterianism was so closely associated, and rather than conform to Presbyterianism, after the

[1] Appendix F.

death of the Rev. Donald Macrae, many of them joined the Roman Catholic Mission which had recently been established among them by the Rev. Alexander Macrae already mentioned. The Rev. Donald Macrae married Catherine Grant[1] of Glenmoriston, by whom he had issue.

(1). ALEXANDER, mentioned below.

(2). MR JOHN, who married a daughter of the Laird of Chisholm, but left no issue. The Mr prefixed to his name suggests that he was a University graduate. He appears to have been well educated, and was tutor to Norman Macleod of Macleod, with whom he is said to have travelled abroad, and who settled on him and his heirs the sum of " 1000 pounds Scots per bond." Mr John died in 1741, leaving this sum to his youngest brother, John Og.

(3). DUNCAN married and left issue.

(4). COLIN ; (5). CHRISTOPHER, both killed at Sheriffmuir.

(6). JOHN OG, who, on the death of his father, and the final suppression of Episcopacy in Kintail, became a Roman Catholic, and was the fourth to join the mission referred to above. He died young,

---

[1] The tradition in Kintail is that this Catherine Grant was a daughter of John Grant, Laird of Glenmoriston, 1703-1736, commonly called *Ian a' Chragain*, by his second wife, Janet, daughter of Sir Ewen Cameron of Lochiel. Janet died in 1759, aged 80 years. This places her birth in 1679, so that in 1715, the year of the Battle of Sheriffmuir, she was 36 years of age. Now, the Rev. Donald Macrae had two sons and a son-in-law killed at Sheriffmuir. These, according to the Kintail tradition, would be the grandchildren of Janet Cameron, who, at the time of their death, was only 36 years of age. The son-in-law (John of Conchra), who was killed at Sheriffmuir, left two children ; this would make Janet Cameron a great grandmother at the age of 36, and, therefore, if the Rev. Donald was married only once, the probability is that Catherine Grant was a sister, and not a daughter, of *Ian a' Chragain.*

and was attended by Father Farquharson of Strath-glass on his death-bed. He married Barbara Mac-rae, daughter of Farquhar, son of Christopher, son of Alexander of Inverinate, and by her had issue—

(*a*). ISABELLA, who married Alexander Macrae of Achtertyre, of whom hereafter.

(*b*). HELEN, who married Duncan Macrae, Fa-doch, also mentioned hereafter.

(*c*). CATHERINE, who married John Macrae, a descendant of John Breac, son of the Rev. Farquhar Macrae.

(*d*). CHRISTINA, married with issue.

John Og's widow afterwards married Donald, son of the Rev. Finlay Macrae of Lochalsh, with issue.

(7). MARY.

(8). ISABELLA, who married, first, John Macrae of Conchra, who was killed at Sheriffmuir, and of whom hereafter. She is said to have married, secondly, Alexander Mackenzie of Applecross, son of John, who was killed at Sheriffmuir, and thirdly, George Mackenzie of Fairburn.

(9). KATHERINE married Donald Macrae of Tor-lysich.

On the other hand, it is stated in an old Genealogical Tree of the Macraes, that the Rev. Donald had a daughter, Mary, by " his first marriage with Chisholm's daughter." In that case, it may be possible that he was twice married, and that his second marriage was with Catherine, daughter of *Ian a' Chragain*. The disparity of their years, however, would be very great, and they might have had one child, John Og, mentioned below. This explanation may be regarded as not altogether improbable, as the tradition is certainly an old one, and was related to the writer in a very circumstantial manner by one of John Og's descendants, a man whose information he has invariably found reliable. Janet Cameron must have married at a very early age, and some of her descendants must have done so also, because we read that there were great-great-grandchildren at her funeral.

(10). CHRISTINA married Donald Macrae of Morvich, son of Farquhar, son of Alexander of Inverinate.

(x.) ALEXANDER, eldest son of the Rev. Donald Macrae, appears to have lived at Ruroch in Kintail. He married Florence, daughter of Ewen Mackenzie Vll. of Hilton, by whom he had two sons—

(1). FARQUHAR.

(2). JOHN, who married a daughter of Chisholm of Muckarach. His circumstances becoming reduced, he, along with many others from Kintail, emigrated to North Carolina in 1774, where he died, shortly after his arrival, from the bite of a snake, which he received while clearing some ground for a plantation. He left one son there, called JOHN.

Alexander had three daughters.

(xi.) FARQUHAR, eldest son of Alexander, by Florence Mackenzie of Hilton, married, first, the widow of John Macrae of Achyark, by whom he had one daughter. He married, secondly, Margaret (or Mary), daughter of Duncan Macrae of Balnain, by whom he had three sons.

(1). CHRISTOPHER, a sergeant in the regiment which was raised by Lord Seaforth in 1778 (the 78th, afterwards the 72nd). He served abroad, and died in India. He was the author of several Gaelic songs, which used to be very popular, and may still be heard in Lochalsh and Kintail.

(2). COLIN married with issue—ALEXANDER and four daughters.

(3). ALEXANDER was tacksman of Inchcro, in Kintail. He married Mary, daughter of Duncan

Macrae, Fadoch, who was descended from Miles, son of the Rev. Farquhar Macrae, with issue—

(*a*). Christopher, who, along with his brother, was for some time tacksman of Inchcro. He was married, but died, without issue, in or near Dingwall about 1860.

(*b*). Duncan, who died, unmarried, in New Zealand about 1882.

(*c*). A daughter, who married John Macrae, Dornie, who was commonly called Ian Dubh Nan Dorn (Black John of the Fists), so called from the extraordinary strength he possessed in his hands.

5. CHRISTOPHER, third son of Alexander of Inverinate and Mary Mackenzie of Dochmaluag, is mentioned hereafter.

6. FARQUHAR, fourth son of Alexander of Inverinate and Mary Mackenzie of Dochmaluag, lived at Morvich. He married with issue, one of whom—

a. Murdoch, who is mentioned as taking a prominent part in the skirmish at Ath nam Muileach (the ford of the men of Mull), in Glenaffric, on the 2nd October, 1721, when Donald Murchison of Auchtertyre, with about three hundred followers, met and repulsed William Ross of Easter Fearn, near Tain, who was proceeding to Kintail under the escort of a company of soldiers to collect rents on the Seaforth Estates on behalf of the Forfeited Estates Commissioners.[1] Murdoch married Mary, daughter of Farquhar X., and left with other issue—

John, the celebrated Kintail poet, commonly called Ian Mac Mhurachaidh, whose Gaelic songs are

[1] Appendix E.

F

still well known in Kintail and Lochalsh. These
songs are of very high poetical merit, and this,
together with the strong and effective local colour-
ing they possess, helps to account for the deep
and lasting impression which the poet made on
his countrymen, and the prominent place which
his name occupies among the traditions of Kintail.
The poems deal chiefly with the pursuits and de-
lights of such a country life as he himself led among
his native glens and mountains, many of which he
has invested with associations which must continue
classic and sacred to his countrymen so long as any
of them are left in Kintail to speak the Gaelic
tongue. About 1770 a great many of the people
of Kintail emigrated to America, and the poet
resolved to seek his fortune there also. His friends
endeavoured to persuade him to remain at home,
but nothing could shake his resolution. It is said
he was so greatly esteemed in the Highlands that,
when his intention to leave the country became
known, several neighbouring lairds offered him valuable lands on their estates if he would only remain
in the country. But the spirit of adventure was
then abroad in Kintail, and, notwithstanding the
prospects held out to him at home, the poet was
as much as anyone under its influence. There are
various traditions as to the motives which induced
him to leave the country, but the chief motive was
undoubtedly the adventurous desire to seek fortune
in a new field beyond the Atlantic, as so many of
his countrymen did at this time. On the day of his
departure, many of his friends accompanied him to

the heights of Auchtertyre in Lochalsh, and the spot is still pointed out where he took his farewell of them. But things went hard with him in America. When the War of Independence broke out, he cast in his lot with the Loyalists, whose cause soon became the losing one, and, after sharing in the hardships and defeat of the British armies, he at last perished a fugitive among the primeval woods. During the time of his adversity in America, he composed several songs, which were brought back to Kintail, and in which he expresses with much beauty and pathos the yearning of his soul to return to the scenes and the friends of happier days.[1] He married before he left Kintail. It is doubtful who his wife was, but the tradition in Kintail is that she was Christina Macrae, daughter of Alexander Roy of the Torlysich family.[2] He had three sons, Charles, Murdoch, and Donald. He also had a daughter whom he left behind him a child in Kintail, and who afterwards married Finlay Macrae, who was schoolmaster at Fadoch, in Kintail, a grandson of the Rev. Finlay Macrae, with issue, as already mentioned.

b. Farquhar, called Farquhar Og (Farquhar the younger), had, with other issue, a son called Donald Ban, who had a son Murdoch, who had a son, the Rev. Donald Macrae, who was born in 1802,

---

1 Appendix J.

2 In Sir J. D. Mackenzie's genealogical tables of the Mackenzies, it is stated that about this time Winifred Mackenzie, of the Dochmaluag family by her father and the Fairburn family by her mother, married John Macrae, a poet of Kintail. At all events, the poet lived on terms of the closest friendship with the Fairburn family.

ordained a minister of the Free Church by the Presbytery of Lews in 1844, and died at Cross, in Lews, on the 15th November, 1876, with issue, six children.

c Alexander is mentioned as taking part in the affair of Ath nam Muileach.   He appears to have had a son John, who is also mentioned in connection with the same affair.

d. Anne, married Alexander Mac Gillechriosd Macrae, in Strathglass, and had issue—Christopher; Isabel, who married as his second wife Alexander Macra of Ardintoul; Margaret, who married Duncan MacAlister Mac Gillechriosd, and had a son a priest.

7. MURDOCH, fifth son of Alexander of Inverinate and Mary Mackenzie of Dochmaluag, came to an ultimely and tragic end.   He was out hunting in Glenlic one day in the early winter, and, according to tradition, found a man stealing his goats.   Having captured the thief, Murdoch was leading him along, but as they were passing the brink of a precipice called the Carraig (Rock), the prisoner succeeded in pushing Murdoch over the rock, at the foot of which his body was found after a search of fifteen days.   The death of Murdoch was such a mysterious affair that there arose a belief in Kintail that the dark deed was the work of an evil spirit, and the spot where the body was found was long believed to be haunted, but it is said that, many years afterwards, an old man in Strathglass confessed on his deathbed that he was the murderer, and gave a full account of the event.   Another

version of the same tradition says that the goat-stealer was accompanied by his little grandson, who was a witness of the murder, and who afterwards went to America, where he lived to a very advanced age, and related the circumstances of the murder on his deathbed. The Glenlic hunt and the death of Murdoch occupy a very prominent place in the traditions of Kintail.[1] Several elegies composed on the occasion have been preserved, and some of them are of a very high order. The traditions with regard to those elegies are somewhat vague, and it is not easy to arrive at definite facts, but some of them are believed to have been composed by John Macdonald, Ian Lom,[2] the Lochaber Bard, who was the contemporary of the sons of Alexander of Inverinate. It is said that Ian Lom's life being at one time in danger in his own country, he fled for refuge to Kintail, where he was living with the Inverinate family at the time of Murdoch's death, and that on each of the fifteen days during which the search lasted, he composed an elegy. Another tradition says that some of the elegies were composed by Murdoch's brother, Duncan. In any case, the fragments that have been preserved are of great merit, and not unworthy even of such poets as Ian Lom and Donnacha nam Piòs. One of the elegies contains a verse in which all Murdoch's brothers are mentioned, except

[1] See chapter on legends and traditions of the clan.

[2] John Macdonald, or Ian Lom (Bare John), was a celebrated Gaelic poet of the family of Keppoch. He was a personal friend and a devoted supporter of the Earl of Montrose. One of his chief productions is a descriptive poem on the victory gained by Montrose over the Earl of Argyll at Inverlochy, in 1645. Ian Lom died at a very advanced age about 1710.

Alexander, who may possibly have died before :

> 'S tùirseach do sheachd bráithrean gráidh,
> Am *parson* ge h-árd a leugh,
> Thug e, ge tuigseach a cheaird,
> Aona bharr-tùirs air cách gu lèir.

> Bho thus dhiubh Donnachadh nam Piòs.
> Gillecriosda, 's an dithis de'n chléir,
> Fearachar agus Ailean Donn,
> Uisdean a bha trom 'n ad dhéigh.[1]

The *parson* mentioned in the first of these verses was undoubtedly Murdoch's brother — the Rev. Donald of Kintail, who, from the reference here made to him, seems to have written an elegy on this occasion, but the manner in which Donnacha nam Piòs is mentioned would seem to imply that he himself was not the author, at all events of the poem from which these verses are quoted.

Murdoch left a young widow, and at least two sons, who grew up and married with issue.

8. ALLAN, sixth son of Alexander of Inverinate and Mary Mackenzie of Dochmaluag, left no male issue.

9. HUGH, seventh son of Alexander of Inverinate and Mary Mackenzie of Dochmaluag, will be mentioned hereafter.

10. Christina, daughter of Alexander of Inverinate by his first wife, Margaret Mackenzie of Redcastle, married Alexander Matheson of Achtaytoralan, in Lochalsh, an ancestor of the Ardross family.

---

[1] Sad are thy seven beloved brothers,—the parson though profound is his learning,—though his office is one of giving comfort, yet he surpassed the others in his grief.

First among them is Duncan of the silver cups, then Christopher and the two clergymen, Farquhar, Allan of the auburn hair, and Hugh, who was sad after thee.

CHAPTER VI.

IX. Duncan, called Donnachadh nam Piòs.—His Character and
Attainments.—Traditions about Him.—The Silver Herring.—
The Oak Trees at Inverinate.—Duncan as a Poet.—The
Fernaig Manuscript. — A Valuable Contribution to Gaelic
Literature.—Religion and Politics of the Poems contained in
it.—Professor Mackinnon's Estimate of Donnachadh nam Piòs
and his Work.—His Tragic End.—His Marriage and Family.—
X. Farquhar.—His Marriage and Family.—XI. Duncan.—His
Marriage and Family.

IX. DUNCAN, eldest son of Alexander of Inverinate (VIII.), by his first wife, Margaret Mackenzie
of Redcastle, was commonly known as Donnachadh
nam Piòs, which means Duncan of the silver cups,
a name said to have been given to him probably because of the magnificence of his table service.   He
was a man of high character, a poet, and a skilful
mechanician, and many anecdotes and traditions
illustrative of his attainments are still related about
him in Kintail and Lochalsh.   It is said that when
he was a student in Edinburgh he assisted in
forming a plan for bringing the water into that
city.   There is a tradition that on one occasion a
strange ship had her mast broken in passing through
Kyle Rea.   The captain, unable to proceed any
further, was advised to appeal to Duncan for help.

Duncan took the matter in hand himself, and spliced the broken mast so skilfully that the joining could hardly be seen, and in return for this service the grateful captain gave him a silver herring, which remained for a long time an heirloom in the family, and which was commonly believed by the people of Kintail to possess the magic power of attracting herring into Loch Duich. It is also said that the oak trees at Inverinate were reared by him from acorns that he brought from France. There is reason, however, to believe that Duncan's trees have been cut down, and that the present trees are not so old as his time.

It is, however, as a poet that Duncan achieved his greatest distinction. Fragments of poetry ascribed to him still survive orally among the people of Kintail, and Professor Mackinnon of Edinburgh University, has proved[1] beyond any reasonable doubt that he was the compiler of the *Fernaig Manuscript* and the author of many, if not of most, of the poems contained in it. This manuscript, which has recently been printed[2] consists of two small volumes of paper in pasteboard covers, about eight inches long and three broad. The two volumes together consist of one hundred and twenty-eight pages, of which about one hundred and five are closely and neatly written upon in the handwriting of the period. It contains about

[1] Transactions of the Gaelic Society of Inverness, Volume XI.

[2] Reliquiæ Celticæ, left by the late Rev. Alexander Cameron, LL.D., edited by Alexander Macbain, M.A., and the Rev. John Kennedy, and published by the Northern Counties Newspaper and Printing and Publishing Company, Limited, Inverness, 1894.

four thousand two hundred lines. It was commenced in the year 1688, and the latest date
mentioned in it is the year 1693. The spelling
is phonetic and very difficult, if not quite un-
readable, for one who is accustomed only to the
modern Gaelic spelling. In addition to poems by
Duncan himself, the manuscript contains poems also
by writers who can easily be identified as his
relatives and kinsmen, such as his great-grandfather, Macculloch of Park; his father-in-law, Macleod of Raasay; his brother, the Rev. Donald
Macrae of Kintail. There are poems also by Bishop
Carswell of the Isles; Alexander Munro, teacher,
Strathnaver, and others. The history of the
manuscript from the time of the writer until the
present century is unknown. In the year 1807, it
was in the possession of Mr Matheson of Fernaig,
father of the late Sir Alexander Matheson of
Ardross. Hence the name by which it is now
known. We afterwards find it in the possession of
Dr Mackintosh Mackay, on whose death, in 1873,
it was handed over to Dr W. F. Skene. It is
now in the keeping of Mr Alexander Macbain, of
Inverness.

The Fernaig Manuscript is a valuable contribution to Gaelic literature, and next to the Dean of
Lismore's book it is said to be the most important
document we possess for the study of older Gaelic.
But it possesses more than mere philological value.
Its poetry, which is mainly religious and political,
affords an agreeable glimpse of the religion and the
politics of the remote Highlands at the time of the

Revolution.   In Politics the authors of these poems
are Jacobites, in Religion they are ardent Episcopalians, and they evidently had a clear, intelligent,
and comprehensive grasp of the great questions of
the day, not simply as those questions affected their
own local interests, but as they affected the
kingdom as a whole.   Though the poems deal with
the state of the country in unsettled times of
warfare and revolution, they nevertheless breathe,
even against political and religious opponents, a
spirit of kindly toleration which must afford, at
all events to patriotic Highlanders, a pleasing
contrast with the narrow bigotry and religious
intolerance which formed so striking a feature of
this period in the south of Scotland.

"He (Donnachadh nam Pìos) was undoubtedly,"
says Professor Mackinnon, "a remarkable man and
a character pleasant to contemplate.   I have no
reason to doubt that there were many like-minded
Highland gentlemen living in those days—cultured,
liberal, and pious men; but undoubtedly Duncan
Macrae, the engineer and mechanician, the ardent
ecclesiastic,   the   keen   though   liberal-minded
politician, the religious poet, and collector of the
literature of his countrymen, is as different from the
popular conception of a Highland Chief of the
Revolution as can well be conceived.   We have
it on the testimony of Lord Macaulay that Sir
Ewen Cameron of Lochiel was not only a great
warrior, not only eminently wise in council, eloquent
in debate, but also a patron of literature.   It is a
high character to attain in that rude age, and from

4

5

6

7

8

FAC-SIMILE PAGE OF FERNAIG MS.

so severe a judge of Highlanders as Lord Macaulay undoubtedly was.   Duncan Macrae did not possess the great gifts, mental and physical, of Eoghan Dubh.[1]   With . kindly exaggeration the English historian calls Lochiel the Ulysses of the Highlands. By no figure of speech would we be justified in claiming such a high sounding title as this for Donnachadh nam Piòs.   And yet, the Highland chief who, among the distractions of Civil War and in the scanty intervals of leisure wrested from a useful, honoured, and industrious life, sat down to compose Gaelic verse and to collect the poems composed by his countrymen and neighbours, is highly deserving of our affection and admiration. Such a man was Duncan Macrae.

Altogether, the Fernaig Manuscript appears to me to be an important contribution to our stock of Gaelic literature; the political and religious intelligence, the devout and tolerant spirit, the strong sense and literary power displayed by the various writers in rude and turbulent times, are creditable to our people, while the enlightened compiler is a Highland Chief of whom not only the Macraes, but all his countrymen, may well be proud." [2]

But Duncan was not merely a mechanician and a poet, he was also a practical man of the world, and prospered in his affairs.   His end, however, was

[1] Eoghan Dubh (Black Ewen) is the name by which Sir Ewen Cameron of Lochiel was usually known in Gaelic.

[2] Professor Mackinnon, on the Fernaig Manuscript in the Transactions of the Gaelic Society of Inverness, Volume XI.

tragic.   Having gone on one occasion to the "Low
Country" to negotiate the purchase of the lands
of Affric from The Chisholm, he was returning home
accompanied by a single attendant, who possessed
the fatal and involuntary power of causing anyone
whom he might happen to see in the act of fording
a river to be drowned.[1] The homeward journey was
accomplished by Duncan and his servant without
accident or mishap, until they reached Dorisduan in
the Heights of Kintail.   Here it was necessary to
cross the River Conag, which happened to be in
flood.   The servant forded the river in safety, and
then threw himself on his face on the ground lest he
might chance to see his master in the water.   Having remained in that attitude long enough, as he
thought, for his master to gain the bank, he turned
round and caught sight of his master, who was
still struggling in the water, and who immediately
lost his footing in the stream.   Duncan succeeded,
however, in recovering himself, and in getting
sufficiently near the bank to seize hold of the
branch of a tree, but the unfortunate servant,
losing all presence of mind in his anxiety, still felt

---

[1] This fatal power was called, at all events in some parts of the Highlands,
"Or na h'aoine" (the charm of the fast or of Friday), and was believed to be
possessed by some men in Kintail within very recent times.   A man well
known to the author was, on one occasion about forty years ago, returning
home from church, with his wife, on a wet afternoon, in Strathconon. They
were accompanied by a shepherd from Kintail, and on the way they had to
ford a stream which was in high flood.   When they reached the stream the
shepherd plunged in, waded to the other side, and then stood still on the
opposite bank, with his back to the stream, until the other man and his wife,
who had great difficulty in crossing, came up to him.   The man, struck by the
strange behaviour of the shepherd, said to him—"You were going to allow
my wife and myself to get drowned without offering to help us."   "Perhaps,"

constrained to look at his master, who vainly struggled for some time to gain the bank, but finally lost his hold and was drowned. By this accident the family is said to have lost "much property,"[1] as Duncan had valuable papers on his person at the time, and among them the title deeds of Affric. Many local traditions have grown round the death of Donnachadh nam Piòs, and the sad and tragic event has been commemorated both by elegies and pibrochs. The exact date of Duncan's death is not known, but it was some time between 1693 and 1704.

Duncan married Janet, daughter of Alexander Macleod, fifth laird of Raasay, and sister of John, sixth laird, commonly called Ian Garbh. Ian Garbh, who was drowned off the north coast of Skye while returning from a visit to the Lews, left no issue, and so the succession to the estates of Raasay came to Janet and her sister, Giles, who were served heirs in 1688. But Janet and her sister, being anxious to maintain the dignity of their own clan, resigned or sold their rights in 1692 to their cousin, Alexander Macleod, who succeeded as the seventh chief

---

replied the shepherd, "it is a good thing for you and your wife that I did not offer to help you." The shepherd believed that he possessed the same fatal power as the servant who accompanied Donnachadh nam Piòs, and that if he saw the man and his wife in the stream they would both be drowned.

[1] Though there seems to be no documentary evidence of this loss, yet Duncan undoubtedly held lands in the Chisholm country. There is a sasine on charter of apprising under the Great Seal in favour of Duncan Macrae of Inverinate, of the lands of Meikle Comer, Comerroy, and others, in the parish of Kilmorack and shire of Inverness. At Edinburgh, 10th July, 1674, and sasine on 12th September, 1674, in presence of Christopher Macrae, in Beolak, in Kintail, and others. Alexander Macrae, in Achachaik (Achyark ?), as Sheriff and Bailie in that part, gives sasine.

of the family. It is said that the words of the satirical ditty known in the west of Ross-shire as Cailleach Liath Rasaidh (the greyhaired old woman of Raasay) were composed, on hearing of this transaction, by a Kintail wit, who was probably zealous for the dignity of the Inverinate family, and had perhaps hoped that Raasay might come into their possession. Janet herself appears to have possessed poetic talent, and is said to have composed an elegy on the death of her husband. By her Duncan had issue—

1. FARQUHAR, mentioned below.

2. KENNETH, who was one of the ringleaders of the riot at Dingwall Church in 1704, which has been already referred to. He married and left issue.

3. JOHN married and left issue. There is a John Macrae of Inverinate mentioned as taking a prominent part in the affair of Ath nam Muileach, and this was probably the man.

4. MARGARET, who married the Rev. Finlay Macrae of Lochalsh, with issue, as already mentioned.

5. Another daughter, whose name is not recorded.

X. FARQUHAR, eldest son of Duncan IX., about whom very little is known, married, in 1694, Anne, daughter of Simon Mackenzie, first laird of Torridon, and died in 1711, with issue—

1. DUNCAN, mentioned below.

2. CHRISTOPHER, who married and had issue, at least one son, Farquhar, called Ferachar Ban (Fair Farquhar) of Fadoch. He married Mary, a sister of Archibald Macra of Ardintoul. This Mary

died shortly before the 6th June, 1823, after a married life of sixty-two years. Her husband was alive at the time of her death, but he was completely blind and almost deaf with age. He died before 1826. They left issue—Hector; Duncan; Alexander, who appears to have been educated at at Aberdeen, and to have graduated M.A. in 1803; John; and several daughters, one of whom, Isabel, was married to a Duncan Macrae, who was dead in 1826.

3. JOHN, who is said to have been a man of great physical strength, and of whom it is related that on one occasion, at Loch Hourn, he carried away from a boat, across the beach, a large barrel of salt under each arm, one of which a man of ordinary strength could, with difficulty, lift from the ground.[1] John is witness to a sasine by his brother, Duncan Macrae of Inverinate, to Florence Mackenzie, his spouse, at Coul, 10th August, 1725.

4. JANET, married Christopher Macrae, at Drudaig, a descendant of the Rev. Donald, son of the Rev. Farquhar Macrae VII.

---

[1] The following extract from a letter written in Kintail in 1826 refers to this incident, and is worth quoting as an instance of the usual tendency to magnify the "good old days": "I have heard my father remark that the people of his native country are much degenerated in strength, as many anecdotes, still well known, will show. One trial of strength he often spoke of as being particularly well authenticated. John Macrae, uncle to Farquhar Macrae, late Fadoch, was at Loch Hourn with Simon Murchison, brother of Alexander of Auchtertyre, when they observed a man carrying up salt from the seaside to the beach, a barrel at a time. 'Do you see,' says Macrae, 'that man is boasting.' He then went and took up a barrel under his arm. 'Will you,' says he, 'help me to take up this other to my haunch?' Simon did so with very great difficulty, and Macrae swaggered away with both up to the beach. This was related to my father by the above Simon Murchison."

5. MARY, who married Murdoch, son of Farquhar Macrae of Morvich, and had, with other
issue, John, the Kintail poet, already mentioned.

6. ANNE, who married Duncan Macrae, son of
Donald, in Glensheil.

XI. DUNCAN, eldest son of Farquhar X., was
served heir on the 19th March, 1725. He married
Florence, daughter of Charles Mackenzie of Cullen
(Kilcoy family), by his wife, Florence, daughter of
John Mackenzie, second laird of Applecross, and
died in 1726, leaving issue—

1. FARQUHAR, mentioned below.

2. ANNE, who married Captain Horne and
resided with him in France. Mrs Horne is said
to have been the first to bring tea to Kintail. The
caddy in which the tea was brought is now in the
possession of Mrs Mackenzie, of Abbotsford Park,
Edinburgh, the great-granddaughter of Mrs Horne's
brother, Farquhar of Inverinate.

CHAPTER VII.

XII. Farquhar, Last of Inverinate.—His Marriages and Family.—
Alexander.—Captain Duncan Macrae and his Descendants.—
Colonel Kenneth Macrae.—Jean married the Rev. John
Macqueen of Applecross. — Her Descendants. — Dr John
Macrae and his Descendants. — Dr Farquhar Macrae.—
Represents Colin Fitzgerald in Benjamin West's Painting
in Brahan Castle.—Killed in a Duel.—Madeline Married
the Rev. John Macrae of Glensheil.—Her Descendants.—
Anne married Lachlan Mackinnon of Corriechatachan.—Her
Descendants.—Florence married Captain Kenneth Mackenzie
of Kerrisdale.—Her Descendants.—XIII. Colin.—His Marriage
and Family.—XIV. John Anthony.—His Marriage and Family.
—XV. Colin George.—His Marriage and Family.

XII. FARQUHAR, son of Duncan XI., was the
last of the family who held Inverinate and acted as
Chamberlain of Kintail.   Like so many more of his
Clan, he was an ardent Jacobite, and narrowly
escaped trouble in 1745.   Considering all that the
people of Kintail had suffered at the hands of the
supporters of the House of Hanover, both in 1715
and again in 1719, it is no matter for surprise that
in 1745 they once more showed signs of strong
Jacobite sympathies.   It is said that, notwithstanding Seaforth's loyalty to the House of
Hanover at that time, the army of the Prince was
joined by a number of Macraes, not one of whom

ever again returned to Kintail, and that Farquhar, who was then a very young man, was so strongly suspected of Jacobite sympathies that he was placed for some time under arrest.   There is a tradition that on one occasion he was mistaken by a party of the King's soldiers for the Prince himself, who had recently passed a day or two in Kintail in the course of his wanderings after the battle of Culloden, and that they took him to Fort-William, where his mother succeeded in satisfying the authorities as to his identity, and so secured his release.   Farquhar made some additions to the Rev. John Macrae's Manuscript History of the Clan, but those additions appear to have been limited to the merest outline of his own family.   He married first, on the 22nd April, 1755, Mary, daughter of Alexander Mackenzie, eighth laird of Dochmaluag, on whose death he married, as his second wife, Elizabeth, widow of Richard Ord, of Inverness, and daughter of John Mackenzie, son of Alexander, seventh laird of Dochmaluag, by whom he had no issue.   He died at Inverness in December, 1789, and was buried in Kintail.   By his first wife, Farquhar left numerous issue—

1. ALEXANDER, born 10th May, 1756, and died unmarried in Demerara.

2. DUNCAN, born 8th June, 1757.   He received an Ensign's Commission in the 78th Highlanders, which was raised by Lord Seaforth in 1793, and served with that regiment in India.   He was promoted Captain in 1797, and retired on half-pay in 1805.   He was connected at various times with

other regiments than the 78th.   He died about
1825.   Captain Duncan is said to have been a man
of very handsome personal appearance, a good
Highlander, and a generous man.   He married first,
on the 4th August, 1784, Janet, daughter of Alexander Murchison of Tarradale.   He married, as his
second wife, Christina, daughter of the Rev. William
Bethune of Kilmuir, Skye.   By his first wife he had
issue—

a. Kenneth, born 19th May, 1785.   He was
educated at King's College, Aberdeen, and went
to London in 1803 "to be placed in a mercantile
house."   He was afterwards a planter in Demerara.

b. Mary, born 20th August, 1786, died in infancy.

c. Alexander, born 28th August, 1787.   He was
educated at Aberdeen, and was afterwards a planter
in Demerara, where he was resident for half a
century.   He is the author of a "Manual of
Plantership in British Guiana," which was published
in 1856.   Alexander married and left three daughters
—Christina, Mary, and Flora—but no male issue.
He died at Southampton in 1860 from the effects
of an accident he met with on the homeward
voyage from Demerara.

d. Mary and Margaret, born 1st February,
1789, died in infancy.

Captain Duncan had issue also by his second
wife, as follows—

e. John

f. Duncan, who entered Aberdeen University
in 1820, and attended for four sessions, but did not
graduate.   He died unmarried in Demerara.

g. Mary, who was born at Inverinate, and married Lieutenant-John Robertson-Macdonald of Rodel, in Harris, with issue, one daughter, Jane, unmarried.

h. Jessie, who married Hector Mackinnon of the Island of Egg, with issue :—

*h*1. Duncan, died in Australia.

*h*2. Lachlan also died in Australia.

*h*3. Jessie, who married a Mr Crawford.

*h*4. Flora, who married a Mr Morrison, with issue.

*h*5. Alexandrina, who married a Mr Finlayson.

i. Flora, who, on 2nd February, 1826, married Alexander Macdonald of Vallay, North Uist, with issue—

*i*1. Alexander Ewen, in Australia, married, with issue.

*i*2. William John, a Senator of Vancouver Island, married, with issue—Flora ; Edith ; Christina ; Reginald, in the Royal Artillery ; William, in the Royal Navy ; Douglas.

*i*3. Duncan Alexander Macrae, in Australia.

*i*4. Colin Hector, in Australia, married, with issue.

*i*5. Duncan, in Australia.

*i*6. Christina Mary, married the Rev. John William Tolmie, of Contin, with issue : — (1) John, married Alexandrina, daughter of Donald Macrae, Luskintyre, in Harris, son of the Rev. Finlay Macrae; (2) the Rev. Alexander Macdonald Cornfute of Southend, Kintyre ; (3) Margaret, married the Rev. Archibald Macdonald of Kiltarlity, joint author of the *History of Clan Donald*, with issue, Marion

Margaret Hope; Christina Mary; Flora Amy Macruari; (4) Mary Macrae; (5) Flora, married Charles Hoffman Weatherall, M.R.C.V.S., in India, with issue; (6) Hugh Macaskill, in New Zealand; (7) Gregory, in New Zealand; (8) Williamina Alexandrina.

i7. Harriet Margaret married Alexander Allan Gregory, of Inverness, with issue :—(1) Alexander, married Miss Stewart (of Murdostoun, Lanarkshire), with issue; (2) Margaret Maclean, married Francis Foster, with issue ; (3) Harriett, married William Lindsay Stewart (of Murdostoun); (4) Catherine Christina, married Charles William Dyson Perrins, Esq. of Davenham, Worcestershire, and of Ardross Castle, with issue; (5) William ; (6) Neil; (7) Mary ; (8) John, in the Royal Navy ; (9) Reginald.

i8. Mary Isabella married the Rev. Kenneth Alexander Mackenzie, LL.D., of Kingussie, with issue : — John, died young ; Mary Flora, married Walter Frederick Rodolph De Watteville, M.B., &c., of Edinburgh University ; Elizabeth.

3. KENNETH, born 16th July, 1758. He received a Commission in the old 78th, afterwards the 72nd Highlanders, which was raised by the Earl of Seaforth in 1778. He afterwards served in the 76th Foot, in which regiment he was promoted Major in 1795, and Lieutenant-Colonel in 1804. He served with his regiment in India with much distinction. In one of his dispatches from India, dated 26th December, 1804, and giving an account of the capture of Deig, General Lake says : —" I myself feel under the greatest obligation to

Lieutenant-Colonel Macrae, to whose conduct on this occasion I attribute the ultimate success of the attack" (on Deig, on the 23rd December, 1804). Colonel Kenneth also took a prominent part in the siege and capture of Bhurtpore in the following year. Among the casualties at the siege at Bhurtpore, there was a Lieutenant D. Macrae of the 76th killed, and a Lieutenant J. Macrae of the same regiment wounded, on the 21st January, 1805. Colonel Kenneth Macrae was afterwards Paymaster-General of Jamaica, where he died about 1814. He married a Miss Mackay in Jamaica, but left no issue.

4. JEAN, born 23rd August, 1759. She married, in 1781, the Rev. John Macqueen, of Applecross, and died in 1847. She was called in Kintail "The Sunbeam of Tullochard" because of her beauty. She left issue—

a. Donald, a planter in Demerara.

b. John, a Major in the Army; married a daughter of Judge Bliss, of New Brunswick, and left a son, John, a Lieutenant in the Rifle Brigade, and other issue.

c. George, a Captain in the Rifle Brigade.

d. Archibald, who was Clerk of Arraigns in Demerara, and died unmarried.

e. Dr Kenneth, H.E.I.C.S., married, but left no surviving issue.

f. Farquhar, a Captain in the Indian Navy, married and left issue.

g. Mary; *h*, Jane; *i*, Jessie; *k*, Beatrice.

5. JOHN, born 3rd November, 1760, was a Doctor of Medicine, H.E.I.C.S. (Calcutta and Chittagong).

He married the daughter of a Colonel Erskine, with issue—

a. John, also a Doctor of Medicine, H.E.I.C.S., married and left one daughter. He died at Monghyr, in India, early in 1864.

b. Farquhar, who was a Lieutenant in the Indian Army, served in the first Burmese War, 1824-6, and died in 1847.

c. Ellen married Mr Lee Warner, without issue.

d. Dora married James Fraser of Achnagairn, in Inverness-shire, with issue—

*d*1. Dora, who married Robert Reid, brewer, London, without issue.

*d*2. Jane, who married Eyre Lambert, without issue.

*d*3. Helen, who married, first, Huntly George Gordon Duff of Muirtown, with issue :—(1) Emily Dora, who died young ; (2) Georgina Huntly, who married Francis Darwin of Elston, Notts, and of Muirtown, Inverness, without issue. Helen married, secondly, Charles Middleton of Middleton Lodge, Ilkley, Yorkshire, with issue ; (3) Charles Marmaduke ; (4) Reginald Charles ; (5) Lionel George ; (6) Mary Hilda.

e. Georgina, who married, 3rd March, 1831, Edmund Currie of Pickford, Sussex, with issue—

*e*1. The Very Rev. Edward Reid Currie, D.D., Dean and Vicar of Battle, in Sussex, married, first, Geraldine Dowdeswell, only child of Richard Tyrrell, Esq., with issue ; Edward George. He married, secondly, Frances Emma, only daughter of the Rev. William Frederick Hotham.

*e*2. Georgina married Sir Augustus Rivers Thompson, K.C.S.I., Lieutenant Governor of Bengal.

*e*3. Eliza Fredrica married George William Moultrie, of the Bank of Bengal.

*e*4. Mary Catherine.

*e*5. Dora married Nathaniel Stewart Alexander, Bengal Civil Service.

6. CHARLES, born 26th June, 1762, died young.

7. FARQUHAR, born 30th March, 1764. He was a Doctor of Medicine, and was appointed Medical Officer to Lord Macartney's Embassy to China in 1792-4. He was afterwards killed in a duel with a Major Blair in Demerara in 1802. He left no issue. He is said to have been " handsome and comely in personal appearance, and strong in proportion." His portrait is represented as Colin Fitzgerald, the reputed founder of the House of Seaforth in Benjamin West's celebrated deer hunt painting in Brahan Castle. There is an interesting tradition with regard to the manner in which Farquhar came to be chosen as the model for Colin Fitzgerald. It is said that the artist accidentally saw him one day in Hyde Park, and, being struck by his appearance, asked him if he would sit as a model for the founder of the House of Seaforth, which he readily consented to do. Farquhar was not only a native of the ancestral country of the Seaforths, but was also closely related to that family, and it is a remarkable fact that he should have struck the artist, to whom he is said to have been a perfect stranger, as a suitable representative for the hero of the painting.

8. MADELINE, born 2nd October, 1765. She

married, on the 27th June, 1782, the Rev. John
Macrae, M.A., minister of Glensheil, and died on the
21st January, 1837.   The Rev. John Macrae, who
was a native of the neighbourhood of Dingwall, was
educated at Aberdeen.   He was ordained to the
parish of Glensheil in 1777, and died there in 1823,
aged seventy-five years.   By him Madeline had
issue—

a. Alexander, born in 1783, died young.

b. Mary, born in 1785, married in 1814, Donald
Munro (of the family of Lealty, in Ross-shire), and
died in 1844, leaving issue—

*b*1. Madeline, who married the Rev. Alexander
Fraser Russell, M.A., Free Church minister of Kil-
modan, in Argyleshire, with issue :—(1) Sir James
Alexander Russell, M.D., LL.D., &c., Lord Provost
of Edinburgh, 1891-94.   He married Marianne Rae,
daughter of James Wilson, Esq., of Edinburgh, and
niece of Professor Wilson (Christopher North), without issue ; (2) The Rev. John Munro Russell, M.A.,
B.D., minister of the Scottish Church, Cape Town.
He married Nancy Eliza, daughter of the Rev.
Robert Elder, D.D., Free Church minister of Rothesay, with issue—Alexander Fraser ; Robert Elder ;
Madeline Mary ; Ian Robson ; (3) Donald George, a
tea planter in India, died in Edinburgh in 1897 ;
(4) William John, M.B., died at Wandsworth in
1883 ; (5) Duncan Kenneth Campbell, a Civil
Engineer ; (6) Tindal Mackenzie, died young ; (7)
Alexander Fraser, M.A., M.B., &c., Army Medical
Department, married Laura Charlotte, daughter of
Colonel Frederick Prescott Forteath of Newton,

Elginshire, with issue—James Forteath, Margaret Marianne; (8) Mary Florence Beatrice, died young.

*b*2. Isabella, now (1897) residing at Abbotsford Park, Edinburgh, married John Mackenzie, Leguan, British Guiana, with issue : — (1) Gilbert Proby, Surgeon - Major Indian Medical Service, married Jane Scott, and died in 1890, leaving issue—John, Indian Staff Corps; Thomas Rennie Scott; George Kenneth; Isabella; Emma; Gilbert Proby; (2) Donald George, Captain, Indian Staff Corps, married Mary Ruth, daughter of Captain G. M. Prior, R.A., and died in India in 1885, leaving issue — Isabella Florence Ruth; Ethel Lucy; (3) Charles Tindal Grant, died young.

*b*3. John died unmarried in Australia.

*b*4. Anne married Allan Cameron, with issue.

*b*5. Christina Flora married George Ross in Demerara, with issue.

*b*6. Donald married Maggie Muir, with issue.

c. Isabella, born 1786, married John Campbell, farmer, Duntulm, in Skye, and died in 1849, leaving numerous issue.

d. Florence, born 1788, married Duncan Macrae of the Torlysich family, and died in 1865, with issue, one son, Francis Humberston, who married in Tasmania, and left issue, two sons and one daughter.

e. Beatrice, born 1790, married the Rev. Alexander Campbell, minister of Croy, and died in 1877, with issue—

*e*1. Rev. Patrick Campbell, minister of Killearnan, in Ross-shire, died unmarried.

*c*2. Madeline married James M'Inroy, with issue.

*c*3. Jane married the Rev. James M. Allardyce, D.D., minister of Bowden, in Roxburghshire, with issue, one son, who died young.

*c*4. Duncan died in Calcutta.

*c*5. Charlotte married Captain Hamilton, H.E.I.C.S., with issue, one son, Dr Archibald Hamilton.

*c*6. Rev. Colin A. Campbell, minister of Lyne, Peeblesshire.

f. Duncan, born 1796, died in Florida.

g. Christina, born 1798, married Lieutenant Farquhar Macrae of the 78th Highlanders, Torlysich family, of whom hereafter.

h. Rev. John Macrae, born 21st November, 1799. He succeeded his father as minister of Glensheil in 1823, became minister of Glenelg in 1840, and died on the 7th July, 1875. He married in 1826 Jamesina Fraser, daughter of Norman Macleod of Ellanriach, Glenelg, and by her, who died in 1852, he had issue—

*h*1. John Kenneth, who was Deputy-Commissioner at Rangoon, and married Elizabeth Dunbar, with issue; John Dunbar; Norman Farquhar; Hugh; Madeline; Catherine; Florence.

*h*2. Norman James, an Indian missionary, married Jessie, daughter of Dr John Junor, Peebles, without issue.

*h*3. Alexa married Hugh Bogle, Esq., of Glasgow, with issue :—(1) Margaret Kennedy married Frank Crossman ; (2) Madeline Macrae married Harry Calthorpe, with issue ; (3) Gilbert married Alice

Galloway, with issue; (4) John Stewart Douglas; (5) William Lockhart, a distinguished artist, whose paintings of Highland subjects are well known at the annual exhibitions of the Royal Academy.   He is married to Margaret, daughter of Peter Maclean of Dunvegan, Skye; (6) Rosalind De Vere; (7) Mary Innes married George Kynoch; (8) Norman Archibald died in Burmah in 1894.

*h*4. Madeline Charlotte married the Rev. Colin A. Campbell, minister of Lyne, Peeblesshire, without issue.

*h*5. Forbes.   *h*6. Catherine Christina Sibella.

i. Kenneth, born in 1802, died unmarried in Florida.

9. ANNE, born 21st March, 1768, married in 1794 Lachlan Mackinnon, Esq. of Corriechatachan, in Skye, who died in 1828, aged 56 years, leaving issue—

a. Lachlan, who married, first, Catherine, daughter of Duncan Macdougall of Ardentrive, by whom he had issue, five daughters, one of whom married Archibald Roberts Young, of the Bengal Civil Service, with issue.   He married, secondly, Charlotte, daughter of General Sir John Hope, without surviving issue.

b. Anne, who in 1815 married the Rev. John Mackinnon, minister of Strath, in Skye, with issue—

*b*1. The Rev. Donald Mackinnon, D.D., also minister of Strath.   He married, first, Flora, daughter of Dr Farquhar Mackinnon of Kyle, in Skye, and secondly, Emma Flora, daughter of

Colonel William Macleod, of the Madras Army, and by her had issue—John William Macleod ; Lachlan Kenneth Scobie ; Donald ; Charles John ; Archibald ; Godfrey William Wentworth ; Emma Flora ; Annie Emily.

*b*2. Lachlan, of Melbourne, in Australia, and of Elfordleigh, in Devonshire, who was one of the original founders of *The Melbourne Argus.* He married, first, Jane, daughter of Robert Montgomery, of Belfast, and secondly, Emily, daughter of Lieutenant Bundock, R.N.

*b*3. John Murray Macgregor of Ostaig House, Skye, who married Christina, widow of Archibald Smith, Esq.

*b*4. Charles Farquhar, of Melbourne, Australia, died unmarried.

*b*5. Surgeon-General Sir William Alexander Mackinnon, K.C.B., LL.D., &c., Knight of the Legion of Honour in France, &c., who was born in 1830, and educated at Edinburgh and Glasgow Universities. He joined the army in 1853, and was appointed Assistant-Surgeon to the Forty-Second Highlanders. He served with that regiment during the Crimean War, being present at Alma, Balaclava, Kertch, and Sebastopol, for which he received the medal with three clasps ; was appointed Knight Commander of the Legion of Honour ; and received the Turkish medal. He afterwards served on the personal staff of Lord Clyde in the Indian Mutiny in 1857, taking part in the campaigns of Rohilcund and Oude, and in the actions of Bareilly and others. He served in New

Zealand from 1862 to 1866 as Surgeon of the Fifty-Seventh Regiment; was appointed Sanitary Officer and Field-Surgeon to the New Zealand forces, and was present at various engagements. For these services he received the Companionship of the Bath. He was Assistant-Professor of Clinical and Military Surgery at the Army Medical Hospital from 1867 to 1873. In 1874, he was appointed principal Medical Officer in the Ashantee War, and was promoted to be Deputy-Surgeon-General. He was principal Medical Officer also at Aldershot and Colchester, and in China, Malta, and Gibraltar, and is Honorary Surgeon to the Queen. In 1889, he attained the highest rank in his profession, being appointed in that year Director-General of the Army Medical Department. In 1891, he was created a Knight Commander of the Bath, and finally, after forty-three years of service, retired from the army on the 7th May, 1896. His career has thus been one of great distinction. Lord Clyde, General Sir Duncan A. Cameron, and others have borne the strongest testimony to his fearless and efficient devotion to duty on active service; and on the 3rd July, 1894, the Secretary for War declared in Parliament that " there could be no more efficient or just chief of the Army Medical Department than Sir William Mackinnon."[1]

*b*6. Colin Macrae married Anne, daughter of Robert Saunders Webb, Esq., with issue.

*b*7. Godfrey Bosville, of Melbourne, Australia,

[1] A portrait and biographical sketch of Sir William Mackinnon appeared in the *Celtic Monthly* for August, 1896.

married Maggie, daughter of Charles Macdonald, Esq. of Ord, Skye, with issue :—John ; Annie ; Mary Anne ; Charles Macdonald ; William ; Neilly.

*b*8. Ann Susan, died young.

*b*9. Mary Jane, died young.

*b*10. Catherine Charlotte, died in 1890.

*b*11. Louisa Houptoun, married John Henry Stonehouse Lydiard, son of Admiral Lydiard, R.N., with issue, and is now living in Melbourne.

*b*12. Flora Downie, now of Duisdale House, Skye.

c. Mary, married Lieutenant-Colonel Duncan Mackenzie, with issue :—George and Lachlan, both in the Indian Service.

d. Charles, married Henrietta, daughter of Captain Studd, H.E.I.C.S., with issue—

*d*1. Victoria, married Major-General Colin Mackenzie, of the Indian Army, with issue :—(1) Colin John, Major 2nd Battalion Seaforth Highlanders (Ross-shire Buffs). He served in the Egyptian Campaign, the Burmese Campaign, the Black Mountain Expedition, and the Hunga Nagar Campaign in Cashmere. (2) Charles Alexander ; (3) Ronald Pearson, M.D.; (4) Mary Charlotte ; (5) Henrietta Studd ; (6) Victor Herbert, of the British East Africa Company, died in 1892 ; (7) Kenneth Lascelles ; (8) Frederick William, R.N.; (9) Henry Studd ; (10) Morna ; (11) Annie Stuart.

*d*2. Anne, married General John Stewart, of the Indian Army.

*d*3. Flora Jane, married Dr Clarke, of the Indian Army, with issue.

*d*4. Harriet, married Colonel Prinsep, of the Indian Army, with issue.

*d*5. Jessie, married Captain Poynter, with issue.

*d*6. Mary, married Captain Murray, with issue.

*d*7. Susan Margaret, married, in 1877, Algernon St Maur, fifteenth Duke of Somerset.

*d*8. Henrietta, married a Mr Sargent, with issue.

e. Farquhar, Lieutenant H.E.I.C.S., died at the Cape of Good Hope in 1825.

f. Flora, died unmarried.

g. Margaret, married Captain D. Macdonald, of the 42nd Highlanders, with issue :—

*g*1. Farquhar ; *g*2 Archibald ; *g*3 Lachlan ; *g*4 Christina.

*g*5. Catherine, married, first, Donald Reid, Esq., and secondly, General Macleod.

*g*6. Ann Mary, married M. H. Court, Esq., of Castlemans, Berks.

h. Alexander Kenneth, married, first, Flora, daughter of the Rev. Alexander Downie, D.D., of Lochalsh, with issue—

*h*1. Alister, died in India in 1860.

*h*2. Annabella, married Admiral Rutherford, R.N..

Alexander Kenneth married, secondly, Barbara, daughter of Captain Daniel Reid, R.N., with issue—

*h*3. Flora Downie. *h*4. Catherine.

*h*5. Annie Flora, married Robert Currie, H.E.I.C.S., with issue.

*h*6. Charlotte.

*h*7. Lachlan Charles, of *The Melbourne Argus*, married, as his second wife, Emily Grace Bundock

Mackinnon, adopted daughter of his cousin, Lachlan Mackinnon, of Elfordleigh, with issue.

*h*8. Daniel, died unmarried.

*h*9. Charles, married Constance, daughter of Colonel Wright, with issue.

*h*10. Thomas Mackenzie.

i. Kenneth, a Doctor H.E.I.C.S., married Jessie, daughter of Captain Kenneth Mackenzie, of Kerrisdale, with issue—

*i*1. Catherine Mary, married Robert Scott Moncrieff, with issue :—(1) Jessie Margaret, married George Scott Moncrieff, Sheriff of Inverness, with issue—Colin ; John. (2) Charlotte, married Charles Watson, grandson of the Rev. Thomas Chalmers, D.D., with issue ; (3) Susan ; (4) Mary Catherine, married Wellington Ray, M A., with issue ; (5) Robert Lawrence, in Buenos Ayres, married Victoria Troutbeck ; (6) Kenneth, an electrical engineer in India; (7) William Elmslie, Indian Medical Service ; (8) Catherine, B.A., of London University ; (9) David.

*i*2. Flora Anne, married Major John Ross, of Tilliscorthy, Aberdeenshire, with issue :—(1) John, British Consul, Fiji Islands ; (2) Alexander, British Consul at Biera ; (3) Helen, married W. J. Bundock Mackinnon ; (4) Jessie ; (5) Charles ; (6) Robert.

*i*3. Jessie, married Dr A. Halliday Douglas, Edinburgh, with issue :—(1) Kenneth Mackinnon, M.D., married Florence Amy Leslie, with issue— Jessie Margery ; Kenneth ; Archibald. (2) Rev. Andrew Halliday Douglas, M.A., Presbyterian minister, Cambridge, married Isabel Lumsden Love,

H

with issue ; Margaret Isabel Mackinnon ; (3) Charles Mackinnon, D.Sc., Lecturer, Edinburgh University, married Anne Tod.

*i*4. Charles Kenneth, Colonel in the Indian Army, married Miss Broadfoot.

*i*5. Kenneth Hector, died unmarried.

j. Jessie, married Hugh Macaskill, of Mornish.

k. Johanna, married the Rev. James Morrison, of Kintail, with issue—

*k*1. Rev. Roderick Morrison, born 1839, also minister of Kintail, who died at Kintail Manse 11th June, 1897.

*k*2. Annie, married William Dick, Esq.

*k*3. Jane.

l. Susannah and Jane (twins), died unmarried.

10. HECTOR, born September, 1722, died young.

11 FLORENCE married Captain Kenneth Mackenzie of Kerrisdale, in Gairloch, younger son of Sir Alexander Mackenzie, third baronet of Gairloch, with issue—

a. Alexander, a Captain in the 58th Regiment, married Ellen, daughter of William Beibly, M.D., President of the College of Physicians, Edinburgh, with issue—

*a*1. Kenneth, a planter in Bengal.

*a*2. William, Deputy Postmaster-General in India—retired.

*a*3. Julius, an engineer in Birmingham, married, with issue.

*a*4. Frank, a planter in India, married, with issue.

b. Hector died unmarried in Java.

c. Farquhar went to Victoria, where he married and left issue:—Hector; John; Violet; Mary; Flora.

d. Jean married William H. Garrett, of the Indian Civil Service, with issue—

*d*1. Edward.   *d*2. William.

*d*3. Eleanor, married, first, Dr Calder, H.E.I.C.S., with issue :—(1) William, died without issue ; (2) Edward, Captain, Mercantile Service, married, with issue.

Eleanor married, secondly, Gershom Gourlay, Esq., of the firm of Gourlay Brothers, engineers, Dundee, with issue ; (3) Henry, of the firm of Gourlay Brothers ; (4) Jane, died young ; (5) Miriam, died young ; (6) Frederick, a civil engineer, married Agnes, daughter of the Venerable Archdeacon John Edward Herring, with issue ; (7) Florence, died young; (8) Charles, of the firm of Gourlay Brothers, married Fanny Gordon ; (9) Morris, died young ; (10) Margaret, married J. Campbell Penney, with issue ; (11) Kenneth Mackenzie, married Grace, daughter of D. M. Watson of Greystone, with issue ; (12) Frank, a Doctor of Medicine.

*d*4. Flora died young.   *d*5. Emily.

*d*6. Elizabeth married James Bell, Esq., Dundee, with issue :—(1) James, merchant in Dundee, married, with issue ; (2) Morris, a civil engineer, married, with issue ; (3) Grace married, with issue ; (4) Jane married, with issue ; (5) Thomas; (6) William ; (7) Son.

e. Mary married, first, Dr Macleod, Dingwall, without issue, and secondly, Murdo Mackenzie, Calcutta, also without issue.

f. Christian Henderson married John Mackenzie, solicitor, Tain, a son of George Mackenzie, third of Pitlundie, with issue :—George ; Kenneth.

g. Jessie married Dr Kenneth Mackinnon, of the Corriechatachan family, H.E.I.C.S., Calcutta.

12. COLIN, of whom next.

XIII. COLIN, youngest son of Farquhar Macrae of Inverinate and Mary Mackenzie of Dochmaluag, was born on the 14th March, 1776.   He was a merchant and planter in Demerara, where he rose to a position of importance and prominence.   He was Colonel Commandant of the Colonial Militia, a member of the Colonial Legislation, and one of the negotiators of the cession of Demerara to England after the Peace of 1814.   He married Charlotte Gertrude, daughter of John Cornelius Vandenheuvel,[1] Esq., of Demerara, who was for some time Governor of that Colony when it belonged to the Dutch, and by her had issue, as below.   Colin died in Edinburgh on the 25th October, 1854.

1. CHARLOTTE married Captain Edward Brook Vass, with issue :—Charlotte Gertrude ; Catherine Murat ; Maria Cornelia.

[1] The Vandenheuvel family came originally from Germany, which they were obliged to quit at the time of the Reformation in consequence of their adhesion to the Protestant cause. This they did, however, with the permission of the Emperor Charles V., and settled for a time in Brabant. Shortly afterwards the head of the family rendered an important military service to the Emperor, for which he received a patent of nobility, the addition of a sword to his coat-of-arms, and a medal which was recently, and is probably still, in the possession of his descendants. One of his sons eventually returned to Germany, and, having made profession of the Roman Catholic religion, he obtained possession of the old family estates. The eldest son, however, remained in the Netherlands, and from him was descended in a direct line the said John Cornelius Vandenheuvel, of Demerara.

2. FARQUHAR, drowned in 1838 off Cape Hatteras, in America, while trying to rescue another man.

3. MARIA CORNELIA married Dr James Sewell, son of Chief Justice Sewell, of Quebec, with issue—James ; Justine ; Colin ; Edward ; Hope ; Horace.

4. JOHN ANTHONY, who succeeded as representative of the Inverinate family, and of whom hereafter.

5. COLIN WILSON married Louisa Elliott, without issue.

6. JUSTINE HENRIETTE married, 26th December, 1833, Horatio Ross, Esq. of Rossie, Forfarshire, and Wyvis, Ross-shire, Captain in the 14th Light Dragoons, and some time M.P. for Aberdeen and the Montrose Burghs.   She died at Southsea in 1894, leaving issue—

a. Horatio Senftenberg John, Esq., of the Indian Civil Service, married Caroline Latour St George, daughter of Sir Theophilus St George, Bart., with issue.

b. Hercules Grey, Esq., of the Indian Civil Service, who distinguished himself during the Indian Mutiny, married, with issue.

c. Colin George, Esq., sometime of Wyvis, and later of Gruinards, Ross-shire, married, with issue.

d. Edward Charles Russell, who was winner of the Queen's prize at the first Wimbledon Meeting in 1860, Chairman of the Board of Lunacy, &c., married Margaret Seymour Osborne, with issue.

e. The Rev. Robert Peel, a clergyman of the Church of England, some time Rector of Drayton Bassett, in Staffordshire, married with issue.

7. ALEXANDER CHARLES, M.D., formerly In-

spector-General of Hospitals, Army Medical Department, married Charlotte Reid, with issue—

a. Fanny Catherine Ousley married on the 26th April, 1866, Robert George, son of Sir Frederick Larkins Currie, Bart., and died on the 17th September, 1870, leaving issue, a son and two daughters.

b. Charles Colin, born 1843, M.A. University College, Oxford, barrister-at-law in London, and of Oakhurst, Oxted, Surrey, formerly Secretary of the Legislative Council of Bengal, married Cecilia, daughter of Samuel Laing, Esq., M.P., with issue— Charles Alexander ; Frank Laing.

c. Louisa.

ISAAC VANDENHEUVEL, born 12th June, 1819, a clergyman of the Church of England, and now (1897) Vicar of Brassington, in Derbyshire. He married Elizabeth Johnson, with issue—

a. Christina Elizabeth married, 6th September, 1894, John Eaton Fearn, with issue — Francis ; Russel Colin.

b. Colin John.

9. ROBERT CAMPBELL married, 25th October, 1853, Jane Eliza, eldest daughter of Vice-Admiral Mark John Currie, and died 11th February, 1896, leaving issue—

a. Farquhar Campbell.

b. Mark Reginald married Nancy Dill, with issue.

c. Junita Gertrude married Harry William Antill, with issue.

d. Justine Alice married William Mathias Lancaster.

e. Harold John married Maggie von Broda.

f. Colin Tisdall.

g. Horace Duncan died unmarried in 1885.

h. Marshall.

i. Hilda married William Arthur Warwick Herring, with issue.

j. Mary Edith married Peter Felix Mackenzie-Richards, with issue.

10. MARGARET ELIZABETH married John Kennedy, Esq., of Underwood, Ayrshire, and died in 1893, leaving issue—

a. John, D.L. for County of Ayr, W.S., and a Parliamentary solicitor, Westminster, married and has issue.

b. Neil James, B.A., LL.B. and advocate in Edinburgh, married 10th September, 1895, Eleonora Agnes, only surviving child of Robert William Cochran Patrick, Esq. of Woodside and Ladyland, in the County of Ayr, some time M.P. for North Ayrshire, on whose death, in 1897, Mrs Kennedy having succeeded to the estates, Mr Neil J. Kennedy assumed the name of Cochran Patrick.

c. Charlotte Maria died unmarried, 1896.

d. Justine Henriette married, 1884, Alan John Colquhoun, C.B., son of John Colquhoun, author of "The Moor and the Loch," a nephew of the late Sir James Colquhoun of Luss, Bart.   He was formerly Captain in "The Black Watch," and is now (1897) Lieutenant-Colonel Commanding the Duke of Edinburgh's Own Edinburgh Artillery Militia, and has issue.

e. Elizabeth   Theodora   Mary   married   John

William M'Kerrell Brown, of the Bank of Scotland, Dunfermline.

f. Adelaide Emily Jane.

XIV. JOHN ANTHONY, LL.D., Esquire of Wellbank, Forfarshire, J.P., and a Writer to the Signet in Edinburgh, second son of Colin XIII., was born on the 1st February, 1812. Mr Macrae raised the first Volunteer Company in Scotland in 1859, and, at his death, was Major of the Queen's R.V. Brigade. He married Joanna Isabella Maclean, daughter of John Maclean of Dumfries estate, in the Island of Carriacou, West Indies, and died on the 23rd May, 1868, leaving issue—

1. John Anthony, born 23rd November, 1842 ; died 5th March, 1852.

2. Colin George, of whom below.

3. Horatio Ross, Esquire of Clunes,[1] Inverness-shire, is a Justice of the Peace for the County of Inverness, a Writer to the Signet in Edinburgh, and Lieutenant-Colonel of the Queen's Rifle Volunteer Brigade. He married Letitia May, daughter of Sir William Maxwell of Cardoness, Bart., with issue— Alexander William Urquhart, born 18th April, 1885.

4. Jessidora married in 1884, Sir William Francis Maxwell of Cardoness, Bart., Kirkcudbright-shire, with issue—

William Francis John, born 7th July, 1885 ; Joanna Mary ; Dorothea Letitia May.

---

[1] Mr Macrae's estate of Clunes is situated in the district which, according to tradition, was the original home from which the Macraes migrated to Kintail.—See Chapter I.

XV. COLIN GEORGE, eldest surviving son of John Anthony XIV., is now the lineal representative of the Macraes of Inverinate, and is fifteenth in descent from Fionnla Dubh Mac Gillechriosd, the founder of the Clan Macrae of Kintail.   He was born 30th November, 1844, is a Writer to the Signet in Edinburgh and a Justice of the Peace for the City of Edinburgh and for the County of Forfar. He was educated at the Edinburgh Academy and at the University of Edinburgh, where he had a distinguished career and graduated Master of Arts. As a student, he was for two years President of the University Conservative Club, and since his entry upon public life has taken a prominent part in the affairs of his native city.   At the present time (1897) he is Chairman of the School Board of Edinburgh, a position which he has occupied for the past seven years with conspicuous success and with the cordial support of his fellow-citizens.[1]   He is also a loyal member and supporter of the Church of Scotland, in connection with which he has done much active and valuable work, having sat in the General Assembly almost continuously for twenty years. His interest in the Highlands, and more especially in young Highlanders coming to Edinburgh, has always been great, and has frequently been shown in a kindly and practical manner.[2]   Mr Macrae

---

1 . . . He is a man who, as an educationist, has done much sterling and unselfish work for the city, and his opinions must command respect even from those who disagree with him. . . . It is undeniable that the Edinburgh Board has done admirable public work, and never more than in the time of Mr Macrae himself. . . . —*The Scotsman*, 19th February, 1897.

2 A portrait and biographical sketch of Mr Colin George Macrae appeared in *The Celtic Monthly* for November, 1896.

married, 23rd June, 1877, Flora Maitland, daughter
of John Colquhoun, Esq., author of the well-known
work entitled "The Moor and the Loch," and has
issue—

1. JOHN ANTHONY, born 19th May, 1883.
2. FRANCES MAITLAND DOROTHEA.

CHAPTER VIII.

Christopher, son of Alexander of Inverinate. — Tacksman of Aryugan.—His Marriage and Descendants.—Mathesons of Lochalsh and the Rev. Dr Kennedy of Dingwall Descended from him.—Other Descendants of Christopher.—John, son of Christopher.—His Marriage and Descendants.

IX. CHRISTOPHER, son of Alexander of Inverinate and Mary Mackenzie of Dochmaluag, and ninth in descent from Fionnla Du Mac Gillechriosd, was tacksman of Aryugan, in Kintail, and was commonly known as "Gillecriosd Mor a Chroidh" (Big Christopher of the Cattle). He was alive on the 15th August, 1723, as his signature appears on a bond of caution drawn up on that date for the protection of their rights by the wadsetters on the estates of Macdonald of Sleat, which the "Forfeited Estates Commissioners" were then proposing to sell. It is uncertain who his wife was, but it is said that he was twice married, and that his first wife was of the Murchisons of Auchtertyre, and that his second wife was a Chisholm. He left a large family, all of whom are said to have married and to have left issue. Many of his descendants are still living in Kintail and Lochalsh.

1. DUNCAN. He is witness to a sasine on the 19th March, 1700, and was killed at the Battle of Sheriffmuir in 1715. He is said to have married

Margaret, daughter of John Mackenzie of Lochbroom, and left issue, as below, so far as it has been
found possible to trace them—

a. John, who had a son.

*a*1. Duncan, who married Janet, daughter of
Christopher, son of Finlay, son of John Breac, son
of the Rev. Farquhar Macrae, and had (1) John,
who had issue — John ; Donald ; Farquhar ; Kenneth ; Christopher.   (2) A son called Christopher
Tailor ; (3) Isabella ; (4) Christina.

*a*2. John, who had issue — John, Christopher,
Alexander, Duncan.

*a*3. Anne, who married Christopher, at Druidaig.

*a*4. Christina, who married Ian Mac Callum.

b. Alexander, called Alister Ruadh (Red Alexander), who had issue—

*b*1. John, called the Red Smith, who had sons—
(1) Alexander, who was a blacksmith at Ardelve ;
(2) Finlay.

*b*2. Finlay, who went to America.

2. ALEXANDER had a son Duncan, who had a
son Christopher, a priest, and other issue.

3. DONALD, who had a son Duncan, who had a
son John, who had a son Alexander, admitted to the
Grammar School, Aberdeen, with a Macra bursary
in 1806, entered the University in 1809, and
graduated M.A. in 1813.

4. CHRISTOPHER, mentioned as taking part in
the affair of Ath nam Muileach on the 2nd October,
1721.

5. MURDOCH, also present at the affair of Ath
nam Muileach.

6. FARQUHAR, who was also present at the affair of Ath nam Muileach, married, it is said, a Macdonald of Sleat, and had a daughter, Barbara, who married first, John Og, son of the Rev. Donald Macrae of Kintail, with issue, and secondly Donald, son of the Rev. Finlay Macrae of Lochalsh, also with issue.

7. JOHN, mentioned below.

8. FINLAY.

9. MARY married, in 1695, Farquhar Matheson of Fernaig, and had, with other issue—

a. John, who, in 1728, married, as his second wife, Margaret Mackenzie of Pitlundie, and died in 1760, leaving issue—Alexander, who, about 1763, married Catherine Matheson, and died in 1804, leaving issue—John, who, in 1804, married Margaret, daughter of Captain Donald Matheson of Shinness, and died in 1826, leaving, with other issue—Sir Alexander Matheson, Bart. of Lochalsh, who married, as his second wife, Lavinia Mary, daughter of Thomas Stapleton of Carlton, Yorkshire, and died in 1886, leaving, with other issue—Sir Kenneth James Matheson, Bart. of Lochalsh.

b. Donald, who married Margaret, daughter of Roderick Mackenzie, Sanachan, of the Applecross family, and had a daughter—Mary, who married Donald Kennedy of Kishorn, by whom she had, with other issue—the Rev. John Kennedy of Redcastle, one of whose sons was the Rev. John Kennedy, D.D., who was Free Church minister of Dingwall from 1844 until his death in 1884, and occupied throughout his whole career a foremost place among the greatest preachers of Scotland.

10. MARIAN married John Macrae, a descendant of Miles, son of the Rev. Farquhar.

11. ANNE.

12. CHRISTINA.

13. CATHERINE married Colin Mackenzie, ninth laird of Hilton.   There is a sasine by Colin Mackenzie of Hilton[1] in favour of Catherine Macrae, his spouse, in liferent of his pecklands of Easter Casichan in the parish of Contin and shire of Ross, on the 26th August, 1749.   Catherine left issue—

a. John, who died before his father.

b. Alexander, tenth of Hilton.

c. A daughter who married, as his first wife, John Macdonell, twelfth of Glengarry, and had, with other issue—Alexander, who carried on the representation of that family.

14. JANET.   15. ISABEL.

16. MARGARET, who married Finlay Macrae, Strathglass.

X. JOHN,[2] son of Christopher of Aryugan, called Ian Ban, was educated at Aberdeen, and is mentioned in some copies of the MS. history of the Clan as "Mr John, graduate in Aberdeen."   He is said to have married Annabella, daughter of Duncan Macrae, tutor of Conchra, by his wife Isabel, daughter of the Rev. Finlay Macrae, with issue—

---

[1] The property of this family, which was formerly known as Hilton, was situated in Strathbran, and is now traversed by the Dingwall and Skye Railway between the stations of Achnault and Achnasheen.

[2] The succession of Christopher of Aryugan is continued here in his son John only for convenience of arrangement, and not because John's descendants are the oldest lineal representatives of Christopher.

1. FINLAY, who lived at Achmore, and married Isabella Macrae, daughter of Farquhar Mac Ian of the Torlysich family, with other issue—

a. Alexander.

b. John, who married Kate, daughter of Duncan Macrae, and had, together with several daughters, the following issue—

*b*1. Christopher, who married Mary, daughter of Christopher Macrae, Carr, with issue—(1) Alexander; (2) John, married Isabella, daughter of Duncan Maclennan, Sallachy, with issue—Mary; Jemima; Christopher; Ewen; MaryAnne; Duncan; (3) Christopher; (4) Janet; (5) Isabella; (6) Mary.

*b*2. Finlay. *b*3. Alexander.

*b*4. Duncan, who was for many years a farmer at Kirkton, Lochalsh, and is now (1897) living at Durinish, Lochalsh. He married Jessie, daughter of Alexander Maclennan by his wife Mary, daughter of Alexander Macrae, Achtertyre, and by her, who died 11th April, 1882, aged sixty-seven, had issue— (1) Mary, who married John Maclennan, Strathglass, with issue—Duncan; John; Donald Ewen; Jessie; Annie; Catherine; Mary; Mary Anne; Margaret; Lexy; (2) Catherine, who married Captain William Mackenzie of the Merchant Service, with issue— William; (3) Mary Anne, who died unmarried on the 19th January, 1893.

*b*5. Annabella, married Duncan Macrae, with issue—(1) John, married Mary, daughter of Thomas Macrae, with issue; (2) Finlay married Annabella Macdonald, with issue; (3) Duncan; (4) Annabella married, with issue.

2. DUNCAN married and had issue—at least one son—

a. John, who married, and had, with other issue—

*a*1. Duncan, who married Grace, daughter of Colin Mackenzie, Kishorn, and died at Dingwall on the 19th December, 1895, aged seventy-nine, leaving issue :—(1) Donald, in America, married Jessie Kennedy, with issue ; (2) Marjory married Andrew Robertson, with issue ; (3) Catherine married John Murchison, builder, Dingwall.

*a*2. Alexander, in Kishorn, married a daughter of Duncan Mackenzie of Lochcarron, and sister of the Rev. Murdoch Mackenzie of the Free Church, Inverness, with issue :—(1) Duncan, living at Kyleakin ; (2) Murdoch, a minister of the Free Church of Scotland. Alexander has also three daughters.

*a*3. Murdoch, living at Strome Ferry, married, without issue.

3. FARQUHAR married Mary Macrae, with issue—

a. Duncan married Christina Mackenzie, and died in 1864, with issue—

*a*1. Alexander, a schoolmaster in Lochcarron, married, first, Mary Mackenzie, without surviving issue. He married, secondly, Catherine, daughter of John Macpherson, and died in 1892. By his second wife he had issue :—(1) John, a doctor, married Sarah Wilson, and died at Gateshead-on-Tyne in 1889, leaving issue—Ethel ; Charles ; (2) Alexander married Agnes Reid ; (3) Farquhar, Lieutenant, Army Ordnance Department, married Martha Bessie Rafuse, with issue—Albert Edward ; William Farquhar ; Catherine Macpherson ; James

Norman ; (4) the Rev. James Duncan, minister of Contin, married Catherine, daughter of Peter Robertson, with issue—Catherine Macpherson ; James Peter Robertson ; (5) Mary Elizabeth married John Macleod, with issue.

*a*2. Farquhar, married Mary Macrae and died in 1894.

*a*3. John was holder of the Macra bursary at the Grammar School, Aberdeen, in 1831, and afterwards entered the shipbuilding business and was drowned at the launching of the Daphne, on the Clyde, on the 3rd July, 1883. He married Margaret Gillies, with issue—(1) Alexander, a joiner in Glasgow, married, with issue ; (2) Mary, married, with issue.

*a*4. Donald, married Margaret Macrae, with issue—Colin ; John ; Farquhar.

*a*5. Kenneth, married Flora Macmillan, with issue—Donald; John; Helen; Jane; Christina Anne.

*a*6. Margaret, married Lachlan Matheson, with issue.

*a*7. Helen, married Christopher Macrae, with issue.

*a*8. Christina, married John Macrae, with issue.

b. John, married, first, a Macdonald, with issue—(*b*1) Kenneth, who went to Australia ; (*b*2) Mary ; (*b*3) Jane ; (*b*4) Anne, married John Galt, Elgin.

John married, secondly, Catherine Mackenzie and died in 1867. By his second marriage he had a son.

*b*5. The Rev. Farquhar Macrae, who is now a Presbyterian minister in Manitoba, and is married, with issue—

I

c. Christopher married in 1839, Mary Finlayson, who died on the 17th August, 1897, aged ninety-two. He died in 1872, aged eighty-one years, leaving issue—

*c*1. Alexander, born 15th October, 1843. He married, in 1872, Catherine Maclean, and is now living in New Zealand, with issue—John; Catherine; Mary; Alexandrina; Margaret.

*c*2. Farquhar, born 12th November, 1845, and is now living at Dornie. He is a good genealogist, and is well versed in the legends and traditions of the Macrae country. He married, first, Mary Maclennan, and secondly Margaret, daughter of Duncan Matheson, Dornie.

*c*3. John, born on the 27th June, 1848, married 18th May, 1877, Williamina Macdonald, with issue —Farquhar; Mary Finlayson; Catherine Finlayson, died in infancy; Christopher; Ninian Finlayson; Alexander; Catherine Finlayson; Jessie Isabella Anne Finlayson; Malcolm John Duncan Finlayson.

*c*4. Duncan, born 18th January, 1851, married, in 1883, Catherine Finlayson, with issue — Farquhar; Alexander; Mary; Christopher; Catherine; Donald Roderick; Anne.

d. The Rev. Farquhar Macrae, born at Camus-lunie on the 25th November, 1805. He received his early education from a well-known Kintail schoolmaster, Finlay Macrae, commonly called Finlay Fadoch. In 1816 he was admitted to a Macra bursary at Aberdeen Grammar School, where he had for his teacher the celebrated classical

scholar and Gaelic poet, Ewen Maclauchlan.   He
entered the University in 1819, and after a distinguished career, graduated M.A. in 1823.   He studied
Divinity from 1823 to 1827.   From 1825 to 1833
he was schoolmaster of Lochcarron, and was licensed
by the Presbytery of Lochcarron in 1829.   In 1833
he was ordained to the charge of South Uist, where
he remained for eight years, and in 1841 became
minister of Braemar.   At the Disruption of the
Church of Scotland in 1843 he cast in his lot with
the Free Church, and in 1849 became minister of
the Free Church in Knockbain, in succession to his
well-known fellow-clansman, the Rev. John Macrae.
Here he lived and laboured, trusted and respected
by his people until his death, which occurred at
Nairn on the 20th December, 1882.   He was a man
of much culture and sound scholarship, and an able
and eloquent preacher, equally good both in Gaelic
and in English.   The Rev. Farquhar married Anne
Murray and had issue, one surviving son—Francis
Farquhar.

e. Christina married Roderick Mackenzie at
Camusluinie, with issue.

f. Isabel married Thomas Macrae at Camusluinie,
with issue.

CHAPTER IX.

IX. Hugh, son of Alexander of Inverinate.—X. Alexander of
Ardintoul.—Was at the Battles of Sheriffmuir and Glensheil.
Traditions about Him.—IX. Archibald of Ardintoul.—His
Marriage and Descendants.—Colonel Sir John Macra.—Alex-
ander of Hushinish.—His Marriage and Family.

IX. HUGH, the youngest son of Alexander of
Inverinate by his second wife, Mary Mackenzie
of Dochmaloaig. He is mentioned as one of the
leaders of the disturbance in connection with the
vacancy at Dingwall church in 1704,[1] and took part
in the Jacobite rising of 1715. He was wounded
in the battle of Sheriffmuir, and his name appears on
a list of "Gentlemen Prisoners" taken to Stirling
on the following day. It is said that he was
removed from Stirling to Perth, where he remained
in hospital until he was sufficiently recovered from
his wound to be able to accomplish the homeward
journey. Hugh was living at Sallachy in 1721.
He married Margaret Macleod of Swordlan, in
Glenelg, and by her had issue—

1. ALEXANDER.
2. JOHN, went to America 1774.
3. RODERICK, went to America 1774.
4. DUNCAN.

[1] See note page 71.

5. BARBARA, married Farquhar, son of Alexander, with issue.

6. MARY, married G. Macculloch.

X. ALEXANDER, eldest son of Hugh, was appointed local factor of Kintail, and lived at Aryugan or Ardintoul. He was one of the first to join the Roman Catholic Mission, which has already been referred to. As a young man he fought on the Jacobite side, both at Sheriffmuir and at Glensheil, and is mentioned as taking part in the affair of Ath nam Muileach in 1721. After the battle of Glensheil, he was for three days among the hills without any food except one drink of milk. It is said that on one occasion when "Colonel Alexander Mackenzie, the next Protestant heir to the Seaforth estates, had come to the country with a view to take up the rents, but finding that the people would not come into his views nor pay him the rents they judged belonged to Lord Seaforth, he went up from Ardelve to Kintail with a large boat well manned, that he might arrest some of the people and send them to Fort-William. Alexander was up in Kintail at the time, and observing a fellow carrying his own father on his back to put him into the boat, his indignation was roused. 'You silly, dastardly rascal,' said Alexander, 'is it putting your own father in you are,' and he set the old man at liberty. The Colonel was in the stern of the boat and came up to him. They grappled, and Alexander getting hold of his thumbs, held him there until he yielded,"[1] and

[1] Old letter from Kintail.

left the people alone.   Alexander married, first, a
daughter of Fraser of Guisachan (or Culbokie), and
by her had a daughter, who married John Macrae,
Strathglass.   On one occasion Alexander sustained
such heavy losses through a severe winter that he
became somewhat straitened in his circumstances,
and it is said that his wife, who was unwilling to
share the lot of a poor man, took advantage of a
temporary absence of her husband from home, to
pack up her effects and leave him.   Circumstances,
however, turned out more favourable for Alexander
than his wife anticipated, and the tide of his
prosperity soon turned.   His wife hearing of this,
decided to join him once more, and returned to his
sheiling at Glasletter, but he refused to receive her.
On her death, which occurred shortly afterwards, he
married, as his second wife, Isabel, daughter of
Alexander Macgilchrist (Macrae) of Strathglass, by
his wife, Anne, daughter of Farquhar Macrae of
Morvich, and by her had issue—

1. ARCHIBALD.

2. ALEXANDER.

3, FARQUHAR, who went to America.

4. JOHN, a doctor.   He went as surgeon of an
emigrant ship to America about 1817.   The vessel
was wrecked on the return voyage off Prince Edward Island, but no lives were lost.   In 1821 Dr
John himself left for Canada, along with "Alexander, a brother of Mr Macrae, Dornie," and several
others from Lochalsh and Kintail, and he is mentioned as being at Glengarry in Canada in 1826.

5. ANNE married John Macrae of Conchra.

6. MARGARET married Donald Macrae, Torly-sich.

7. MARY married Farquhar Macrae, Fadoch. She died in 1823, leaving issue.

XI. ARCHIBALD, eldest son of Alexander by his second wife, Isabel Macrae, was born in 1744. He was educated in the house of Archibald Chisholm of Fasnakyle, probably by a priest, to whose instructions he did no small credit. He was a devout Catholic, a man of sound judgment and high character, " a courtly old gentleman, shrewd, practical, but warm-hearted and unobtrusively religious ; able, too, to face difficulties, the common lot of all mortals, with the clear conscience and stout heart of a strong and upright man." For fully half-a-century he occupied a foremost place in the affairs of the Seaforth estates, of which he was for many years chamberlain. He was created a free Burgess and Guild Brother of the Burgh of Dingwall on the 16th October, 1789. Archibald married on the 9th September, 1783, Janet, daughter of John Macleod, the tenth chief of Raasay. John Macleod was one of the Highland chiefs who entertained Dr Samuel Johnson in the course of his celebrated tour in the Hebrides in 1773. Writing of his host on that occasion, Dr Johnson says :— " The family of Raasay consists of the laird, the lady, three sons, and ten daughters. For the sons there is a tutor in the house, and the lady is said to be very skilful and diligent in the education of her girls. More gentleness of manners, or a more pleasing appearance of domestic society is not

found in the most polished countries."[1]   Archibald
died about 1830, leaving issue—

1. FLORA, born 9th September, 1783, died unmarried in 1852.

2. Colonel Sir JOHN MACRA, K.C.H., who was
born on the 14th February, 1786.   He obtained an
Ensign's commission in the 79th Highlanders in
1805, and was promoted to the rank of Lieutenant
in the same year.   His subsequent promotions were
as follows :—Captain, 1812 ; Major, 1818 ; Lieutenant - Colonel, 1821 ; Colonel, 1837.   He was
created a Knight of the Order of Hanover (K.C.H.)
in 1827.   His military career was both distinguished and eventful.   He was present at the siege
and surrender of Copenhagen in 1807, and went to
Sweden with the army under Sir John Moore in
1808.   Later on in the same year he accompanied
the British force which was sent to Portugal, and
was present in all the operations of that campaign,
including the retreat of Sir John Moore and the
battle of Corunna, on the 16th January, 1809.
From Spain he accompanied his regiment in the
Walcheren expedition, and was present at the siege
and capture of Flushing in August the same year.
At Walcheren he suffered from the fever which
caused so much havoc among the British troops,
and from the effects of which he never completely
recovered.   The following year, however, he was in

---

[1] The China tea service used by the Raasay family at the time of Dr
Johnson's visit is now in the possession of Captain John MacRae-Gilstrap of
Ballimore, Tigh-na-bruaich, Argyllshire, great grandson of the above-men-
tioned Janet Macleod.

the Peninsula, and served with his regiment throughout the campaigns of 1811 and 1812, being present at all the operations in which his regiment took part, including the battles of Fuentes D'Onoro, on the 5th May, 1811, and Salamanca, on the 22nd July, 1812, the siege of Burgos in September and October, 1812, and many smaller engagements.   In 1813 he joined the staff of the Marquis of Hastings, then Lord Moira, who in that year was appointed Governor-General of India, and who was married to Sir John's cousin, Flora Campbell, daughter of the fifth Earl of Loudon, by his wife Flora, daughter of John Macleod, tenth chief of Raasay.   The Marquis of Hastings was one of the ablest and most successful of our Indian statesmen, and his rule, which extended from 1813 to 1823, was a period of great importance in the history of that country.   In 1814 and 1815, after some severe fighting, he succeeded in subduing the Goorkhas, who had established a power of considerable strength in Nepaul.   But the circumstances and events to which Lord Hastings owes his great celebrity as an Indian ruler and statesman arose in another quarter.   The centre of India was at this time occupied by the great Princes of the Mahratta nation, who, although partly subdued, were still powerful, and evidently preparing to make an effort to recover their former greatness.   Besides these restless and active enemies there existed also a formidable body of freebooters called the Pindarees, who had established themselves along the south of the Vindhya Mountains. During the Goorkha War the Pindarees, secretly

supported by the Mahrattas, crossed the British
frontiers and plundered and destroyed more than
three hundred villages.   Lord Hastings resolved
to put an end to these robbers, and having
obtained permission to proceed against them on a
great scale, he collected forces from all parts of
India, and brought into the field the "grand army,"
with which, after a war of two years' duration—
1817-18—the Pindarees and the Mahrattas were
completely conquered.   Other native powers were
subdued at the same time, and Lord Hastings had
thus the honour of being the first to render British
authority absolutely supreme in India.   In all these
operations Sir John Macra, who held the post of
Military Secretary to the Governor-General, took
an important part.   He was in the field throughout
the war against the Goorkhas in 1814 and 1815,
and was with the grand army in 1817 and 1818.
At the end of 1818 he was sent home with despatches announcing the successful termination of
the war, and returning immediately to India, he
continued to serve under the Marquis of Hastings,
who was now in a position to rule in peace and
to effect wise and useful changes for the good of
the people of India.   The importance of Lord Hastings' measures, which have been fully justified by
time, was not then appreciated by the Directors
of the East India Company, and this, together
with failing health, for he was now an old man,
induced him to leave India in 1823.   In the following year he was appointed Governor of Malta, where
Sir John, after a short visit home, joined him once

more in the capacity of Military Secretary, until
the death of the Marquis, which took place in 1825.
Sir John retired in May, 1826, after a most distinguished career of more than twenty years, which
were nearly all passed in active service.   After his
retirement he lived chiefly at Ardintoul and Raasay,
where he is still remembered by old people as a
man of frank and generous disposition and a genuine
Highlander.   He was an excellent performer on the
bagpipes.   He was also an amateur maker of bagpipes, and it is said that some of those which he
made are still to be found in the West Highlands.
He died on the 9th August, 1847, and was buried
in Kintail.   A plain iron cross, which has been
placed by his nephew, Captain A. M. Chisholm, on
the wall of the old ruined church of Kilduich, marks
the place of his last rest.

3. ALEXANDER was born on the 3rd of May,
1787.   He obtained an Ensign's commission in the
75th Highlanders in 1806.   He joined that regiment the following year and served with it for
some time.   He was for many years tacksman of
Hushinish in Harris, and was a Justice of the
Peace and a Deputy-Lieutenant of the county of
Inverness.   He was a good Catholic, and was well
known in the West Highlands as a liberal and
large-hearted man.   He was " pre-eminently a man
without guile," and it was said of him at the time
of his death, that the poor on the West Coast
lost in him "a friend who always kept his heart
open to their wants, and assisted them without
ostentation."   As an amateur musician he possessed

unusual taste and cultivation, and was an excellent violinist. He had also a keen appreciation of the national music and poetry of the Highlands, and was himself an excellent type of the old Highland gentleman, dignified, cultured, generous almost to a fault, and in full and kindly sympathy with all that was best and noblest in the character and traditions of his countrymen. He died on the 25th January, 1874, and was buried at Kilduich. He married Margaret, daughter of Farquhar Macrae, and by her, who died at Strathpeffer on the 10th July, 1896, and was buried at Kilduich, had issue—

a. Janet Macleod.

b. Isabella Christian married Alister Macdonald Maclellan of Portree, Ceylon.

c. Archibald Alexander.

d. John.

e. Marion Flora.

4. ISABELLA was born on the 6th April, 1789, and married, in 1808, Major Colin Macrae (75th Highlanders), Conchra family, with issue.

5. JANE was born on the 8th April, 1791, and married, at the end of 1816, or beginning of 1817, Donald Macrae of Achtertyre, with issue.

6. CHRISTINA, born 11th January, 1793, died unmarried.

7. MARY, who was born in June, 1794, married in 1821, Dr Stewart Chisholm, of the Royal Artillery, who was at the battle of Waterloo, and attained the rank of Deputy Inspector-General of Army Hospitals. He died at Inverness in 1862, leaving issue—

a. Archibald Macra, born 6th July, 1824, late Captain 42nd Royal Highlanders, now of Glassburn. He is a J.P. for the counties of Ross and Inverness. He married, 14th October, 1853, Maria Frances, only daughter of William Dominic Lynch, and granddaughter of the late Lewis Farquharson Innes of Balmoral and Ballogie,[1] without issue.

b. Loudon, who served in the 43rd Regiment H.E.I.C.S., and was killed in the Burmese War in 1853.

c. Mary Stewart, who married Philip Skene, Esquire of Skene, and died at Inverness on the 4th January, 1895, aged 72 years, without issue.

d. Jessie Macleod married Charles O. Rolland of Ste. Marie Monnoir, near Montreal in Canada, with issue.

8. JAMES, born 30th October, 1796, was an Army Surgeon, and died, unmarried, in India, in 1832.

9. ANNE, born 1st October, 1798, married Captain Valentine Chisholm, with issue, John and Jessie.

---

1 A biographical sketch, with a portrait, of Captain Chisholm, appeared in the *Celtic Monthly* for February, 1893.

CHAPTER X.

VIII. JOHN, son of the Rev. Farquhar Macrae of
Kintail, was born at Ardlair on the 13th March,
1614.   He received his early education at Fortrose
Grammar School, and thence proceeded to St
Andrews, where he studied under Mr Mungo
Murray, and became one of the most distinguished
students of the University.   We read that he had
for his "antagonist" at St Andrews the Duke of
Lauderdale, who afterwards played so prominent a
part in public affairs during the reign of Charles II.
Upon completing his course, and taking the degree
of M.A. at St Andrews, he went to Aberdeen, where
he studied Divinity for three years under Dr Robert
Barrow, and became "a great divine and profound
schoolman."   In 1638, when the Presbyterians
gained the ascendancy in the Church of Scotland

and deposed the clergy who would not subscribe the National Covenant,[1] Mr John wished to leave the country, but was prevented by his father, who kept him with himself in Kintail. He had several offers of a living at this time, but refused to accept any because of the necessity of signing the National Covenant, an act which would mean the abjuration of Episcopacy. In 1640 the severity of the Presbyterian measures was somewhat relaxed, and George, Earl of Seaforth, presented Mr John to the living of Dingwall, from which the previous incumbent had been ejected for refusing to acknowledge the Acts of the General Assembly of the Church of Scotland, which met in Glasgow in 1638. Mr John entered into possession of the living of Dingwall without subscribing the Covenant, and continued a staunch Episcopalian until his death. His learning and force of character soon brought him to the front, and he became the leader of his own party in the Presbytery, so that there was frequent and sharp contention between himself and the Presbyterian party. In 1654 the noted Covenanter, Mr Thomas Hogg, became minister of Kiltearn, and three years later his almost equally noted friend, Mr John Mackillican, became minister of Fodderty. To Mr John and his followers these two men and their

---

1 In 1638 the Presbyterians of Scotland drew up and signed *The National Covenant*, by which they bound themselves to defend their religion and their freedom of conscience with their lives. Hence the term *Covenanter*. In 1643 this term received a further meaning in consequence of an alliance entered into by the Covenanters and the English Parliament, called *The Solemn League and Covenant*, by which both parties pledged themselves to mutual defence against the king.

views on Church government were specially objectionable, and the strife between the opposing parties
soon became very bitter. In 1658 Hogg's party
appear to have been in the majority. He himself
was Moderator of the Presbytery, while his friend
Mackillican was Clerk, and they took their
revenge on their opponents by recording against
them in the minutes several entries which show
much personal animosity and very little of that
spirit of Christian charity which is sometimes
claimed in Ross-shire for Mr Hogg and his party.
In these entries they record Mr John's "needless
strife, his great miscarriage deserving censure,
his litigiousness, needless contention and intract-
ableness, his stubbornness and wilfulness, his
wearying tediousness, his misapplication of scrip-
ture, and his pertinacity and loquaciousness."[1]
Matters had come to such a pass that some of the
brethren were forced to declare that the meetings of
Presbytery were "bitterness to them," and to wish
the Presbytery to be dissolved and annexed to other
Presbyteries. It was probably as a result of this
quarrel that there was no meeting of the Presbytery
from April, 1658, to May, 1663. The restoration of
Charles II. led to the establishment of Episcopacy
once more. One result of the change was the
deposition of Hogg and Mackillican, and when the
Presbytery met again in 1663[2] the objectionable

---

[1] Inverness and Dingwall Presbytery Records, edited by William Mackay.

[2] The clergy still continued to meet as a Presbytery after the Restoration
of Charles II. and the re-establishment of Episcopacy, but it appears that
their acts, in order to have any force, had to receive the sanction of the Bishop.

minutes recorded against Mr John were deleted and
marked on their margin as "shameless lying" and
" the spirit of lieing and malice."   Mr John's party
was now in the ascendant, and as far as ecclesiastical matters were concerned the remainder of his
days were passed in peace.   It is said of him that
"he was more fit for the chair" of a Professor "than
for the pulpit," and that " he gave such evidence of
his learning as the place wherein and the society he
was among would allow, and of his piety and vigilance such as they could desire or expect from any,"
while his public life was creditably free from that
religious intolerance which formed so marked a
feature of the age in which he lived.   He appears
also to have been a man who prospered in his
worldly affairs.   He held the wadset rights of
Dornie, Aryugan, Inig, and other places in Kintail
for some years in succession to his father, and there
is a sasine in his favour, on the 18th April, 1672, of
three Oxgates of the town and lands of Craigskorrie
and several others, including the quarterlands of
Balnain in the parishes of Contin, Fodderty, and
Urray.   Mr John married, first, Agnes, daughter
of Colin Mackenzie, first laird of Kincraig, and,
secondly, Florence Innes,[1] heiress of Balnain.   He
died in 1673, and was buried in Dingwall.   His
tombstone was to be seen in Dingwall Churchyard
until very recently, but a search made in 1897
failed to discover any trace of it.   By his first wife
he had issue—

[1] After the death of Mr John, Florence Innes married, as her second
husband, Colin Mackenzie, uncle of Murdoch Mackenzie of Fairburn.

K

1. ALEXANDER, mentioned hereafter.

2. DUNCAN, who was some time Bailie of Ding-wall. He was attorney for his father in the above-mentioned sasine on the 18th April, 1672. He appears to have been the father of Harry Macrae, Bailie of Dingwall, who is mentioned in 1697, and also subsequently, as lawful son of the late Duncan Macrae. Bailie Harry Macrae is frequently men-tioned in the Burgh Records of Dingwall. He is said to have left no male issue.

3. CATHERINE married Donald Ross of Knock-artie. By the marriage contract, dated 25th March, 1672, " the said Donald Ross disposed to the said Catherine Macrae in liferent the lands of Culrichics, in the parish of Kilmuir and shire of Ross." There is a "renunciation by Catherine Macrae, with con-sent of Donald Ross, late of Knockartie, and now of Rosskeen, her spouse, in favour of the Laird of Bal-nagown, of her liferent right by contract of marriage of the lands of Tormore, Gartie, and Knockartie, &c. At Apidale, 26th February, 1699."

4. ISABEL, married Lachlan Mackinnon of Corrie-chatachan, with issue. There is a tombstone to her memory in the old Church of Kilchrist, in the parish of Strath, Skye, bearing the date 1740.

Mr John is said to have had another daughter by his first wife, who married Mr George Tuach.

By his second wife, Florence Innes, Mr John had issue—

5. JOHN, of whom below. .

6. JAMES, who succeeded, in right of his mother, to the estate of Balnain, his elder brother John

being for some reason passed by. There is a sasine on the 11th June, 1673, on disposition by his father, dated at Fortrose, 15th August, 1672, to James and the "heirs male to be gotten of his body, whom failing, to return to any other son to be gotten betwixt the said Mr John Macrae and his said spouse (Florence Innes), and the heirs to be gotten of that child's body; whom failing, to John Macrae, eldest lawful son procreated between the said Mr John Macrae and his said spouse, his heirs male and assignees whomsoever, of the Quarterland of Balnain, in the parish of Urray and shire of Ross." James married Isabel, third daughter of Alexander Mackenzie of Ballone. Contract dated 29th June, 1697. He is mentioned in 1703 as having been invited to the funeral of Hugh Munro of Teaninich, which took place on the 23rd September of that year. He left no issue.

On the death of James, the estate of Balnain passed to a Murdoch Macrae, who, in the manuscript history of the Clan, is said to have been a brother of James. On the other hand, it is stated in the above-mentioned contract of marriage between James and Isabel Mackenzie, dated 29th June, 1697, that James was the "only lawful son now on life procreated between the late Mr John Macrae, minister of Dingwall, and Florence Innes, his second spouse." Again, in Mr John's disposition of the lands of Balnain, in favour of his son James, dated 15th August, 1672 (that is to say, a few months before Mr John's death), only two sons by Florence Innes are mentioned, viz., John and James, and James at that

time was, or very nearly was, of age, as he was
infefted in the lands of Balnain the following June,
so that in all probability Mr John had only two
sons by his second wife, Florence Innes. Taking
these documentary evidences into consideration, and
comparing them with the traditions of Kintail,
which are very clear on this point, the probability is that the Murdoch who is said to have
succeeded to Balnain was a son of John, the eldest
son of Mr John and Florence Innes.

(x.) MURDOCH, who was probably tenth in
descent from Fionnla Dubh Mac Gillechriosd, "finding the lands of Balnain much encumbered, was
tampering about the disposal of them to Seaforth
when he died." Murdoch is said to have married
Mary, daughter of Donald Mac Fhionnla Mhic Gillechriosd, by whom he had issue—

(1). DUNCAN, who disposed of the estate of Balnain to Seaforth " for a verbal promise of a free
liferent tack of Fadoch, in Kintail, which he held
rent free only for five years, though he lived about
forty years thereafter. Thus the estate of Balnain
fell into the family of Seaforth for little money."
He appears to be the Duncan Macrae of Fadoch
who is mentioned in the Valuation Roll of the
Seaforth estates in 1756. Duncan married and left
a large family—

(a). John.

(b). Donald, who had sons : — (b1) Donald,
whose descendants are still living in Kintail; (b2)
Farquhar, who is mentioned in a genealogical tree
of about 1820 as " Dr Downie's herd."

(*c*). Farquhar.

(*d*). Mary or Margaret, who married Farquhar, son of Alexander, son of the Rev. Donald Macrae.

(*e*). Isabel, who married Alexander Macrae, called Alister Buidh, in Fadoch, a descendant of Miles, son of the Rev. Farquhar Macrae, of whom hereafter.

(2). FARQUHAR.

(3). DONALD, of whom next.

(4). CHRISTOPHER.

(XI.) DONALD, son of Murdoch of Balnain, was called Donald Ban. He is said to have married Mary, daughter of Alexander Macrae, with issue—

(1). JOHN married, with issue.

(2). CHRISTOPHER married, with issue.

(3). FINLAY, of whom next.

(XII.) FINLAY, who was called Fionnla Buidh (yellow-haired Finlay), was a farmer at Coilrie about 1760, and was married, with issue—

(1). DONALD, of whom below.

(2). CHRISTOPHER.

(3). ALEXANDER, who married and left issue—

(*a*). Donald, who lived at Bundalloch, married and left issue, at least one son—Donald, also at Bundalloch, who married Christina, daughter of Duncan Macrae, Camusluinie, with issue.

(*b*). Finlay, went to America.

(*c*). Duncan, who lived at Carndu, near Dornie, and married Christina, daughter of Murdoch Macrae.

4. MALCOLM, who left issue—

(*a*) Donald, who had (*a*1) Kenneth, who lived at Sallachy; (*a*2) John, who went to America.

(*b*). John died unmarried.

(XIII.) DONALD, son of Finlay, was called Donald Ban. He married Christina, daughter of Angus Macmillan, at Killelan, and by her, who died in 1836, had issue as below. Donald died at Sallachy in 1840, and was buried at Killelan.

(1). DONALD, called Domhnull Ruadh (Red-haired Donald), married, with issue, and went to Canada.

(2). DUNCAN, a farmer at Sallachy. He gave evidence before Lord Napier's Crofter Commission at Balmacara in 1883, and died at the advanced age of ninety-four in 1890. He married Margaret Macrae, with issue—(*b*1) Alexander; (*b*2) Donald; (*b*3) John; (*b*4) Christina; (*b*5) Anne; (*b*6) Margaret. .

(3). FINLAY.

(4). ANGUS, born at Coilrie. He was for many years tacksman of Achnault, and subsequently leased the farms of Newhall Mains and Kinbeachie, in the Black Isle. He married Isabel, daughter of Donald Mackenzie, Lochcarron, who died at Kinbeachie on the 17th April, 1892, aged seventy-five years, and was buried at Cullicudden, by whom he had issue as below. Angus died at Kinbeachie on the 8th August, 1877, aged seventy-two years, and was buried at Cullicudden.

(*a*). Murdoch, who by purchase acquired the estate of Kinbeachie in 1897.

(*b*). Christina, married John Macniell, and died in Australia in 1891, without issue.

(*c*). Helen, married Roderick Tolmie, and died in Queensland in 1890, with issue—(*c*1) Isabella;

(*c*2) James ; (*c*3) Christina ; (*c*4) Mary ; (*c*5) Ella ; (*c*6) Sarah ; (*c*7) Agnes ; (*c*8) Maggie; (*c*9) Roderick.

(*d*). Margaret, married on the 7th February, 1868, John Macdonald, Invergordon, with issue— (*d*1) Donald Alexander ; (*d*2) Isabella Christina Mackenzie Macrae ; (*d*3) Margaret Jane, married a Mr Graham, and died at Belize, British Honduras, 27th February, 1895, aged twenty-three years ; (*d*4) Angus, died young ; (*d*5) Hannah ; (*d*6) John Evan ; (d7) Duncan Donald ; (*d*8) Grace Maclennan, died in infancy ; (*d*9) Joseph ; (*d*10) Helen, died in infancy ; (*d*11) Murdoch Evan Macrae.

(*e*). Donald, married Jeannie Hooper without issue, and died in New Zealand.

(*f*). The Rev. Duncan Mackenzie, M.A., minister of the Free Church, Lochearnhead, married, 27th August, 1890, Jeanie Cooper, only daughter of Andrew Watters, Esq. of Inchterf, Glenample, Perthshire, with issue—(*f*1) Jean Cooper McWhannell ; (*f*2) Angus ; (*f*3) Andrew Thomas Watters ; (*f*4) Duncan Mackenzie.

(*g*). Sarah.

(*h*). Evan Mackenzie, now of Brahan Mains.

(*i*). Jane, married, first, John Macdonald, of Achnacloich, Nairnshire, without issue. She married, secondly, the Rev. Duncan Finlayson, Free Church, Kinlochbervie, Sutherlandshire, with issue—Isabel Mary.

(5). Christina married Donald Macrae, and went to Canada about 1849.

(6.) Mary married Ewen Maclennan, and went to Australia.

IX. ALEXANDER, eldest son of the Rev. John of Dingwall and his first wife, Agnes Mackenzie of Kincraig, received a wadset, dated 13th and 24th January and 26th February, 1677, of the lands of Conchra and Ardachy, in the parish of Lochalsh, which was held by his family for some generations. There is a sasine on the 6th March, 1683, in favour of Alexander, eldest son and heir, "served and retoured" to the late Mr John Macrae, minister of Dingwall, of a portion of the lands of Easter Rarichies, in the parish of Nigg. There is also a sasine by Alexander, on the 14th April, 1699, in favour of Hugh Baillie, writer in Fortrose, and John Tuach, writer in Dingwall, of the towns and lands of Little Kindease, in the parish of Nigg. He appears to have been a man of considerable means, and is said to have been "a sensible, good countryman," and to have lived to an advanced age. He married Florence Mackinnon of Corrichatachan, by whom he had at least two sons—

1. JOHN, who succeeded him.

2. DUNCAN, commonly called the "Tutor of Conchra," because he acted as guardian to the children of his brother John, who was killed at Sheriffmuir. In this capacity his name appears frequently in connection with the proceedings of the Forfeited Estates Commissioners in Lochalsh and Kintail, after the Rebellion of 1715. Duncan married Isabel, daughter of the Rev. Finlay Macrae of Lochalsh, with issue—

a. Farquhar.

b. Alexander.

c. Isabel, said to have married Duncan, son of the Rev. Donald Macrae of Kintail.

d. Annabel.   *e.* Mary.

f. Janet, who married Alexander Matheson, at Sallachy, where he died in 1793, leaving a son, Roderick, who was farmer of Immer, in Lochcarron, and wrote a manuscript history of the Mathesons. He married and left issue.

X. JOHN, eldest son of Alexander, succeeded to the wadset rights of Conchra, and is commonly known as " John of Conchra." He took a prominent part in the Jacobite rising of 1715, and was Captain in one of Seaforth's regiments on that occasion. He was one of the famous " Four Johns of Scotland "[1] who so greatly distinguished themselves at the battle of Sheriffmuir, where he fell along with many of his clansmen. The memory of John of Conchra still enters largely into the traditions of Lochalsh and Kintail, and many anecdotes about his strength and prowess are preserved in that country. It is said that on the march to Perth, where the Highlanders assembled in 1715, a horse carrying provisions fell into a hole. The men who were near at the time endeavoured to lift it out, but all their efforts were in vain until the arrival of John of Conchra, who succeeded in pulling the horse out by himself. This incident made him known at once to the Highlanders as one of the strongest men

[1] The " Four Johns of Scotland," *Ceither Ianan na h' Alba*, were so called by Highlanders from their valour at the battle of Sheriffmuir. They were John Macrae of Conchra, John Murchison of Auchtertyre, John Mackenzie of Applecross, and John Mackenzie of Hilton. All of them were officers in Seaforth's regiments, and fell in the battle.

among them, and a man of whom great deeds would
be expected in the day of battle.   The Highlanders,
however, were but poorly supplied with firearms,
and while discussing the expectations formed about
him, with Alexander of Ardintoul, John of Conchra
remarked—" If it was to measure manly strength of
arm that we were going to meet the Whig rabble I
should meet them with good courage, but I fear the
little bullets." [1]   It is said that on the day of the
battle the herdsmen of Conchra saw an apparition
of their master walking about among the cattle, and
that when they went home and told his wife about
it, she at once concluded that he was slain.   The
fate of the " Four Johns of Scotland " is lamented in
a Gaelic elegy by Kenneth Macrae of Ardelve, who
was an old man when the battle of Sheriffmuir was
fought, and who makes the following reference to
John of Conchra :—

G'un thuit an t' oganach anns an t' srcup,
An t' Ian o Chonchra 's bu mhòr am beud,
An curaidh laidir le neart a ghairdean,
A cur nan àghannan diubh gu feur.
Bc sud Ian Chonchra a bha gun sgàth,
Bé 'n duine marbhteach e anns a' bhlar,
Ri sgoltadh cheann fhad's a mhair a lann da
'S bha fir gun chaint ann as deigh a laimh.[2]

[1] Old letter from Kintail.

[2] And there fell in the combat the young hero, John of Conchra, and
great was that loss ; the strong warrior who by the strength of his arm laid
heaps of them down on the grass.   Such was John of Conchra, the dauntless,
a deadly man was he in the fight, cleaving skulls as long as his blade lasted,
and behind him lay men made speechless by the work of his hand.

See also Appendix J.

The dirk worn by John of Conchra at Sheriff-muir has been preserved by his descendants. It was taken to America about 1770 by one of his grandsons, in whose family it remained until 1894, when it came into the possession of Duncan Macrae, Esq. of Kames Castle. John of Conchra married, as her first husband, Isabel, daughter of the Rev. Donald Macrae of Kintail, by his wife Catherine Grant of Glenmoriston, with issue.

1. ALEXANDER, who died young and unmarried. His name is frequently mentioned in connection with the proceedings of the Forfeited Estates Commissioners on the Seaforth estates, after the Rebellion of 1715. He is mentioned as a minor under the guardianship of his uncle, Duncan, Tutor of Conchra, on the 29th July, 1728, and probably lived for some years after.

2. JOHN, of whom next.

XI. JOHN is said to have been an active, industrious man who prospered in his affairs. There is, under date 12th April, 1754, a renunciation by him in favour of Kenneth, Lord Fortrose, of the town and lands of Conchra, Croyard, &c., in which he is described as John Macrae of Conchra, eldest son and heir of the late John Macrae of Conchra, and grandson and heir of the late Alexander Macrae of Conchra, eldest lawful son of the late Mr John Macrae, Minister at Dingwall. He married[1]

---

[1] There is some confusion in the Mackenzie Genealogies with regard to this marriage, and also with regard to the marriage of James Macrae of Balnain with another Isabel Mackenzie of Ballone (page 147). See Sir J. D. Mackenzies' Genealogical Tables, sheet 10, and Mackenzie's History of the Mackenzies, pages 575-6.

Isabel, daughter of Alexander Mackenzie, third of Ballone, and died in 1761, with issue :—

1. JOHN, described in an old "Tree" as last of Conchra, a Captain in the 80th Regiment, was killed on the 8th February, 1804, on board the Admiral Applin, in the Bay of Bengal, by the French, while returning as a passenger to India to join his regiment. His son, James, who was with him at the time, was taken prisoner to Mauritius, along with the ship. Captain John married Anne, sister of Archibald Macra of Ardintoul, who, on the death of her husband, received two pensions, one from the Government and another from the East India Company. By her Captain John left issue :—

a. James, Captain in the 11th Devon Regiment, was drowned off the Lizard on the 21st February, 1811, while on his way to the Peninsular War.

b. Florence, married Captain James Grant, with issue :—*b*1. Patrick James, Major 7th Fusiliers, married Sarah Graham ; *b*2. Anne, married Allan Ord, with issue :—Thomas, Captain 2nd Dragoon Guards, died 1870 ; Jane ; Patrick ; Catherine.

2. DUNCAN, born at Conchra, 26th April, 1754, and died 27th November, 1824. He married, first, in 1785, Sarah Powell, with issue :—

a. Flora, born 1786.

b. Powell, born 1788.

He married, secondly, in 1789, Mary Chesnut, with issue :— *a.* Isabella Scota, who married John Macrae of Conchra ; *b.* Margaret ; *c.* Harriet ; *d.* Flora ; *e.* Duncan ; *f.* Sarah ; *g.* Mary ; *h.* Sarah ; *i.* John.

3. COLIN, of whom below.

4. FLORENCE, married Murdoch Matheson, with issue :—

a. Alexander, who settled in Charleston, U.S.A., about 1830, and married a daughter of Captain Bate, with issue :—Murdoch ; Alexander ; John ; Flora.

XII. COLIN, son of John of Conchra and Isabella Mackenzie of Ballone, was Major in the 75th (Abercromby's) Highlanders. He served in India, and came home in command of the regiment in 1806. He married, in 1808, Isabella (who died in 1827), daughter of Archibald Macra of Ardintoul, by his wife Janet, daughter of John Macleod, tenth Baron of Raasay, with issue as below. Major Colin died at Banff on the 10th March, 1821, and by his own dying request was buried with his forefathers in Kintail. His father-in-law, Archibald Macra of Ardintoul, and his brother-in-law, Donald Macrae of Auchtertyre, went to Banff to arrange the funeral. The men of Lochalsh and Kintail went as far as Cluanie to meet the hearse, and bore the coffin for the rest of the way on their shoulders.[1]

1. JOHN went to South Carolina about 1828. He married his cousin, Isabella Scota, daughter of Duncan Macrae and his wife, Mary Chesnut, and died without issue.

2. ARCHIBALD lived at Bruiach, in Inverness-shire, married Fanny Taylor of Alding Grange, Durham, and died at Kemerton Priory, in Gloucestershire, with issue, Mary and Flora, both of whom died young.

[1] Letter from Kintail, 1821.

3. James died young at Banff, and was buried there.

4. COLIN went to South Carolina about 1850, and lived with his brother John until the death of the latter, when he succeeded as lineal representative of the Conchra family, and thirteenth in descent from Fionnla Dubh MacGillechriosd, the founder of the Clan Macrae of Kintail. He lives at Camden, in South Carolina, and is unmarried.

5. DUNCAN, born 8th October, 1816. He served in the H.E.I.C.S., and married, November, 1852, Grace, daughter of Donald Stewart, representative of the Stewarts of Overblairich (cadet of the Stewarts of Garth), with issue as below. Mr Macrae resides at Kames Castle, Rothesay, and is a J.P. and D.L. for the County of Bute.

a. Stewart, married December, 1891, Ethel Evelyn, eldest daughter of Martin Ridley Smith, of Hayes Common, Kent, and his wife, Emily, daughter of Henry Stuart of Montford, Bute, with issue :—*a*1. Kenneth Stewart; *a*2. John Nigel; *a*3. Grace Emily.

b. Sophia Fredrica Christina Hastings, married 13th November, 1879, R. P. Henry-Batten-Pooll, of Road Manor, Somersetshire, and Timsbury, Wiltshire, with issue :—*b*1. Robert Duncan, died 12th August, 1894; *b*2. Walter Stewart; *b*3. Mary Margaret; *b*4. John Alexander; *b*5. Arthur Hugh.

c. John MacRae-Gilstrap, of Ballimore, Argyleshire, Captain Forty-Second Royal Highlanders, The Black Watch, served in 1884 and 1885 in Egypt, the Soudan, and the Nile Expedition, was present at all the engagements in which his regiment took part, and was mentioned in dispatches. Captain MacRae-Gilstrap[1] married on the 4th March, 1889, Isabella Mary, daughter of the late George Gilstrap of Newark-on-Trent, and niece of the late Sir William Gilstrap, Bart. of Fornham Park, Suffolk, under whose will he assumed, 9th January, 1897, by Royal Licence, the additional surname and arms of Gilstrap, and has issue :— c1. Margaret Helen ; c2. Janet Isabel ; c3. Ella Mary ; c4. Elizabeth Barbara Katherine ; c5. Flora Sybil ; c6. John Duncan George.

d. Anna Helena.

e. Isabella.

f. Colin William, Lieutenant in the Forty-Second Highlanders, The Black Watch. Lieutenant Colin, who is an accomplished performer on the bagpipes, is possessor of the " fedan dubh " or Black Chanter of Kintail.[2] This chanter, which was one of the heirlooms of the " High Chiefs " of Kintail, was given by the last Earl of Seaforth to the late Colonel Sir John Macra of Ardintoul. By him it was given to his nephew, Captain Archibald Macra Chisholm of Glassburn, late of the Forty-Second Royal Highlanders, The Black Watch, who, in 1895, gave it to Lieutenant Colin.

6. FRANCIS died young.

7. JESSIE died young at Banff, and was buried there.

---

[1] A portrait and biographical sketch of Captain MacRae-Gilstrap, and also a portrait of Mrs MacRae-Gilstrap, appeared in the *Celtic Monthly* for July, 1896.

[2] Appendix I.

CHAPTER XI.

VIII. The Rev. Donald Macrae, son of the Rev. Farquhar.—Vicar
of Urray.—Chaplain to Seaforth's Regiment.—Commissioner to
the General Assembly.—Vicar of Kintail.—His Marriage and
Descendants.—The Drudaig Family.

VIII. REV. DONALD, son of the Rev. Farquhar
Macrae of Kintail, became Vicar of Urray in 1649.
He was chaplain to the regiment contributed by
Seaforth to the expedition which ended in the
defeat of the Royalist troops at Worcester on the
3rd September, 1651, but does not appear to have
accompanied it to England, as he was chosen
Commissioner to the General Assembly of the
Church of Scotland in that year, and was present,
after his return from the Assembly, at a meeting of
the Dingwall Presbytery at Contin on the 19th
August in that year, when the brethren expressed
their satisfaction with the manner in which he had
performed his duties as their Commissioner. In
1656 he was translated to Kintail as fellow labourer
and "conjunct" minister with his father, under
circumstances which have already been referred to
in some detail.[1] On the death of his father in 1662
Mr Donald became sole Vicar of Kintail until his
own death, which occurred about 1681. Mr Donald

---

[1] See page 64.

married Isabel, daughter of Murdoch Mackenzie, fifth of Hilton, and by her had issue—.

1. ALEXANDER, of whom below.

2. JOHN, who left one son, Kenneth, who married and had two sons. After the death of their father these two sons went to North Carolina in 1774 with their mother, who had married a second husband.

3. COLIN married and left, together with daughters—

a. Kenneth.

b. Alexander was tacksman of Achantighard, where his widow was living in 1756. He married Janet, daughter of Donald Macrae, and had issue—

*b*1. Christopher, who was for some time tacksman of Leachachan. He afterwards lived at Kyleakin. He married Janet, daughter of Donald Macrae, Dornie, with issue :—(1) Christopher ; (2) Alexander, died in Demerara, leaving issue ; (3) Colin, died in Demerara ; (4) Donald ; (5) James ; (6) Christina, who married Christopher Macrae, Kyleakin; (7) Janet,[1] who, on the 13th March, 1838, married Malcolm Macrae, Dornie, and died on the 25th October, 1893, leaving issue—Jean, died young; Jessie; Barbara, married Thomas Paton, Glasgow ; Christopher, died in America ; Jane ; Murdoch, died young ; Christina ; Isabella, married Roderick Matheson, Totaig ; John, now living at Dornie ; Christina ; Mary Anne.

*b*2. Mary, married Murdoch Macrae.

*b*3. Christina, married Fionnla Og Mor of Corriedhomhain.

---

[1] Mentioned also on page 48.

L

*b*4. Anne, married Duncan Macrae.

4. MARY, married John Matheson of Bennets-field, with issue.

IX. ALEXANDER, son of the Rev. Donald, was settled by his father in the lands of Drudaig, where his descendants lived for some generations. He is said to have married a daughter of Fraser of Belladrum, and had issue—

1. CHRISTOPHER, of whom below.

2. DONALD, who married Anne Matheson of Fernaig, with issue—

a. Donald, who had at least four sons—Alexander ; Donald ; Christopher ; Duncan.

b. Duncan, who was living at Achantighard in 1756. He married Isabel, daughter of Maurice Macrae, with issue—

*b*1. Donald, who had at least four sons—Christopher ; Duncan ; Allan ; John.

*b*2. Farquhar.

*b*3. Alexander, who was in the Seventy-Eighth Highlanders.

*b*4. Christopher, also in the Seventy-Eighth Highlanders, was killed in India on the 29th November, 1803.[1]

X. CHRISTOPHER, son of Alexander, is mentioned in an old letter, as having been at the Battle

---

[1] The following extract is from a letter written by a cousin of Christopher at Bombay, and refers to his death :—"You will no doubt be sorry for poor Christopher's fate, who was killed in battle on the 29th November, 1803. You heard, I daresay, of his marriage. He left a promising young daughter, with a pretty good fortune of £600 sterling. His fate was unexpected, so that he left his affairs unsettled. His wife is now married to another man in the military service, and has the guardianship of the child."

of Sheriffmuir. He is described as "a tall, slender man, but very spirited." He was one of the first adherents of Presbyterianism in Kintail, and was one of the first and firmest supporters of the Rev. John Bethune, who was appointed first Presbyterian minister of the newly-formed parish of Glenshiel in 1727. Christopher married Janet, daughter of Farquhar Macrae of Inverinate, and died in 1765, leaving issue—

1. CHRISTOPHER, of whom below.

2. MARGARET married Farquhar Macrae.

3. FLORENCE married Christopher Macrae at Dall, son of Finlay, son of John Breac, with issue.

4. ANNE married Duncan, son of Maurice Macrae of Achyuran, with issue.

XI. CHRISTOPHER, son of Christopher, was tacksman of Drudaig and Glenundalan.[1] He married Anne, daughter of John Macrae, son of Duncan, and died young, leaving issue—

1. DONALD, who lived at Drudaig, and afterwards went to America. He married Margaret, daughter of Farquhar Macrae, Fadoch.

2. DUNCAN married Christina Macrae, with issue at least three sons—John; Christopher; Alexander.

3. CHRISTOPHER married Margaret, daughter of Alexander Macrae of Auchtertyre, and went to Canada about 1816, where he died, leaving issue—

a. Donald, married Mary Macgregor about 1841, and died at Woodside, Manitoba, on the 18th July, 1886, leaving a large family, one of whom is called Duncan, by whom the information here given about

---

[1] Glenundalan is in Glensheil, above Sheil House.

the family of Christopher and Margaret Macrae was communicated to the author in 1896.

b. Alexander, who went to France as a young man and was never again heard of.

c. Margaret, married Kenneth Macgregor, and died at Ashfield, Ontario, leaving issue—two sons and two daughters.

d. Isabella, married Donald Macgregor, and died also at Ashfield, Ontario, leaving a large family.

e. Duncan, married and had a large family. He died about 1891, and was the last survivor of the family.

f. Annie, married John Macrae, with issue.

g. John, died in Indiana about 1866, leaving a large family.

4. ALEXANDER, married Flora Macrae, with issue—

a. Duncan.   *b.* Donald.

c. Alexander, who was living in 1887 with his son, a chemist in Edinburgh.

5. ANNE, married Donald Macrae at Achnagart, and had, with other issue, the Rev. John Macrae of Knockbain, of whom hereafter.

6. MARGARET.

7. MARY.

8. JANET.

9. ISABEL.

CHAPTER XII.

VIII. MILES or MAOLMOIRE, son of the Rev. Farquhar Macrae of Kintail, received, about 1646, a joint wadset with his brothers Murdoch and John Breac, of Camusluinie, which the family held until 1751, when the wadset was redeemed. He married, it is said, a Murchison, and left issue, at least one son.

IX. DONALD, who is said to have been "an active and spirited man." He married and left issue, at least one son.

X. JOHN, who married Marian, daughter of Christopher Macrae of Aryugan, by whom he had issue—

1. ALEXANDER, of whom below.

2. FARQUHAR, who had two sons, Donald and Farquhar.

3. DUNCAN died unmarried.

XI. ALEXANDER, son of the above-mentioned John, was called Alister Buidh. He married, first, Isabel, daughter of Duncan Macrae of Balnain, by whom he had issue—

1. DUNCAN, of whom below.

2. JOHN, called Ian Ruadh (Red-haired John), married Isabella Macrae, with issue—

a. Donald, who married, first, Christina Maclennan, by whom he had a son.

*a*1. Duncan, who went to New Zealand. He married Isabella, daughter of Farquhar Maclennan, Camusluinie, with numerous issue.

Donald married, secondly, Christina, daughter of Christopher Macrae, Carr, and died in 1883, leaving issue.

*a*2. John, a farmer at Ardelve, married Mary Macrae, with issue—Jessie; Donald; Isabel; Christina; Alexander; Duncan; John.

*a*3. Christopher died at Ardelve in 1887.

*a*4. Alexander, a farmer at Ardelve, married 16th December, 1886, Zeller, daughter of Donald Macrae, Auchtertyre family, with issue—Farquhar; Frederick; Donald; Margaret; Duncan.

b. Farquhar died unmarried at Ardelve in 1887.

Alexander, called Alister Buidh, married, secondly, Mary, daughter of Alexander Macrae, Camusluinie, with issue- -

3. FARQUHAR, called Ferachar Ban. He was a Sergeant in the Seventy-Eighth Highlanders, served in India, and afterwards lived as a Pensioner at Dornie. He married Anne, daughter of Murdoch Murchison, with issue—

a. Alexander, a Roman Catholic Priest, was for some time at Beauly, and was afterwards drowned at Cape Breton.

b. Janet; *c.* Mary.

XII. DUNCAN, eldest son of Alister Buidh, is spoken of as "an industrious and religious man." He lived at Fadoch, and afterwards at Ardelve. He married Helen, daughter of John Og, son of the Rev. Donald Macrae of Kintail, with issue.

1. MARY, born 14th September, 1774, married Alexander Macrae, Inchcro, with issue.

2. ALEXANDER, who went to Canada in 1821. He married Anne, daughter of John Mackenzie, by his wife, Christina, daughter of Alexander Macrae, Auchtertyre, and had, with other issue —

a. Duncan.

b. John Alexander, an American Railway Contractor, now living at Niagara Falls. He married, first, Agnes Anne Ross, who died on the 22nd August, 1891, and was buried at St Catherine's Cemetery, Ontario. She left one son, William. John Alexander married, secondly, Julia Perham.

c. Christopher.

3. JOHN, called Ian Ban, born at Ardelve 30th January, 1777, died 14th August, 1848, and was buried at Kilduich. He married Isabel, daughter of Alexander Macpherson, Gairloch, and by her, who died on the 6th March, 1861, had issue—

a. Duncan, died unmarried 8th May, 1886, aged seventy-two years.

b. Anne, died unmarried 18th July, 1858, aged forty-one years.

c. Kate, died unmarried 10th February, 1883, aged sixty-two years.

d. Hannah, died unmarried.

e. Margaret, died unmarried.

d. Alexander, for many years Postmaster at the Strome Ferry, died unmarried on the 25th June, 1896, aged seventy-one years.

VIII. MURDOCH, son of the Rev. Farquhar Macrae of Kintail, had a joint wadset with his brothers, Miles and John Breac, of Camusluinie. He married and had issue, at least one son.

IX. DONALD, who married and left issue, at least one son.

X. MURDOCH, who married Giles or Julia, daughter of Kenneth Mackenzie, merchant, Dingwall, by whom he had issue two sons, as mentioned below, and four daughters, of whom nothing appears to be known.

1. DONALD, who married Anne, daughter of Alexander Mackenzie of Lentran, second son of Simon Mackenzie, first laird of Torridon. Donald died at an advanced age about 1790, and had issue—

a. Murdoch, who emigrated to North Carolina in or about 1773. He was engaged on the Loyalist side in the American War of Independence, and "was killed in the engagement 'twixt the Loyalists and the Americans at More's Bridge in that country in February, 1776."

b. John, who was a planter in Jamaica.

c. Colin, who was a printer in London.

d. Alexander, who was a merchant in New York.

e. Abigail ; *f,* Giles or Julia ; *g,* Florence. These three daughters were married. *h,* Janet.

2. ALEXANDER, who married a Maclean, niece of the Rev. John Maclean, first Presbyterian Minister

of Kintail, by whom he is said to have had issue, one son and four daughters.

It has been found impossible, so far, to trace the descendants of Murdoch, son of the Rev. Farquhar Macrae, any further.

CHAPTER XIII.

VIII. John Breac, son of the Rev. Farquhar.—Foster Brother of Kenneth, third Earl of Seaforth.—Under Factor or Chamberlain of Kintail.—His Marriage and Descendants.—The Auchtertyre Family.—Finlay, son of John Breac.—Killed at the Battle of Glensheil.—His Marriage and Descendants.—The Carr Family.

VIII. JOHN, probably the youngest son of the Rev. Farquhar Macrae of Kintail, was called Ian Breac. He was tacksman of Achyaragan in Kintail, and is spoken of as "an active and successful farmer, who left means behind him." He also had a joint wadset of Camusluinie with his brothers Miles and Murdoch, for which his father gave ten thousand marks to George, second Earl of Seaforth. With regard to this wadset the clan historian says that "whether the other two paid off John or not, his successors got none of the money when the wadset was redeemed in 1751." In addition to being an "active and successful" farmer, John Breac was under factor or chamberlain of Kintail under Kenneth Mor, third Earl of Seaforth, who, it will be remembered, was brought up as a boy and received his early education in the family of the Rev. Farquhar Macrae.[1] John Breac was Kenneth Mor's

[1] See page 59.

foster brother, and there is some reason to believe that the reputation which Kenneth had of being the best chief in the Highlands of Scotland was in some measure due to the influence of his foster brother, to whose strong sense of justice and kindly consideration for the rights and the feelings of the people the traditions of Kintail and Lochalsh still testify. It is said that about the year 1670, while there was a rearrangement of farms and a revision of leases being made on the Seaforth estate of Kintail, John Breac was ill of a fever and unable to take any part in the proceedings. On hearing, however, that a certain Kenneth Mackay of Sallachy was to be removed against his own wish from a farm which his family had held for several generations, John Breac, ill as he was, got out of bed, wrapped himself well up in a blanket and set out across the hills of Attadale in pursuit of Seaforth, who had, only that day, left Kintail for Brahan. John Breac overtook him at Camalt Inn, Attadale, and refused to part with him until he promised to let Mackay remain in undisturbed possession of his ancestral home. It is said that this Mackay's descendants are still living at Sallachy. From all accounts John Breac was a man of weight and influence among his countrymen, and his death was lamented in an elegy, of which a few fragments have been orally preserved in Lochalsh and Kintail to the present day.[1]

John Breac was married, but it is uncertain who his wife was. He had at least three children, and

[1] Appendix J.

his eldest son, Duncan, was born before his marriage. One tradition says that the mother of this Duncan was a daughter of Munro of Foulis, who was living at the time with Lady Seaforth at Ellandonan Castle. Another tradition, which can be traced back among Duncan's descendants for more than a hundred years, and which, for other reasons also, appears to be a more authentic one, says that Duncan's mother was a daughter of Mackenzie of Hilton, and that she afterwards became John Breac's wife. This tradition is to a certain extent supported by the Manuscript History of the Clan, in which it is stated that John Breac "had a son by his wife before marriage," but does not say who his wife was. In any case it was Finlay, the second son, who was served heir to John Breac, who died before the 28th of July, 1696, that being the date of the service. John Breac left at least the following issue—

1. DUNCAN, of whom below.

2. FINLAY, of whom hereafter.

3. CATHERINE, who married Murdoch Matheson, and had a son John, who had a son Kenneth, who married a daughter of Roderick Mackenzie of Rissel, Lochcarron, and had a son John, who died without issue at Kishorn in 1849, aged seventy-two years.

IX. DUNCAN, son of John Breac, is mentioned on an old genealogical tree as "Mr Duncan," and was probably educated for the Church. There is a tradition that he occupied some post of importance[1] on the Seaforth estate of Kintail. He lived at Coilrie, was married, and left issue—

[1] Gaelic, "Fear drèachd," which means a man holding an office of trust and rank.

1. ALEXANDER, of whom below.

2. MURDOCH, who had issue—

a. Alexander, mentioned as a Schoolmaster in Easter Ross.

b. John.

3. DONALD, married and had issue—

a. John, who had a son called John Roy Og, who had two sons, viz., Thomas, who was drowned, and John, who had two sons, John and Thomas, who resided at Dornie in the first half of the present century.

b. Alexander.   *c.* Duncan Roy.

4. BEATRICE, who married Donald Macrae, and had a son Alexander, who had a son Alexander Og, who lived at Dornie.

X. ALEXANDER, son of Duncan, married and had issue—

1. DONALD, of whom next.

2. DUNCAN, married with issue.

3. MARY.

4. CATHERINE, married with issue.

5. REBECCA, married with issue.

XI. DONALD, son of Alexander, was called Domhnull Mhic Alister. Having quarrelled for some reason with Seaforth, he left Kintail and went to Rannoch, in Perthshire. After a brief and apparently not very satisfactory sojourn in that part of the country he returned home, and afterwards took a grazing farm on Bein na Caillich, in Skye, where he lived for some time. He was drowned while crossing Kylerea Ferry during a storm, and his body was never found. He married Flora, daughter of

Kenneth Mackenzie, Culdrein, Attadale (Dochma-luag family), by his wife Flora Mackenzie, whose father was Roderick, son of John, second laird of Applecross, and whose mother was Isabel, daughter of Kenneth Mackenzie, sixth laird of Gairloch.   By her he had issue—

1. ALEXANDER, of whom below.

2. DUNCAN, who married, and had issue.

a. Flora, who, on the 17th March, 1788, married John Macrae, Sallachy, with issue—Duncan; Donald; Isabel.

b. Isabel, who married Malcolm Macrae, with issue—

*b*1. Duncan, who went to America, married, and had issue.

*b*2. John, who died young.

*b*3. Margaret.   *b*4. Kate.

*b*5. Flora, who married George Finlayson at Avernish, with issue—Duncan ; Kenneth, now living at Avernish ; John.

XII. ALEXANDER, eldest son of Donald, was called Alister Donn (Brown Alexander).   He was co-tacksman of Auchtertyre, with the famous Coll Macdonell, fourth of Barisdale,[1] and was in his own day one of the leading men of the parish.   He had a house built for himself at Auchtertyre, which is said to have been the first " white house " in the parish of Lochalsh, except the Minister's Manse.   He married Isabel,[2] daughter of John Og, son of the Rev.

---

[1] For several references to Coll of Barisdale, see Antiquarian Notes (Second Series) by Charles Fraser Mackintosh, LL.D.

[2] See page 79.

Donald, son of Alexander of Inverinate, and by her had issue as below. He lived to a very advanced age, and was the oldest man in the parish for several years before his death, which occurred in June, 1832. He was buried at Kirkton, Lochalsh.

1. DUNCAN, of whom below.

2. DONALD, born at Auchtertyre in 1775. He was a planter at Demerara, and afterwards tacksman of Auchtertyre, and factor for Macleod of Raasay and Matheson of Attadale. He married, about the end of 1816 or the commencement of 1817, Jane, daughter of Archibald Macra of Ardintoul, by whom he had issue as below. He died on the 15th November, 1843, and was buried at Kirkton.

a. John, a Doctor of Medicine, was surgeon in the East India Company's service, and died unmarried at Cawnpore on the 21st January, 1857.

b. James died unmarried.

c. Archibald died unmarried.

d. Jessy, who, in 1849, married John Stewart of Ensay (of the Stewarts of Garth), and died on the 26th of October, 1860, leaving issue—

d1. Jane Macrae.

d2. William, a Captain in the 91st Highlanders.

d3. Isabella Christian married, in 1882, Gordon Fraser, and has issue.

d4. Mary died in 1891.

d5. Donald Alexander married, in 1894, Isabella Mary Anderson, with issue—Mary.

d6. Jessy Chisholm married, in 1888, Thomas Scott.

*d*7. Archibald died in childhood.

3. ALEXANDER, who died while studying medicine at Aberdeen on the 14th June, 1810, aged twenty-two years, and was buried at Kirkton.

4. JOHN, died unmarried, and was buried at Kirkton.

5. FARQUHAR went to Canada about 1833, and was for some time a schoolmaster there. He is spoken of as "an excellent teacher and a most loveable man."[1] After a few years spent in Canada he returned to Lochalsh, and died unmarried on the 4th October, 1839. He was buried at Kirkton.

6. CHRISTINA married John Mackenzie, Auchmore, and had, with other issue, Anne, who married Alexander Macrae in America, a descendant of Miles, son of the Rev. Farquhar Macrae of Kintail, with issue as already mentioned.[2]

7. MARY married Alexander Maclennan, and had, with other issue, a daughter Jessie, who married Duncan Macrae, farmer, Kirkton, with issue as already mentioned.[3]

8. MARGARET married Christopher Macrae (Drudaig family), went to America, and had issue as already mentioned.[4]

9. BARBARA married Malcolm Ross, a native of Easter Ross. He was a road contractor, and made, among other roads, the one leading from Strome Ferry to Lochalsh. Barbara and her husband subsequently went to America. She died on the 11th February, 1870, and her husband died on the

---

1 Letter from one of his old pupils.
2 Page 167.   3 Page 127.   4 Page 163.

22nd April, 1877, both at a very advanced age. They left issue—

a. John, who was born at Auchmore, in Lochalsh, before his parents emigrated. He is a railway contractor in America.

b. Catherine died at the age of twenty-one, on the 9th May, 1846, and was buried at Russelton Flats, Quebec.

c. Alexander, married with issue.

d. Isabella.

e. Christina, married with issue.

f. Donald Walter married Susan Macdonald. He died on the 26th December, 1877, and was buried at St Catherine's Cemetery, Ontario.

g. Agnes Anne married John Alexander Macrae of Niagara Falls, with issue, and died on the 22nd August, 1891,[1] as already mentioned.

10. FLORA died unmarried.

XIII. DUNCAN, eldest son of Alexander of Auchtertyre, was for some time a Sergeant in the Seventy-Eighth Highlanders. He was a farmer at Auchmore, and afterwards lived at Auchtertyre, where he died at a very advanced age on the 13th February, 1860, being for some time before his death the oldest man in the parish. He was buried at Kirkton. He married Christina, daughter of Murdoch Mackenzie, farmer at Braintra,[2] and by her, who died on the 10th of October, 1874, aged

---

1 See page 167.

2 The family to which this Murdoch Mackenzie belonged lived at Braintra for many generations, and is said to have been descended from Sir Dougal Mackenzie, Priest of Kintail, who was killed by Donald Gorm Macdonald of Sleat in 1539.—See page 26.

M

ninety years, and was buried at Kirkton, he had issue—

1. DONALD, born at Auchmore on the 15th of January, 1808.   He lived at Avernish, where he died on the 3rd of April, 1888, and was buried at Kirkton. He married, on the 23rd of January, 1845, Margaret, daughter of Murdoch Matheson, and by her, who died on the 22nd of April, 1893, aged seventy-two years, had issue—

a. Margaret, born on the 12th of November, 1845, married on the 31st July, 1873, Ewen Matheson, at Plockton, with issue—

*a*1. Annabella Mary ; *a*2, Margaret Mary ; *a*3, Farquhar ; *a*4, Frederick Donald ; *a*5, Hectorina.

b. Donald, born on the 22nd of January, 1847, a Sergeant of Police in Glasgow, married on the 5th of April, 1870, Janet, daughter of Thomas Maclennan, with issue—

*b*1. Margaret, born on the 27th of March, 1871, married on the 15th October, 1896, Colin Campbell, in Glasgow, with issue.

*b*2. Jessie, born on the 22nd of April, 1873.

*b*3. Jane, born on the 14th of September, 1876.

*b*4. Catherine, born on the 18th of October, 1880.

*b*5. Frederick Donald, born on the 4th of April, 1883.

c. Murdoch, born on the 25th of May, 1849, died unmarried in Minnesota, in the United States, in 1872.

d. Catherine, born on the 10th of October, 1851.

e. Frederick George, born on the 7th of December, 1853 ; a Captain in the Merchant Service, drowned at sea in 1882.

f. John Alexander, born on the 11th of March, 1856.

g. Farquhar, born on the 17th of October, 1858.

h. Zeller, born on the 26th of October, 1860, married Alexander Macrae, at Ardelve, with issue as already mentioned.[1]

2. MARGARET, married on the 25th of April, 1844, John Matheson, and died on the 2nd of January, 1846, without surviving issue.

3. JOHN, born at Auchmore in March, 1814. He lived for many years at Aultdearg in Kinloch-luichart,[2] and afterwards moved to Easter Ross. He died at Bridgend of Alness, in the parish of Rosskeen, on the 15th of April, 1865, and was buried at Kirkton, in Lochalsh.   He married, on the 10th April, 1851, Flora,[3] born 13th September, 1825, daughter of Alexander Gillanders, some time tacks-man of Immer and Attadale in Lochcarron, and left issue—

a. Rev. Alexander, born on the 23rd of April, 1852, a clergyman of the Church of England, now (1898) Assistant Master of Emanuel School, Wands-worth Common, and Curate of St Helen's Church, Bishopsgate, in the City of London.   He is the author of this book.

b. Margaret, born on the 12th October, 1853.

c. Duncan, born on the 29th of July, 1855, and

1 Page 166.

2 Kinlochluichart is a quoad sacra parish situated near the centre of the county of Ross, and traversed by the Dingwall and Skye Railway.

3 Appendix F.

now in America, married on the 19th July, 1887, Mary Anne, daughter of Roderick Macdonald, Dingwall, and by her, who died the following year at Toronto, Canada, had issue, one son, Roderick John, born on the 15th of March, 1888.

d. Annie, born on the 14th of June, 1857, married, on the 3rd of December, 1886, Ivan Ingram Mavor, of Newcastle-on-Tyne (son of the Rev. James Mavor, M.A., Glasgow) who was shortly afterwards killed in an accident at Birkenhead, and by whom she had issue, one son, Ivan, born on the 12th of September, 1887.

e. Jeannie, born on the 20th of August, 1859, married, on the 12th of August, 1896, Farquhar Matheson, Dornie.

f. Farquhar, born on the 20th of October, 1862, M.B. and C.M., of Aberdeen University, now living at Alness.

g. John, born on the 31st of October, 1865.

IX. FINLAY, son of John Breac, son of the Rev. Farquhar Macrae. He was served heir to his father in July, 1696.[1]

Finlay is said to have "lived in plentiful circumstances at Dullig," and was killed in the battle of Glensheil in 1719, fighting on the Jacobite side. "During the retreat he loitered behind to have a shot at two troopers who were following up close behind.

---

[1] Finlaus M'Cra in Achgargan haeres Joannis M'Cra nuper in Achgargan, filii legitimi quondam Magistri Farquhardi M'Cra aliquando Ministri verbi Dei apud ecclesiam de Kintaill patris.—*Register of Retours*, 28th July, 1696.

Under the same date Finlay is entered as heir to his uncles Christopher and Thomas, legitimate sons of Mr Farquhar Macrae, formerly Minister of Kintail.

He killed one of the troopers, but the other killed him."[1]   It is uncertain who his wife was, but she is mentioned on an old genealogical tree as Janet Nighean Lachlain Mhic Thearlich (daughter of Lachlan, the son of Charles), and by her he had issue—

1. FARQUHAR, of whom hereafter.

2. Christopher, who lived at Dall, and is mentioned as "a religious, honest man."   He married Florence, daughter of Christopher Macrae, Drudaig, with issue—

a. John, called Ian Ban, a carpenter or builder. He married Catherine, daughter of John Og, son of the Rev. Donald Macrae, with issue—

*a*1. Christopher, who had sons—(1) Farquhar, who had a son, Alexander ; (2) Donald ; (3) John.

*a*2. Flora, who married Duncan Macrae,[2] a descendant of the Rev. Finlay Macrae, Lochalsh.

b. Janet, who is said to have married Duncan, grandson of Christopher of Aryugan.[3]

c. Flora, married Alexander Macrae, of the Merchant Service.   He was called the Captain Dubh (the Black Captain).

d. Anne, is said to have married "Farquhar of the Smith family."

3. Flora, married Neil Mackinnon of Kyleakin, and had issue at least a son—

a. John, who married a Miss Macdonald, and had a son—

*a*1. Dr Farquhar Mackinnon of Kyleakin, who married and had issue—(1) John, who lived at Kyleakin.   (2) The Rev. Neil Mackinnon of Creich,

1 Old letter from Kintail.   2 Page 50.   3 Page 124.

who married Elizabeth Flora Anne, daughter of
James Thomas Macdonald of Balranald, with issue—
Farquhar; Catherine, married James Ross, Pollo,
Kilmuir, Easter Ross, with issue; James Thomas;
Jane; Jemima; Christina.   (3) Margaret.

4. ISABEL, married, first, Kenneth Macleod of
Arnisdale, Glenelg, commonly called Kenneth
Mac Alister, with issue.   She[1] married, secondly,
Neil Mackinnion of Borreraig, one of the Corri-
chatachan family.   From this marriage were de-
scended the Mackinnons of Strath.

X. FARQUHAR,[2] son of Finlay, married, first,
a daughter of Duncan Macrae of Aryugan,[3] who was
killed at the Battle of Sheriffmuir, and had issue—

1. FINLAY, called Fionnla Ban, lived at Bundalloch; married, and had issue.

2. DONALD, who went to America in 1774.

3. DUNCAN, who also went to America in 1774.

Farquhar married, secondly, a daughter of
Alister Mor Mac Ian Mhic Dhonnachidh, and had
issue.

4. CHRISTOPHER, of whom below.

5. ISABEL, who married Christopher Macrae,
Achyark, with issue—

a. Farquhar, who lived at Ardelve and married
Anne, daughter of John, son of Alister Ruadh
Macrae, already mentioned,[4] and had issue—

---

[1] There is some reason to believe that this, and not the daughter of the
Rev. John Macrae of Dingwall, is the Isabel whose name is mentioned on the
tombstone referred to on page 146.

[2] The succession of Finlay is continued here in his son Farquhar only for
convenience of arrangement.   It is not maintained that he was the eldest son.

[3] Page 123.   [4] Page 124.

*a*1. Duncan, now living at Ardelve, by whom this statement of the descendants of his grandparents, Christopher and Isabel Macrae, was given to the author in 1890. Duncan gave evidence before Lord Napier's Crofter Commission in 1883. He married Mary, daughter of Duncan Macrae, with issue :—Anne ; Anne ; Duncan, who died at Dornie in 1883 ; Kate ; Farquhar ; Maggie.

*a*2. John.

*a*3. Farquhar, married Janet Macrae, with issue: —Anne ; Janet ; Maggie ; Isabel ; Mary ; Alexander.

*a*4. Christopher, married Kate Macrae, with issue :—Anne ; Duncan ; Margaret married Hector Macdonald ; Farquhar ; Christina ; Catherine ; Mary.

b. Farquhar.

c. Duncan, who was a soldier and served in India.

d. Alexander.

e. John, who was for many years a schoolmaster at Sleat, and a well-known Gaelic scholar, folklorist, and genealogist. He married Catherine Macrae of the Torlysich family, and had issue—

*e*1. John ; *e*2, Christopher ;

*e*3. The Rev. Codfrey, Minister of Cross, in the Island of Lews ;

*e*4. Isabel ; *e*5, Annabel ; *e*6, Christina ; *e*7, Flora.

f. Finlay, married a Miss Finlayson, with issue : —Mary ; Christopher ; Roderick ; Kenneth ; Farquhar ; Duncan ; Annabel ; Isabel.

6. Christina, married Duncan Macdonald, at Carr, with issue.

7. MARY, married Farquhar Maclennan, a native of Kintail, and had issue at least one son.

a. Roderick, called Ruaridh Mor (Big Roderick), who lived in Glenurquhart, and died in 1884. He married Mary Grant, and had, with other issue—

*a*1. Alexander, who lived in Kingussie, where he died in 1892. He married Helen, daughter of Duncan Macrae,[1] with issue ; (1) The Rev. Duncan, M.A. of Edinburgh, Free Church, Laggan, married, in 1893, Isabella, daughter of Donald Macpherson, Factor of the Island of Eigg, by his wife, Mary, daughter of Farquhar Macrae of Camusfunary, with issue, Norman ; (2) Mary, died young ; (3) Roderick, M.A. of Aberdeen, now Headmaster of the Public School, Kingussie, married Flora, eldest daughter of the Rev. Neil Dewar, Free Church, Kingussie ; (4) John ; (5) Jane ; (6) Helen ; (7) Kenneth, M.A. of Aberdeen ; (8) Mary Anne ; (9) Alexander.

XI. CHRISTOPHER, son of Farquhar, was a farmer at Carr. He married Isabel Macrae, with issue—

1. WILLIAM, lived at Carr. He married Anna-

---

[1] Some time during the last century two brothers of the name Macrae migrated from Kintail to Badenoch, where their descendents, who were men of good position, were known as Na Talich (the Kintail Men). From one of these brothers is descended the Rev. Alexander Macrae, Minister of the Scottish Church, Crown Court, London. From the other brother were descended, in the second or third generation—(1) the above-mentioned Duncan, who, in addition to his daughter, Helen, had two sons : (*a*) John, S.S.C., Procurator-Fiscal of Kirkwall, who died a comparatively young man, in 1890, leaving a widow and family, one of whom, Robert, is in the Indian Civil Service ; and (*b*) Kenneth, now living in London. (2) Kenneth, who had a son, John, a Doctor of Medicine, for many years Medical Officer of the Parish of Laggan, and now living with his family in Edinburgh.

bel, daughter of Murdoch Macrae, Achnagart, and died in July, 1879, leaving issue—

a. Alexander, went to South America ; *b*, Mary; *c*, Donald ;

d. Isabel, married Murdoch Macrae at Camuslunie, with issue—William ; Elizabeth ; Alexander ; Donald ;

e. Christopher ;

f. Murdoch, now living at Seabank, in Gairloch.

2. CHRISTOPHER, a farmer at Carr, died in 1895. He left a son, Alexander.

3. FINLAY, a farmer a Carr. He married Mary, daughter of Donald Macrae, with issue—*a*, Mary ; *b*, Kenneth ; *c*, Christopher ; *d*, Isabel ; *e*, Jessie ; *f*, Donald.

4. CHRISTINA, married Donald Macrae at Ardelve, as already mentioned.[1]

5. CATHERINE, married Farquhar Macrae, Camusfunary, with issue, of whom hereafter.

6. JANET, married Donald Macrae, Inverness, without issue.

7. MARY, married Christopher Macrae, Durinish, with issue—*a*, Alexander ; *b*, John ; *c*, Christopher ; *d*, Mary ; *e*, Isabel ; *f*, Janet.

[1] Page 166.

CHAPTER XIV.

V. Farquhar, son of Constable Christopher Macrae of Ellandonan Castle.—Progenitor of the Black Macraes.—Fearachar Mac Ian Oig.—The Rev. Donald Macrae of Lochalsh.—Tradition about Ancestry of Governor James Macrae of Madras.—Domhnull Og. —High-handed proceedings of Garrison placed in Ellandonan by the Parliament after the Execution of Charles I.—Fight between the Garrison and the Kintail men.—Domhnull Og's Descendants.—Donnacha Mor Mac Alister killed at Sheriff-muir.—Maurice of Achyuran.—His Marriage and Descendants. —The Rev. John Macrae of Knockbain.—Eonachan Dubh and his Descendants.—Domhnull Mac Alister, Progenitor of the Torlysich Family.—Killed at Sheriffmuir.—His Marriage and Descendants.

V. FARQUHAR, son of Christopher,[1] who was fourth in descent from Fionnla Dubh Mac Gille-chriosd, and was Constable of Ellandonan Castle in the time of John of Killin, ninth Baron of Kintail, was progenitor of the branch of the clan which was known as Clan 'ic Rath Dhubh (the Black Macraes). He married and had issue—

1. DONALD, of whom below.

2. MAURICE, who left issue.

3. CHRISTOPHER, whose descendants appear to have been well known in Kintail about the end of the seventeenth century, and of whom the Rev.

---

[1] Page 24.

John Macrae of Dingwall says, in his manuscript history of the clan, that others in Kintail could give a more satisfactory account than he could.

VI. DONALD, eldest son of Farquhar, married a daughter of Alexander Bain of Inchvanie, and by her had five sons, who are spoken of as "all bold, pretty, forward men."

1. ALEXANDER, mentioned as "an understanding active man."   For some time he was "principal officer" or Chamberlain of Kintail, "a desirable and lucrative post."   It is said that Sir Kenneth Mackenzie, first Baronet of Coul, was fostered and brought up in his house, and that this led to "a friendship 'twixt the family of Coul and the Macras."   Alexander left no lawful son, but he had two illegitimate sons—John, who lived and died at Leault in Kintail, leaving numerous issue;   and Murdoch, who lived and died with Sir Kenneth Mackenzie at Coul.

2. JOHN, called Ian Og, married, and had issue—

a. Alexander, who had issue :

*a*1. John, who had a son, John, who lived at Coul.

*a*2. Duncan, who had several sons, one of whom, John, was a gunsmith in Kintail.

*a*3. Alexander, who left issue.

b. Duncan, who was killed in the Battle of Auldearn in 1645, leaving issue, one son, Christopher, who was for some time principal officer of Kintail, and left issue.

c Farquhar, called Fearachar Mac Ian Oig, whose name figures prominently in the traditions of

Kintail. It is said that on one occasion, while Farquhar was out hunting, the ground officer or bailiff of Kintail entered his house, and seized some of his chattels in payment of certain dues, which the bailiff was endeavouring to levy on his own account, and which Farquhar strenuously opposed. When he returned home his wife tauntingly informed him of what had happened, and he, giving way to the impulse of the moment, immediately set out in pursuit of the bailiff, whom he soon overtook and killed. For this deed of blood he was obliged to flee the country, but he soon returned, and for seven years concealed himself among the hills of Kintail. At the end of that time he made peace with the bailiff's friends, and paid them a ransom. He was now able once more to appear in public among his friends and his countrymen, who welcomed him back with great delight. The chief of Kintail, perhaps Colin, first Earl of Seaforth, refused, however, to allow Farquhar to come into his presence, but during a rebellion in the Lews, of which there were more than one at this time, Farquhar joined the expedition sent there, unrecognised, and, being a man of great valour, he conducted himself in a manner which led to a complete reconciliation between himself and his chief. Farquhar possessed considerable poetic talent, and is said to have composed several songs during his exile.[1] Whatever truth there may or may not be in this tradition of Farquhar's exile, we know that during the chieftainship of Colin, first Earl of Seaforth, who lived in far greater state than any of his predecessors,

[1] Appendix J.

the people of Kintail suffered greatly from the excessive rents which were then levied upon them, and as Farquhar Mac Ian Oig is specially mentioned as one of those who suffered from the exorbitant raising of rent, it is quite possible he may have been a leader of resistance and opposition to the exactions of the chief and his officials, and may have been obliged in consequence to spend part of his life as an outlaw.   The Rev. John Macrae of Dingwall, in his Manuscript History of the Mackenzies, explains, as an instance of the "grievous imposition" of Earl Colin's time, how the yearly rent of the tack of land called Muchd in Letterfearn, which was held by Farquhar Mac Ian Oig, was in a short time raised from sixty merks Scots to two hundred and eighty. It appears that while this process of rent-raising was going on, Farquhar left Muchd and moved to Achyark.   At all events tradition says it was at Achyark he was living when the bailiff seized his property.   In the poem ascribed to Farquhar, as mentioned above, he calls his wife Nighean Dhonnachidh (Duncan's daughter), and by her he had, with other issue, a son.

c1. The Rev. Donald of Lochalsh, who was educated at Aberdeen, where he graduated M.A. in 1653.   He was minister of Lochalsh before the 11th August, 1663, and was still there on the 12th April, 1688.   He is said to have lived until 1710.   He married Annabel, daughter of William Mackenzie of Shieldaig, and by her had issue:—Mr John; Donald; Duncan ; Farquhar ; Maurice ; and Christopher.

d. John, called Ian Dubh Mac Ian Oig, who

went to Greenock, and was, according to a Kintail tradition,[1] the grandfather of Governor James Macrae of Madras, of whom hereafter.

3. DONALD, mentioned below.

4. DUNCAN, left a daughter but no male issue. " He was a pretty man and lived to a great age."

5. FINLAY, left issue, and his descendants were numerous in Kintail and Lochalsh.

VII. DONALD, son of Donald VI., had five sons, "all pretty men, who outlived their father."[2]

1. JOHN, was " bred a scholar," but does not appear to have profited much by his learning, as he became one of Earl Colin's menial servants. He had a son called John, who married and had issue.

2. CHRISTOPHER, mentioned below.

3. DUNCAN, who was eighth in descent from Fionula Dubh Mac Gillechriosd, married and had issue at least three sons—John, who is described as " a great natural orator," and was accidentally killed in Strathconon in 1698 ; Ronald ; and

(IX.) FARQUHAR,[3] who left a son.

(X.) CHRISTOPHER, who is said to have married a Maclennan, with issue—

---

[1] Tradition communicated to the author by Mr Alexander Matheson, shipowner, Dornie, in 1897.

[2] It is interesting to note how frequently the Clan historian refers to the good looks and handsome personal appearance of the different members of this branch of the Clan, who were his own contemporaries, and with whom he was perhaps personally acquainted This is a characteristic which some members of this branch of the Macraes are said to have retained until the present time.

[3] The Rev. John Macrae's account of this family terminates with Farquhar (IX.) The continuation of the genealogy here given was communicated in outline to the author in August, 1896, by Councillor Alexander Macrae, Inverinate.

(1). FARQUHAR, of whom below.

(2). CHRISTINA, who married Donald Macrae, a farmer at Inverinate, and had, with other issue—

(a). Duncan, commonly called Donnacha Sealgair (Duncan the Hunter), who married and had issue.

(b). Alexander, who was Quarter-Master Sergeant in the Seventy-Eighth Highlanders. He served with his regiment in India, and took part in the Battle of Assaye on the 23rd of September, 1803, and several other engagements. He was also present at the capture of Java in 1811, and retired from active service in 1815, "after twenty-five years of faithful, zealous, and gallant good conduct."[1] On the occasion of his retirement he was presented by his regiment with a valuable gold watch, in recognition " of his long and faithful services to his good King and country." Sergeant Macrae afterwards lived at Kirkton, Lochalsh, where he died at the age of eighty-four, on the 16th of June, 1855, and was buried in Kirkton Churchyard. He married Elizabeth, daughter of Alexander Mackenzie,[2] fifth laird of Cleanwaters, by whom he had issue—

[1] Letter from Lieutenant-Colonel D. Forbes, Commanding 1st Battalion 78th Highlanders, dated Java, 1st March, 1815.

[2] Cleanwaters was formerly the name of a small estate on the south side of Dingwall. The above-mentioned Alexander was a son of Alexander, fourth of Cleanwaters, son of Charles, son of John, son of Colin, second laird of Kilcoy, son of Alexander, first laird of Kilcoy, younger son of Colin, eleventh baron of Kintail, son of Kenneth, tenth baron of Kintail, by his wife the Lady Elizabeth Stewart of Athole, for whose descent from the Royal families of England and Scotland see Appendix F. For some account of the Mackenzies of Cleanwaters see Mackenzie's History of the Mackenzies, new edition, page 584.

(*b*1.) Alexander, who married Jane Macdonald, and died in Australia, leaving issue.

(*b*2.) Donald, who died at Inverness in 1891, unmarried.

(*b*3.) Jessie married Robert Forbes, with issue.

(*b*4.) David, in Australia.

(*b*5.) Christina married Alexander Macintosh, with issue—(1) John died unmarried in Dingwall in 1896 ; (2) Elizabeth married Thomas Nicol, a well-known citizen and Magistrate of Dingwall, and has issue ; (3) Margaret married John Macrae, a solicitor and Magistrate of Dingwall, with issue ; (4) Annie ; (5) Alexander ; (6) Mary ; (7) Donald, who was in the Seaforth Highlanders, and was killed in India ; (8) Robert ; (9) Charles ; (10) David.

(*b*6.) Charles, a supervisor of Inland Revenue, died at Rothesay on the 16th of September, 1885, aged fifty-four years, and was buried in Rothesay Cemetery. He was twice married. By his first wife he left a daughter, and by his second wife two sons and five daughters.

(XI.) FARQUHAR lived at Inchcro. He married Margaret (?), sister of Alexander Macrae of the Merchant Service, commonly called the Captain Dubh (the Black Captain), and by her had issue—

(XII.) CHRISTOPHER, who lived at Fadoch, married Isabella Macrae. He was drowned in one of the rivers of Kintail, and left issue.

(1). DUNCAN, who died at Glenose, in Skye, on the 19th August, 1877, aged seventy-two years. He married Margaret Maclennan, with issue—

(*a*). Alexander in Australia.

(*b*). Christopher, also in Australia.

(*c*). Jessie Hannah.

(2). ALEXANDER, who married Flora, daughter of Duncan Macrae (the above-mentioned Donnacha Sealgair), and had issue—

(*a*). Alexander, living at Inverinate, and now the County Councillor for the Parish of Kintail. He married Anne Maclennan, and has issue :—Mary ; Alexander ; Donald ; Farquhar ; Duncan ; Flora.

(*b*). Donald married Mary Anne Macrae, with issue : — Anne ; Farquhar ; Duncan ; Alexander ; Duncan ; Alexander ; Flora.

(*c*). Isabella.

(3). JOHN died in Australia in 1888, married with issue.

(4). JAMES, who was commonly known as Seumas Ban (James the Fair). He was the author of several Gaelic songs[1] which are well known in Lochalsh and Kintail. He lived for many years at Ardroil, in Lews, where he was the neighbour and friend of the Rev. John Macrae, some time of Carloway, Lews, and formerly of Knockbain. James died at New Kelso, Lochcarron, on the 16th January, 1888, aged seventy-five years, and was buried in Lochcarron Churchyard. He married Flora, daughter of Duncan Mackenzie, by his wife Christina, daughter of John Macrae,[2] and by her, who died at Hemel

[1] Appendix J.

[2] This John Macrae, commonly known as Ian Mac a Gobha—John the Son of the Smith—was the man who brought Ian Mac Mhurachaidh's poems and songs from America (page 83). He died at Carndu, Dornie, in 1839, aged ninety-three years. See also Appendix J.

N

Hempstead, Hertfordshire, on the 18th of March, 1895, and was buried in Lochcarron, had issue—

(*a*). John, who is also a Gaelic poet[1] of considerable talent, now living at Timsgarry in Lews. He married Elizabeth Fraser, with issue—John Fraser ; Duncan ; James ; Isabel Anne ; Alexander.

(*b*). Isabella married Kenneth Murchison, Lochcarron, with issue—Margaret ; Roderick Impey ; James Alexander ; Flora ; Christina ; Isabella ; Finlay ; Kenneth ; Barbara.

(*c*). Flora.

(*d*). Christina, whose name was included in the Women's Roll of Honour for the Victorian Era in the Earl's Court Exhibition of 1897, for having been the means of saving the crew of a Danish ship—the Grana—which was wrecked on the coast of Lews on the 21st of October, 1896. For her conduct on that occasion the Danish Government presented her, through the Prime Minister, Lord Salisbury, with a marble clock, bearing a suitable inscription.[2] Christina is married to Donald Mackay, Mangersta, Lews, and has issue — Flora Helen ; Andrina ; John ; Jemima ; Farquhar Alexander.

(*e*). Barbara.

(*f*). Farquhar, a graduate of Aberdeen University, now a Medical Practitioner in London.

(*g*). Alexander Mackenzie, now a student at the Presbyterian College, London.

4. DONALD, called Dahitar or Dyer, so called

---

1 Appendix J.

2 An account of the heroic conduct of Mrs Mackay on this occasion, together with a portrait of herself, appeared in *The Strand Magazine*, December, 1897.

because he was taught the trade of dyeing, though he never followed it.   He left sons and daughters.

5. DONALD, who was eighth in descent from Fionnla Dubh Mac Gillechriosd, being the second member of the family who bore this name, was called Donald Og.   He greatly distinguished himself in a skirmish which took place in 1650 between the men of Kintail and a garrison which had been placed in Ellandonan Castle by the Scottish Parliament after the execution of Charles I., with whose cause George Earl of Seaforth, after much wavering, finally cast in his lot.   The garrison treated the people with great insolence, and among other things, as the autumn drew to a close, they insisted that the people should furnish them with a sufficient store of fuel for the winter.   Accordingly, a party of soldiers, under a certain John Campbell and a Sergeant of the name Blythman, proceeded to the residence of the Chamberlain at Inverinate in order to enforce their commands.   The soldiers were met by a small party of ten men, probably a deputation appointed to remonstrate against this new imposition.   The remonstrance soon gave place to high words, and the officer in command ordered the soldiers to fire.   This the soldiers did, but without doing the men any injury.   The Kintail men, however, had old scores to settle, especially against John Campbell, who, it seems, had on a former occasion attacked and wounded some people at Little Inverinate, so they immediately drew their swords, fell upon the soldiers, killed several of them, including John Campbell and Sergeant Blythman, and put the rest to flight.

Donald Og, who was evidently the leader of the
Kintail men, singled out Campbell for attack, and with
one fierce stroke of his sword, "cut off his head, neck,
right arm, and shoulder from the rest of his body."
The place where this occurred was long known as
Campbell's Croft. Sergeant Blythman was killed while
attempting to cross a stream of water between Little
Inverinate and Meikle Inverinate, at a spot which
was afterwards called Blythman's Ford. Thus the
ten Kintail men, without losing any of their own
number, fought against the thirty soldiers, and put
them to flight. After this the garrison made no
further demand for fuel, nor did they make any
effort to avenge their defeat. On the contrary,
they felt so uneasy and so much afraid of the men of
Kintail that shortly afterwards they left the country,
and no further notice was ever taken of the matter.
Donald Og left issue,[1] Duncan, and

(IX.) ALEXANDER, who had a son.

(X.) DUNCAN, called Donnacha Breac, who had
a son.

(XI.) JOHN, who had a son.

(XII.) JOHN, who had a son.

(XIII.) KENNETH, who had a son.

(XIV.) ALEXANDER, who lived in Lochcarron,
and married Anne Macrae, with issue.

(1). ALEXANDER, who married, and had issue.

(2). DONALD, who married Helen, daughter of

---

[1] The succession of Donald Og, as here given, was communicated to the
author in 1897, in Kintail, by two independent genealogists, whose statements
were in entire agreement, and were further confirmed by some family notes
in the possession of the Rev. Donald Macrae of Lairg.

Joseph Riddoch of Skeith, near Cullen, and afterwards of Fowlwood, Grange, and died in 1889, leaving issue.

(*a*). Joseph Riddoch, born on the 4th of July, 1855, and died on the 27th of August, 1874.

(*b*). Anne, married Hugh Stewart, who died in 1889, leaving issue—Jane ; John ; Nelly, who died in childhood.

(*c*). The Rev. Donald, born on the 10th of January, 1864, M.A. of St Andrews, B.D. of Aberdeen, Minister of the Parish of Lairg in Sutherlandshire, to which he was ordained in 1890. He married on the 15th of January, 1891, Anne, daughter of William Stephen of Culrain House, and has issue :—

(*c*1). Donald Alastair, born on the 26th of October, 1891.

(*c*2). Ronald Stephen Bruce, born on the 15th March, 1893.

(*c*3). Colin Frederick, born on the 19th of February, 1895.

(*c*4). Charles Eric, born on the 16th of February, 1897.

(*d*). Alexander, born on the 18th September, 1866, married Marie Don, and is now living in East Liverpool, Ohio, in the United States.

(*e*). Helen.

(3). KENNETH, in Kansas in the United States, married, with issue.

(4). FLORA married John Macdonald, in Skye, with issue.

VIII. CHRISTOPHER, son of Donald VII., is said to have been "a prudent and facetious man." He married and left a son.

IX. ALEXANDER, who lived about the time of the Revolution of 1688. He married Margaret, daughter of Alexander Macdonald, of the Glengarry family, by whom he had six sons, " all pretty men."

1. DONALD, who was killed at the Battle of Sheriffmuir, and of whom hereafter.

2. DUNCAN, who was called Donnachadh Mor or Donnachadh Mac Alister. He was noted for his prowess and strength, and was killed at the Battle of Sheriffmuir. It is said that as the Kintail men were passing through Glensheil, under the leadership of Duncan, to join the Jacobite Rising which ended in that battle, they came upon six men who were struggling to place a large stone in a wall they were building. Duncan told the men to stand aside, and, seizing hold of the stone, lifted it up and placed it in the desired position, and at the same time expressed a fervent hope that the Macraes would never be without a man who could lift that stone as he had done. This stone is still pointed out at Achnagart. Duncan's sword was picked up on Sheriffmuir after the battle, and was exhibited for many years in The Tower of London as " the great Highlander's sword." There are men still alive who remember seeing this sword in The Tower. It is not there now, however, and what has become of it is no longer known, though the probability is that it may have been lost in the fire by which The Tower Armoury was destroyed in 1841. In the time of William Earl of Seaforth, Duncan was Captain of the Freiceadan or Guard, whose duty it was to protect the marches of the Seaforth estates

from the plundering raids of the Lochaber cattle-lifters, and many are the traditions of his adventures and feats of arms against the Fir Chaòla (the thin or lean men), as the Lochaber marauders were usually called in Kintail.[1]   Duncan was also a poet, but it has been found impossible so far to recover any more than the merest fragments of his productions.[2] He was married, and left issue.

3. MAURICE, son of Alexander, was tenth in descent from Fionnla Dubh Mac Gillechriosd. He lived at Achyuran, in Glensheil, and is said to have married Christina, daughter of Alexander Macrae, Camusluinie, with issue at least two sons, Alexander and Duncan.

(XI.) ALEXANDER, son of Maurice, was called Alister Ruadh (red-haired Alexander), and was ground officer of Kintail.   It is said that while at school at Fortrose he married a Margaret Fraser of Belladrum, by whom he had one daughter, who married Duncan Macrae, Achnashellach. Alexander married, secondly, a daughter of John Macrae, Inversheil, with issue :—

(1). DONALD, called Domhnull Ruadh, who was a farmer at Achnagart, and in 1794 moved to Ard-elve, in Lochalsh, where he lived for nineteen years. In 1813 he moved to Morvich, in Kintail, where he died the same year.   He married Anne, daughter of Christopher Macrae of Drudaig,[3] and by her had a large family, of whom at least four sons reached manhood, and there was a daughter alive and

1 See chapter on the legends and traditions of the clan.
2 Appendix J.   3 Page 164.

unmarried in 1830.   The four sons had the farm of
Immer, in Lochcarron, between them for some time,
and they were there as late as 1823.

(*a*). Alexander is mentioned as the eldest of
Donald Roy's sons in a letter written by himself to
the Honourable Miss Mackenzie of Seaforth, on the
22nd May, 1830.   He married Isabella Crichton,
who was descended from a Covenanting family, and
had issue : — Marion, Donald, William Crichton,
Alexander, John, Farquhar.

(*b*). Christopher married and left a son, Donald,
who is now living at Bundalloch, in Kintail, and is
married with issue.

(*c*). Farquhar.

(*d*). The Rev. John, some time of Knockbain,
and better known in the Highlands as Macrath Mor
a Chnuicbhain (the great Macrae of Knockbain),
said to have been the youngest of the sons, was
born either at Achnagart or at Ardelve in May,
1794.   In his youth he was noted not only for
physical strength but also for his mental capacity
and intelligence, and numerous anecdotes about his
great personal strength and courage are still floating
about the Highlands.   While living at Immer with
his brothers he made the acquaintance of the Rev.
Lachlan Mackenzie, of Lochcarron, who is said to
have formed a high opinion both of his character
and of his abilities.   After leaving Immer he
received a share in the farm of Ratagan, on the
south side of Lochduich, and while there he acted
for some time as superintendent of the workmen
who were engaged on the construction of the road

THE HISTORY OF THE CLAN MACRAE.   201

leading from Kintail across Mam Ratagan to
Glenelg and Kyle Rhea. He afterwards held an
appointment as teacher in a school at Arnisdale, in
Glenelg, where he became a centre of much influence
for good. Upon deciding to enter the Church he
succeeded in obtaining a bursary for Mathematics at
Aberdeen University. In this subject he took a
high position during his course, but failed to make
a good appearance in Latin and Greek, having
commenced the study of those languages too late in
life to be able to acquire the familiarity which is
necessary for a complete mastery of their construction and idiom. He was, however, a very proficient
student of Hebrew. On completing his college
course and obtaining licence, he acted for some time
as assistant to the Rev. James Russell, of Gairloch.
He became minister of Cross, in Lews, in 1833.
Here he continued until 1839, when he became
minister of the parish of Knockbain, in the Black
Isle.[1] The great controversy which led to the
Disruption of the Church of Scotland in 1843 was
then at its height, and Mr Macrae soon became one
of the ablest and most energetic of the leaders of
the popular party in the Highlands. In 1843 he
cast in his lot with the Free Church, and remained
at Knockbain for some years longer. In 1847, the
death of his intimate friend, the Rev. Alexander
Stewart, of Cromarty, made him wish for a change
of locality, and in 1849 he accepted the Gaelic
Church at Greenock, where he continued until town

[1] The Black Isle is the peninsula lying between the Beauly and Cromarty
Firths, on the north-east coast of Scotland.

life and labour began to tell so much on his health
that he found it necessary to move to a quieter
scene. Accordingly in 1857 he moved to the parish
of Lochs in Lews, and then in 1866 to Carloway,
also in Lews. Here he remained until 1871, when
he retired from active duty, generously declining to
accept the retiring allowance to which he was
entitled from the Church. He died at Greenock on
the 9th October, 1876, leaving behind him a
memory and a name which Gaelic-speaking Highlanders will not readily allow to perish. Mr
Macrae's powers as a preacher were undoubtedly of
the very highest order, and his influence among the
people and his brother clergy was very great. It
was said of him at the time of his death that no
minister in the Highlands during the last two
hundred years had made so great an impression on
so large a number of people. One writer says that
Mr Macrae, " who was of fine personal appearance,
was the type of a genuine Kintail man, well propor-
tioned, beautifully shaped head and shoulders,
herculean limbs, and deep chest, an excellent voice,
and an impressive manner. The effects he produced
upon his hearers were such as no preacher of the
time except Dr Chalmers was known to produce.
In Gaelic his powers came fully out, yet in English
he often thrilled his hearers as he did when he
spoke in his native tongue. His preaching was
characterised by richness of thought, beauty and
simplicity of illustration. He was a large-hearted
man, sound in doctrine, liberal in sentiment, and
esteemed by all." Another writer says that " His

appearance as he presented himself before a congregation at once arrested attention, it suggested to his hearers the thought that this was a messenger from God." The Rev. John Macrae married Penelope, daughter of Captain Mackenzie of Bayble in Lews, and by her, who died on the 9th December, 1859, aged fifty-four years, he had four sons and two daughters.

(d1). John went to Australia, married.

(d2). Donald went to New Zealand.

(d3). Jane married the Rev. Donald Macmaster of Kildalton, in Islay, with issue:—John; Donald; Mary; Hugh; Æneas; Alexander; Ebenezer; Jane.

(d4). Ebenezer, in New Zealand, married, with a large family.

(d5). Annie married the Rev. Alexander Macrae of Clachan, in Kintyre, with issue:—John; Alexander; Ebenezer James; Duncan Graham.

(d6). Alexander Stewart.

(2). FARQUHAR, married Finguela, daughter of Duncan Macrae of the Torlysich family, with issue—

(a). Donald, married Catherine Maclennan, with issue—

(a1). Donald.

(a2). Murdoch,[1] now living at Cairngorm, in Kintail, married Margaret Finlayson, with issue—Donald; John; Alexander; Murdoch; Farquhar; Duncan.

---

[1] Mr Murdoch Macrae's name came into considerable prominence throughout the Highlands during the crofter agitation about 1884, in connection with proceedings instituted against him for damage alleged to have been done by a pet lamb belonging to him, in the deer forest of Kintail, then leased by a wealthy American, the late Mr W. L. Winans.

(*a*3). Farquhar, now living at Sallachy, married Anne Mackay.

(*a*4). Isabella.

(*b*). John married, and had issue.

(*c*). Alexander, killed in Egypt.

(*d*). Farquhar married Catherine Maclennan, and had issue.

(*d*1). Alexander, who died at Strome Mor, Lochcarron, on the 28th August, 1895, aged 80 years. He is the author of a treatise on " Deer Stalking," published by Blackwood & Sons, Edinburgh. He married Anne, daughter of Duncan Macrae of Leachachan, with issue — Catherine ; Mary ; Christina, married Alexander Macrae, in New Zealand ; Duncan, at Strome Mor, Lochcarron ; the Rev. Farquhar, M.A., minister of the parish of Glenorchy, in Argyllshire; Donald, in New Zealand; Flora, married Joseph Ramsay, in Glasgow ; Alexander, in Western Australia ; Kate Anne ; Ewen.

(*d*2). Flora, married Duncan Maclennan, with issue—

(*d*3). Catherine ; (*d*4). Farquhar.

(3). Christina (?), who, according to the traditions of Kintail, married Ian Mac Mhurachaidh, the poet.[1]

(4). Anne, who married Donald Macrae, of the Torlysich family, and had issue—a son, Maurice, and daughters.

(xi.) DUNCAN, son of Maurice, son of Alexander IX., married Anne,[2] daughter of Christopher Macrae of Drudaig by his wife Janet, daughter of Farquhar Macrae of Inverinate, son of Duncan

---

[1] Page 83.   [2] Page 163.

of Inverinate, son of Alexander of Inverinate by his first wife, Margaret Mackenzie of Redcastle,[1] and by her had issue at least one son—

(1). DUNCAN, called Donnachadh Og. He lived at Carr, and married Anne, daughter of Duncan Maclennan, Inchcro, and by her had issue—

(a). Donald lived at Fernaig, and died 2nd December, 1858. He married Janet, daughter of Alexander Macrae of Morvich, and by her, who died on the 20th of May, 1897, aged seventy-eight years, had issue—

(a1). Peter, late of Morvich.

(a2). Catherine, married Dr Cameron.

(a3). Mary, married Roderick Macrae.

(a4). Anne, married Duncan Maclennan of Achederson, in Strathconon.

(a5). Jessie, married Dr Duncan Macintyre, of Fort-William. She died in Edinburgh on the 30th of January, 1898.

(a6). Duncan Alexander, late of Fernaig and Monar, married Barbara Mitchell, with issue—

(b). Farquhar, who was tacksman of Camus-funary, in Skye, married Catherine, daughter of Christopher Macrae, Carr, with issue—

(b1). Alexander, married Madeline, daughter of Captain Farquhar Macrae of Inversheil, with issue, a son, Farquhar, who is married, with issue ; and three daughters.

(b2). Duncan, died in America.

(b3). Ewen, now at Fernaig, in Lochalsh.

(b4). John, also at Fernaig.

1 Appendix F.

(*b*5). Thomas, in Leith.

(*b*6). Donald, in Australia.

(*b*7). Mary, married Donald Macpherson, Eig, with issue—(1) John ; (2) Catherine, married the Rev. John Smyth Carroll, M.A., Glasgow ; (3) Isabella, married the Rev. Duncan Maclennan, M.A., Laggan[1]; (4) Mary, married David Boyd, Aberdeen ; (5) Farquharina, married John Macrae, Portree.

(*b*8). Jane, married Mr Mackintosh, with issue.

(*b*9). Anne. (*b*10). Catherine.

(*c*). Ewen, died at Fernaig.

(*d*). Duncan, was a farmer at Leachachan. He married Mary, daughter of Donald Maclennan, Conchra, and died on the 15th of January, 1862, aged sixty-four years, leaving issue—

(*d*1). Christina, married Alexander Macrae, Achlorachan, in Strathconon.

(*d*2). Ewen, now at Borlum, near Fort-Augustus.

(*d*3). Anne, married Alexander Macrae, with issue.

(*d*4). Isabella, married Robert Blair, with issue.

(*d*5). Lachlan, in Inverness, married, with issue.

(*d*6). Christina.

(*d*7). The Rev. Duncan, now minister of the parish of Glensheil.

(*d*8). Donald, a doctor, died in Bristol in 1889.

(*e*). John, was tacksman of Braintra, in Lochalsh, where he died on the 1st of May, 1874, aged seventy-three years. He married Flora, daughter of Roderick Finlayson, Achmore, and by her, who died on the 6th of May, 1867, aged forty-five years, had issue—

1 Page 184.

(e1). Anne, married Murdoch Matheson, of the Hudson Bay Company, with issue, Flora Catherine; Joan Alexandrina Mary.

(e2). Duncan, J.P., of Ardintoul.

(e3). Roderick, M.D. of the University of Edinburgh, Surgeon-Lieutenant-Colonel in the Indian Medical Service. He served in the Afghan War in 1878-1880, at the close of which he received a special staff appointment "for excellent services in the field," and now holds the important appointment of Chief Medical Officer of the District of Dacca, under the Bengal Government.[1]

(e4). Ewen, in New Zealand, married in 1891, Mary Eleanor Fantham, with issue—Flora Mary; Annie Ethel Frances; Robert Cunningham Bruce.

(e5). Donald John, in Assam, married, 12th October, 1894, Catherine Isabella Gibbs, Daisy Bank, Portobello.

(e6). John Farquhar, M.B. and C.M., Brighton, married, in 1886, Edith Lily Johns.

4. CHRISTOPHER, son of Alexander IX., and tenth in descent from Fionnla Dubh Mac Gillechriosd, was called Gillecriosd Glas (Pale Christopher). He married and left issue—

(XI.) DONALD, who is said to have married Marion (?), a sister of the poet Ian Mac Mhurachidh, and had a son.

(XII.) JOHN, called Ian Dubh na Doiraig (Black John of Doiraig). He married Catherine Macrae, and had with other issue—

---

[1] A biographical sketch, with a portrait of Surgeon-Lieutenant-Colonel Macrae, appeared in the *Celtic Monthly* for December, 1896.

(1). Donald, who was a farmer in Glengarry, where he died in 1860.

(2). Alexander, who was a soldier in the Seventy-Eighth Highlanders.

(3). Duncan, of whom next.

(XIII). DUNCAN,[1] called Donnacha Ban Brocair (Fair Duncan the Foxhunter), lived for many years at Tulloch, near Dingwall, and was afterwards a farmer at Kernsary, near Poolewe, where he died in November, 1851. He married Margaret, daughter of John Macrae, farmer and miller in Lochbroom, by his wife Catherine, daughter of Alexander Macvinish of Achilty, in the parish of Contin, and by her, who died in Dingwall in 1859, aged fifty-three years, had issue—

(1). CATHERINE, born in 1827, married Charles Macleod, a Free Church missionary, with issue, two daughters.

(2). ISABELLA, born in 1829. She married Duncan Mackenzie, and died in 1891, leaving issue, two sons and three daughters.

(3). DUNCAN, born in 1832, now of Strathgarve, Dalveen, Queensland. He married on the 21st of September, 1869, Charlotte Jane, daughter of Loudon Hastings Macleod, with issue[2]—

(a). Margaret Jane.

(b). Addie Sophia.

(c). Loudon Hastings Duncan, born on the 1st of August, 1876.

---

[1] The descent of this Duncan from the above-mentioned Christopher, son of Alexander IX., was communicated to the author in August, 1897, by Mr Alexander Matheson, shipowner, Dornie.

[2] A biographical sketch, with a portrait of Mr Duncan Macrae, appeared in the *Celtic Monthly* for May, 1897.

(4). ALEXANDER, born in 1834, now of Brixham, Devonshire, married in 1871, Anne Lorrimer, who died on the 5th of December, 1897, aged sixty-seven years, without issue.

(5). FARQUHAR, born in 1836, now of Killiemore, in the Island of Mull. He married, in 1870, Maggie, daughter of Donald Macdougall of Port Ellen and Tyndrum, in the Island of Islay, and by her, who died in 1887, aged forty-two years, had issue—(a). Duncan ; (b). Kate Cameron ; (c). Grace Maclennan.

(6). JOHN, born in 1838, was for some time a farmer at Ardlair, on the shores of Loch Maree. He went to Queensland in 1873, and was killed there by a horse in 1880. He married and left issue—(a). Duncan ; (b). Ian ; (c). Grace.

(7). COLIN, born in 1843, married, in 1880, a Miss Young, and died in 1892 without issue.

5. FARQUHAR, son of Alexander IX., was severely wounded at the battle of Sheriffmuir, and brought home by his nephew, John, who is mentioned below. Next day as this John was going over the field of battle he found his father and his uncle Duncan among the slain, and his uncle Farquhar lying wounded with a fractured leg. John tried to catch one of the stray horses that were wandering over the field in order to carry his wounded uncle away; but without success. It is said that the wounded man succeeded, however, by hailing one of the horses in English, to draw it near enough to seize it by the bridle, which he held until his nephew came up to him. But the horse, on hearing the beating of drums in the distance, became very restive, and the young man

o

had great difficulty in managing it. He succeeded, however, at last in getting his uncle mounted. They then set out on the homeward journey, and never halted until they reached Fort-William, where Farquhar remained for three months, until his wound was quite healed. He then returned to Kintail, taking the horse along with him. The horse was carefully kept until it became weak with age and at last died through sinking accidentally in a bog. The iron shoes it wore at Sheriffmuir were kept for many years in the Torlysich family as an heirloom, and were last in the possession of the late Alexander Macrae of Morvich.

6. JOHN, who was known as Eonachan Dubh (Black little John), is said to have been the youngest of the sons of Alexander IX. He was tenth in descent from Fionnla Dubh Mac Gillechriosd. He is said to have been a man of short stature, but of great strength, and there are traditions still preserved of his deeds of daring and prowess against the Lochaber marauders, with whom, in his time, the men of Kintail had many a stout contest.[1] John married, and had issue at least one son.

(XI.) CHRISTOPHER, who lived at Malagan, in the Heights of Kintail, and in whose house Prince Charles passed a night, or part of a night, during his wanderings in that part of the country about the end of July, 1746. He is said to have married Anne,[2] daughter of Christopher Macrae of Aryugan, and had issue at least one son—

---

1 See chapter on the legends and traditions of the clan.
2 Page 126.

(XII.) ALEXANDER, who married Anne Macrae, Camusluinie, and had issue.

(1). MURDOCH, of whom below.

(2). CHRISTOPHER, who married Janet Macrae, with issue.

(a). Isabel married Alexander Macrae at Reraig, in Lochalsh, and had issue.

(a1). Christopher died in Canada, married, with issue.

(a2). Malcolm died in Canada.

(a3). Christina married Alexander Finlayson, Lochcarron.

(a4). Duncan, who was ground officer of Lochalsh, and died in 1866, aged fifty years.

(a5). Mary, married James Macrae, Kirkton, Lochalsh, without issue.

(a6). Hugh, in the Inland Revenue, died at Kirkton, Lochalsh, in 1891. He was married, but left no issue.

(a7). Agnes, married Murdo Finlayson, of Kyle Inn, Lochalsh, with issue :—Catherine, who married Alexander Maclennan, of whom hereafter.

(a8). Roderick, married Mary, daughter of Donald Macrae, Fernaig,[1] with issue, and died in 1893.

(a9). Flora married Alexander Mackenzie, Oban.

(a10). Alexander died young.

(b). Annabella married Kenneth Maclennan, Sallachy.

(c). Alexander, who died at Reraig, Lochalsh, and left a son.

1 Page 205.

(*c*1). John, living in Paisley, and married with issue, a son, Alexander, and several daughters.

(3). ALEXANDER, married and had issue at least one son.

a. John, who married Isabella, daughter of Farquhar Macrae of Torlysich, and had, with other issue—

*a*1. Christopher, who lived in Glensheil, married and had issue.

*a*2. Alexander, who was a farmer in Glenmoriston from 1844 to 1868, when he removed to another farm in Badenoch, which he occupied until 1884. He married Anne, daughter of Duncan Macrae, Attadale, and died in Edinburgh, leaving issue—(1) John, living at Islip, New York, by whom this information about his own family was communicated to the author in 1898. (2) Duncan, living in North Wales, married with issue, a son, James Alexander. (3) Jane, married Colin Maclennan, Islip, New York. (4) Catherine, married William Russell, New York.

(XIII.) MURDOCH, lived at Sheil House, and died at Achnagart on the 17th of December, 1846, aged eighty-six years. He married Annabella, daughter of the Rev. Donald Mackintosh, of Gairloch, by his wife Catherine, daughter of William Mackenzie, fourth laird of Gruinard,[1] and by her, who died on the 15th of April, 1861, aged seventy-eight years, had issue—

(1). CATHERINE, died young.

(2). ALEXANDER, died in Montgomery County, in Ohio, about 1856. He was married and left issue.

---

1 Mackenzie's History of the Mackenzies, new edition, page 618.

(3). ANNE, married Donald Macrae, a merchant in Jeantown, Lochcarron.

(4). DONALD, of whom next.

(5). ANNABELLA, married William Macrae, Carr, with issue.[1]

(6). ALEXANDRINA, died unmarried on the 31st of January, 1860, aged forty-two years.

(7). ISABELLA, died at Seabank, Gairloch, on the 2nd of November, 1896.

(8). CHRISTOPHER, a wool broker in Liverpool, died on the 15th of January, 1856, aged thirty-five years.

(9). CHRISTINA, married John Mackenzie, Ardroil, Lews.

(XIV.) DONALD, was for some time tacksman of Achnagart, and afterwards became proprietor of the estate of Kirksheaf, near Tain. He was a Justice of the Peace for the County of Ross. He married Anne Magdalen Gordon, only daughter of Thomas Stewart, J.P., of Culbo, and died in 1884, with issue one son.

(XV.) CHRISTOPHER ALEXANDER of Kirksheaf, born in 1864, Captain in the 3rd Battalion Seaforth Highlanders. He died at Dover, while on the way to Algiers, on the 20th of December, 1894, and was buried in the St Duthus Cemetery, Tain. He married, in 1888, Helena Margarette, third daughter of the late Edward Griffith Richards, J.P., of Langford House, Somerset, with issue—

(1). DONALD CHRISTOPHER, born on the 3rd of March, 1889.

[1] Page 184.

(2). KENNETH MATHESON, born on the 11th of September, 1890.

(3). ELEANOR MARJORIE, born on the 2nd of August, 1893.

X. DONALD, son of Alexander IX., and his wife, Margaret Macdonald, was the first of this family who lived at Torlysich. He married Rebecca (?), daughter of John Macrae, a former occupier of the lands of Torlysich, called Ian Mac Ian,[1] and was killed at the Battle of Sheriffmuir. By his wife Donald had issue—

1. DONALD, of whom below.

2. JOHN, who as a young man was at the Battle of Sheriffmuir, and brought his wounded uncle, Farquhar, home, as already mentioned. John was afterwards tacksman of Inversheil, and lived to a very advanced age, his descendants to the fourth generation being at his funeral in Kildnich. He married Anne Macrae, and had issue at least four sons—

a. Alexander, who married Marion, probably a sister of Ian Mac Mhurachaidh the poet, and lived at Achyuran. He had a son.

a1. Duncan, who had two sons, Duncan and Farquhar.

b. Donald, called Domhnull Buidh (yellow-haired Donald), who married and had issue :—

---

[1] Ian Mac Ian of Torlysich was the Chief of the Clann Ian Charrich Macraes (see pages 22-23). He is said to have been killed in a fight between the Kintail men and the Lochaber cattle lifters, at a place called Carndhottum, between Glenmoriston and Glengarry. His body was brought back to Kintail for burial, and Donald married his daughter and took possession of Torlysich.

*b*1. John, who married Isabella, daughter of Farquhar Macrae of Sheil Inn, and went to Canada.

*b*2. Donald, who married and went with his family to Australia.

*b*3. Duncan.

c. Christopher, was a farmer at Achnagart, and married a daughter of John, son of Duncan Macrae of Glenelchaig, with issue at least three sons :—

*c*1. Farquhar, and *c*2, John, who both went with their families to Canada.

*c*3. Alexander, who was for some time a farmer at Achnagart, and married a daughter of Donald Macrae, Inchcro, with issue :—(1), Christopher ; (2), Alexander ; (3), Donald ; (4), Catherine, who married John Maclennan, with issue—Alexander, tacksman of Linassie, in Kintail, of whom hereafter; (5), Mary, who married John Macrae (Ian Ruadh) of the Torlysich family ; and (6) Isabella, who married his brother Allan. Both Mary and Isabella went to Australia with large families.

d. Farquhar married and had issue—

*d*1. Donald, a soldier.

*d*2. Malcolm, who was sheriff-officer for Kintail.

3. DUNCAN lived in Glensheil. He married, first, a Macrae, without surviving issue.

He married, secondly, Annabella, daughter of Donald Matheson of Craig, Lochalsh, by whom he had issue—

a. Donald, who married Anne, daughter of Alexander, son of Maurice of Achyuran,[1] and by her had issue, a son Maurice and several daughters.

1 Page 204.

Duncan married, thirdly, a daughter of Christopher Macrae, by whom he had, with other issue— *b*, Christopher ; *c*, Alexander ; *d*, John, a soldier, who served in India, and obtained a pension. He married and left issue.

XI. DONALD, son of Donald X., succeeded his father in Torlysich, and had Glenquaich in joint wadsett with some cousins from Glengarry.   He married Katherine,[1] daughter of the Rev. Donald Macrae of Kintail, with issue—

1. FARQUHAR, of whom below.

2. DUNCAN married and left issue.

3. JOHN married Abigail Macrae, Camusluinie, with issue—

a. John married Mary, daughter of Donald Maclennan, with issue—

*a*1. Christopher died in the West Indies.

*a*2. Donald, who lived for several years at Avernish, Lochalsh.   He married Elizabeth, daughter of Donald Macrae, and died at Carnoch, in the Heights of Kintail, on the 22nd of March, 1892, aged eighty-five years, leaving issue :—(1) Mary married Donald Mackenzie, with issue, and died on the 5th of July, 1878 ; (2) John, in Wales, married Lilla Andrews; (3) Donald, at Killelan, married Janet Maclennan ; (4) Farquhar, in New Zealand ; (5) Christopher, at Carnoch ; (6) Anne married, on the 6th of January, 1898, John Macrae, of Dornie, son of Malcolm and Janet Macrae.[2]

*a*3. Farquhar went to Australia.

---

[1] Page 79.   [2] Page 161.

*a*4. Catherine married John Macrae,[1] schoolmaster at Sleat, in Skye, with issue.

*a*5. Helen, married Malcolm Macrae, and went to Australia in 1852 with her husband and family. She died there shortly after their arrival, and her husband died in 1872.   They left, with other issue, a son Duncan, now a farmer at Donnybrook, in Victoria.

b. Donald, married Hannah, daughter of John Macrae, with issue—

*b*1. John, who married Isabel, daughter of Roderick Matheson, with issue.

*b*2. Farquhar.

*b*3. Donald, a gamekeeper at Cailleach, in Skye, married Catherine Munro, with issue.

c. Alexander, married Anne, daughter of John Macrae, with issue.

*c*1. John, went to Australia.

*c*2. Donald, lived at Inversheil.   He married Catherine, daughter of John Macrae, Durinish, with issue.

*c*3. Farquhar, went to Australia.

*c*4. Catherine, went to Australia.

d. Christopher, died without issue.

John and Abigail Macrae had two other sons in the Seventy-Eighth Highlanders. He had also some daughters.

4. MARGARET, married Duncan, son of Alexander, son of Farquhar.

5. HELEN, married Kenneth Maclennan, in Morvich.

[1] Page 183

XII. FARQUHAR, son of Donald XI., succeeded his father at Torlysich. He married "Helen Grant of Dundreggan, in Glenmoriston, whose mother was a daughter of Colonel Grant of Shewglie, whose wife was a daughter of John Grant, commonly called Ian a Chragain,[1] by his second wife, Janet, daughter of Sir Ewen Cameron of Lochiel,"[2] and by her had issue—

1. DUNCAN, called Donnacha Mor, succeeded to Torlysich, and was extensively engaged in cattle dealing. When Seaforth sold the south side of Glensheil to Mr David Dick, Duncan left the old family home at Torlysich, about 1820, but got the farm of Achnagart, which still formed part of the Seaforth property. He married Florence,[3] daughter of the Rev. John Macrae, of Glensheil, with issue one son, Francis Humberston, who married in Tasmania, and left issue, now the lineal representatives of the old Torlysich family.

2. DONALD, tacksman of Cluanie, in the Heights of Kintail. He married Margaret, daughter of Alexander Macra of Ardintoul, with issue—

a. Alexander, some time tacksman of Glenquaich, died unmarried in Australia.

b. Hannah married Donald Macdonald, Lochaber.

c. Isabella married Donald Stewart of Luskintyre, in Harris, with issue—

---

[1] For an interesting account of Ian a Chragain, who was Laird of Glenmoriston from 1703 to 1736, see Mackay's "Urquhart and Glenmoriston."

[2] Letter.   [3] Page 106.

*c*1. John, now of Ensay, married Jessy Macrae of Auchtertyre, with issue as already mentioned.[1]

*c*2. Donald died unmarried.

*c*3. William died unmarried.

*c*4. Robert died unmarried.

*c*5. Alexander married Anne, daughter of Captain Mackenzie.

*c*6. Grace married Duncan Macrae of Kames Castle, with issue as already mentioned.[2]

*c*7. Mary married, first, the Rev. Robert Mackintosh of Kirkmichael, and, secondly, Robert Anderson of Lochdhu, with issue.

*c*8. Helen Grant married, in 1846, William Hill Brancker of Athline, in the Island of Lews. She died in October, 1897, and left with other issue, William Stewart, barrister-at-law, of the Inner Temple.

*c*9. Richmond Margaret married John Macdougall of Lunga, with issue:—Stewart, now of Lunga, late Major in the Ninety-Third Highlanders, and married with issue.

*c*10. Hannah married Captain Ronald Macdonald (Aberarder family) of the Ninety-Second Highlanders.

d. Janet married Duncan Macrae of Linassie, who went with his family to Canada.

Donald of Cluanie had also a natural son, John, who was a Sergeant in the Seventy-Eighth Highlanders, and was killed after greatly distinguishing himself at the battle of El Hamet, in Egypt, in 1807. Sergeant John Macrae is mentioned by

---

[1] Page 175.   [2] Page 158.

General David Stewart of Garth in his *Sketches of the Highlanders.*[1]

3. ALEXANDER, tacksman of Morvich, married Jessie Cameron of Clunes, in Lochaber, who died on the 12th of March, 1858, aged eighty-two years. Alexander died on the 27th of January, 1852, aged ninety-two years, and by his wife left issue—

a. Janet married Donald Macrae, Fernaig, with issue as already mentioned,[2] and died at a very advanced age on the 20th of May, 1897.

b. Helen, married Ewen Maclennan of Killelan, with issue—

*b*1. Alexander, in Canada.

*b*2. Anne Charlotte, married Alexander Maclennan,[3] tacksman of Linassie, with issue—Ewen Donald ; Percy Cameron ; Katie Christina ; John.

Alexander of Morvich had also two natural sons —(1) Alexander, who was for many years a farmer

---

[1] In Volume II., page 317, General Stewart, in speaking of the battle of El Hamet, says :—Sergeant John Macrae, a young man about twenty-two years of age, but of great size and strength of arm, showed that the broadsword, in a firm hand, is as good a weapon in close fighting as the bayonet. . . . . Macrae killed six men, cutting them down with his broadsword (of the kind usually worn by sergeants of Highland corps), when at last he made a dash out of the ranks on a Turk, whom he cut down ; but as he was returning to the square he was killed by a blow from behind, his head being nearly split in two by the stroke of a sabre. Lieutenant Christopher Macrae, whom I have already mentioned as having brought eighteen men of his own name to the regiment as part of his quota of recruits for an ensigncy, was killed in this affair, with six of his followers and namesakes, besides the Sergeant. On the passage to Lisbon in October, 1805, the same sergeant came to me one evening, crying like a child, and complaining that the ship's cook had called him English names, which he did not understand, and thrown some fat in his face. Thus, a lad who in 1805 was so soft and childish, displayed in 1807 a courage and vigour worthy a hero of Ossian.

[2] See page 205, where her age is erroneously stated to have been seventy-eight—she was much older.   [3] Page 215.

at Achlorachan, in Strathconon. He married, first, Maria Margaret, daughter of Kenneth Mackenzie of Langwell and Corrie, in Lochbroom, with issue, a son, Kenneth Farquhar, late of Achlorachan, and now living in the State of Oregon, in America, and a daughter, Alice, who married Murdoch Mackenzie of Glenbeg, Kishorn. He married, secondly, Chistina, daughter of Duncan Macrae, Leachachan.[1] (2) Duncan, who married and had issue.

4. JOHN, called Ian Ruadh, was for some time tacksman of Dalcataig, in Glenmoriston. He married Mary, daughter of Allan Grant of Dundreggan, and sister of Captain Grant of Reraig, Lochalsh, with issue—

a. John, married Mary Macrae of Achnagart, with issue, and went to Australia.

b. Allan, married Isabella Macrae of Achnagart, with issue, and went to Australia.

c. Duncan, died unmarried.

d. Angus, died unmarried.

e. Jessie, married Duncan Macrae of Sheil House, and went as a widow to Australia with her three sons—Duncan; Christopher, who died on the voyage; Alexander.

f. Donald, who died at Inversheil in 1896, at a very advanced age, and whose portrait was painted some years before his death by Mr William Lockhart Bogle.

5. CHRISTOPHER, was a Lieutenant in the Second Battalion of the Seventy-Eighth Highlanders, which was raised in 1804, and joined by many young men

1 Page 206.

from Kintail. Coming back to the district as a recruiting officer, Christopher brought twenty-two recruits to his battalion, and, in recognition of his services, obtained an Ensign's Commission for his brother Farquhar. The departure of these men was commemorated in a pibroch called Lochduich. Lieutenant Christopher was killed, along with seven other Macraes, as already, mentioned, at the battle of El Hamet, in Egypt, in 1807.

6. FARQUHAR joined the Seventy-Eighth High-landers at a very early age, and obtained an Ensign's Commission, as stated above, shortly after the rais-ing of the Second Battalion. He was promoted Lieutenant in 1808. He was present at the battle of Maida, in Italy, in 1806, and at El Hamet the following year. He served also in India and in Java, and was with the portion of his regiment which was wrecked in the Bay of Bengal while sailing from Java to Calcutta in November, 1816, and had to remain nearly five weeks on the Island of Preparis, where they suffered great hardships before they were finally rescued.[1] He retired about 1825. On returning home he lived first at Cluanie, and afterwards became tacksman of Inversheil. He married, on the 12th of January, 1826, Christina, daughter of the Rev. John Macrae of Glensheil,[2] and died on the 18th of November, 1858, aged about seventy-two years, leaving issue as below. His wife died in Bute on the 4th of August, 1887, and was buried at Kilduich.

---

[1] Historical Records of the 78th Highlanders, by James Macveigh, page 84.
[2] Page 107.

a. Donald John, born on the 18th of April, 1830, who was tacksman of Inversheil and Cluanie, and who, according to the obituary notices of him which appeared at the time of his death, was one of the best known and most highly esteemed farmers in the North of Scotland. He married Margaret, daughter of Archibald Wallace, Esq. of Conrick, in Dumfriesshire, and died on the 14th of June, 1877, leaving issue—

*a*1. Margaret Wallace.

*a*2. Farquhar, in India.

*a*3. Christian Isabella Stewart married, in 1894, R. D. Tipping, in India, with issue—Richard Percy Macrae.

*a*4. Archibald Wallace.

*a*5. Fanny.

*a*6. Donald John.

*a*7. William Alexander Mackinnon.

*a*8. Agnes Wallace.

b. Helen Elizabeth Grant, born 13th of March, 1828, married Farquhar Finlayson, of Rothesay, with issue—Christina Madeline; Duncan; Mary Catherine.

c. Madeline, born 18th of April, 1832, married Alexander Macrae, as already mentioned.[1]

7. ISABELLA, married John Macrae, as already mentioned.[2]

8. JANET, married John, son of Duncan Macrae, farmer, Conchra, with issue at least one daughter, Mary, who married a Mr Fraser, with issue.

9. CATHERINE, married Alexander Maclennan Culagan, Lochcarron, with issue—

1 Page 205.   2 Page 212.

a. John, died in Trinidad. He was married and left issue, a son and a daughter.

b. Farquhar, lived in Lochcarron, where he died in 1869, aged fifty-eight years. He married Janet, daughter of Kenneth Mackenzie, Morvich, by his wife, Anne Macrae, and left issue—

b1. Alexander, now living at Craig House, Lochcarron. He married Catherine, daughter of Murdoch Finlayson, as already mentioned,[1] and has issue—Farquhar, now a Medical Student at the University of Aberdeen; Agnes; John; Murdo Roderick Finlayson; Duncan Lachlan.

b2. Hannah, married James Macleod in Australia.

b3. John, died in Australia in 1869.

b4. Lachlan, in Queensland.

b5. Kenneth, at Monar.

b6. Annie, married to Joseph Williams in Hereford. *b7.* Catherine.

c. Christopher, died in Australia, was married, and left issue.

d. Duncan, died in Australia, unmarried.

e. Lachlan, living at Clunes, Victoria, in Australia, is married, and has a large family.

---

[1] Page 211.

CHAPTER XV.

Finlay, son of Christopher of Aryugan.—Settled in Lochcarron.
—Fionnla nan Gobhar.—His Family.—Donald Macrae of
Achintee.—Ruling Elder of the Parish of Lochcarron.—His
Marriage and Descendants.

X. FINLAY,[1] son of Christopher of Aryugan,
and tenth in descent from Fionnla Dubh Mac
Gillechriosd, left Kintail and settled in the neighbourhood of New Kelso, in Lochcarron, and there is
no reasonable doubt that this was the Finlay Macrae
known in Lochcarron as Fionnla nan Gobhar (Finlay
of the goats), who lived at a place called Frassan,
near New Kelso, during the first half of the eighteenth
century, and was a man of means.   This identity is
further confirmed by the traditions of Fionnla nan
Gobhar's descendants, who claim Christopher of
Aryugan as their ancestor.   Fionnla nan Gobhar
married, and left issue at least two sons—

1. DUNCAN, of whom next.
2. FINLAY, who married, and had issue at least
one son, Duncan, who married Rebecca Macaulay,
and had a daughter, Mary.

XI. DUNCAN, son of Finlay, married, and had
issue—

1. DONALD, of whom next.

1 Page 125.

P

2. CHRISTOPHER, who emigrated to North Carolina about the end of the last century, and was living there in 1810. He married, and had issue at least one son and several daughters.

XII. DONALD lived at Achintee in Lochcarron, He is said to have been a man of "great piety and much force of character," and was ruling elder of the parish of Lochcarron under the ministry of the well-known Mr Lachlan Mackenzie. He married Mary, daughter of his cousin, Duncan Macrae, who is mentioned above, and by her had issue as below. He died on the 3rd of January, 1821, aged eighty years, and was buried in Lochcarron.

1 DUNCAN, who died unmarried in 1804.

2. THE REV. FINLAY, born in 1792. He was educated at King's College, Aberdeen, graduated Master of Arts in 1812, and became minister of North Uist in 1818. "Amid the bitterness and strife engendered by the veto controversy he was accused of maintaining erroneous opinions in a sermon preached at the opening of the Synod (of Glenelg). The case came before the General Assembly (of the Church of Scotland) in 1841, who referred it to a committee, who reported on the 31st of May, unanimously, that unsoundness of doctrine was not chargeable."[1] He was not only acquitted of the charge of heresy, but was also complimented by the Assembly on the general ability of the sermon. He continued minister of North Uist until his death on the 15th of May, 1858. He married on the 16th of July, 1824, Isabella Maria (born 1800, died in

---

[1] Fasti Ecclesiæ Scoticanæ.

Edinburgh 1882), daughter of Colonel Alexander Macdonald of Lynedale, Skye, and Balranald, North Uist, and by her had issue—

a. Donald, born at Baleloch, in North Uist, in August, 1825.   He married in March, 1851, Annabella, daughter of Captain David Miller, Royal Marines, of Pow, Perthshire, and died in 1893, leaving issue—

*a*1. David Miller, born in 1851, and died unmarried in 1893.

*a*2. Annabella Douglas, born in 1853.

*a*3. Isabella Maria, born in 1855, died in childhood.

*a*4. John Miller, born in 1857, died, unmarried, in 1882.

*a*5. Elizabeth Anne, born in November, 1859, married, in 1887, Charles Gordon Mackay, M.B., Lochcarron, with issue.

*a*6. Alexandrina Cornfute, born in November, 1859, married, in 1887, John Tolmie,[1] of H.M. Register House, Edinburgh.

*a*7. Isabella, born in 1861, died in infancy.

*a*8. Finlay Alexander, born in 1863, of the firm of Jackson, Gourlay, Taylor, & Macrae, Chartered Accountants, London and Glasgow.   He married, in 1886, his cousin, Mildred Augusta, daughter of Surgeon-Major Alexander Macrae, of whom below, with issue—(1) Florence Annabella, born in 1887; (2) Rita Mildred, born in 1888 ; (3) Dorothy Mary, born in 1890 ; (4) John Finlay Noel, born in 1891 ; (5) Nina Elizabeth, born in 1893.

*a*9. Mary Jane Harris, born in 1865.

[1] Page 100.

*a*10. Caroline Isabella Craigdaillie, born in 1867, married Percy Maclean Rogers, London, with issue.

*a*11. Somerled James, born in 1870, died unmarried, in 1893.

b. Alexander, born at Baleloch, in North Uist, in 1828, a Doctor of Medicine. He was surgeon in the Army, first in the Ninety-Third Highlanders, and afterwards in the Ninth Lancers, with which regiment he served in the Indian Mutiny. He was afterwards promoted Surgeon-Major of the Ninety-Seventh Regiment, and died in London on his return from India, in May, 1862. He married, in 1851, Florence, daughter of Dr William Henry Maclean of the Royal Hospital, Greenwich, with issue—

*b*1. Lachlan, born in 1858, married, with issue.

*b*2. Mildred Augusta, born in 1859, married her cousin, Finlay Alexander, as mentioned above.

*b*3. Eva Florence Impey, born in 1862, married, in 1894, Thomas Southwood Bush, Bath.

c. Duncan, born at Vallay, in North Uist, in 1829, went to Australia, was married, and died in 1866, leaving issue, two sons, Duncan and Finlay.

d. John Alexander, born at Vallay, in 1832. He succeeded his father as minister of North Uist, and died unmarried in 1896.

e. James Andrew, born at Vallay in 1834, Major in the Inverness Highland Light Infantry, died unmarried in 1873.

f. Jane Ann Elizabeth, born at Vallay in 1838, married Captain Edward William Hawes, R.N., who served in the Crimean War and died in December, 1874, and by whom she had issue :—Isabella Georgina

Emily; Mary Margaret; Elizabeth Alexandrina Macdonald.

g. Godfrey Alexander, born at Vallay in 1840, a Doctor of Medicine, died unmarried in Edinburgh in 1884.

3. CHRISTOPHER, who in his youth was a great favourite of the Rev. Lachlan Mackenzie, succeeded to his father's farm, and in 1842 became tacksman of Glenmore, in Kishorn, where he lived for many years.   He was extensively engaged in cattle dealing, and was the first man who sold cattle on the present site of the Muir of Ord Market.   He married Margaret, daughter of John Gillanders, of Kishorn, and by her had issue as below.   Christopher died on the 5th of October, 1875, aged over eighty years. His wife died on the 26th of July in the same year, aged seventy-five, and both were buried in Lochcarron.

a. Mary, married John Maclennan, and succeeded to her father's farm at Achintee.   She has issue—.

*a*1. Duncan, married with issue.

*a*2. Anne, married Alexander Maclennan, with issue.

*a*3. John, died while studying at the University.

*a*4. Christopher.

*a*5. Christina, married, with issue.

b. Flora, married Alexander Mackenzie, with numerous issue, one of whom is the Rev. Colin Mackenzie, of the Free Church, St Ninians, Stirling.

c. Margaret, married Kenneth Macdonald, factor for Lord Dunmore, in Harris.   She died on the 22nd October, 1863, without issue.

d. Rebecca, died unmarried in Liverpool.

e. Donald, a Doctor of Medicine, of The Firs, Beckenham, Kent, and a Justice of the Peace for the county of Inverness. He married on the 2nd of June, 1874, Harriet Parker Garth, daughter of Arthur Michel, Esq., of Eaton Square, London, with issue, one daughter.

Emily Elizabeth Mary, married, on the 15th of September, 1897, Edward Oliver Kirlew, B.A., of Christ Church, Oxford.

f. Jane, married William Coghill, of the Royal Engineers, without surviving issue.

g. John, died in New Zealand on the 12th of July, 1895.

h. Kate ; *i.* Isabella.

4. JOHN, a farmer at Achintee, married Kate Maciver, and died in 1835, leaving issue—

a. Donald, born in 1826, succeeded to his father's farm. "He was a religious and a highly respected man." He married in 1850 Margery, daughter of Donald Macdonald, Lochcarron, by whom he had issue as below. He died in 1887.

*a*1. John, died young.

*a*2. Mary, born in 1852, married, in 1877, John Mackenzie, Lochalsh.

*a*3. Donald, born in 1854, was a schoolmaster at Dunblane, and died in 1879.

*a*4. John, born on the 25th of June, 1856, ordained minister of the Free Church at Aberfeldy in 1884. He married on the 20th of April, 1887, Catherine Campbell Mackerchar, with issue, Donald, born on the 16th of September, 1888.

*a*5. Margaret, born in 1858, died in 1867.

*a*6. Catherine, born in 1861, married, in 1882, to Murdoch Mackenzie, Auchnashellach, Lochcarron.

*a*7. Isabella, born in 1865, married, in 1894, to John Stewart, Slumbay, Lochcarron.

*a*8. Alexander, born in June, 1867, a minister of the Free Presbyterian Church at Kames, in Argyllshire.

*a*9. William, born in 1869, succeeded to his father's farm at Achintee.

*a*10. Margaret Isabella, born in October, 1873.

b. Alexander, born in 1828, went to Australia in 1852, settled near Ballarat, and died in 1890. He was married, and left a large family.

c. Mary, born in 1830, died young.

5. THE REV. DONALD, born on the 12th of January, 1801. He was educated at King's College, Aberdeen, and graduated Master of Arts in 1823. He became minister of Poolewe, in Ross-shire, in 1830. At the Disruption of the Church of Scotland in 1843, he cast in his lot with the Free Church, and was followed by his entire congregation. In 1845 he became minister of the Free Church at Kilmory in Arran, where he continued until his death on the 6th of August, 1868. He married on the 2nd of August, 1834, Jessie, daughter of the Rev. James Russell, M.A., of Gairloch, and by her had issue—

a. Mary Johanna, married the Rev. John Stewart, for many years Free Church minister of Pitlochry, who died in 1882, and by whom she had issue—

*a*1. Jessie Russell.

*a*2. Alexander, in South Africa.

*a*3. Donald Macrae, a Presbyterian minister in Melbourne.

*a*4. Margaret, married James Arthur Thompson, Lecturer in Biology in Edinburgh University.

*a*5. William, in the United States.

*a*6. Ella ; *a*7. Douglas ; *a*8. Ian.

b. Donald, a medical practitioner in the city of Council Bluffs, Iowa, U.S.A., was for three years Mayor of that city. He married Charlotte Angelica, daughter of Joseph Bouchette, Surveyor-General of Canada, with issue, one son, Donald, who is also a medical practitioner, in partnership with his father, and is married, with issue.

c. Isabella, died young in 1855.

d. Jessie Russell, married the Rev. John Teed Maclean, minister of the Free Gaelic Church, Govan, Glasgow. She died in 1888, leaving issue.

e. James Russell, a farmer near Council Bluffs, U.S.A., married, with issue.

f. Rev. John Farquhar, sometime minister of the Free Church, Cockpen, near Edinburgh, and afterwards of the Free Church, St Andrews. He is now minister of the Toorak Presbyterian Church, Melbourne, one of the most important Presbyterian Churches in Australia. He married Bertha, daughter of Thomas Livingstone Learnmouth, of Park Hall, Polmont, with issue—Frederick ; Norman ; Ethel ; Muriel ; Marjory Bertha.

g. Rev. Duncan, now minister of the Presbyterian Church, Wood Green, London. He married Alice, daughter of Alfred Hawkins, solicitor, London, with issue—Irene, died in childhood ; Russell Duncan ; Winifred Alice ; Kathleen Doris.

h. Finlay Alexander, now living at Wood Green,

London, married Myra, daughter of the Rev. Colin Campbell, minister of the parish of Lamlash, in Arran.

6. ANNE, married George Mackenzie, with issue.

7. JESSIE, married Finlay Matheson, a Senator of Canada, with issue.

8. REBECCA, married Kenneth Macleod, with issue.

9. MARY, married in 1806, Christopher Macdonald, Lonellan, Kintail, with issue—

a. Kate, married, first, in 1826, Alexander Macrae, shipowner, Dornie, with issue.

*a*1. Donald, born in 1827, died in Australia.

*a*2. Margaret Catherine, married in 1859, Alexander Bremner, of the Inland Revenue, now in Dunblane, with issue, three sons, one of whom is Dr A. M. Bremner, Alyth, Perthshire.

Kate, married, secondly, in 1841, John Murdoch, of the Inland Revenue, with issue—

*a*3. John; *a*4. Mary; *a*5. Christopher; *a*6. Caroline.

b. Duncan, born in 1809, died in 1831.

c. Mary, married Roderick Mackenzie, shipowner, Shieldaig, with issue—

*c*1. Isabella, married Duncan Macrae, Dornie, with issue.

*c*2. Mary, married Christopher Macdonald, New Zealand, with issue.

*c*3. Anne.

*c*4. Christopher, merchant, Shieldaig.

*c*5. Margaret, married Roderick Macrae, Lochcarron.

d. Christina, married, in 1841, Charles Mackenzie, Lonellan, with issue—

*d*1. Alexander Colin, born in 1842, schoolmaster, Maryburgh, near Dingwall, Major, First Volunteer Battalion Seaforth Highlanders, and a Justice of the Peace for Ross and Cromarty.

*d*2. Christopher Duncan, born 1843, now in business in Middlesbrough, Yorkshire, married, in 1870, Margaret Sclanders, daughter of John Macmillan, Glasgow, with issue.

*d*3. Annabella, married, in 1875, John Bell, at Bishop Auckland, Durham, with issue.

*d*4. Mary, died in 1894 ; *d*5. Margaret.

e. Finlay of Drudaig, a Justice of the Peace for the County of Ross, married, in 1860, Jessie Margaret, daughter of Lieutenant John Macdonald, North Uist, and died in 1892, leaving issue—

*e*1. John Christopher, a planter in India.

*e*2. Johanna Matheson.

*e*3. Alexina Flora, married Dr Robert Moodie, of Stirling, with issue.

*e*4. Mary Catherine, married James Gerrard, of Coorg, in India.

*e*5. Jemima Margaret.

*e*6. Duncan Alexander, died young.

*e*7. James Andrew, died young.

f. Alexander, born in 1820, drowned in 1834.

CHAPTER XVI.

Governor James Macrae of Madras.—Tradition about his Ancestry.
—His Humble Birth.—Boyhood.—Goes to Sea.—Mission to
Sumatra.—Governor of Madras.—Return to Scotland.—His
Death.—His Heirs.—Their Marriages and Descendants.

THERE have been very few men who had a more
romantic or a more successful and honourable career
than Governor James Macrae of Madras, who, though
by birth a native of the County of Ayr, is sometimes
claimed as a descendant of the Macraes of Kintail.
There is a Kintail tradition to the effect that some
time during the first half of the seventeenth century a
certain John Macrae, known in Kintail as Ian Dubh
Mac Ian Oig[1] (Black John, son of John the younger),
migrated to the south and settled for some time at
Greenock, that either he or one of his sons afterwards moved farther south to the town of Ayr or
its neighbourhood, and that he was the grandfather
of Governor James Macrae of Madras. At the same
time, the name Macrae or M'Cra appears more than
once in connection with Ayr [2] many generations
before the time to which this tradition refers, and it
is quite possible that, notwithstanding the Kintail

[1] Pages 189-190.

[2] In the Register of the Great Seal, 25th August, 1534, mention is made
of Thomas M'Cra, Sergeant or Constable of the Sheriff of Ayr, but the name
occurs in Ayr as far back as 1477.

tradition, Governor Macrae may have belonged to an old Ayrshire family of that name.   But, on the other hand, it may be mentioned that, besides this Kintail tradition, there are traditions [1] also among other families of the name to the effect that they are descended from certain Macraes who left Kintail and settled in the south-west of Scotland about the middle of the seventeenth century.

Of Governor Macrae's ancestry, however, nothing beyond the Kintail tradition appears to be known. He was born in the neighbourhood of Ayr about the year 1677.   His parents were in poor circumstances, and at an early age James was employed in herding cattle.   He lost his father while still very young, and his mother then moved to a small thatched cottage in one of the suburbs of Ayr.   Here she earned her living as a washerwoman, while her son added to the earnings by serving as an errand boy in the town.   By some means or other he contrived to acquire an education—perhaps through the kindness of a fiddler of the town of Ayr called Hugh Macguire, and about 1692 went to sea.   It is generally supposed that he was not heard of again in Ayr until he returned home after an absence of about forty years.   In 1720 he is mentioned as Captain Macrae, then serving under the Honourable East India Company, and conducting a special mission to the English settlement on the West Coast of Sumatra.   So successfully did he fulfil the object of that mission, and deal with certain commercial abuses which prevailed there at the time,

_____

[1] These traditions are again referred to in Chapters XX., XXI.

that he was appointed Deputy-Governor of Fort St David, with reversion of the Governorship of Fort-George. He was afterwards appointed Governor of the Presidency of Madras, and assumed charge of office on the 15th of January, 1725. His rule is said to have been stern and arbitrary, but highly acceptable to the Company, as he reformed many abuses, reduced expenditure, and greatly increased the Company's revenues. The first Protestant Mission was inaugurated at Madras during his rule in 1726, and in the following year a general survey of the town and suburbs was made under his direction. He is said to have been emphatically a commercial Governor, effecting fiscal reforms on all hands, correcting various abuses and greatly developing and increasing the commerce of the Presidency, while many improvements of various kinds were carried out as the result of his intelligent and energetic policy. The old records of Madras reveal many facts most creditable to the rule of Governor James Macrae, who thus occupies a high and honourable place in the long list of eminent statesmen who have made our Indian Empire what it is. He resigned the Governorship on the 14th of May, 1730, and on the 21st of January, 1731, set sail for Scotland.

On his return to Scotland he found himself a perfect stranger, but a diligent search led to the discovery of some relatives or friends, whom he treated with great kindness, and among whom he made a liberal distribution of his wealth. He bought several estates in the West of Scotland, and fixed his own residence at Orangefield, in Ayrshire. He was admitted a burgess of Ayr on the 1st of August, 1733, and in 1735 he presented Glasgow with a bronze statue of William III.   He died on the 21st of July, 1744, and was buried in Monktoun Churchyard, where he is commemorated by a monument which was erected in 1750.   Governor Macrae died unmarried, and the exact degree of relationship between himself and the family which he adopted appears to be somewhat doubtful.   They were the grandchildren of Hugh Macguire, to whose kindness, as already mentioned, Governor Macrae is said to have been indebted for such education as he received in his childhood, and they are also mentioned as his sister's children.   It is quite possible that a son of Hugh Macguire, also called Hugh, may have married Governor Macrae's sister.   In that case, then, both descriptions might be correct.[1]

On obtaining some information about her, Governor Macrae is said to have written to his sister, Mrs Hugh Macguire, at Ayr, enclosing a large sum of money, and offering to provide for herself and family.   The surprise of Mrs Macguire and her husband, who is said to have been a poor man, earning his living partly as a carpenter and partly as a fiddler, was, of course, unbounded, and "they are said to have given way to their delight by indulging in a luxury

---

[1] The writer of the article on Governor Macrae in the *Dictionary of National Biography* speaks of the family he adopted simply as the grandchildren of his old benefactor, Hugh Macguire, but in J. Talboys Wheeler's *Madras in the Olden Time* (a work to which the author is indebted for most of the information contained in this chapter) they are mentioned as the children of Governor Macrae's sister, Mrs Hugh Macguire.

which will serve to illustrate both their ideas of happiness, and the state of poverty in which they had been living. They procured a loaf of sugar and a bottle of brandy, and scooping out a hole in the sugar loaf they poured in the brandy, and supped up the sweetened spirit with spoons until the excess of their felicity compelled them to close their eyes in peaceful slumber."[1] Governor Macrae made liberal provisions for the Macguire family, as follows :—

1. The eldest daughter married Mr Charles Dalrymple, Sheriff-Clerk of Ayr, and received the estate of Orangefield.

2. MARGARET married Mr James Erskine, who received the estate of Alva, and was afterwards elevated to the bench under the title of Lord Alva.

3. ELIZABETH married William Cunningham, thirteenth Earl of Glencairn, in August, 1744, and died at Coats, near Edinburgh, on the 24th of June, 1801, leaving issue—

a. William, Lord Kilmaurs, died unmarried in 1768.

b. James, fourteenth Earl of Glencairn, died unmarried on the 30th of January, 1791. This was the Earl of Glencairn so frequently referred to in the works of Robert Burns, and on whose death the poet wrote his well-known " Lament for James, Earl of Glencairn."

c. John, fifteenth and last Earl of Glencairn, born in 1750, was an officer in the 14th Dragoons, but afterwards took orders in the Church of England. He married, in 1785, Lady Isabella Erskine,

1 J. Talboys Wheeler's *Madras in the Olden Time.*

second daughter of the tenth Earl of Buchan, and widow of William Leslie Hamilton. He died without issue on the 24th of September, 1796, when the title became extinct.

d. Harriet married Sir Alexander Don, Bart. of Newton-Don, Roxburgh, and had a son—Sir Alexander Don, Bart., who succeeded to the barony of Ochiltree on the death of his grandmother, the Countess of Glencairn, in 1801.

4. The fourth daughter married James Macrae, of whom next.

JAMES MACRAE, who married the fourth daughter of Hugh Macguire, received the barony of Houston, in Renfrewshire. He appears to have been a young gentleman of doubtful origin, said to have been the nephew of Governor Macrae, but supposed to have been his natural son.[1] He was a Captain in the Army, and on the 4th of April, 1758, was served heir general to Hugh Macguire of Drumdow, who is there mentioned as his father, and who died in 1753. Captain Macrae died on the 16th of October, 1760, leaving issue, at least, one son—

JAMES, of Houston, and afterwards of Holmains, in Dumfriesshire, was also a Captain in the Army. In consequence of an insult which Captain Macrae received, or thought he had received, one night at the theatre door in Edinburgh, from one of the

---

[1] This account of James Macrae is from J. Talboys Wheeler's *Madras in the Olden Time*, but the writer of the article in the *Dictionary of National Biography* says that he was the son of Hugh Macguire (in which case he was probably the nephew of Governor Macrae), and that he adopted the name Macrae as one of Governor Macrae's heirs. This would seem to be borne out by his service of heirship, and in that case he could not, of course, have married a daughter of Hugh Macguire, as stated by J. Talboys Wheeler.

servants of Sir George Ramsay, Bart. of Bamff, in Perthshire, a quarrel arose between Sir George and himself. The quarrel led to a duel between them on Musselburgh Links, in which Sir George Ramsay was killed, in 1790. After this Captain Macrae appears to have lived abroad. He married, about 1787, Maria Cecilia, daughter of Judge Le Maistre, of the Supreme Court of Judicature in India, and by her, who died in 1806, had issue as below. Captain Macrae died in France on the 10th of January, 1820.

1. JAMES CHARLES, Esq. of Holmains, J.P. and D.L., was born on the 2nd of January, 1791. He married on the 26th of June, 1820, Margaret Elizabeth, daughter of Sir Alexander Grierson, Bart. Mr Macrae sold Holmains, and went to live at Reading, where he died about 1876. He appears to have been the last representative in the male line of this family.

2. MARIE LE MAISTRE married J. P. Davis, Esq., of London.

CHAPTER XVII.

A Romance of Sheriffmuir.—The Rev. James Macrae of Sauchieburn.—The Rev. David Macrae of Oban, and afterwards of
Glasgow.—The Rev. David Macrae of Gourock, and afterwards
of Dundee.

AMONG the Macraes who fought at the battle of
Sheriffmuir, a certain young man, covered with
wounds and apparently dead, with his sword still
in his grasp, was found on the field after the battle.
On its being discovered that life was still in him, he
was taken to a neighbouring farm house, where he
was kindly cared for until his wounds were healed.
Instead of returning home he settled in the neighbourhood and married the farmer's daughter. By
her he had at least one son,

DUNCAN, who joined the Highland army in
1745 on its way south under Prince Charlie. Duncan married and had at least one son,

JAMES, who became a carpenter in the Perthshire Highlands, married and had issue, at least one
son,

JAMES, who was trained for the ministry of the
Established Church, but, owing to his objections to
the Confession of Faith, left and became an Independent minister at Sauchieburn, in the parish of
Fettercairn, in 1775. During the latter part of the

century he made considerable stir in the Scottish
ecclesiastical world as a vigorous and able champion
of religious freedom and equality.   He was in many
respects considerably in advance of his times.   His
preaching is said to have been evangelical and full
of power, and people flocked to his church from all
the adjacent parishes.   After a long and honourable
course of labour he was forced by the increasing
infirmities of old age to resign his pastorate, and
shortly afterwards died at Laurencekirk in 1813.
He had married Jean Low of Fettercairn in 1777,
by whom he had a large family, one of whom was

DAVID, born on the 14th of October, 1796.   He
was educated at Aberdeen University, and graduated M.A. in 1820.   For some time he was teacher
of Mathematics in one of the schools of Aberdeen,
where he had as one of his pupils the late Professor
John Stuart Blackie of Edinburgh University.   He
joined the Presbyterian (Secession) Church in Aberdeen; was trained for the ministry of that denomination, and on the 6th of March, 1827, was ordained
minister of the Secession (now United Presbyterian)
Church at Lathones, in Fife.   Here he laboured for
eleven years, when he accepted a call from the
congregation of the United Presbyterian Church at
Oban, and was inducted there on the 25th of April,
1838.   At Oban Mr Macrae engaged in many important labours, and the energy and ability with
which he set himself to work among the people
during the famine which visited the Highlands in
1845-47, had the effect not only of providing for the
poor during a time of great trial and destitution,

but also of creating habits of industry and independence among them. The memory of his good works is warmly cherished by the people of that district, and many anecdotes of the earnestness and saintliness of his life may still be heard among them. Mr Macrae continued at Oban until 1852, when, at the urgent solicitation of the United Presbyterian Presbytery of Glasgow, he transferred the scene of his labours to that city. He commenced his work in Main Street, Gorbals, where he built up a large and flourishing church, and laboured with much success until 1873, when he moved along with his congregation to a new church in Elgin Street. The jubilee of his ministry was celebrated in Glasgow amid many signs of respect, gratitude, and devotion by his congregation and numerous friends in April, 1876. He died on the 19th of July, 1881, and was buried at Craigton, Glasgow. He had married on the 15th of April, 1828, Margaret, daughter of Gilbert Falconer, of Aberdeen, and sister of Forbes Falconer, the distinguished Orientalist, and Professor of Oriental Languages in King's College, London, and by her (who died on the 29th of November, 1874, aged seventy-four years) had issue as below—

1. JAMES GILBERT, born at the Manse of Lathones in 1833; was at Umballa, in India, at the time of the Mutiny. He married, but without issue, and died in London on the 22nd of September, 1886.

2. JANE FALCONER, born at the Manse of Lathones in 1835. At a pic-nic party on the Island of Kerrara, in Argyllshire, on the 30th of July, 1875, she slipped down a steep place, ruptured a blood vessel,

and died on the hillside.   A cross was erected to mark the spot where she expired.

3. REV. DAVID, who is now one of the best known and ablest of the ministers of Scotland, was born at the Manse of Lathones on the 9th of August, 1837, and taken to Oban when he was only seven months old.   At Oban he spent his boyhood, and received the rudiments of a liberal education, which was afterwards continued at the Universities of Glasgow and Edinburgh.   In 1859 he was lamed for life by a fall on Arthur Seat.   A serious illness followed, but he was able to resume his studies the following year.   While going through the Theological course of the United Presbyterian Hall in Edinburgh, he travelled abroad between the Sessions, and to those early travels he no doubt owes in some degree the sympathetic and enlightened knowledge of men and things which has formed so marked a feature both of his public life and of his writings.   He was ordained minister of the United Presbyterian Church at Gourock, in Renfrewshire, on the 9th of April, 1872.   He very soon came into prominence as a leading man in his own denomination, and in 1873 he commenced a movement which resulted in a reform of the United Presbyterian Theological Hall. In 1876 he commenced another movement for the Revision of the Confession of Faith, which led to the adoption of what is now known in Scotland as the Declaratory Act, first by his own denomination, afterwards by the Presbyterian Church of England, and more recently by the Free Church of Scotland. For going further still, and demanding a right to set

aside the dogma of eternal punishment, Mr Macrae
was expelled from the United Presbyterian Church,
at a special meeting of its Supreme Court in Edinburgh, in May, 1879. In the meantime he had been
called to Dundee as successor to the Rev. George
Gilfillan, who died in 1878, and, on being expelled
from his own denomination, the call was renewed,
Gilfillan's congregation declaring itself ready to leave
the denomination with him. The call was accepted,
and Mr Macrae commenced his ministry in Dundee
in October, 1879, when the Rev. Baldwin Brown,
Chairman of the Congregational Union of England
and Wales, travelled specially from London to
preach the induction sermon. In Dundee Mr
Macrae organised a large congregation of more
than thirteen hundred members, built the Gilfillan
Memorial Church, and laboured there for eighteen
years. From this ministry he retired in November,
1897, and is now living in Glasgow. When leaving
Dundee, he was presented with a remarkable testi-
monial by his congregation, and with a public address
from the citizens, which was presented to him in the
Town Hall by the Lord Provost. In 1880, and subsequently, he took a leading part in the movement
for the maintenance of Scotland's National Rights, including the petition addressed to the Queen in 1897,
and signed by over one hundred thousand Scottish
people of all ranks and classes, protesting against
"the violation of the Treaty of Union in the un-
warrantable substitution of the terms 'England' and
'English' for 'Britain' and 'British,' even in official
utterance and in treaties with foreign powers." Mr

Macrae is the author of numerous books and pamphlets, including *The Americans at Home*, originally published in two volumes by Edmonston & Douglas, Edinburgh, giving the results of his observations during a long tour in America, from Canada to the Gulf States, at the close of the war, and when the coloured people had newly emerged from slavery, —and recording also his interviews with Longfellow, Emerson, Lowell, Henry Ward Beecher, General Grant, Confederate General Lee, and other noted soldiers both of the North and South. This book, which was most favourably reviewed by the press, both at home and in America, has passed through several additions, and has been translated into French and Italian. Amongst his other works are *George Harrington; Dunvarlich; Diogenes among the D.D.'s*, a book of ecclesiastical burlesques, beginning with the " Trial of Norman Macleod for the murder of Moses Law;" *Quaint Sayings of Children; Voices of the Poets; Reminiscenes of George Gilfillan; Lectures on Robert Burns; New Parables;* &c. Mr Macrae married, on the 23rd of February, 1875, Williamina Burton Craig, without issue.

4. MARGARET FORBES, born in Oban in 1839, a lady of "rare gifts and far-reaching sympathies." She was intimately associated in after years with her brother, David, in his work, and died suddenly of heart disease at Maryland House, Glasgow, on the 20th of October, 1881.

CHAPTER XVIII.

The Macraes of Wilmington.—Connection with the Macraes of Kintail.—Ruari Donn.—His Descendants.—General William Macrae.

ABOUT the year 1770, a certain Roderick Macrae emigrated from Kintail to America, and landed at Wilmington, in North Carolina. He was only one of many who left Kintail for America at that time, but he was a man of importance among them, and his descendants have since occupied a prominent and honourable place in the affairs of his adopted country. What his exact connection with the main stock of the Clan may have been is not fully known,[1] but he was closely related to the Rev. Donald Macrae,[2] the last Episcopalian Minister of Kintail. He may have been a son of Alexander, eldest son of the Rev. Donald, or he may have been a son of Hugh,[3] youngest brother of the Rev. Donald. At all events, Hugh is said to have had a son, Roderick, who went to America about 1770 or 1774, and he is the only Roderick Macrae of whom there appears to be any

[1] An American account of the Macraes of Wilmington says that they are descended from a certain Rev. Alexander Macrae of Kintail, who had two sons killed at Culloden. This, of course, is incorrect, and is clearly a mistake for the Rev. Donald Macrae who had two sons killed at Sheriffmuir.

[2] Page 76.   [3] Page 132.

record as having gone from Kintail to America about that time. The Roderick who landed at Wilmington, and of whom below, is said to have been accompanied by a brother and two sisters, viz.:—

PHILIP (or Finlay), who is said to have served as a Lieutenant in the Army of Prince Charles in 1745, and who cherished such a hatred of the English, in consequence of the atrocities of the Duke of Cumberland, that he would never speak the English language, but spoke only Gaelic as long as he lived.

MARY, who married a Macrae (?) with issue, and settled in Moore County.

CATHERINE, who married Donald Macrae, who settled with his family in Georgia, where their descendants still live.

RODERICK, called Ruari Donn (Brown Roderick), landed at Wilmington, about 1770, as mentioned above. Thence he proceeded to Chatham County, and lived for a time at Pocket Creek. Soon afterwards he moved to Crane's Creek, in the same County, and eventually settled at Little Rockfish, a few miles south of Fayetteville, in Cumberland County, North Carolina. Roderick married, first, Catherine Burke, apparently a widow, and by her had issue—

1. COLIN, of whom below.

2. JOHN, settled at or near Augusta, in Georgia. He married, and left issue.

Roderick married, secondly, Christina Murchison, with issue.

3. JOHN, who was for a number of years teller of

the Commercial Bank of Wilmington, and died unmarried in 1863.

COLIN, son of Roderick, was a farmer at Little
Rockfish, where all his family were born. He was a
man of sound sense and good education, was for
many years a prominent Magistrate of his County,
and "was esteemed by all who knew him as an independent, upright, and honest man." He married
Christian, daughter of Duncan Black, and sister of
John Black, some time Sheriff of Cumberland County,
by whom he had issue as below. He died at a very
advanced age on the 8th of July, 1865—

1. ALEXANDER, of whom below.

2. ARCHIBALD, born on the 17th of January,
1798.

3. ISABELLA, born on the 9th of January, 1800.

4. DONALD, born on the 19th of January, 1802.

5. ANNE, born on the 26th of January, 1804.

6. JOHN, born on the 26th of July, 1806, died
in 1883.

7. CATHERINE, born on the 6th of July, 1808.

8. RODERICK, born on the 11th of October, 1810,
died in 1882.

ALEXANDER, son of Colin, was born at Little
Rockfish, North Carolina, on the 26th of March,
1796. When he was about eighteen years of age he
moved to Wilmington, where he engaged in various
pursuits. He was for many years president of the
Wilmington and Weldon Railroad Company, and
being a man of great energy and much public spirit
was connected with most of the affairs of Wilmington
during his long, useful, and honourable life. He

volunteered as a private in the war of 1812-14, was soon made Sergeant, and was about to be promoted to a lieutenancy when the war ended. When the War of Secession broke out in 1861, although he was then sixty-five years of age, he was called upon because of his popularity and influence to raise a company to aid in the defence of Wilmington. So ready was the response to his appeal for recruits that instead of a company he raised a whole battalion, which became known as " Macrae's Battalion of Heavy Artillery," and which served under him with much distinction throughout the war. He died at Wilmington on the 27th of April, 1868.

Alexander married first, on the 30th of April, 1818, Amelia Ann, daughter of John Martin. She died on the 24th of August, 1831, leaving issue—

1. John Colin, born at Wilmington, on the 10th of March, 1819, was a Colonel in the Confederate Army, and died unmarried on the 9th of February, 1878.

2. Archibald, born at Smithville, on the 21st of September, 1820, was a Lieutenant in the United States Navy, and died on the 17th of November, 1855.

3. Alexander, born at Wilmington, on the 1st of March, 1823, and died on the 18th of December, 1881. He married Elizabeth Chambers, with issue—

   a. Caroline Amelia.

   b. Elizabeth, married J. Fairfax Payne, with issue.

4. Donald, born at Wilmington on the 14th of October, 1825, and died on the 15th of September, 1892. He married, first, Mary Savage, with issue—

a. Mary Savage, born on the 11th of December, 1851, and died on the 10th of May, 1896.

He married, secondly, Julia Norton, with issue—

b. Norton, died in childhood.

c. Agnes, born on the 20th of November, 1859, married Walter Linton Parsley, with issue—

*c*1. Julia, born on the 2nd of March, 1882.

*c*2. Anna, born on the 14th of January, 1886.

*c*3. Mary, born on the 25th of March, 1890, died in infancy.

*c*4. Walter Linton, born on the 12th of January, 1892, died on the 8th of December, 1897.

*c*5. Donald Macrae, born on the 5th of October, 1895.

d. Donald, born on the 3rd of May, 1861, now living at Wilmington, and by whom most of this information about the Macraes of Wilmington was communicated to the author in 1898.

e. Julia, born on the 15th of December, 1862, died in infancy.

f. Hugh, born on the 30th of March, 1865, now living in Wilmington. He married Rena Nelson, with issue—

*f*1. Dorothy, born on the 26th of December, 1891.

*f*2. Nelson, born on the 5th of June, 1893.

*f*3. Agnes, born on the 7th of October, 1897.

5. HENRY, born at Wilmington on the 8th of May, 1829. He was a Major in the Confederate Army, and died on the 22nd of April, 1863. He was married and left issue—Alice ; Mary.

Alexander married, secondly, on the 15th of March, 1832, Anna Jane, daughter of John Martin

(his first wife's father) and his wife, Zilpah Mac-
Clammy, and by her, who died on the 17th of
October, 1842, aged thirty-five years, had issue—

6. ROBERT BURNS, born at Wilmington on the
15th of December, 1832.   He was a Major in the
Confederate Army, and died on the 28th of December, 1864.   He was married, but left no issue.

7. WILLIAM, born at Wilmington on the 9th of
September, 1834.   He was a Brigadier-General in the
Confederate Army, and one of its most distinguished
soldiers.   At an early age he displayed great apti-
tude for mathematics and mechanics, and, having
received an excellent education, he took up the
profession of Civil Engineer.   In this capacity he
was employed for some time in surveying lines for
projected railways in North and South Carolina, and
also in Florida.   On the outbreak of the war between
North and South, in 1861, he volunteered as a private, but was soon elected Captain of a company of
the Fifteenth North Carolina Regiment, which was
placed at first in General Cobb's Brigade, and transferred the following year to General Cook's Brigade.
Macrae was promoted Lieutenant-Colonel in 1862,
Colonel in 1863, and Brigadier-General in August,
1864.   His brigade consisted of five North Carolina
regiments, and had already become famous in the
war.   Macrae never left it from the day he took over
the command of it until the fighting ceased, with the
surrender of General Lee, at Appomattox on the 9th
of April, 1865.   Under his command it attained the
very highest degree of discipline and efficiency, and
so unbounded was the confidence of the men in their

leader, that they considered no foe too numerous to
be attacked, nor any position too strong to be
assailed, if the order came from General William
Macrae. He fought in almost all the great battles
of the war, and was repeatedly complimented by
General Lee in general orders for personal valour
and able handling of his troops. At the battle of
Malvern Hill, he led into action a regiment three
hundred strong, and came out with only thirty-five.
At the battle of Fredericksburg, he was posted on a
hill under terrific fire, but held the ground though
he lost nearly half his men. He was in the great
battles of the Wilderness in May, 1863. At the battle
of Ream's Station, on the 25th of August, 1864, he
captured nine pieces of artillery and more men than
he had in his own command. In April, 1865, when
General Lee, with the remnants of his brave army, was
attempting to make his way from Petersburg to the
mountains, Macrae's Brigade covered the retreat
near Farmville, and, while advancing towards Appomattox, where preparations for surrender were
already being made, he attacked and drove off a
Northern force which had fallen on the waggon
trains. This is said to have been the last fight in
Virginia, and his brigade was the last of the Confederate troops to stack arms and surrender. General
Macrae was undoubtedly a soldier of the highest
order, and a born leader of men, possessing in an
eminent degree the power of imparting his own
courage and enthusiasm to others. Though indifferent to danger himself, he was most careful of the
lives of the soldiers who fought under him and were

always ready to follow him with implicit trust.   He was a stern disciplinarian, yet not one murmur was ever heard in his brigade against the most stringent orders issued by him.   " It was said of his company, when he was Captain, that it was the best company in the regiment.   It was said of his brigade, when he was Brigadier-General, that it was the best brigade in the division.   It was truthfully said of Macrae that the higher he rose the more magnificent his character appeared." [1]

After the close of the war General Macrae filled some important appointments as superintendent of railways.   In these positions he displayed the highest order of ability, both as an engineer and as an organiser of men, and was widely known and universally respected as a man of humane and generous disposition, and wide and enlightened sympathies.   He died unmarried at Augusta, Georgia, on the 11th of February, 1882, and was buried at Wilmington.[2]

8.   MARION, born on the 30th of November, 1835, died in childhood.

9.   RODERICK, born on the 13th of September, 1838.

10.   WALTER GWYN, born on the 27th of January, 1841, Captain in the Confederate Army.

Alexander married, as his third wife, Mary Herring, without issue, and as his fourth wife, Caroline A. Price, also without issue.

1 Memorial Address on General William Macrae, delivered at Raleigh, North Carolina, by the Honourable B. H. Bunn.

2 The above sketch of the career of General William Macrae is compiled mainly from a " Memorial Address " delivered at Wilmington, North Carolina, on the 10th of May, 1890, by the Honourable Charles M. Stedman, and from the Rev. David Macrae's book on " The Americans at Home."

CHAPTER XIX.

Ian Mac Fhionnla Mhic Ian Bhuidhe.—A Sheriffmuir Warrior.—
His Descendants.

AMONG the Kintail warriors who fought at Sheriffmuir, and around whose names have gathered traditions of that fatal day, was a certain John Macrae,
known as Ian Mac Fhionnla Mhic Ian Bhuidhe
(John, son of Finlay, son of Yellow John). In the
course of the fight, he received no fewer than seven
sword cuts on his head, and was left for dead on
the field. But during the night he revived, and
resolved to make an effort, under cover of the darkness, to commence the homeward journey. Having
had the misfortune to lose his shoes in the battle, he
began to search for another pair with which to equip
himself for the journey, and while thus engaged, came
across Duncan Mor Mac Alister,[1] who was lying near
him mortally wounded, and suffering from intense
thirst. John recognised him by his voice, and having
no other means of fetching water, he took one of
Duncan's shoes and brought him a drink in it.
Before Duncan expired he gave John an account of
how he received his wounds, and this account is

1 Page 198.

still preserved in the traditions of the Clan.[1] John recovered from his own wounds, and made his way back to Kintail, where he lived to a very advanced age. He was a great hunter, and possessed a famous gun called An Nighean Alainn (the beautiful daughter), which he always carried with him, even in his old age, wherever he went. On one occasion, as he was passing down the hills, probably about Scatwell, on his way to Brahan Castle, he observed a magnificent stag, which he shot and carried on his shoulders all the way to Brahan as a present to Seaforth. John was married, and had issue at least one son,

DONALD, who was a soldier, and was killed in battle in the Netherlands, probably at Fontenoy, in 1745. He was married, and left one son,

DUNCAN, who married, and left also an only son,

JOHN, who was twice married. By his first wife he had a large family, all of whom went to Canada and settled in the district of London. By his second marriage also he had a family, the eldest of whom was

ALEXANDER, who lived at Dornie, and went to Australia in 1852. He married in 1842 Christina, daughter of Donald Macmillan (a connection of the Torlysich family), and his wife, Helen, daughter of Alexander, son of Farquhar Macrae, a younger son of the Inverinate family,[2] and by her had issue—

1 See chapter on legends and traditions of the clan.

2 A comparison of dates leads to the conclusion that Alexander, the grand-father of the above-mentioned Christina, who married in 1842, could hardly have been Alexander, son of Farquhar of Morvich, mentioned on page 84 as having been present at the affair of Ath nan Muilcach in 1721. He might possibly have been a grandson of Farquhar of Morvich, that is to say, a son of Farquhar Og (page 83), son of Farquhar of Morvich, younger son of Alexander of Inverinate.

R

1. JOHN, living in Victoria, Australia, married, with issue, four sons and one daughter.

2. DONALD, living at Gelantipy, near Melbourne, and by whom the information contained in this chapter was communicated to the author in 1898. He is married to Agnes, daughter of Hector Armour of Stewarton, Ayrshire, without issue.

3. JOHN (the younger), living in Victoria.

4. DUNCAN, living in Victoria.

5. ALEXANDER, living in Victoria.

6. HELEN, married Angus Gillies, in Victoria, with issue.

Mc Crea.

CHAPTER XX.

The McCreas of Guernsey.—Descended from the Macraes of Kin-
    tail.—Connection with Ulster.—Emigrated to America.—Jane
    McCrea, "The Bride of Fort Edward."—Major Robert McCrea
    in the American War of Independence.—Governor of Chester
    Castle. — Connection with Guernsey. — His Marriages and
    Descendants.

THE McCreas of Guernsey are descended from the
Macraes of Kintail, and their connection with the
main branch of that Clan, though now lost, was
known so recently as sixty or seventy years ago.[1]
This connection is borne out, not only by the traditions of the family, but also by their personal
appearance and features, which, in many instances,
are strikingly typical of the Macraes of Kintail.
The family tradition is that in the time of the
Covenanters a certain Macrae of Kintail, who had
adopted Puritanic principles, left his own country,
where those principles were held in great disfavour,
and eventually made his way to Ireland and settled
among the Puritans of Ulster.   It may be pointed out

---

[1] Mrs Carey, who was born in 1819, and of whom mention is made hereafter, a daughter of Major Robert McCrea of Guernsey, was shown her own
name on a family tree while on a visit as a young girl to the country house of a
gentleman of the name Macrae in Scotland.   Mrs Carey died in 1878, and
there does not appear at present to be any possibility of ascertaining who that
gentleman was.

that this tradition is not at all without an appearance of probability, for, although no trace of Puritanism appears in Kintail until well into the eighteenth century, yet the Macraes of Kintail were closely associated with Dingwall during the whole of the Covenanter period, and as they were deeply interested in the political and religious movements of the time, it is not at all unlikely that some of them might come under the religious influence of the neighbouring family of Munro of Fowlis, who were among the most active supporters of the Covenanter movement in the Highlands, and to whom the chief Macrae families of the time were closely related.[1] The adoption of Puritanic principles would, of course, be extremely distasteful not only to the Macrae vicars of Dingwall, but also to the leading Macrae families of Kintail, who were such ardent Episcopalians. A Macrae holding such principles could hardly feel comfortable among his own people, and would not unnaturally seek a new home among people to whom his views would be more acceptable than they were to his own countrymen. Whether it was the man, who left the Highlands, himself, or one of his descendants that afterwards went to America, is uncertain, but it was probably one of his descendants. At all events, some members of the family remained behind in Ulster, where their descendants are still living. There is a tradition among the McCreas of Guernsey that one of their ancestors took part in the defence of Londonderry during the famous siege

---

[1] Appendix F.—Alexander Macrae of Inverinate married as his second wife a granddaughter of Hector Munro of Fowlis, who died in 1603.

of 1689, but this ancestor may have been on the female side, as there is a further tradition of some family connection with the Rev. George Walker,[1] who organised the defence of Londonderry on that occasion, and was afterwards killed at the Battle of the Boyne, in 1690, shortly after being nominated to the Bishopric of Derry by King William III. From Ulster a certain William McCrea[2] emigrated to America, and from him the Guernsey family trace their descent as below. The McCreas of Guernsey are a family of soldiers, and have served with much distinction in every war we have been engaged in during the present century. There is perhaps no other family in the United Kingdom that has held a greater number of commissions in the Army and Navy during the reign of Queen Victoria than the descendants of Major Robert McCrea of Guernsey.

WILLIAM McCREA went to America about 1710 or 1715, and was an elder in White Clay Creek Church, near Newark, Delaware. His watch and seal were in the possession of his descendants in America in 1831. He married a Miss Creighton, and had a son,

THE REV. JAMES McCREA, who was born at Lifford, in the county of Londonderry, in Ireland,

---

1 One version of this tradition is, that the Rev. George Walker himself was a McCrea by birth, and that the surname Walker was only an adopted one.

2 There is a tradition in the family that the ancestor who fled from Ross-shire changed his name from Macra or Macrae to McCrea, as a mark of his complete religious severance from his family, but the spelling of the name is a matter of no genealogical consequence whatever. At that time there was frequently no fixed spelling of names, and this name appears in various forms, M'Crea included, in Ross-shire documents of the period.

before his father left that country.   He is mentioned
as a Presbyterian Clergyman of Scotch descent and
devoted to literary pursuits.   He married, first, a
Miss Graham, who was dead before 1754, and,
secondly, Catherine Rosebrooke, who, after his death,
married Richard Macdonald.   She died in July, 1813,
and was buried next her son Philip at Sanaton.   By
his first marriage the Rev. James had issue—

1. JOHN, who was educated for the law, and
settled in the city of Albany.   "A man highly
respected in his day."   He was a Colonel in the
American Army during the War of Independence,
and was the Colonel John McCrea mentioned in
connection with the murder of his sister Jane,
of whom below.   He died in May, 1811.   He married Eva Bateman, by whom he had issue—

a. Sally, who was dead in 1831.

b. James, a Councillor at Law.   He settled on a
large estate at Balston, Central Saratoga, in the
Province of New York, about 1816, and was alive in
1842, but appears to have left Balston for Ohio.
He married and had issue—

*b*1. John Beckman (or Bateman), who was a
lawyer at Balston in 1831.

*b*2. James, who was living at Balston in 1831,
and was then twenty-four years of age.

*b*3. Catherine Mary, who was living at Balston
in 1831, and was then eighteen years of age.

*b*4. Stephen, who was also living at Balston in
1831.   He was then fourteen years of age, and
was the possessor of a watch and seal which had
belonged to his great-great-grandfather, William
McCrea.

2. MARY, who married the Rev. Mr Hanna, an American, and had with other issue—

a. James, who was "settled in Pensylvania" in 1816, an Attorney-General.

b. John, who was a "Member of Congress." He had a house and land "three miles south of Balston Spayor Springs," and was dead in 1816.

3. WILLIAM, who also had a house and land three miles from Balston Spayor Springs, and was dead in 1816. He married "General Gordon's sister." She was alive in 1816, and had two children, one of whom was called

a. Maria. She married a Mr Macdonald, who was dead in 1833, and by whom she had two children, who appear to have both died young. She married, secondly, a Mr Staat, apparently without issue. She was living in 1842.

4. JANE, died young.

5. JAMES, who was born in 1745. He lived at Balston, and died on the 7th May, 1826. He married, and his wife was dead in 1816. He had issue, at least, one son,

a. John, who was a Clergyman in Ohio in 1831, and was married and had daughters.

6. SAMUEL, married a Miss Sloane, of New Jersey, who was dead in 1816. He settled at Balston, and had issue—

a. Samuel, who with his wife and four daughters were living at Balston in 1842. He is mentioned in that year as the only member of the McCrea family then living at Balston. According to another account, there were descendants of the McCrea

family still living at Balston and in other parts of
the State of New York in 1888.[1]   In 1842 he had
issue—Mary Ann, Caroline, Elizabeth, Jane.

  b. William, dead in 1830.

  c. John, living in Virginia in 1831.

  d. Mary, married Judge Betts.

  e. Another daughter, unmarried in 1831.

  7. GILBERT, married a Miss Meshet, and had
several children.   He settled in Kentucky, and was
dead in 1816.   His widow was alive in 1842.

  8. JANE, who is said to have been born at Bed-
minster (now Leamington), New Jersey, in 1753,
though there is some reason to believe that she was
born before that date.   She is known as " The bride
of Fort Edward," and was killed on the 27th of July,
1777, at Fort Edward, near Albany, on the Hudson
River, by an Indian, under circumstances which have
given her name a very prominent place in Anglo-
American history.   She is described, on the authority
of persons who knew her, as " a young woman of
great accomplishments, great personal attractions,
and remarkable sweetness of disposition.   She was
of medium stature, finely formed, and of a delicate
blonde complexion.   Her hair was of a golden brown
and silken lustre, and, when unbound, trailed on the
ground."   It would be quite impossible in the limited
compass of the present notice to give even a summary
of all that has been written about the death of this
young woman, or of the various versions which exist
of that tragic occurrence.   The outstanding facts

---

[1] Appleton's Cyclopædia of American Biography, published at New York
in 1888.

are as follows :—After the death of her father, Miss
McCrea, who was engaged to a young man named
David James, an officer in the British Army, appears
to have lived with her eldest brother, John, who, as
already mentioned, was a Colonel in the American
Army.   As a natural result of opposite sympathies
with regard to the war, there arose an estrangement
between Colonel McCrea and David James.[1]   Miss
McCrea resolved, however, to remain faithful to her
lover, and when the time appointed for their marriage
arrived, he sent a body of loyal Indians to escort her
safely from her home to the British Camp, where the
marriage was to take place.   But on the way two of
the Indians appear to have quarrelled as to who
should have the honour of presenting her to the
bridegroom and receiving the promised reward.   In
the course of the quarrel one of the Indians became
furious, and resolving that if he himself could not
receive the reward neither should his opponent,
struck Miss McCrea on the head with his tomahawk,
and killed her on the spot.   He then carried the
scalp of his victim into the British Camp, where it
was soon recognised by the length and the beauty of
the hair.   On the following day her body was recovered, and buried by her brother, Colonel John
McCrea.   David James never recovered from the
shock caused by the tragic death of his bride.
Shortly afterwards he resigned his Commission in
the Army, and though he lived for many years he

[1] In "The Tartans and the Clans of Scotland," with historical notes by
James Grant, he is named "Jones."   See also "Pictorial Field Book of the
American Revolution," by B. J. Lossing.

never married. Miss McCrea's remains were removed
in 1852 to the Union Cemetery, between Fort
Edward and Sandy Hill, where their resting-place
is marked by a marble tombstone erected by her
niece, Sarah Hanna Payne, and bearing a suitable
inscription.

9. STEPHEN, a Surgeon-General in the American
Army.   He married a Miss Rudyers, and was dead
in 1816.   He had two children, one of whom died
young ; the other, a daughter, married and appears
to have had issue.

By his second marriage, also, the Rev. James
McCrea had issue—

10. ROBERT, of whom below.

11. PHILIP, "killed in the war."   He married
and had a son Philip, who was living in Ohio in
1831, and had a daughter.

12. CREIGHTON, formerly of New Jersey.   He
was a Captain in the 75th Highlanders, and was at
the capture of Seringapatam.   The family possesses
a jewelled watch said to have been given to Captain
Creighton by Tippoo Sahib.   He also served on the
Loyalist side in the American War of Independence,
and was an Ensign in the 1st American Regiment
(or Queen's Rangers) in 1782.   At one time he
resided at Guernsey, where he made a will, but he
died in America on the 10th December, 1818.

13. CATHERINE, who married a Mr Macdonald,
son of a Colonel Macdonald, of the British Army,
and was alive in Ohio in 1842.   She had a large
family, and her husband was "just dead" in July,
1813.

ROBERT, son of the Rev. James McCrea by his second wife, Catherine Rosebrooke, was born on the 2nd November, 1754. He fought on the Loyalist side in the American War of Independence, and was Major in the 1st American Regiment (or Queen's Rangers) in 1782. He was severely wounded at the battle of Brandywine in 1777, and received a " pension for wounds." He was for some time Governor of Chester Castle, and in 1788 was Captain of one of six Companies of Invalides stationed in Guernsey. He afterwards became Major Commanding the 5th Royal Veterans. He is mentioned as a man of fine presence, and at the age of seventy-five years is said to have looked like a man of fifty.[1] He died at Paris on the 2nd July, 1835, and was buried at Père la Chaise, Paris. He married, first, Jane Coutart, a Guernsey lady of Huguenot descent, who was born on the 20th December, 1767, and died on the 8th April, 1796. He married secondly, on the 12th June, 1804, Sophia Le Mesurier, who was born on the 23rd January, 1780, and died on the 8th March, 1860. She was a sister of General William Le Mesurier,[2] of Old Court, Guernsey, who served in the Peninsular War. Major McCrea had issue by both marriages as below. By the first wife he had—

1. CATHERINE MARIA, born on the 28th December, 1786, married Colonel Frederick Barlow, of the Sixty-First (Gloucestershire) Regiment, at the head

---

[1] Letter dated 1831.

[2] A branch of these Le Mesuriers were formerly Hereditary Governors of the Island of Alderney.

of which he was killed at the Battle of Salamanca, on the 22nd of July, 1812, and by him had issue one daughter,

a. Jane, who married Philip de Sausmarez, Captain R.N., a younger brother of the Seigneur de Sausmarez, a fief for centuries in the possession of the family.[1] Captain Philip de Sausmarez entered the Royal Navy on the 18th of June, 1823, saw much service, including the China War, and retired on the 31st of March, 1866. By him Jane Barlow had issue—

*a*1. Philip Algernon, born 1841, Captain West African Mail Service, and afterwards Consul at Rouen. He is married, and has issue—

*a*2. William Howley, born 1845, died young.

*a*3. Lionel Andros, born 1847, entered the Royal Navy 1860, Sub-Lieutenant 1866, and was for some time engaged in the suppression of the slave trade in South East Africa. He was present at the Bombardment of Alexandria in 1882, was mentioned in despatches, and received the Egyptian medal with the clasp for Alexandria, the Khedive's bronze star, and the Order of Osmanjeh (fourth class). He received special promotion, and the Albert and Royal Humane Society's medals for having, while acting as officer of the watch on the 1st of June, 1868, on H.M.S. Myrmidon, lying in Banana Creek, River Congo, jumped overboard into the shark-infested river and rescued a seaman who could not swim. He retired

---

[1] The founder of the De Sausmarez family received from Henry II. the fief of Jerbourg, in the Island of Guernsey, and was appointed hereditary Captain of Jerbourg Castle, which was situated within the limits of the fief.

with the rank of Commander in 1883. He married his cousin, Mary, daughter of Frances Charlotte McCrea and George Bell, and has issue—

Lionel Wilfred, Lieutenant in the King's Royal Rifles, and daughters.

*a*4. Frederick Barlow, born in 1849, M.A., Pembroke College, Oxford, appointed one of Her Majesty's Inspectors of Schools in 1878.

2. MARY AUGUSTA, born on the 9th of February, 1788, married at Kinsale on the 27th of December, 1814, Lieutenant-Colonel Chilton Lambton Carter,[1] of the Forty-Fourth Regiment, by whom she had issue—

a. John Chilton Lambton, Captain in the Fifty-Third Regiment, sold out in 1852, and went to New Zealand. He married and left issue.

b. William Frederic, Lieutenant-Colonel of the Sixty-Third Regiment, Knight of the Legion of Honour and of the Order of Medjidie, served in the Crimea in 1854-5, including the Battles of the Alma, Balaclava, and Inkerman, the Expedition to Kerch, the Fall of Sebastopol, succeeding to the command of his Regiment at the last attack and the capture of Kimburn. He married, with issue, and died in 1867.

3. RAWDON (so named after his godfather, Francis Rawdon, Marquis of Hastings[2]), born on the 5th of

1 Colonel Carter was descended from Robert Chilton of Houghton-le-Spring, who married Anne Lambton.—See Burke's Peerage, Earl of Durham.

2 Francis Rawdon, Marquis of Hastings, known successively through his career as Lord Moira and Earl of London, was descended from Sir Arthur Rawdon, Bart. of Moira, in County Down, a man who distinguished himself in the defence of Londonderry and Enniskillen in the reign of William III. The Marquis of Hastings was not only a distinguished soldier, but also one of the most eminent of our Indian statesmen. Born 1754, died 1825. For his connection with the Macraes of Kintail, see page 137.

April, 1789, Captain in the Eighty-Seventh Regiment, served in the Peninsular War. He was one of the storming party at the taking of Monte Video in 1807, where he received five wounds. He was killed at the battle of Talavera on the 28th of July, 1809.

4. ROBERT COUTART,[1] born on the 13th January, 1793. He was an Admiral in the Royal Navy. He was at the battle of Trafalgar, 21st October, 1805, on H.M.S. Swiftshire, and saw much other service. He married, on the 10th of April, 1822, Charlotte, daughter of the Rev. Nicholas Dobrée, Rector of Ste. Marie-de-Castro, Guernsey (by his wife, who was a sister of the first Lord de Saumarez), and by her, who died on the 8th December, 1897, in her 103rd year, had issue—

a. Robert Barlow, born on 9th of January, 1823, Major-General Royal Artillery. He was present in the Revolution in Hayti, in 1859, when he landed in command of three batteries of the Royal Artillery and a detachment of the Forty-First Regiment, for the protection of Europeans. For his conduct on that occasion he received the brevet rank of Major, and the thanks of both the English and French Governments. He married, on the 9th August, 1850, Harriet, daughter of John Maingay of Grange Villa, Guernsey, and died at Ewell, Surrey, on the 11th February, 1897. He was buried at Candie Cemetery, Guernsey.

b. Frances Charlotte, married on the 3rd Febru-

---

[1] Admiral McCrea acquired land in Australia known as McCrea Creek, Victoria, and still held by the family.

ary, 1848, George Bell, of The Merrienne, Guernsey, eldest son of Thomas Bell, mentioned below, and died on the 11th July, 1854, leaving issue—one daughter, Mary, who married her cousin, Commander L. A. de Sausmarez, as already stated.

c. James, born on the 19th of February, 1825, a Captain in the Forty-Fifth Regiment, served in the Kaffir Wars of 1846-7 and 1852-3. He was Colonel Assistant-Adjutant-General of the Royal Guernsey Militia, and died at Grange Villa, Guernsey, on the 2nd September, 1885, in his 65th year. He married Mary Brock Potenger, and by her, who died at Guildford on the 27th January, 1886, had issue—

*c*1. Victor Coryton Dobrée, died in infancy.

*c*2. De la Combe, born 15th March, 1857, died unmarried in Ceylon in 1878.

*c*3. Flora, married Henry Roome, with issue.

*c*4. Constance, died unmarried.

d. Richard Charles, born on the 18th of April, 1826, Captain in the Sixty-Fourth Regiment. He was killed in action near Cawnpore on the 28th November, 1857. He is mentioned in Major-General Windham's despatch on that occasion as " that fine gallant young man," and was promised the Victoria Cross, had he lived to receive it. He married, on the 5th June, 1850, Anne De la Combe, daughter of Thomas Bell, of The Merrienne, Guernsey, and by her had issue—

*d*1. Rawdon, born 28th February, 1851, late Captain 28th Regiment, now living in Guernsey.

*d*2. Julia, married Colonel Anthony Durand,

Bombay Staff Corps, who served in the Indian Mutiny, 1857-8; Abyssinian Expedition, 1867-8; and the Afghan War, 1880. She died in India.

*d*3. Charles Brooke Potenger, born in 1855.

e. John Dobrée, an Admiral in the Royal Navy, saw much war service, including the Baltic, 1855 (medal). He married, on the 9th May, 1857, Marion, daughter of J. Anderson, of Cox Lodge Hall, Northumberland, and died on the 18th March, 1883, leaving issue—

*e*1. Richard Francis, a Major in the Royal Artillery, married Mabel Romney.

*e*2. Charles Dalston, died young.

*e*3. Charles, a Lieutenant in the Royal Navy, died at Gibraltar in 1896.

*e*4. John Henry, married Olive Macdonald, with issue—John Dobrée, died young; Lena Marion, born 1893; Francis Dobrée, born 1894.

*e*5. Frederic, died young.

*e*6. Alfred Coryton, Lieutenant Indian Staff Corps, served in the Hazara Expedition in 1891, medal with clasp; and in Chitral in 1895, was with the Relief Force at the storming of the Malakand Pass, and in the action at Khar—medal with clasp. He married Emma Priestley.

*e*7. Florence Marian.

*e*8. Mary Evelyn, married Frederick W. D. Fisher, of the India Forest Service.

*e*9. Frances Edith, died in 1890.

f. Katharine Carterette, married on the 17th April, 1854, Major-General John Cromie Blackwood de Butts, R.E., son of the late General Sir A. de Butts, R.E., K.C.H., with issue.

*f*1. Arthur John, born 1855, M.D., formerly Captain Third Royal Guernsey Light Infantry Militia, married Alice, daughter of Colonel Martindale, R.E., C.B., with issue. He died at Folkestone in February, 1898, and was buried at Ewell, Surrey.

*f*2. Katharine Mary McCrea, born in 1855, married, in 1880, Edward Kenyon,[1] Major Royal Engineers, with issue—Herbert Edward ; Roger de Butts, died in childhood ; Kenneth, died in childhood ; Catherine Mary Rose ; Ellen Blackwood ; Winifred Lillian ; Frances Margaret.

*f*3. Harriet Olivia, born in 1856, married E. Fairfax Taylor, Principal Clerk and Taxing Officer, House of Lords, with issue.

*f*4. Annie Georgina Louisa, born in 1858, married Major Norton Grant, R.E., with issue.

*f*5. Alice Maud Martindale, born in 1860, married Major James Henry Cowan, R.E., with issue.

*f*6. Frederick Robert McCrea, born in 1863, Captain Royal Artillery, served in the Burmese War in 1886-7, was with the Indian Contingent at Suakim in 1896, and was killed in action at the Sampagha Pass, on the North-West Frontier of India, on the 29th of October, 1897. He married Katharine, daughter of Captain Travers of the Seventeenth Regiment, with issue.

*f*7. Brownlow Stanley Cromie, born in 1865, M.D., M.R.C.S.

*f*8. Isobel Rhœta, born 1867.

*f*9. Ellen Dobrée, born 1872.

g. Rawdon, died young.

---

[1] See Burke's Peerage, Kenyon.

h. Mary Coutart, married on the 10th September, 1856, the Rev. Haydon Aldersey Taylor, M.A., St John's College, Oxford, Army Chaplain, who served in the Crimea. She died on the 13th of September, 1890, leaving issue—

*h*1. Lilian Aldersey, died on the 4th of June, 1873.

*h*2. Charlotte McCrea, married Commander Edward Lloyd, R.N.

*h*3. Anna Katharine De Sausmarez.

*h*4. Haydon D'Aubrey Potenger, Major in the Gloucestershire Regiment, married.

*h*5. Oswald Albon Aldersey, Captain in the Duke of Wellington's Regiment, married.

*h*6. Marion Louise, married Lieutenant-Colonel Davidson, of the Black Watch.

*h*7. Harriette Mary, married the Rev. William Philip Hurrell, M.A., Oriel College, Oxford, St James' Vicarage, Northampton.

*h*8. Frances Arabella Joyce, married George Adams Connor of Craigielaw, Long Niddry, N.B.

*h*9. Coutart De Butts.

*h*10. Leonora Eliot.

i. Harriet Amelia, married, on the 4th of September, 1861, Brownlow Poulter, M.A., Barrister-at-Law of Lincoln's Inn, a Justice of the Peace, and formerly Fellow of New College, Oxford, and has issue—

*i*1. Rev. Donald Francis Ogilvy, M.A., of Lincoln College, Oxford.

*i*2. Mabel Catherine, M.B., Ch.B.

*i*3. Creighton McCrea, Captain Indian Staff Corps, died March, 1896.

*i*4. Aline Marian.

*i*5. Arthur Brownlow, Cape Mounted Rifles.

*i*6. Muriel Alice.

*i*7. Douglas Ryley, Lieutenant in the Royal Artillery.

*i*8. Julia Harriette.

*i*9. Richard Charles McCrea, solicitor.

5. JANE, born 9th March, 1794, married on the 5th October, 1815, Colonel George Augustus Eliot, who held a command in the British service in the American War of 1812, believed to have been then attached to the Royal Engineers.   He left one son, who died young.

6. JAMES CREIGHTON, died in infancy in 1796.

By his second wife, Sophia Le Mesurier, Major Robert McCrea had issue—

7. SOPHIA MARIA CREIGHTON, born on the 19th June, 1805, married Sir Charles Payne, Bart., Captain 25th Regiment of Light Dragoons, with issue one son, died young.

8. ROBERT BRADFORD, born on the 18th of June, 1807.   He was Captain in the Forty-Fourth Regiment, and was killed at Cabul on the 17th of November, 1841.   He married, on the 7th of August, 1832, Margaret Bushnan, and had issue—

a. Frederick Bradford, born on the 4th of December, 1833, a Major in the Eighth (The King's) Regiment, who served at the taking of Delhi in 1857, and was afterwards present in the following actions, viz., Bohundshur, Ackabad, Mynpoorie, Battle of Agra, actions of Karonge and Alumbagh, relief of the garrison of Lucknow, battles of the 2nd and 6th December at Cawnpore, action of Fattehghur, and the Oude campaign of 1858. Also, was in command of details of a force of about two thousand strong at Meerun-ka-Serai for about four months, and prevented the Nana Sahib and Feroh-Shah, the son of the King of Delhi, each, on two occasions, from crossing the Ganges, and so getting into Central India. For the services rendered on those two occasions, he was thanked by the General Officers of three Divisions. He has the Indian Mutiny medal with clasps for Delhi and the Relief of Lucknow, and is a F.R.G.S., F.R.H.S., and F.I.I. In 1871 Major McCrea founded "The Army and Navy Co-operative Society," of which he has been a Managing Director ever since, and with a capital of £60,000 the Society has up to the 31st of January, 1898, paid in bonuses and interest, £1,297,508, and accumulated reserve funds amounting to £270,449. Major McCrea married, on the 24th of January, 1864, Frederica Charlotte (who died on the 10th of June, 1894), only daughter of Captain John Francis Wetherall, 41st Regiment, and has issue—

*a*1. Frederick Augustus Bradford, born on the 8th of October, 1865, late Captain in the Hampshire Militia.

*a*2. Robert George, born on the 24th of February, 1867.

*a*3. Francis Bramston, born on the 3rd of November, 1868 ; married, on the 2nd October, 1897, Edith, daughter of Charles Arthur Patton, Marpole House, Ealing.

*a*4. Henrietta Mary, born on the 3rd of June, 1872.

b. Osborn Leith.

c. Henry Nepean died young.

9. HENRY TORRENS (so called after his godfather, Sir Henry Torrens [1]), born 15th June, 1812, Ensign 2nd Queen's Royals, was drowned at Bombay on the 21st April, 1831, unmarried.

10. ELIZABETH CAREY, born 10th June, 1813, married, on the 14th June, 1854, William Jones (an author) of Brent House, Brentford, Middlesex. He was Vice-Consul at Havre, and was instrumental in helping the flight of Louis Philippe, King of the French, in 1848. She died in London on the 31st of December, 1856, without issue.

11. LOUISA CREIGHTON, born on the 3rd of May, 1816, and married H. M. Arthur Jones, who afterwards took the name of Owen, a Welsh squire of Wepré Hall, near Flint. Issue—Lewis, who died young.

12. HALE SHEAFF (so called after his godfather, Sir Hale Sheaff), born on the 17th of April, 1817, and died on the 20th September, 1820.

13. MARTHA ELIZA, born on the 3rd of December, 1819, and married, on the 29th of June, 1850, the Rev. Carteret Priaulx Carey, M.A., Oxon, eldest son of John Carey [2] of Castle Carey, Guernsey. She died on the 15th of April, 1878, leaving issue—

1 Major-General Sir Henry Torrens, K.C.B., a native of Londonderry, who was, in 1798, Aide-de-Camp to Lieutenant-General Whitelock, second in command to the Earl of Moira (Note, page 269) at Portsmouth, was Secretary to the Duke of Wellington during the Peninsular War. He was afterwards appointed Adjutant-General, and, while holding that office, he revised the Army Regulations and introduced many important improvements. Born 1779, died 1828.

2 The Careys of Guernsey have held a leading position there for upwards of six hundred years.

a. John Herbert Carteret of Castle Carey, Guernsey, born on the 11th of April, 1851. He was for some time a Lieutenant in the Sixtieth Royal Rifles, afterwards Captain and Adjutant First Royal Guernsey Infantry, and was engaged in the reorganisation of the Royal Guernsey Militia ; retired on War Office pension as Major (Army rank) in 1894 ; Honorary Lieutenant-Colonel of the Royal Guernsey Militia, 1894. He is a member of the Societé Jersiaise and a member of the Council of the Guernsey Historical and Antiquarian Society. He married, on the 24th of February, 1877, Isabella Anne, sole surviving child of the late James S. Scott, J.P., formerly of Lawnsdowne, Queen's County, Ireland, with issue, twin daughters, Eleanor Katherine Matilda and Marguérite Blanche Isabel.

b. Abdiel Archibald McCrea, born on the 4th of July, 1852, died young.

c. Carteret Walter, born on the 13th December, 1853, Lieutenant in the Seventy-Fourth Highlanders, 12th November, 1873, Equery to H.R.H. the Duchess of Edinburgh in Malta, Captain 1882, Major 1890. He served in the Egyptian Expedition in 1882 as Adjutant of his battalion, and was present at the Battle of Tel-el-Kebir, where his horse was wounded. He received the Egyptian War medal with clasp, the Khedive's bronze star, and the Order of Medjidie, Fourth Class. In 1892, out of eighty competitors, he received the first prize—£100— awarded by Lord Wolseley for the best essay on the " Reorganisation of the Volunteer Forces." He served as Second in Command of the Second Bat-

talion of the Highland Light Infantry (74th Highlanders), in the North-West Indian Frontier War,
1897-98, including operations against the Boners,
commanding the infantry in the reconnaisance in
the Milandri Pass, operations against the Mah-
munds, Pelarzais, and Shamozais, and was with the
Reserves during the operations against the Utman
Khels ; also in the Bonewal Campaign, 1898, including storming and capture of the Tangu Pass,
and the capture and occupation of Kingergali, Jowar,
Tursak, and Ambeyla. He married, on the 11th
December, 1890, Florence Margaret, daughter of
William Ravenhill Stock, with issue—Vera Carteret
Priaulx.

.*d.* Samuel Robert, born on the 16th of March,
1855, died young.

e. William Wilfred, born on the 23rd of August,
1856. Formerly Major in the First Royal Guernsey
Light Infantry Militia. He was appointed Secretary
to the British Commissioners, Egyptian States
Domains, 1882, was present at the bombardment of
Alexandria, and was attached to the Intelligence
Department under Sir J. Goldsmid from July to
September, 1882, receiving the thanks of Her
Majesty's Government for his services. In 1883 he
was appointed Inspector, and in 1897 Inspector-
General of the Egyptian States Domains. He holds
the Egyptian War medal, the Khedive's bronze
star, the Order of Osmanlieh, Fourth Class, and the
Order of Medjidie, Fourth Class. He married, in
1880, Louisa Sophia, daughter of the late General
Broadly Harrison, Colonel of the Thirteenth Hussars.

14. CHARLOTTE, born on the 9th of January, 1822, and died on the 16th of January, 1884. She adopted the three orphan children of her brother, Herbert Taylor.

15. HERBERT TAYLOR (so called after his god-father, Lieutenant - General Sir Herbert Taylor, K.C.B.), born on the 3rd of May, 1827. He was a Lieutenant in the 94th Regiment and Paymaster in the 43rd Light Infantry. He served in the Kaffir War 1851-52-53. He married, on the 5th of January, 1851, Elizabeth, daughter of John Carey, Castle Carey, Guernsey, and died at the Cape of Good Hope, on his way home from India, on the 8th of April, 1855, leaving issue as below. His wife died in the Neilgherry Hills, Kotagherry, on the 28th July, 1855—

a. Herbert Carey Howes, born on the 28th of October, 1851. He married Maria, daughter of General Rolandi, of the Spanish Army, and has issue—Constance Isabella Rolandi.

b. John Frederick, born on the 1st of April, 1854, at Fort George, Madras. He was Surgeon-Major in the Cape Mounted Rifles. He saw much service in the Cape, won the Victoria Cross in the Basuto War, and was severely wounded in the action at Twee Fontein. He married, in 1887, Miss E. A. Watermeyer, and died on the 16th July, 1894, without issue.

c. Elizabeth Charlotte, born on the 20th of June, 1855, and died on the 20th of December, 1896.

CHAPTER XXI.

A Tradition of the Time of Montrose.—Macraes in Galloway.—
Alexander Macrae of Glenlair married Agnes Gordon of
Carleton.—Their Descendants.

There is a tradition to the effect that after the
defeat of Montrose at Philiphaugh, near Selkirk, on
the 12th of September, 1645, two Highland brothers
of the name of Macrae who served in his army,
sought refuge in Galloway because it was the nearest
place where Gaelic was then spoken. There they
settled down and prospered. The same tradition
relates that from one of these brothers was descended a certain

ALEXANDER MACRAE, who, in 1744, married,
as his first wife, Agnes, daughter of Alexander Gordon, fifth of Carleton, by his wife Grizzell, daughter
of Sir Alexander Gordon, Baronet of Earlston,[1] by
his wife Marion, daughter of Alexander Gordon,
fifth Viscount Kenmure, and sister of William, Earl
of Kenmure, who was executed in 1716. Agnes
Gordon brought him as her dowry the farm of
Glenlair, in the parish of Parton, in Kirkcudbright.
He is said to have married three other wives, and
to have had issue, at least by some of them. By his
first wife, Agnes Gordon, he had a son,

---

[1] See Burke's Peerage and Baronetage, Gordon of Earlston.

ALEXANDER, born in 1745, in the parish of Parton, in Kirkcudbright, of Moreland estate, in the Island of Jamaica, where he lived for many years. He married, on the 17th of September, 1767, Mary, daughter of Thomas Harvie, Professor of Greek in the University of Glasgow, and by her, who died in Jamaica, and was buried at Old Harbour, parish of St Dorothy, had issue as below. Alexander himself died in Edinburgh on the 14th of March, 1796, a few months after his return from Jamaica—

1. WILLIAM GORDON, of whom next.

2. ALEXANDER, a Captain in the First Royals.

3. JAMES, in the Thirteenth Light Dragoons, killed at Martinique in 1821.

4. THOMASINE married the Rev. Mr Maddison.

WILLIAM GORDON McCRAE[1] was born near Ayr in 1768. He married Margaret Morison,[2] who was descended from the family of Lord Forbes of Pitsligo, and by her had issue—

1. MARY HARVIE, born 1797, married Dr Cobham, Barbadoes, with issue—

a. Francis McCrae married, with issue.

b. Richard married, with issue.

[1] He changed the spelling of the name from Macrae to McCrae.

[2] Margaret Morison was connected with the Pitsligo family as follows :— Rev. John Forbes (born 1643, died 1708), described on a marble slab on the wall of the old church of Kincardine O'Neill, Aberdeenshire, as of the noble family of Pitsligo (ex nobile Dominorum de Pitsligo oriundus familia), married Margaret Strachan, and had issue one daughter, Nichola Helen, who, on the 30th October, 1707, married John, youngest son of Sir John Forbes, Bart. of Craigievar, and had a daughter, Margaret (baptised 17th October, 1710), who married George Herdsman, factor to the Earl Marischal, and had a daughter, Mary (born on the 28th of July, 1740), who married Andrew Morison, Clerk to the Court of Session, and had, with other issue, the above-mentioned Margaret, who married William Gordon McCrae.

c. Elizabeth married Hon. Mark Nicholson, with issue.

d. Mary married Hon. James Graham, with issue.

2. ALEXANDER, born in 1799, Captain in the Eighty-Fourth Regiment, commanding the Grenadier Company, and afterwards Postmaster-General of Victoria, in Australia. He married Susanna Dannay, with issue—

a. Alexander died unmarried.

b. George died unmarried.

c. Margaret married Edward Graham without issue.

d. Sarah Agnes married Dr W. G. Howitt with issue :—Sarah Muriel Susanna ; Phœbe ; Godfrey ; William Godfrey ; Alexander McCrae ; John Bakewell ; George Ward Cole ; Charles Hugh.

e. Katherine Susannah married Thomas W. Palmer with issue :—Catherine Wrangham married H. R. Anthony ; Ethel McCrae married George Ogle Moore ; Agnes McCrae married Charlton Howitt ; Margaret Annie.

f. Mary Harvie married W. F. Freeman with issue : — Susanna McCrae ; Clara Annie married George Jennings ; Alfred William ; Marion Kate ; Harry Randall.

g. William Gordon died unmarried.

h. John Morison, born 1848, now living at Perth, West Australia, and by whom this information about his own family was communicated to the author in 1898. He married, first, in 1870, Eleanor Harrison Atkin, with issue—Alexander ; John Morison. He married, secondly, in 1893, Bessie Fraser Brock, widow of F. A. Brock.

i. Union Rose died in infancy.

j. Thomasanne Cole married Maurice Blackburn with issue :—Maurice McCrae ; James ; Gertrude ; Elsie.

k. Agnes Bruce married George Loughnan with issue :—Marion ; Muriel ; John Hamilton ; George Richmond ; Agnes ; Valory.

3. ANDREW MURISON, born in 1800. He was a Writer to the Signet in Edinburgh, and practised for some time as a Parliamentary Agent in London. He went to Australia in 1838. On arriving in Melbourne (after staying some time in Sydney) he was admitted a solicitor, and practised there for several years. He was afterwards a Stipendiary and Police Magistrate, and in that capacity served on several stations. He was also a Warden of the Gold Fields, a Commissioner of Crown Lands, and Deputy Sheriff. He died in 1874. He married, in 1830, Georgina Huntly Gordon, and by her, who died on the 24th of May, 1890, aged eighty-six years, had issue—

a. Margaret Elizabeth Mary, born in 1831, died young.

b. George Gordon, born in Scotland in 1833, a retired Civil Servant, now living at Hawthorn, near Melbourne, and by whom most of the information contained in this chapter was communicated to the author in 1896. Mr George Gordon McCrae is a poet of recognised merit and standing. He married Augusta Helen Brown, with issue.

c. William Gordon, born in Scotland in 1835, now living in West Australia.

d. Alexander Gordon, born in Scotland in 1836, now living in New South Wales.

e. Farquhar Peregrine Gordon, born in England in 1838, Inspector, Bank of Australasia, Sydney, New South Wales. He married Emily Aphrasia Brown, and has issue.

f. Georgina Lucia Gordon, born in Australia in 1841, married Robert Hyndman, with issue.

g. Margaret Martha, born in Australia, married Nicholas Maine, with issue—Margaret Isabella.

h. Octavia Frances Gordon, born in Australia, married George Watton Moore, with issue.

i. Agnes Thomasina, died in infancy.

4. AGNES, born 1802.

5. JOHN MORISON, born in 1804, Lieutenant Seventeenth Native Infantry, Bengal.

6. FARQUHAR, born in 1806, Surgeon in the Enniskillen Dragoons. He afterwards went to Australia, and died in Sydney. He married Agnes Morison, with issue.

7. AGNES, born in 1808, married William Bruce, and had issue.

8. THOMAS ANNE, born in 1810, married Commander George Ward-Cole, R.N., with issue.

9. MARGARET FORBES, born in 1812, married Dr David John Thomas, with issue.

CHAPTER XXII.

Legends and Traditions of the Clan Macrae.—How the Macraes
first came to Kintail.—How St Fillan became the Greatest of
Physicians and made the Inhabitants of Kintail Strong and
Healthy.—How Ellandonan Castle came to be built.—How
Donnacha Mor na Tuaigh fought at the Battle of Park.—
How the Great Feud between Kintail and Glengarry began.—
How Ian Breac Mac Mhaighster Fearachar made Lochiel
retract a vow against the Men of Kintail.—Tradition about
Muireach Fial.—Tradition about Fearachar Mac Ian Oig.—
Tradition about the Glenlic Hunt.—Traditions about Donnacha
Mor Mac Alister.—Traditions about Eonachan Dubh.—How
Ian Mor Mac Mhaighster Fionnla killed the Soldiers.—A
Tradition of Sheriffmuir.—How a Kintail Man was innocently
hanged by the Duke of Cumberland.—Some Macrae Traditions
from Gairloch.

Like every other clan, the Macraes of Kintail had
their own legends and traditions, and in olden time
their country was more than usually rich, even for
the Highlands, in poetry, legend, and historic lore.
It was formerly a well-known and universal custom
in the Highlands for the people of a township to
meet together in some central house in the long
winter evenings, and pass much of the time in
singing songs and reciting tales. This custom, which
has survived to a certain extent in some districts
down to our own times, was called the Ceilidh, a
word which means a meeting for social intercourse

and conversation, and it is needless to say that at such meetings the Seanachaidh or reciter of ancient lore, who could relate his tales in fluent, sonorous language, and with a due admixture of homely, dramatic dialogue, a thing to which the Gaelic language so effectively lends itself, was a man whose company was always welcome.   The Seanachaidh has now given place very largely to the political newspaper and other cheap forms of literature, and it may be questioned if, in itself, the change is altogether for the better.   At all events, the reciter of Highland folklore endeavoured to entertain his listeners with tales of the courage, devotion, and chivalry which go to make a true hero, and to young, impressionable minds the effect of this could hardly fail to be, at least, as wholesome as the ceaseless appeal to human selfishness and covetousness which too frequently forms the chief stock-in-trade of the political newspaper.

In this chapter an effort is made to preserve a few of the old legends and traditions of Kintail, and they are given almost in the very words in which they were communicated to the author by men who know Kintail and its people, and who, in almost every case, heard them related by old men at the Ceilidh many years ago.[1]   There is no attempt made

[1] The author has great pleasure in acknowledging his indebtedness for most of the information contained in this chapter to Mr Alexander Matheson, shipowner, Dornie (p. 48) ; Mr Farquhar Macrae, Dornie (p. 130) ; Mr John Alexander Macrae, Avernish (p. 179) ; Mr Farquhar Matheson, Dornie (p. 49) ; Mr Alexander Maclennan, Craig House, Lochcarron (p. 224) ; Mr Donald Macrae, Gelantipy, Victoria (p. 258) ; Mr John Macrae, Islip, New York (p. 212) ; and Mr Alexander Macmillan, an old man of Dornie, who died on the 13th May, 1896.

to harmonise them, even when possible to do so, with
the actual facts of the historic incidents to which
they refer, and the reader will readily recognise some
of them as local versions of legends which may be
found in other lands as well as in the Highlands,
but they are interesting as showing the light in
which the people of the country looked upon their
own history, and they serve to illustrate the wholesome pride of the clan in its own heroes, as well as
their appreciation of the man of courage, presence of
mind, and prompt action, who was bold and fearless
in the face of a foe, loyal to his chief, true to every
trust, as well as humane and gentle to the weak and
helpless who were in any sense dependent upon him.
It is not pretended for a single moment that such
traits of character were universal in the Highlands
any more than in other places, but they constituted
the standard of life and conduct at which the true
man was expected to aim, and it was only in as far
as he succeeded in reaching that standard that his
memory was held worthy of an honoured place in
the traditions of his clan and country.

HOW THE MACRAES FIRST CAME TO KINTAIL.

Once upon a time, in Ireland, three young men of
the Fitzgerald family, called Colin Fitzgerald,[1]
Gilleoin na Tuaigh, and Maurice Macrath were present
at a wedding, and partook somewhat freely of the

---

[1] Colin Fitzgerald was the reputed founder of the Clan Mackenzie, and
Gilleoin na Tuaigh of the Clan Maclean.

good cheer which was provided for the guests.   On the way home they got so seriously implicated in a quarrel that they thought it prudent to seek safety in flight.   While crossing a ferry they took violent possession of the ferryman's boat, and putting out to sea with it they sailed across to Scotland.   They landed at Ardnamurchan, and gradually made their way across the country to the Aird of Lovat.   On arriving there late in the night, and very tired, they lay down under a hedge to rest until the morning before deciding what their next step was to be.   But in the early morning they were awakened from their sleep by the clang of arms, and found two men engaged in a fierce fight quite near them.   It turned out that one of these men was Bissett, the Lord of Lovat, while his antagonist was a redoubtable bully who, in consequence of some dispute, had challenged him to mortal combat.   Maurice, observing that Bissett was on the point of being vanquished, proposed to go to his aid, but the other two thought it would be wiser and more prudent not to do so, as they did not know the merits of the case, and had already been obliged to leave their country through thoughtless interference in a quarrel which did not concern them.   Maurice, however, would not be persuaded, and going to Bissett's assistance he cut off the bully's head with one blow.   Bissett then invited his unexpected deliverer to his house, and being favourably impressed by him he offered him an important post in his service, and gave him the lands of Clunes to settle on.   When the Frasers became Lords of Lovat the Macrae family was still living at

T

Clunes, and the head of the family was appointed
Lord Lovat's chief forester. One day there happened to be a great hunting expedition in the Lovat
forest, and among those who took part in it was a
bastard son of Lovat, who began to abuse Macrae for
not giving his hounds a better chance. One of
Macrae's sons, called John, who happened to be
present at the time, took up the quarrel on behalf of
his father, who was an old man, and settled the
matter by killing the bastard. As the old man had
rendered him so much loyal and valuable service in
the past Lovat decided to overlook this unfortunate
mishap, but at the same time advised him to send his
sons out of the country, at all events for a time, for
fear of the vengeance of the Fraser family. The four
sons took the hint and quietly left the Lovat country.
They journeyed together as far as Glenmoriston, and
at a place called Ceann a Chnuic (the end of the
hillock) they parted. One of them, called Duncan,
went to Argyllshire, married the heiress of Craignish,
and became the ancestor of the Craignish Campbells.
Another, called Christopher, went to Easter Ross.
The third, who was called John, went to Kintail and
spent his first night there in the house of a man
called Macaulay, at Achnagart. He was such a
restless man that they called him Ian Carrach, which
means twisting or fidgety John. Macaulay's
daughter, however, fell in love with him and persuaded him to remain there. In course of time they
were married. Their first child was born at Achnagart, and he was the first Macrae born in Kintail.
The family of Ian Carrach was one of the chief families

of Kintail until Malcolm Mac Ian Charrich, Constable of Ellandonan, lost his influence by supporting
Hector Roy's claim for the estates of Kintail against
John of Killin.[1]   A fourth son of Macrae of Clunes,
called Finlay, after wandering about for some time,
finally made his way to Kintail and settled there
near his brother John.   He was called Fionnla Mor
nan Gad.[2]   Fionnla Mor nan Gad was the ancestor
of Fionnla Dubh Mac Gillechriosd, with whom the
recorded genealogy of the Macraes of Kintail com-
mences.

HOW ST FILLAN BECAME THE GREATEST OF PHYSICIANS, AND MADE THE INHABITANTS OF KINTAIL STRONG AND HEALTHY.

While St Fillan was travelling on a pilgrimage in
France with a hazel staff from Kintail in his hand,
he went one day into the house of an alchemist.
The alchemist told the Saint he would give him a
fortune if he would bring him to France what was
under the sod where the hazel staff grew.   Upon
being questioned by St Fillan the alchemist explained
that under that sod there was a white serpent, of
which he wished very much to get possession.   St
Fillan then undertook to go in search of the serpent,
and the alchemist gave him the necessary instructions how to capture it.   When St Fillan reached the

1 Pages 22, 23, and Footnote page 214.

2 The meaning of Gad here is doubtful, it usually means a withe or switch,
but in this case it may possibly mean spear.   See Macbain's Gaelic Dictionary.

spot where the hazel staff had been cut, at the north-east end of Loch Long, he kindled a fire and placed a pail of honey near it.   The warmth of the fire soon brought a large number of serpents out of their holes, and among them the white serpent, which was their King.   Being attracted by the smell of the honey, the white serpent crawled into the pail.   Fillan then seized the pail and ran away with it, followed by an ever-increasing number of serpents, anxious to rescue their King.   The saint knew he would not be safe from their pursuit until he had crossed seven running streams of water.   The river Elchaig was the seventh stream on his way, and when he crossed it he felt that he was now safe.   When he reached the top of a small hill called Tulloch nan deur (the hill of tears) he paused for a short rest, and composed a Gaelic hymn or song, of which the following verse is all that appears to be known—

> 'S mi 'm sheasidh air Tulloch nan deur,
> Gun chraicionn air meur na bonn,
> Ochadan ! a rhigh nan rann,
> 'S fhada 'n Fhraing bho cheann Loch Long.[1]

St Fillan then continued his journey, and when he arrived at the end of it, the alchemist took the pail containing the honey and the serpent, put it in a cauldron to boil, and left the Saint alone for a little to watch over it, giving him instructions at the same time that if he saw any bubbles rising to the surface he was on no account to touch them.   The alchemist was not long gone when a bubble rose, and Fillan

---

[1] Standing on the hill of tears with skinless soles and toes,
Alas ! O King of verses, far is France from the head of Loch Long.

thoughtlessly put his finger on it.   As the bubble
burst it gave out such a burning heat that he
suddenly drew his finger back and put it in his
mouth to allay the pain, but no sooner did he do so
than he felt himself becoming possessed of miraculous
healing powers.   This was how St Fillan became
the greatest physician of his age.   The alchemist
intended to get this power from the white serpent
for himself, but when he returned to his cauldron he
found that all the virtue had gone out of it.   St
Fillan then returned to Kintail with his newly-
acquired power, which he used among the people in
such a way that in watching over their spiritual
health he remembered their bodily health also, and
so made them strong and well-favoured among their
neighbours.

HOW ELLANDONAN CASTLE CAME TO BE BUILT.

In olden times there lived in Kintail a wealthy chief
of the same race as the Mathesons, who had an only
son.   When the son was born he received his first
drink out of the skull of a raven, and this gave him
the power to understand the language of birds.   He
was sent to Rome for his education, and became a
great linguist.   When he returned to Kintail his
father asked him one day to explain what the birds
were saying.   "They are saying," replied the son,
"that one day you will wait upon me as my servant."
The father was so annoyed at this explanation that
he turned his son out of the house.   The son then

joined a ship which was bound for France.   Having
learned on his arrival in France that the King was
very greatly annoyed and disturbed by the chirping
of birds about the palace, he went and offered to help
the King to get rid of them.   The King accepted
the offer, and the adventurer explained to him that
the birds had a quarrel among themselves, which
they wished the King to settle for them.   By the
help of his visitor the King succeeded in settling the
dispute to the entire satisfaction of the birds, and was
troubled by them no more.   In gratitude for this
relief the King gave his deliverer a fully-manned
ship for his own use, and with this ship he sailed to
far distant lands, but no land was so distant that he
could not understand and speak the language of the
people.

On one occasion, in the course of a very long
voyage, he met a native King, whom he greatly
pleased with his interesting conversation.   The King
invited him to dine at the royal palace, but when he
got to the palace he found it was so infested with
rats that the servants had the very greatest difficulty
in keeping them away from the table.   Next time
the adventurer visited the palace he brought a cat
from the ship with him, under his cloak, and when
the rats gathered round the table he let the cat
loose among them.   The King was so pleased with
the way in which the cat drove the rats away, that
in exchange for the cat he gave his guest a hogshead
full of gold.   With this gold the wanderer returned
to Kintail, after an absence of seven years, and
anchored his ship at Totaig.   The arrival of such a

magnificent ship caused a considerable sensation, and when the owner presented himself at his father's house, as a man of rank from a distant country, he was received with great hospitality. His father, who failed to recognise him, waited upon him at table, and thus fulfilled the prophecy of the birds. The son then made himself known to his father, and a birth mark he bore between his shoulders proved his identity to the entire satisfaction of the people, who received him with enthusiasm as the long lost heir. His ability and knowledge of the world afterwards brought him into the favour and confidence of King Alexander II., who commissioned him to build Ellandonan Castle to protect the King's subjects in those parts against the encroachments of the Danes.

HOW DONNACHA MOR NA TUAIGH DISTINGUISHED HIMSELF AT THE BATTLE OF PARK.[1]

Shortly before the battle a raw but powerful looking youth from Kintail was seen staring about among the Mackenzies in a stupid manner as if looking for something. He ultimately came across an old, rusty battle axe of great size, and setting off after the others he arrived at the scene of strife just as the combatants were closing with each other. This youth was Donnacha Mor na Tuaigh, and Hector Roy, observing him, asked him why he was not taking part in the fight and supporting his chief and clan. Duncan replied : " Mar a faigh mi miadh

1 Page 17.

duine, cha dean mi gniomh duine" (Unless I get a
man's esteem I will not perform a man's work).
This reply was meant as a hint that he had not
been provided with a proper weapon. Hector
answered him, " Dean sa gniomh duine 's
gheibh thu miadh duine " (Do a man's work
and you shall get a man's esteem). Duncan
at once rushed into the combat exclaiming,
"Buille mhor bho chul mo laimhe 's ceum leatha,
am fear nach teich romham teicheam roimhe " (A
heavy stroke from the back of my arm and a step
to enforce it; he who does not get out of my way
let me get out of his). Duncan soon killed a man,
and, drawing the body aside, coolly sat down on it.
Hector Roy, observing this strange proceeding,
asked Duncan why he was not still engaged along
with his comrades. Duncan answered: " Mar a faigh
mi ach miadh aon duine cha dean mi ach gniomh
aon duine " (If I get only one man's due, I will
do only one man's work). Hector told him to
do two men's work and he would get two men's
reward. Duncan, returning again to the combat,
soon killed another man, and pulling the body aside
placed it on the top of the first one, and again
sat down. Hector repeated his question once more,
and Duncan replied that he had killed two men,
and earned two men's reward. " Do your best,"
replied Hector, "and let us no longer dispute about
your reward." Duncan instantly replied : "Am fear
nach biodh a cunntadh rium cha bhithinn a cunntadh
ris " (He that would not reckon with me, I would
not reckon with him), and rushed into the thickest

of the battle, where he did so much execution among the enemy that Lachlan Maclean of Lochbuy (Lachlainn Mac Thearlaich), the most redoubtable warrior on the other side, placed himself in Duncan's way to check him in his destructive career. The two met in mortal strife, and Maclean being a very powerful man, clad in mail, and well trained in the use of arms, seemed likely to prove the victor; but Duncan, being lighter and more active than his heavily mailed opponent, managed, however, to defend himself, watching his opportunity, and retreating backwards until he arrived at a ditch. His opponent, now thinking that he had him in his power, made a desperate stroke at him, which Duncan parried, and at the same time jumped over the ditch. Maclean then made a furious lunge with his weapon, but instead of entering Duncan's body it got fixed in the opposite bank of the ditch. In withdrawing his weapon Maclean bent his head forward, and thus exposed the back of his neck, upon which Duncan's battle axe descended with the velocity of lightning, and with such terrific force as to sever the head from the body. This, it is said, was the turning-point of the battle, for the Macdonalds, seeing the brave leader of their van killed, gave up all for lost, and began at once to retreat. Duncan was ever afterwards known as " Donnacha Mor na Tuaigh" (Big Duncan of the Battle Axe). That night as Mackenzie sat at supper he inquired for Duncan, who was missing and could nowhere be found. " My sorrow," said Mackenzie, " for the loss of my scallag mhor (big servant) is greater than my satisfaction for

the success of the battle." " I thought," replied one
of those present, " that as the Macdonalds fled I saw
him pursuing four or five of them up the burn."
The words were hardly spoken when Duncan came
in with four heads bound together with a rope of
twisted twigs. " Tell me now," said Duncan, as he
threw the heads down before his master, " if I have
not earned my supper."

HOW THE GREAT FEUD BETWEEN KINTAIL AND GLENGARRY BEGAN.[1]

There was once a famous archer of the Clan Macrae
called Fionnla Dubh nam Fiadh[2] (Black Finlay of
the Deer).   He was forester of Glencannich.   While
Finlay was occupying this position, a certain Macdonald of Glengarry, who had fled from his own
home for murder, took refuge in the forest, having
obtained permission from one of the chief men of the
Mackenzies, not only to take refuge there, but even
to help himself to anything he could lay his hands
on unknown to Finlay.   One day Finlay and another
man went out to hunt in a part of the forest which
was the usual haunt of the best and fattest deer.
To their great surprise they found Macdonald hunting there also.   Finlay asked him who gave him

---

1 Pages 34, 35.

2 Fionnla Dubh nam Fiadh belonged to a tribe of Macraes called Clann a
Chruitear (the descendants of the harper).   Those belonging to this tribe
were generally of a very dark complexion.   It is said they were not of the
original stock of Macraes, but were descended from a foreign harper, who was
brought into the country by one of the Mackenzies, and who settled down
there and adopted the name Macrae.

permission to be there. "That's none of your business," replied Macdonald ; "I mean to kill as many
deer as I please, and you shall not prevent me."
Thus a quarrel arose between them, and the end of
it was that Finlay shot Macdonald through the
heart with an arrow, and cast his body into a lake
called Lochan Uine Gleannan nam Fiadh (the green
lake of the glen of the deer). After a time Macdonald's friends in Glengarry began to wonder what
had become of him, but at last a rumour reached
them that he had been killed by Fionnla Dubh nam
Fiadh.

On hearing this they formed a party of twelve
strong and able men to go to Glencannich to make
inquiries, and, if necessary, to take vengeance on
Finlay. On arriving at Glencannich the first house
they came to was Finlay's. His wife met them at
the door, and as they did not know that this was
Finlay's house, they stated the object of their visit,
and asked if she could give them any directions or
information. She told them to come in and rest.
They did so, and as they were tired and hungry they
were not sorry to see her making preparations to
show them hospitality. Meantime Finlay, who was
in the other end of the house, began to amuse himself by playing on his trump or Jews' harp. The
Glengarry men were so engrossed and interested in
the conversation of their hostess that they took no
notice of Finlay's music. She, however, listened
attentively to it, and from the tune he was playing
she understood that he wished her to poison her
guests. She accordingly contrived to mix a certain

kind of poison, used by her husband to kill foxes, in the rennet with which she was preparing some curds and cream which she set before them. They partook freely of this dish, and eleven of them died from the effects of the poison shortly after they left the house. Finlay then went out and buried them. The twelfth man, however, managed to make his way back to Glengarry, where he told his fellow clansmen what had happened.

The chief, hearing of it, chose eleven strong and brave men to return to Glencannich with this sur- vivor, who undertook to act as their guide and lead them straight to Finlay's house. Now, though this man had already been to Finlay's house, he had not actually seen Finlay himself, and would therefore be unable to recognise him. In due time the Glengarry men reached the brow of a hill opposite to Finlay's house, where they found a man cutting turfs. This was Finlay himself, but he received them with such calm indifference that they never suspected who he was. They asked him if he knew where Finlay was, or if he was at home. "Well," replied Finlay, pointing to his own house, "when I was at that house just now, Finlay was there too." The Glen- garry men, thinking the prize was now within their grasp, hurried to the house without looking behind, and so did not observe that Finlay was following after them. As they crowded in at the door, Finlay called to his wife through the back window to hand him out his bow and quiver. His wife did so, and Finlay then took his stand in a convenient position with his bow and arrows. "Come out," shouted he to the Glengarry men, "the man you want is here.". They rushed out, but he shot them dead one after another before they were able to reach him. He then buried them along with his former victims, and shortly afterwards moved down to his winter quarters at Achyaragan in Glenelchaig.

After a time Glengarry began to wonder what had become of his messengers, and so he sent yet another twelve to make enquiries about them and to punish Finlay. As these men were passing by Abercalder, in the neighbourhood of Fort-Augustus, on their way to Glencannich, they got into conversation with a man who was ploughing in a field. The man innocently told them that he was Finlay's brother, whereupon they immediately struck their dirks into him and left him dead in the shafts of the plough. On finding that Finlay had left Glencannich they followed him to Glenelchaig, where it so happened that the first man they met was Finlay himself, who was out hunting on Mamantuirc. They began to ask him questions about the man they were in search of, which he answered to their satisfaction, and as they walked along he conversed with them with a freedom which prevented any suspicion on their part. But on parting with them he quickly took up his stand in a favourable position, and shouting out that he was the man they wanted, killed them all with his arrows before they could lay hands on him. The last of the twelve took to flight and was killed while in the act of leaping across a waterfall. His name was Leiry, and the waterfall is called Eas leum Leiridh (the waterfall of Leiry's

leap) to this day.   When Mackenzie of Kintail
heard of the murder of Finlay's brother at Abercalder he applied for a commission of fire and sword
against Glengarry, who was also making preparations
on his own account to retaliate for the slaughter of
his men by Finlay.   The Mackenzies and the Macdonalds met and fought their first battle at the Pass
of Beallach Mhalagan, in the heights of Glensheil.
During the fight Finlay took shelter with his bow
and quiver behind a large stone, which is still
pointed out, and continued to pour a deadly shower
of arrows among the Macdonalds until at last they
took to flight.   After the fight was over, Mackenzie
made his men sit down to rest and to partake of
some food.   Observing Finlay among them he turned
round to him and charged him with cowardice
for taking shelter behind the stone during the fight.
" You are very good," said he, " at raising a quarrel,
but you are a very poor hand at quelling it."
" Don't say more," replied Finlay, " until you have
examined your dead foes."   When the dead Macdonalds were examined it was found that no fewer
than twenty-four of the chief men among the slain
had fallen to Finlay's arrows.

One day, as Finlay lay ill in bed at Fadoch,
suffering from a wound in the head, a travelling
leech from Glengarry happened to visit the district.
He was called in to see Finlay, who felt much
relieved by his treatment.   As the leech continued
his journey in the direction of Camusluinie, he met
a woman, who asked him how the patient was.
" He is much better, and will soon be quite well,"

replied the leech.   " Agus leigheis thu Fionnla
Dubh nam Fiadh " (And you have cured Black
Finlay of the Deer), replied the woman.   The leech
did not know until now who his patient was, and
upon learning that it was Fionnla Dubh nam Fiadh,
he returned again to the house, and on a pretence
of having neglected something that ought to have
been done, in order to make the cure certain,
proceeded to examine the wound in the patient's
head once more.   In the course of the examination
he drove a probing needle through the wound into his
brain, and as the blood gushed out some of it flowed
into Finlay's mouth.   " Is milis an deoch a thug thu
dhomh " (Sweet is the drink you have given me),
said he, and with these words he expired.   The
leech then left the house, and continued his journey.
When the sons of Duncan returned and found their
father dead, they set out at once in pursuit of the
leech.   They overtook him among the hills above
Leault, killed him, and buried him on a spot which
is still pointed out.   Finlay himself was buried at
Killelan.

HOW IAN BREAC MAC MHAIGHSTER FEARACHAR MADE LOCHIEL RETRACT A VOW HE HAD MADE AGAINST THE MEN OF KINTAIL.

John Breac[1] used sometimes to go in attendance on
Seaforth to the meeting of the Scottish Parliament
at Perth, and on one of those occasions Seaforth's
sword was stolen from the hall of the house where

[1] Page 170.

he was living in the town.   The next time Seaforth
went to the meeting of Parliament John Breac, who
was with him, recognised the stolen sword in the
possession of one of the followers of Lochiel.   John
charged the man with the theft, beat him soundly,
and took the sword from him.   When Lochiel heard
of the ignominious treatment to which his man had
been subjected he swore that he would execute summary vengence on any Kintail man afterwards found
among the Camerons in Lochaber.   Shortly after his
return to Kintail John Breac missed three of his
horses from his farm at Duilig.   He at once set out
on their track, and traced them all the way to Lochaber, where he found them in a field, and some men
trying to catch them.   John went into the field and
helped the men to catch the horses, for which they
thanked him, but they had no suspicion who he was,
nor did he tell them the object of his visit.   He
asked them, however, if Lochiel was at home, and
they told him he was.   He then went to the house,
but it was early morning and Lochiel was still in
bed.   John told the servant that his business was
very urgent, and desired to be conducted to Lochiel's
bedroom.   "Who are you, and where do you come
from?" asked Lochiel when he saw the stranger
entering his bedroom.   "I come from Kintail," replied John.   "From Mackenzie's Kintail or Mackay's
Kintail?"[1] asked Lochiel.   "From Mackenzie's,"
replied John.   "Then you are a very bold man,"
continued Lochiel. "Are you not aware that I have
vowed vengence against any Kintail man found in

1 See Note, page 16.

my country ?"   "I am well aware of it," replied
John, "and what is more, I believe I was the cause
of your vow."   John then quietly took possession of
Lochiel's sword, which was hanging on the wall by
the bedside, and, explaining who he was, swore that
he would deal with him as he dealt with his man in
Perth if he did not at once retract his vow against
the men of Kintail, and order the stolen horses to
be sent back to Duilig.   Lochiel, who clearly saw
that John Breac was a man who meant what he
said, readily granted both requests, rather than run
the risk of being ignominiously beaten like a dog.

TRADITION ABOUT MUIREACH FIAL.

About the time of the battle of Sheriffmuir there
lived in Kintail a certain Maurice Macrae, known as
Muireach Fial (Maurice the Generous).   He was a
man of some means, and lent money to the Chisholm
of Strathglass, in return for which he received certain
grazing rights on the lands of Affric.   Maurice and
his wife used to go once a year to Inverness to sell
butter and cheese, which they carried on horseback
through the Chisholm country.   On one occasion,
as they were returning home, they were met by a
party of Strathglass men, who invited Maurice to
drink with them in Struy Inn.   Maurice accepted
the invitation, and being of a convivial disposition,
was in no hurry to leave.   His wife, having vainly
endeavoured to induce him to resume his journey,
started leisurely alone, expecting that her husband
would soon overtake her.   But Maurice did not

U

follow, and his wife, at last becoming anxious on his account, hurried home to Kintail, where a party was immediately organised to go in search of him. They searched all over Strathglass, and having made many inquiries without obtaining any information, they returned back to Kintail. On returning home one of their number disguised himself as a poor idiot, and went to Strathglass, where he wandered about begging his way from door to door, but at the same time keeping a careful watch for any trace or talk of the missing Maurice. One night, while lying at the door of a house, he heard someone tapping at the window. He listened attentively, and soon heard the man at the window and the master of the house talking about the bradan tarragheal (the white-bellied salmon), which was tied to a bush and concealed in a certain pool in the river. When the conversation ceased and the visitor took his departure, the Kintail man, wondering what was meant by the salmon, stole quietly away to the pool mentioned, and there found the body of Maurice, who had been murdered by some of the Strathglass men, and whose body had been hidden in the river in a dark pool under a thick bush. He drew the body out of the water, carried it some distance away to a safe hiding-place, and then set out in all haste to Kintail.

When the people of Kintail heard what had happened they formed a large party and went to fetch the body home to Kilduich. As they were passing by Comar churchyard, in Strathglass, on the way back to Kintail, they came upon a large funeral party who were in the act of burying one of the principal men of Strathglass. As the stone was being placed on the grave, four of the Kintail men stepped into the churchyard and carried the stone away. This was done in order to provoke a fight, that they might have an opportunity of avenging the death of Maurice. As the challenge was not accepted they carried the stone all the way to Kilduich and placed it over Maurice's grave, where it is still pointed out. Maurice might have been murdered for the sake of the money he was carrying home with him from Inverness, but the people of Kintail suspected that the murder was instigated by some one connected with the Chisholm, who did not like to see a stranger's cattle grazing on the hills of Affric, and the tradition further says that as soon as Maurice was dead all his cattle were stolen from their grazing by the Chisholm's men. Years afterwards, when Maurice's son, then an old man, was lying on his death-bed, a certain neighbour called Murachadh Buidh nam Meoir (yellow Murdoch of the fingers) went to see him. It was a cold day, and as Murdoch, who was asked to replenish the fire, was in the act of breaking up an old disused settle for fuel, he found concealed in it the parchment bond of the above-mentioned agreement between the Chisholm and Muireach Fial.

TRADITION ABOUT FEARACHAR MAC IAN OIG.

Fearachar Mac Ian Oig[1] lived at Achyark, and was a man of note in Kintail. It was in the time of Colin Earl of Seaforth, and the rents were very

1 Page 187.

heavy. To make matters worse, the bailiff who collected them was a very unpopular man, and was in
the habit of exacting certain payments on his own
account. A quarrel having arisen about a certain
tribute which Farquhar refused to pay, the bailiff
went to Achyark one day while Farquhar was out
hunting, and, taking advantage of his absence,
carried away a cow and a copper kettle in payment
of the disputed tribute. When Farquhar returned
home, his wife told him that if he were half a man
the bailiff would not dare to do what he did. This
taunt roused him to such fury that he immediately
set out with his loaded gun in pursuit of the bailiff,
whom he overtook at the river Conag. As the
bailiff was crossing the river, with the kettle on his
back, Farquhar shot him dead. When he returned
home he told his wife what he had done. "You
silly woman," said he, "you have caused me to work
my own ruin. I must now look to my safety, and
you must take care of yourself the best way you
can." He then fled for safety in the direction of
Loch Hourn, where he had an uncle living. When
he reached Coalas nam Bo (the strait of the cows),
on Loch Hourn, in the dead of the night, he began
to shout across the ferry to his uncle, who was living
on the other side. When the uncle heard him he
recognised his voice, and roused his own sons, who
were asleep in bed. "Get up," said he, "I hear
Farquhar, my brother's son, shouting to be ferried,
with a tone of mischief in his voice." The young
men at once got up, and brought Farquhar across
the ferry. When his uncle asked him what the

matter was, Farquhar told him that he had killed
Domhnull Mac Dhonnachaidh Mhic Fhionnlaidh
Dhuibh nam Fiadh (Donald, the son of Duncan, the
son of Black Finlay of the Deer). "If that is all,"
replied the uncle, "it does not matter much, for if
you had not killed him, I should kill him myself."
Farquhar hid with his uncle for some months, and
then took up his abode in a cave in Coire-Gorm-a-
Bheallaich, in Glenlic. This he made his hiding-
place for seven years, careful never to appear to any
but his most trusted friends. He never left his
hiding-place without placing a copper coin in a
certain position on a stone at the mouth of the cave,
his idea being that if anyone had visited and discovered his hiding-place in his absence they would
be sure either to take the coin away or, at all events,
to handle it, and move it from the position in which
he had left it. It is said that in those times, if
a murderer succeeded in evading the law for seven
years, he could not afterwards be punished, and so,
at the end of seven years, Farquhar, considering
himself a free man, suddenly appeared one day at a
funeral in Kilduich. His friends were delighted to
see him again, and having paid a ransom to the
representatives of the murdered man, he was henceforth able to go about the country in safety. On
one occasion, when taunted on being a murderer by
one of the bailiff's friends, Farquhar replied, "Ma
mharbh mis 'e nach d' ith sibh fhein e?" (If I killed
him, have you not eaten him yourselves?) This
reply referred to the ransom which in those days
would probably consist of food and cattle. Seaforth,

however, would not forgive the murderer of his bailiff, and so he sent a message to caution Farquhar never on any account to come into his presence. Shortly afterwards, Seaforth was fitting out an expedition for the Lews, and gave instructions that his men should meet on a certain day at Poolewe. When Seaforth arrived there he was disappointed to find so few of his men waiting for him. "How," said one of the Kintail men, "can you expect your men to respond to you, when you won't allow the bravest of them to come into your presence?" "And who is the bravest of them?" asked Seaforth. "Fearachar Mac Ian Oig," was the reply, "and he would soon be here if you would only restore him to the position he occupied before the murder of the bailiff." Seaforth consented to do this, and Farquhar, who was in concealment near by, was immediately introduced, and became reconciled to his chief there and then. The tradition says that in the course of this expedition Farquhar proved himself one of the bravest and best of Seaforth's followers.

TRADITION ABOUT THE GLENLIC HUNT.

There was hardly any event in the past history of Kintail around which there gathered more legendary and traditional lore than the famous Glenlic hunt, in which Murdoch, son of Alexander of Inverinate, lost his life, and which has been already referred to.[1] The reason for this was no doubt the mystery surrounding Murdoch's death, and the series of

---

1 Pages 84-85.

elegies composed during the fifteen days that the
search for his body continued.   His death was supposed by many people to have been the work of
some evil spirit, and for many generations it was
considered unsafe to pass at night by the spot where
the body was found, as strange sights were seen
there and strange noises heard, and, most convincing
of all, mysterious marks, as of a round foot with
long claws, used to be seen on the otherwise smooth
unbroken surface of the snow that fell there in
winter.   But there was one man in the district who
was proof, at all events, against any fear of the evil
spirit by which the scene of the tragedy was believed
to be haunted.   This was a redoubtable weaver
called Am Breabadair Og (the young weaver), who
lived at the Cro of Kintail, and who always carried
a brace of pistols with him wherever he went.
Having resolved to challenge the evil spirit to meet
him, he carefully loaded his pistols with silver
buttons—silver being, according to a well-known
belief of olden times, a metal which for shooting
purposes was proof against the power of witches and
evil spirits alike.   Thus fortified, he set out as the
night came on to the haunted spot, determined to
challenge and shoot any thing, whatever it might be,
that chanced to come across his path.   Nothing
happened, however, the first night, and so he
repeated his watch the second night also without
any result.   This went on for fourteen nights in
succession, and still the weaver's watches were
disturbed by neither voice nor vision.   But on the
fifteenth night, which, it may be observed, corre-

sponded with the number of days the search for
Murdoch's body lasted, the weaver returned home
crestfallen, exhausted, and silent.   Nobody was
ever told what he saw or heard on that night, but
he had evidently failed to drive away the evil spirit,
which continued to haunt the place as before.

TRADITIONS ABOUT DONNACHA MOR MAC ALISTER.

Of all the Macrae heroes there is no one whose name
enters so largely into the later traditions of Kintail
as Donnacha Mor Mac Alister.[1] It is said that when
Duncan was a mere lad he went on one occasion
with his mother to sell butter and cheese at Inverlochy (Fort-William).   On the way home Duncan
sulked and fell behind, because his mother refused
to give him money to buy a " bonnet" for himself.
As they continued the homeward journey along
Locharkaig side the mother was attacked by three
Lochaber robbers, who not only took her money
from her, but also a silver brooch, an heirloom which
she prized very greatly.   The conduct of her son,
who refused to give any help, annoyed her so much
that she called out to one of the robbers that she
had still one coin left, and she would give it to him
if he would thrash her son for her.   " Easan am bog
chuilean" (he, the soft whelp), contemptuously replied the robber, and going up to Duncan, struck
him on the face with the back of his hand.   This
was more than the sulking lad could stand, and

[1] Page 198.

being now roused to action, he fell upon the robbers, beat them, and recovered his mother's money and brooch.

Duncan once went to see his aunt in Lochaber, and after wading the Garry river, he continued his journey across the Pass of Coire 'n t' Shagairt. As the darkness came on he arrived at a lonely sheiling, and asked permission to pass the night there. The mistress of the sheiling received him very coldly, and refused his request, but Duncan had made up his mind to remain, and refused to go. Presently the daughter of the mistress came in from the milking of the cows, and proceeded to turn Duncan out by force. A struggle ensued, but Duncan's chivalry led him to acknowledge himself beaten. His strength, however, gained him the respect of the mistress, and he received permission to remain overnight. He then sat down and took off his shoes and stockings to cool his feet. When the mistress of the sheiling saw his feet she recognised him, by some mark or peculiarity about them, as a connection of her own family. It turned out that she was the aunt he had come to Lochaber to see. Next morning his cousin, who wanted to put his skill as a hunter to the test, told him there was a herd of deer among the cattle. Duncan went out, killed two of them, and brought them in for breakfast. On returning home, after spending a few pleasant days with his aunt and her daughter, he found the Garry river in flood. At the river he met his mother's foster brother, Dugald Macdonald, who, on being asked by Duncan if the river was

fordable, taunted him for hesitating to wade across.
Duncan then plunged in, but was very nearly
drowned before he got to the other side. Dugald
afterwards went to Glensheil to see Duncan's mother.
He met Duncan fishing on the River Sheil, which
was in flood, but did not recognise him. Dugald
told him where he was going, and asked him to show
the way. Duncan pointed out his own father's
house on the other side of the river. Dugald then
attempted to ford the river, but would have been
drowned if Duncan had not come to his rescue.
Thus Duncan proved himself to be the stronger of
the two. When Dugald was leaving Glensheil,
Duncan's father gave him a thrashing for tempting
Duncan to run the risk of wading the Garry river
when it was in such high flood, and reminded him
that if Duncan had been drowned then, he would
not be alive to save Dugald from drowning in the
River Sheil. Duncan's mother always used to say
ever after this that though her husband was so good
to her she could not forget how he thrashed her
foster brother.

It has already been mentioned [1] that William
Earl of Seaforth appointed Duncan Captain of the
Freiceadan or Guard, whose duty it was to protect
the marches of Kintail from the plundering raids of
the Lochaber cattle lifters. Seaforth had heard of
Duncan's strength and courage, but before entrusting
him with such a difficult and responsible post he
resolved to satisfy himself as to the truth of what
he had heard about him. He accordingly invited

[1] Page 198.

Duncan to come to see him in Brahan Castle. When Duncan arrived at Brahan, Seaforth received him alone in a room in the Castle. After some conversation, Seaforth locked the door of the room, drew his sword, and called upon Duncan to clear himself at once of some imaginary charge, or he would take his life. Duncan, who had left his sword in the hall of the Castle, had no weapon to defend himself with, but Seaforth's hound was lying on the floor close by. Duncan seized it by the legs and threw it at Seaforth, and, before Seaforth could recover from his surprise, Duncan took his sword from him. Seaforth was so pleased with Duncan's promptness and coolness that he at once decided to make him the Captain of his Guard.

At one time a band of Camerons came to Lochalsh and stole a large number of cattle from Matheson of Fernaig. When this became known, Duncan and his men set out in pursuit. They soon discovered the track of the spoilers, and they overtook them on the borders of Lochiel's country. A fight ensued, in which the Camerons had the worst of it. Not only was the cattle recovered, but in the course of the fight Duncan, assisted by his brother Eonachan and Matheson of Fernaig, the owner of the cattle, overcame Lochiel's three chief warriors, and led them prisoners to Kintail. When Seaforth heard of this he sent a bantering message to Lochiel asking him to come and ransom his champions from their prison. Lochiel sent for the prisoners, but at the same time replied to Seaforth that the Kintail men could never have taken the Cameron champions prisoners in fair

fight. Seaforth then offered to send three men from
Kintail to Lochiel to challenge any three of the
Camerons to a friendly contest of feats of strength.
Seaforth wanted the same three men to go, but his
father would not allow Eonachan to be one of the
three because he was too young, and because his
impulsive and hasty temper might cause the friendly
contest to end in a quarrel. Eonachan's place
had to be taken by his brother Donald. Duncan,
Donald, and Matheson of Fernaig then set out for
Lochiel's castle at Achnacarry. On the way it
occurred to Duncan that his brother Donald had
not yet tried the strength of any of the Cameron
champions, and so, when next they stopped to rest,
Duncan proposed to his brother that they should
wrestle together. They did so, and Duncan was
soon satisfied that his brother was equal to the best
of the Camerons. When they arrived at Achnacarry Castle they were received with much hospitality, and liberally supplied with food and drink.
In due time the hall of the castle was cleared, and
a large number of men who had come together to
witness the contest were brought in. The opposing
champions stood forth and began a wrestling match.
The Camerons in each case had the worst of it, and
Lochiel was so much disgusted with his champions
that he kicked them out at the door. He then invited the Kintail men to join in the feast with his
other guests, which they did. As the cup circulated
freely and the evening wore on, some of the Camerons began to betray their real feelings towards the
vanquishers of their champions, and occasionally cast

threatening glances at Duncan and his companions. But Lochiel's lady, being anxious to avoid bloodshed, contrived to warn the Kintail men of their danger. Duncan took the hint, and taking advantage of the first favourable opportunity, he quietly got his companions out without exciting any suspicions, while he himself was engaged in conversation with Lochiel. Shortly afterwards he slipped out also and joined them. The night was dark and stormy, but they betook themselves to the mountains of Glengarry. When they reached the river Garry towards break of day, they found the Camerons in close pursuit with firearms. The Kintail men plunged into the flooded river and with much difficulty gained the other side; but the Camerons would not venture to try the river, and so they returned home after following the Kintail men for many miles to no purpose.

Another version of this legend says that during the feast some of the Camerons made the door fast to prevent the escape of the Macraes, and that a servant girl (perhaps from Kintail) made them aware of this by whispering to one of them to get out by the window, and that on a signal from Duncan they rushed for the door, broke it open, and escaped into the darkness, challenging the Camerons at the same time to follow them.

When Duncan was a young man, he lived for some time at Killechuinard, and at night used to swim across Lochduich to Inverinate to see his sweetheart. On one occasion, as he was half-way across, he suddenly came into collision with a bull swimming in the opposite direction. The angry bull tried to gore him, and though Duncan was a powerful swimmer, he did not think he could swim against a Highland bull. So he cleverly contrived to get on the bull's back, and, seizing hold of his horns, he compelled the animal to swim back with him to Inverinate.

Though Duncan was a warrior of renown and a mighty hunter, he was also very tender-hearted, and always ready to help anyone in distress. On one occasion a servant at his father's sheiling at Caorun, in the Heights of Cluanie, was taken ill of a virulent fever, and while others were afraid to go near her, Duncan took her in his arms and carried her all the way down to Glenshiel, where she received proper attendance and recovered from her illness. She afterwards composed a song about Duncan's kindness, of which the following is the only verse that now seems to be known :—

> Se nigh'n Alastair Rhuaidh
> A rug a bhuaidh,
> 'S cha be na fuar mhic greananach ;
> Se fear mo ghaoil
> A macan caomh,
> A rinn sa Chaorun eallach dhiam.[1]

It has already been stated[2] that Duncan was killed at Sheriffmuir, where, according to tradition, he fought in command of the Kintail contingent of

---

[1] It was the daughter of Alister Roy (Duncan's maternal grandfather) that brought forth virtue (or blessing) and not cold and surly sons—the man of my love is her gentle son, who took me up as a burden at Caorun.

[2] Page 198.

Seaforth's regiments. Mention has also been made of the stone which he set up at Achnagart as he and his followers were leaving Kintail on that occasion. It is said that in the retreat after the battle he killed seven troopers, one after another, with his claymore, until at last one of them came upon him with a pair of loaded pistols, shot him, and left him for dead on the field.[1] During the night another Kintail man called John Macrae, and commonly known as Ian Mac Fhionnla Mhic Ian Bhuidhe,[2] who had lost his shoes in some marshy ground, and was also severely wounded, revived sufficiently to think of leaving the fatal field under cover of the darkness, and commence the homeward journey. He accordingly began to search among the dead for a pair of shoes. In the course of the search he came upon Duncan, who was still alive and able to speak, and whose voice John immediately recognised. "Oh, Dhonnachaidh bhoc," said John, " 'n tusa tha so, ciod e a thachair riut ? " (O, poor Duncan, is that you ; what has happened to you ?)   " Thug iad a nasgaidh mi le 'n cuid peileiran beag " (They have done for me without any trouble with their little bullets, replied Duncan.)   He then asked for a drink, and John, having no other means

---

1 In *British Battles on Land and Sea*, James Grant, in his description of Sheriffmuir, gives a slightly different account of the death of Duncan Mor. He says that :—"Under Duncan Mor the Macraes made a desperate resist-. ance, and are said to have died almost to a man. During the struggle, and while his people were falling around him, and ere he fell himself, he was frequently seen to wave his reeking sword on high, and heard to shout, " Cobhair ! Cobhair ! an ainm Dhe agus Righ Seumas " (Help ! Help ! in the name of God and King James). Before Duncan fell he slew fifteen with his own hand, which was so much swollen in the hilt of his claymore that it could with difficulty be extricated."

2 Page 256.

of fetching a drink, took one of Duncan's shoes, and
brought it to him full of water. The water revived
him so much that he was able to give John a full
account of his adventures during the battle, but
before the morning dawned Duncan was numbered
among the slain. John lived to accomplish the
homeward journey, and it was he who brought to
Kintail an account of the manner of the death of
Donnacha Mor Mac Alister. There is a tradition in
Kintail that a sketch of Duncan in the battle was
made by one of the officers of the Royalist troops,
and that it was exhibited along with his sword in
the Tower of London.

TRADITIONS ABOUT EONACHAN DUBH.

Eonachan Dubh,[1] Duncan's youngest brother, is also
frequently mentioned in connection with Duncan's
adventures with the Lochaber cattle lifters. It is
related of Eonachan that on one occasion he pursued
a party of Lochaber raiders who had stolen cattle
from Macleod of Glenelg, and recovered the spoil single
handed. As the Glenelg men were returning home
from an unsuccessful pursuit they met Eonachan,
and when they told him where they had been, and
how they had failed to discover any trace of the
raiders, Eonachan volunteered to set out at once,
and alone, in search of them. Late at night he
discovered them in an empty sheiling house, where
they had arranged to take shelter for the night, and
were then roasting a huge piece of beef on a spit

1 Page 210. .

for their supper. Eonachan presented himself as a
benighted traveller, and asked to be allowed to
share the shelter of the hut for the night. This
request was readily granted. After sharing in their
hospitality he entertained them for some time with
his conversation, and at last went out to the door to
see what the night was like. It was very dark, and
as soon as he got outside he shouted to the men
within that the cattle had all gone away. One of
the men then went out to see, but no sooner was he
outside the door than Eonachan, who was prepared
for the occasion, threw his plaid over his head,
knocked him down, and gagged and bound him
before he had time to utter a word. Shortly afterwards another went out to see what had become of
their companion, but Eonachan dealt in the same
manner with him also. After a little time a third man
went out, but only to receive the same treatment as
his companions. There were now only two men left in
the hut, and Eonachan, knowing that he was quite
a match for both of them together, called upon them
to yield, which they did without further resistance.
These two men he gagged and bound also. The
Lochaber men had some guns, which Eonachan
rendered useless by breaking off the stocks. He
then told them to make their way the best they
could, with gagged mouths and bound hands, to
their chief, Lochiel, with Eonachan's compliments.
Having thus disposed of the thieves, he collected
the cattle and drove them back to their owner in
Glenelg.

Eonachan was once on a visit to Brahan Castle,

v

and while talking with the Countess, who had a fire of cinnamon in her room, she asked him if ever he saw such a fine fire as that. " No," replied Eonachan, " the fragrant smell of that fire reaches all the way to the cattle folds of Kintail." " How is that ?" asked the Countess. Eonachan pointed out to her that her extravagant ways had make it necessary for her husband to increase the rents which his Kintail tenants paid for their cattle folds. The Countess took Eonachan's pointed reply in good part and discontinued the cinnamon fires. When Seaforth heard of this he told Eonachan that the Countess insisted on having a fresh ox tongue on her table at dinner every day of the year, and that if Eonachan could cure her of this extravagance, as he had done in the matter of the cinnamon, he should feel deeply indebted to him. Shortly afterwards Eonachan was going to Dingwall with a large herd of cattle, and, as he approached Brahan, he directed his herdsmen to drive three hundred and sixty-five of the cattle past the front of the Castle, in such a way as to make the number appear as large as possible. Having given these instructions, he himself hurried on in advance. When he arrived at the Castle he was kindly welcomed by both Seaforth and his lady. As he sat by one of the windows talking with the lady the herd of cattle began to pass by. "What a very large herd of cattle," remarked the lady. "Not at all," replied Eonachan, "it is only as many as you require for your own dinner in the course of the year." She could not believe that she required so many, and she asked Eonachan what he meant. He explained to her that as she wanted an ox tongue every day for her dinner, and as an ox had only one tongue, it was necessary to kill three hundred and sixty-five oxen every year for her dinner, and that was exactly the number of the herd then passing by.

Eonachan once dreamt that his sister, who was married in Lochaber, was dead. He was so impressed by this dream that he tried to persuade his brothers to go with him to Lochaber to see how she fared. His brothers made light of his fears and refused to go, so he set out alone. When he arrived at his sister's house he found that she was not only dead, but that she was being buried on that same day. He then started after the funeral party, and overtook them as they arrived at the churchyard. Here there arose a dispute as to where she ought to be buried, which greatly annoyed her brother. "What are you disputing about?" said he; "if there is no room in Lochaber for her, there is plenty of room in Kintail; lift the coffin on my back." They did so, thinking he could not carry it very far. For a long time they watched him, expecting every moment to see him lay down his burden, until at last he disappeared over the crest of a hill. They then set out in pursuit of him to recover the body and bring it back to the proper place of burial, but before they could overtake him he accidentally fell in with some men from Kintail, who helped him to carry the body all the way to Kilduich, where it was buried with all due ceremony.

HOW IAN MOR MAC MHAIGHSTER FIONNLA KILLED THE SOLDIERS.

John, son of the Rev. Finlay Macrae of Lochalsh, was considered one of the best swordsmen of his own time in the Highlands. One Sunday, while Mr Finlay was conducting divine service in Lochalsh Church, a party of four or five soldiers came across from Glenelg,[1] and began to plunder his house. While this was going on John, who was returning home from a journey, arrived at an inn above Auchtertyre, and went in to rest. But he had hardly sat down when word reached him of what was going on at his father's house, and, setting out at once with all speed, he overtook the soldiers on the way to their boat with the plunder. He told them to return everything they took, and that they would be allowed to depart without being further interfered with. It so happened, however, that as John was hurrying along to catch the soldiers, one of his garters came undone, and, instead of returning their booty, the soldiers began to make fun of his hose, which had slipped down about his ankle. This was more than John could stand, and falling upon the soldiers with his sword, he killed them one after another before they could reach their boat. The place where the soldiers were buried is still pointed out. It is quite near Lochalsh Parish Church, and is known as Blar nan Saighdear (the Soldiers' Field).

1 The military barracks at Glenelg were built in 1722, but in all probability there were soldiers stationed in that neighbourhood from the time of the battle of Glenshell in 1719 onwards.

A TRADITION OF SHERIFFMUIR.

Many years after the Battle of Sheriffmuir, a Highland drover, who was conducting his herd of cattle to the Southern markets, arrived late one night near a gentleman's house in the Braes of Stirling. The gentleman was a Captain Macdougall, who had fought on the Royalist side at Sheriffmuir. The drover called on the Captain to ask permission to halt with his cattle for the night on the terms which were then usual in such circumstances. The permission was granted, and the Captain being struck by the manner and appearance of the old drover, invited him to pass the night as his guest. The invitation was accepted, and, in the course of conversation, the Captain, learning that his guest was from Kintail, asked him if he knew a place called Corriedhomhain. The drover replied that he did, and the Captain then proceeded to relate the following incident of the Battle of Sheriffmuir : "In the course of the pursuit after the battle," continued the Captain, " I followed a stout Highlander with three well-mounted troopers. The Highlander, perceiving our approach, faced about, took off his plaid, and, carefully folding it, placed it on the ground that by standing on it he might have a firmer footing. My desire being to take him prisoner and not to kill him, we closed upon him with brandishing swords, and commanded him to surrender. This, however, he was not disposed to do, and one of the troopers, approaching too near, had his skull cleft in two by a stroke of the

Highlander's claymore. As another instantly shared a similar fate, the third trooper and myself thought it prudent to keep at a more respectful distance. I was so greatly struck by the Highlander's bearing and swordsmanship that I asked him who he was, but the only information he would give me was that he was from Corriedhomhain, in Kintail." "I know the man as well as I know myself," replied the drover, "his name is Duncan Macrae." "Well then," replied the Captain, "give him my compliments, tell him I commanded the troopers who attacked him in the retreat from Sheriffmuir, that I have ever since been curious to know the name and condition of such an excellent swordsman and brave man, and that I wish him well." "I will do so with much pleasure," replied the drover, who was himself the same Duncan Macrae, of Corriedhomhain, who had fought the four troopers.

This Duncan Macrae, of Corriedhomhain, was known in Kintail as Donnacha Mor nan Creach (Big Duncan of the Spoils). He belonged to a family called Clann a Chruiter (the descendants of the Harper), and said to be descended from a minstrel, probably of Irish origin, who settled in Kintail and adopted the name Macrae. Fionnla Dubh nan Fiadh was of the same tribe.[1]

HOW A KINTAIL MAN WAS INNOCENTLY HANGED BY THE DUKE OF CUMBERLAND.

There was once a lady in Assynt who owned a piece of land which she proposed to give to some neigh-

[1] Page 298.

bouring laird, on condition that he should maintain
her in comfort for the rest of her life.   Seaforth
offered to maintain her in Brahan Castle on the
terms she proposed, but the old lady, preferring to
remain near her own home, rejected Seaforth's offer
and came to terms with Macleod of Assynt.   Seaforth was annoyed at this, and, by way of retaliation,
sent Murdoch Macrae[1] (Murrachadh Mac Fhearachair),
one of his under factors, and Coll Ban Macdonell
of Barisdale, with a party of Kintail men, on a
harrying expedition to Macleod's estates of Assynt.
In the course of their raid they plundered Macleod's
house, and, among other things, they carried away
a web of beautiful tartan.   They also took away two
mares, which were afterwards found and recognised
on the farm of Barisdale.   When Macleod heard of
this he commenced proceedings against Coll of Barisdale for the theft of the horses.   When the trial
came on, the horses were brought to Fort-Augustus
to be identified, and were kept there in the military
stables.   But when it became known to the men of
Kintail, among whom Coll of Barisdale was very
popular, that the horses were being taken to Fort-
Augustus to be used as evidence against him in the
trial, they resolved to make some effort to put the
horses out of the way.   Accordingly, Ian Mor Mac
Mhaighster Fionnla (Big John, son of the Rev.
Finlay), Ian Mac Fhearachair (John, son of Farquhar)
of Morvich, and Donnacha Dubh Mac Dhonnachidh
Mhic Choinnich Mhic Rhuari (Black Duncan, son of

[1] This Murdoch (see page 81) was the father of the Kintail poet, Ian Mac
Mhurachaidh.

Duncan, son of Kenneth, son of Roderick), a Mackenzie of Lochcarron, set out for Fort-Augustus.
Passing through Strathglass, they arrived at Tomich
Inn early in the evening and went to bed.   They
then called the innkeeper to come in to them and
offered him a glass of whisky.   In the morning,
before they got up, they called him in again and
offered him another glass.   This they did that in
the event of any trouble he might be a witness that
they spent the whole night in his house.   But as
soon as the people of the inn retired to rest, the
three visitors quietly got up and set out in all haste
to Fort-Augustus.   They entered the stables by a
hole which they made in the roof, and when they
found Macleod's stolen mares they cut off their
heads, which they took away with them and sank in
Loch Ness.   They then returned to Tomich Inn and
went to bed again before daylight, without having
been missed by the innkeeper or any of his people.
The trial of Coll of Barisdale fell through because
the headless horses could not be identified as Macleod's lost property.

One day, a long time after, Murdoch Macrae was
in Inverness, and had on a pair of hose made out of
Macleod of Assynt's stolen web of tartan.   It so
happened that Macleod was in Inverness on the same
day, and, meeting Murdoch in the street, he recognised the stolen tartan in the hose, and naturally
concluded that Murdoch was one of the Seaforth
party by whom his house had been pillaged.   Macleod resolved to be avenged upon him, and communicated the matter to Macleod of Dunvegan and

Sir Alexander Macdonald of Sleat, both of whom were on the Government side, and there the matter rested for some time. But one night, about a month after the Battle of Culloden, when Murdoch happened to be in the house of Macdonald of Leck, in Glengarry, where a party of the Skye Militia was stationed at the time, he was suddenly seized by a party of soldiers under Macleod of Dunvegan, and sent with a letter from Sir Alexander Macdonald to Lord Loudon, who was then stationed at Fort-Augustus. Loudon sent him to Inverness in charge of an escort of soldiers. On his arrival at Inverness, Murdoch was brought before the Duke of Cumberland, who, at the instigation of Macleod of Assynt, ordered him to be hanged at once as a spy from the Pretender. Murdoch was hanged on an apple tree which grew at the Cross of Inverness, and which immediately afterwards withered. His body, which, after his death, had been stripped naked, was left hanging on the tree for two days, and then buried at the back of the Church.[1] While thus exposed, he is said to have "appeared all the time as if he had been sleeping, his mouth and eyes being shut close—a very uncommon thing in those who die such a death." This execution of a man, believed to have been innocent, appears to have made a deep impression in Inverness. There are several contemporary references to it, and in a poem entitled "The Lament of the Old Cross of Inverness," in 1768, reference is made to the withering of the tree,

[1] For a fuller account of the hanging of Murdoch Macrae, see Charles Fraser-Mackintosh's *Antiquarian Notes*, first series, pp. 206-210.

and Murdoch himself is mentioned "as a man of fame and reputation," who enjoyed the esteem of men of rank and worth, and had never deserted his King or his country.

MACRAE TRADITIONS OF GAIRLOCH.

The early connection between the Macraes and the Mackenzies of Gairloch has been already referred to (pages 9, 10), and some Macrae traditions from Gairloch will be found in Appendix K.

KILDUICH CHURCHYARD, THE ANCIENT BURIAL PLACE OF THE MACRAES.
Bidan Fhuda (Ben Attor) in the Distance.

G. W. Wilson & Co.]

APPENDIX A.

REV. JOHN MACRAE'S ACCOUNT OF THE ORIGIN OF THE MACRAES.

As to the origin of the Macras, tradition tells us of a desperate engagement 'twixt two of the petty Princes of Ireland, in which a certain young man signalized himself by his prowess, defending himself from a particular attack of the enemy, which others, observing, said in Irish words signifying he was a fortunate man if he could award the danger; from whence he was afterwards called Macrath, *i.e.*, the fortunate son.

It is allowed this clan were an ancient race of people in Ireland, and had of old great estates there, have produced eminent men, and are still numerous in that island.

The pronunciation of the name here spelled Macra, varying with the dialect of the country where any of the clan generally reside, has occasioned various ways of spelling this word, as is the case with several others; thus in Ireland they use Macrath and Magrath; in the North of Scotland, Macrah, Macrae, Maccraw, Macrow. In England and the south of Scotland the Mac is left out, from an ill-founded prejudice, and the name Rae, Craw, Crow, and such like, retained as being of the same stock. A more particular account might be had from such as conversed with and have known those historians and genealogists, such as Fergus, Macrourie, Mildonich, Maclean, &c., who were good scholars, and acquainted with the manuscripts and records of Ireland kept for giving an account of the tribes who came from Ireland to Scotland, and became heads of families and chiefs of clans; and from them I heard it confidently said and affirmed, that the Mackenzies, Macleans, and Macraes were of the same people in Ireland. Yea, I heard Sir Allan Maclean of Doward, who was curious and taught in these things, being at Dingwall in the year 1663, say no less,

and it is as certain as tradition and the authorities of the fore-
mentioned antiquaries can make it, that a Macra had his tomb, as
well as Mackenzie and Maclean, in Icolmmbkill, and that close by
one another.   Doctor George Mackenzie, who has wrote a genealogical and historical account of the Mackenzies, mentions that
when Colin Fitzgerald came from Ireland in the year 1263, a
number of the Macras were of his party at the battle of Largs, in
Ayrshire, which, it is natural to think, was in consequence of a
friendly attachment then known to have been 'twixt their ancestors,
as is since continued 'twixt their descendants.   But whether
thére were any Macras before then in Scotland I cannot determine,
only that tradition says there were some of them on the estate of
Lovat, when the Bizets were lords of that place, which titles and
estate they forfeited and lost, according to Buchanan, in the
following manner:—Anno. 1242.—King Alexander the Second, with
many of the nobility, being at Haddington, Patrick Cuming, Earl
of Athole, his lodging was burnt in the night time, and he, with
two of his servants, perished in the flames.   This fire was judged
not to be accidental, and because of an enmity 'twixt him and
William Bizet, nephew to King William The Lyon, and eldest son
of John Bizet, the first Lord Lovat of that name, the suspicion was
fixed upon him.   William endeavoured to exculpate himself by
offering to prove his being in Forfar the night of the burning, and
also offered to vindicate himself by combat, as the custom then
was.   But neither would do, so that he was summoned criminally
to a certain day, when, finding the interest and power of his
adversaries too great for him, or being conscious of his own accession to the crime, he did not appear, so was sentenced and forfeited,
but, by reason of his connection with the Royal Family, the King
gave him a reprieve, with liberty to go to Ireland, where he had
an estate in a place called Glenns of Glenmores, the rents of
which estate were on certain occasions before this forfeiture collected by persons sent on purpose from the estate of Lovat, as
they were in like manner sent to raise the rents of Glenelg when
in possession of this family.

The ruin of this William Bizet did not satisfy the Cumings.
They level next at his brother, John, Lord Lovat, who, by his own
folly, hastened what they desired, for in the next year, 1243, he
joined Macdonald in his rebellion against the King, and when

Macdonald was forced to return to the Isles, the King commanded the Earl of Ross to apprehend John Bizet, Lord Lovat, which he, having heard, went and lurked in Achterlies, but a price being set on his head, he was taken by George Dempster of Moorhouse in the wood of Achterlies, and sent to the King, by whom he was sentenced and forfeited, but was reprieved, as was his brother William, with liberty to go to Ireland.   This John Bizet had no children but three daughters, on whom the King bestowed the estates as their portions because of their relation to the Royal family—Agnes, the daughter of King William the Lyon, being the mother of this John. The eldest daughter, Mary, with the greatest part of the lordship of Lovat and title of Lord Lovat, was given by the King to Sir Simon Fraser of Kinnel, second son of Alexander Fraser of Tweedale, Anno. 1247.   Elizabeth, the second daughter, was married to Andreas Aboses of Spitewood, and Cecilia, the youngest, to William Lord Fenton, whose portion of the estate with her was the Braes of the Aird, Ercliss, Strathglass, Buntaite, Guisachan, and Glenelg, all which fell in again to the next Lord Fraser of Lovat with Janet, daughter to Lord Fenton, Anno. 1279.

When I lived at Kilmorack, in the year 1672, a strong wind having cast down the top stone of the easter gable of the Kirk of Beauly, it fell on the altar and broke to pieces, whereof I laid most together, and found the letters M. B., supposed to be the initials of Mary Bizet, raised on it in large letters.   She was thought to have caused build or at least finish this gable and side walls adjoining the length of St Catherine and St Cross' Chapels.

In the year 1249, King Alexander the Second died, and William and John Bizet having gone to Ireland and settled their families there, their three brothers, Walter, Malcom, and Leonard, who lived in Killiechuimen and Abertarff, finding the Bizets greatly hated, followed them to Ireland.

All this time the Macras continued on the lordship of Lovat, and Mary Bizet having been fostered in the house of Macra of Clunes, had a kindness for him, and a deference to his counsel and advices, which was a means of bringing him to the favour of her husband, Simon, the first Lord Fraser of Lovat, and from him continued 'twixt their successors till the Macras removed.   Nor was it afterwards forgot, as will appear in the sequel.

The Macras were faithful and serviceable adherents of the family, an instance of which was thus :—There was in Ardmeanach about this time a man of numerous kindred and followers called Loban, agnamed Gilligorm, who had a claim or quarrel against the family of Lovat, and in their repeated attacks, and while Lord Lovat was frequently from home and at Court, the Macras opposed them valiantly and with open hostility. But the second or third Lord Fraser of Lovat, judging it for his interest to put an end to so troublesome a quarrel, brought from the south country twenty-four gentlemen of his name, some of whose posterity, as I'm informed, live yet in the Aird. With these and the Macras, and such others as he could get and thought necessary, he marches directly against Gilligorm, who, with all the forces he could make ready, were prepared to receive him, and after some proposals of peace made and rejected, did in end engage in set fight upon the Moor of Drimderfit, above Kessock, called since, from the dismal effects of that fight, Drimdeair, *i.e.*, the Ridge of Tears.

Both parties fought resolutely, and Gilligorm being killed, his kindred and followers were almost totally cut off.[1] Lovat carried away the spoil, and Gilligorm's relict, who was with child, and thought was related to the family of Lovat, where it was resolved, if she would bring forth a male child, he should be destroyed lest he should remember and revenge his father's death. But by the time she was delivered, and that of a son, humanity prevailed over their first intended cruelty so far as that they were satisfied with having his back broken that he might not be a man of arms. He was given to the monks of Beauly to be taught and learned there. He made a good progress, and, coming to perfect age, entered into Orders and became a priest, and was called Croter or Cratach Mac Gilligorm. He travelled to the West Coast and the Isle of Skye. He laid the foundation of, and built the church of Kilmore, in Slate, and of Kilichoinen, in Glenelg, and though he lived about the time of Pope Innocent the Third, who possessed the Chair in the beginning of the 13th century, he did not observe his decree against the marriage of the clergy, for this Pope was the first who made that law, and although before his

[1] In a note added to a transcript copy of the Rev. John Macrae's MS., in 1785, it is stated that there were several cairns of stones then on the site of the battle, and that the largest of them was believed to mark the grave of Gilligorm himself.

time many churchmen did abstain from marriage and led a single life, yet it was free for any churchman of the Superior or Inferior Order to marry, as appears by the story of St Hylaric. He was Bishop of Poictiers, in France, and having gone to the East to reform the Arian Heresy, heard that a young nobleman treated with his daughter, Abra, for marriage, he wrote to his daughter not to accept of the offer, since he had provided for her a far better husband. The daughter obeyed, and before he returned the father prayed that his daughter might die quietly, wherein God heard his prayer, which, when his wife, her mother, understood, she never ceased importune him till she obtained the like favour, as Baptista Mantuanns writes of him.

But, to return to Croter MacGilligorm; he did not, I say, observe the Pope's said decree, but married and had children ; and in memory of Finanus, then a renowned saint, called one of his sons Gillifinan, usually pronounced Gillinan, the letters turning quiescent in the compound, and the son of that man again was patronimically called MacGillinan, whose successors are now in the North of Scotland called Maclinans.

Now, to compensate for this long and, perhaps you may think, needless digression, there are two vulgar errors discovered. The first is that the battle of Drumderfit was fought 'twixt the Macras and Maclinans, and that Lovat had sent his men only to assist the Macras, whereas there were not such a race of men then in being as Maclinans, and what the Macras did was only as followers of Lord Lovat. The other error is that the Macras came to Kintail as soon as Colin Fitzgerald, of whom the Mackenzies are descended, which cannot hold, as Simon, the first Fraser Lord Lovat, married Mary Bizet, Anno. 1247, which was but nineteen years before Colin Fitzgerald got his charter of Kintail from the King, Anno. 1266 ; and the Macras, living on the Lordship of Lovat, during the time at least of three Lords of that name, cannot be supposed to have come to Kintail till a considerable time thereafter. But why or how the Macras removed so totally from the Lordship of Lovat and from Urquhart, where, being in alliance with the Macleans, they likewise possessed several lands, is not at this distance of time easily accounted for, especially as it was never known that there was any misunderstanding betwixt Lovat or his friends and them. On the contrary such of the Macras as lived in the neighbourhood of the Frasers still kept up a good and friendly correspondence, and Lovat likewise had a grateful remembrance of their good services and fidelity to him and his family, so that we may conclude they did not remove at once, but at different times, as circumstances favoured them."

The Rev. John Macrae then proceeds to give an account of the migration of the Macraes to Kintail. This account is summarised in Chapter I.

THE MACLENNANS OF KINTAIL.

The name Maclennan (in Gaelic Mac Gillinnein), the traditional origin of which is incidentally given in the above extract, means son of the servant of Finnan. St Finnan, who flourished about A.D. 575, was a native of Ireland, and one of the companions of St Columba. Others derive the name Maclennan from Mac Gille Adhamhnain. Adamnan, who became Abbot of Iona in 679, was the author of a famous life of St Columba. The first derivation, which is the one given by the Rev. John Macrae in the above extract, seems the more probable,[1] though the name of Adamnan appears in so many different forms that it is difficult to say what names may or may not be derived from it. The Maclennans were at one time numerous in Kintail, and tradition has preserved the name of Domhnull Buidhe Mac Gillinnein as one of the chief of the Kintail warriors in the feud with Glengarry. There is a well-known tradition that eighteen of the chief Maclennans of Kintail were killed in the Battle of Auldearn, in 1645, and that their widows were afterwards married by Macraes, who thus acquired possession of the Maclennan holdings, and so became the leading name in Kintail. But it is a tradition that has no trace of any foundation in fact. We have full contemporary accounts of the Battle of Auldearn, where only four Kintail men were killed, two Maclennans and two Macraes, viz.:—Roderick Maclennan, called Ruari Mac Ian Dhomh'uill Bhain, the chief standard-bearer of Kintail; his brother, Donald Maclennan; Malcolm Macrae,[2] son-in-law of the Rev. Farquhar Macrae; and Duncan Macrae, called Donnacha Mac Ian Oig.[3] It had been arranged before the battle that Sea-

1 See Macbain's Gaelic Dictionary.   2 Page 68.   3 Page 187.

forth, who was ostensibly fighting against Montrose, but had already resolved to change sides, should withdraw his men without fighting. But the men themselves were not aware of this, and consequently, when they received the order to retreat, many of them refused to do so. Maclennan, the standard-bearer, indignant at the thought that the banner which had so often been victorious should flee in his hands, fixed the staff in the ground, and stood by it with his two-handed sword drawn. A number of Seaforth's men rallied round him and refused to surrender until the brave standard-bearer was shot. Several others were killed during this incident, but only the above-mentioned four were from Kintail.

There is a tradition that when Colin, first Earl of Seaforth, built Brahan Castle and fixed his residence there, most of the Maclennans left Kintail and settled in the neighbourhood of Seaforth's new home.[1] This is not at all improbable, as the name Maclennan was, and still is, fairly common in the country round about Brahan. There are only a few Maclennans mentioned in the Rent Rolls given in Appendix H, so that at that time they could not have occupied a very important position in Kintail. We are told that there were several Maclennans in Glensheil about 1790, and that though there were many points of difference between themselves and the Macraes, yet they were always ready to join the Macraes in defence of their common country against every foe.[2]

[1] Tradition communicated to the author by Mr Alexander Maclennan, Craig House, Lochcarron.

[2] Old Statistical Accounts of Kintail and Glensheil.

W

APPENDIX B.

THE following account of Gregory, or, as he is called in The Prophecy of St Berchan, Grig the Mac Rath, a contemporary of Alfred the Great, and one of the greatest of the early Kings of Scotland, is abridged from Chronicles of the Scots, edited by William Forbes Skene, LL.D. :—

The Prophecy of St Berchan consists of two Irish manuscripts, written probably about the time of Donald Bane, who was King of Scotland from 1093 to 1098. It contains a list of Kings of Scotland from Kenneth Macalpin to Donald Bane in the form of a prophecy attributed to St Berchan, who lived towards the end of the seventh century. The names of the kings are concealed under epithets, and Grig, the son of Dungal, who reigned during the last quarter of the ninth century, is called Mac Rath. The following is a translation of some of the parts of the prophecy which refer to him :—

> Till the Mac Rath shall come,
> He shall sit over Alban as sole chief ;
> Low was Britain in his time,
> High was Alban of melodious cities.

> Pleasant is it to my heart and body,
> My spirit relates good to me,
> As King the Mac Rath in the Eastern land,
> Under ravenous misfortune to Alban.

> Seventeen years of warding valour,
> In the sovereignty of Alban ;
> There shall be slaves to him in the house—
> Saxons, Galls, and Britons.

Grig founded a church among the Picts of Maghcircin (or Mearns).

Long afterwards there was a church in Mearns dedicated to St
Cyricus, and called in old charters Ecclesgreig (Grig's Church).
Grig and St Cyricus were probably not the same, but they appear
to have been in some way connected.

In the Chronicle of the Scots and Picts we find the following
entry :—

Grig Mac Dungal xii annos regnavit et mortuus est in
Dundurn et sepultus est in Iona insula.   Hic subjugavit sibi
totam Yberniam et fere totam Angliam et hic primus dedit
libertatem ecclesiac Scoticanae que sub servitute erat usque ad
illud tempus ex consuetudine et more Pictorum.[1]

After a reign, variously stated from eleven to eighteen years, of
great prosperity and dutiful devotion to the interests of the Church,
Gregory is said to have been slain in battle at Dundurn, which,
according to Skene, was situated somewhere about the east end of
Lochearn, but as a matter of fact, the place and manner of his
death, as well as the date of it, are somewhat uncertain.   The
time in which he lived is roughly fixed by a great eclipse of the
sun, which, according to the Pictish Chronicle, occurred in the
ninth year of his reign.   The eclipse is known to have occurred
on the 16th June, 885.   This, so far as known, is the earliest
recorded instance of the name Mac Rath in Scotland.   He was
a Son of Grace in his devotion to the Christian Church, and
he was also a Son of Fortune in his wars with the neighbouring
tribes, as well as with the Danes, whom he drove out of his kingdom.   Though he was nominally King of Scotland, his actual rule
was probably limited to the countries round about Scone, in Perthshire, which was the Capital of those early Scottish Kings, and it is
interesting to note that the name Mac Rath appears to have been
somewhat common in that part of Perthshire in the fourteenth
and fifteenth centuries.   Gregory is also said to have built the
city of Aberdeen.

[1] " Grig, son of Dungal, reigned twelve years and died at Dundurn, and
was buried in the Island of Iona.   He subdued to himself Ireland and nearly
all England, and he first gave freedom to the Scottish Church, which until
that time was in servitude according to the constitution and custom of the
Picts."   There is some reason to believe that he invaded the Kingdom of
Northumbria, which at this time was harassed by the Danes, but there does
not appear to be any foundation for the statement with regard to Ireland.

The following legend is from the Dean of Lismore's Book :—
On one occasion Fionn and six of the chief princes were all
drinking together at Alvie. They were accompanied by their
wives, and as the cup circulated and took effect the women began
to talk among themselves of their chastity. No women on earth
could be more chaste than they. While this talk was going on a
maid was seen approaching the company. Her covering was a
single scamless robe of spotless white from end to end. Fionn
asked what virtue was there in her seamless robe. She replied—
"My seamless robe has the strange power, that such women as are
not chaste can find no shelter in its folds. It shields none but the
spotless wife." The princes then insisted that their wives, each
one in her turn, should try on the seamless robe. They did so, but
the robe would not fit them or spread out over them or cover their
persons. "Give my wife the seamless robe," said M'Raa,[1] "for I
have no fear as to the result." M'Raa's wife took the robe, which
fitted her and spread over her so easily that no part of her person
remained exposed.

[1] The name is so spelled in the original text ; in the English translation it
is rendered MacRea. It has been questioned on competent authority whether
this is the same as the modern name Macrae.

APPENDIX C.

"At Ballachulish, in Lochaber, upon the eighth day of October, one thousand seven hundred and two years, it is condescended and agreed to betwixt the parties following, viz.:—George Campbell of Craignish, on the one part, and Farquhar Macra of Inverinate ; Master Donald Macra, minister of the Gospel, in Kintail ; Donald Macra of Camusluiny ; John Macra, in Achyark ; Duncan Macra, son of Christopher Macra, in Ariyugan ; and Kenneth Macra, brother german to the said Farquhar Macra of Inverinate, all in Kintail, in name and behalf of the hail remnant, gentlemen and others of the said name of Ra, in Kintail and elsewhere, lineally descended of their forbearers and predecessors on the other part ; that is to say—Forasmuch as the said George Campbell of Craignish, and the saids Farquhar, Mr Donald, Donald, John, Duncan, and Kenneth Macras, have at date hereof seriously considered what relation, firm friendship, and correspondence has been of old and hitherto continued betwixt the Campbells of Craignish, the said George Campbell, now of Craignish, his predecessors, and the forebearers and predecessors of the said Farquhar Macra of Inverinate, and others above written, and all others of the said name of Ra, and the great love and favour each of them did bear to other, both by the said George Campbell of Craignish and his predecessors, taking the part of any of the said name of Macra, in all lawful causes, defending the samen against others when occasion required, and the firm, stable, and sure love and favour the said Farquhar Macra and others foresaid, of the said name of Macra, and their predecessors, did and doth bear to the said George Campbell of Craignish and his predecessors, and the acts of kindness and friendship done by the said name of Macra to the said family of Craignish, when occasion offered, in all time bygone. And now for the more firm and sure upholding and maintaining of the said relationship, friendship, and correspondence, and for the better keeping and preserving the samen on record, in all time coming, the said George Campbell of Craignish, by their presents, binds and obliges him, his heirs and successors, to maintain, and in hand take the part of any of the said name of Macra in all lawful causes, and defend the samen, to the uttermost of their power, against any other person, their duty to Her Majesty and Her Highness' successors and Council, and their immediate lawful superiors, alwise excepted. And sicklike the saids Farquhar Macra, Mr Donald, Donald, John, Duncan, and Kenneth Macra, in name and behalf foresaid, for them, their heirs, and all others lineally descending of their bodies, by their presents, binds and obliges them and their foresaids, so far as they may do by law, to own, maintain, and in hand take the part of the said George Campbell of Craignish or his foresaids, or any others lineally descending of his family, in all lawful causes, and defend any of the said family, to the utmost of their power, against all other person or persons, their duty to Her Majesty and Her Highness' successors and Council, and their immediate lawful superiors, all is excepted. And both the said parties obliges them and their foresaids to renew and reiterate their presents, as oft as they will be required thereto, that the samen may be kept in record and memory ad futuram rei memoriam.

"In testimony hereof (written by John Campbell, younger of Balmillin), both parties have subscribed their presents, place, day, month, and year, foresaid, before these witnesses :— Ronald Campbell of Lagganlochta ; Ronald Campbell, brother german to the said George Campbell of Craignish ; Archibald Campbell, merchant in Kilvoran, in Islay ; and the said John Campbell, writer hereof.

(Signed)	" Geo. Campbell.	Farqr. Macra.
	" Mr Dond. Macrah.	D. Mackra.
	" John Macrah.	Dun. Macra.
	" Ken. Macra.	

| " Ron. Campbell, Witness. | Ron. Campbell, Witness. |
| " Arch. Campbell, Witness. | J. Campbell, Witness." |

FAC-SIMILE OF SIGNATURES TO THE BOND OF FRIENDSHIP.

APPENDIX D.

THE two regiments now linked together as the Seaforth High-landers are the 72nd Highlanders (the Duke of Albany's Own Highlanders) and the 78th Highlanders (the Ross-shire Buffs). The 72nd, now the First Battalion of the Seaforth Highlanders, was raised by Kenneth, Earl of Seaforth. It was inspected and passed at Elgin on the 15th of May, 1778, and was numbered the 78th. In 1786 it was re-numbered the 72nd, and in 1822 received the additional name of The Duke of Albany's Own Highlanders, Albany being the second title of the Duke of York, then the Commander-in-Chief of the British Army. It is usually stated that this regiment was recruited largely from the Macraes, but an examination of the muster roll of the men who were inspected and passed in Elgin in May, 1778, shows that although there were several Macraes among them, yet they formed but a small proportion of the whole regiment. The Ross-shire names on the roll are comparatively few, and so far as can be judged from names, the recruits might have been brought together from all parts of the United Kingdom. The majority were in all proba-bility Highlanders, and the Macraes became so prominent in this regiment, not because of their number, but because of the part they took as ringleaders in the Mutiny, which is known as "The Affair of the Macraes."

From Elgin the regiment proceeded to Edinburgh, where it was ordered to be kept in readiness to embark for India. During their sojourn in Edinburgh, many of the men were billeted in the Canongate and other parts of the city, and among them there arose a rumour that the regiment had been sold to the East

India Company. But this was not the only grievance. The bounty money promised, and also their pay, were in arrears, and the result was that on Tuesday, the 22nd of September, 1778, when the regiment assembled, and were about to proceed to Leith to embark there, a large number of men refused to march until their grievances were attended to. The officers were insulted and stoned by the populace, who were in complete sympathy with the men. A scene of great confusion ensued, and, notwithstanding Seaforth's efforts to allay the mutinous feeling by promising that their demands should be complied with as soon as possible, five hundred Highlanders shouldered their arms, set off at a quick pace, with pipes playing and two plaids fixed on poles for colours, to Arthur's Seat, where they took up a position of such natural strength that, with the arms of those days, it would be no easy matter to compel them to surrender. Here they remained for some days, being liberally supplied with food and even ammunition by the people of Edinburgh and Leith, among whom they had many sympathisers. They appointed officers, and placed sentries in regular order, so that any attempt to surprise them was seen to be clearly hopeless. Two accidents occurred among them. One man was killed by falling over a rock, and another man, who was accidentally shot through the thigh, was removed to the Royal Infirmary. Meantime the authorities were assembling a considerable force in the city, but at the same time efforts were being made to induce the mutineers to come to terms. On the second day, General Skene, who was second in command in Scotland, visited them, but they insisted on their former conditions, and the dismissal of certain officers. On the third day they were visited by the Duke of Buccleuch, Lord Dunmore, Lord Macdonald, and several gentlemen and clergymen, but with the same result. On the next day, however, a settlement was arrived at, and the following conditions were accepted by them, viz. :—A general pardon for all that had passed ; that all arrears should be paid before embarkation ; and that they should never be sent to the East Indies. These are the conditions as stated in the newspapers of the day, but it is quite possible the third condition may have been that they were not to be disposed of to the East India Company, as they readily sailed to India three years afterwards. The conditions were signed by the Duke of Buccleuch, Lord Dunmore,

Sir Adolphus Stoughton, Commander-in-Chief for Scotland, and General Skene, second in command in Scotland.

On Friday, the 25th of September, at 11 a.m., they marched down from Arthur Seat, headed by Lord Dunmore, and assembled in St Anne's Yard, near Holyrood, where they were addressed by General Skene, who gave them some good advice, and promised that a Court would be held next day to inquire into the complaints against some of the officers. These complaints were pronounced by the Court to be without foundation, but not one of the mutineers received punishment of any kind. After the meeting in St Anne's Yard, the men were billeted in the suburbs of Edinburgh, and on the following Monday they embarked at Leith.

This amicable settlement did not give satisfaction to all the officers, some of whom blamed Lord Dunmore for acting as he did on behalf of the mutineers, and urged the necessity of severe measures as the only guarantee for the maintenance of discipline. The public, however, applauded the wisdom and prudence of the reconciliation, as there was a general feeling that the mutineers were not without some real grievances. Several disturbances of a similar nature had recently taken place in the Highland regiments, and all about breaches of the conditions of enlistment. It is quite possible that, in the anxiety to gain recruits, promises were sometimes made which could not easily be fulfilled; but the fact that the disputes were frequently about arrears of pay, which the Government were well able to afford, shows an inexcusable carelessness with regard to one of the most practical of all the conditions of employment. And when, in addition to these grievances, the men had to serve under officers who neither knew their language nor appreciated their character, it can easily be understood that their lot was not always free from provocation.[1]

---

[1] "A Highland regiment, to be orderly and well disciplined, ought to be commanded by men who are capable of appreciating their character, directing their passions and prejudices, and acquiring their entire confidence and affection. The officer to whom the command of Highlanders is entrusted must endeavour to acquire their confidence and good opinion. With this view he must watch over the propriety of his own conduct. He must observe the strictest justice and fidelity in his promises to his men, conciliate them by an attention to their disposition and prejudices, and at the same time by pre-

Of these disturbances, "The Affair of the Macraes" was by far the most formidable, and had it not been so wisely and so judiciously settled, it might have had a very disastrous effect on the efforts being then made to recruit the army from the Highlands. It showed once for all that Highland soldiers meant to insist at whatever cost upon being dealt with in good faith, and henceforth we hear less about breaches of the conditions of enlistment.

The idea of sending the regiment to India was for a time abandoned, and from Leith they sailed to Jersey and Guernsey, where they were stationed for some time to resist any attempt at invasion by the French. In 1781 they proceeded to India, accompanied by the Earl of Seaforth as their Colonel. The voyage, which lasted from the 12th June, 1781, to the 2nd April, 1782, proved a disastrous one. Illness broke out among the men, and before they arrived at St Helena, to their utter dismay, their Colonel died. His death had a most depressing effect upon the men, of whom no fewer than two hundred and forty-seven died before they reached India. Traditions of this disastrous voyage still survive in Kintail. The subsequent career of the 72nd Highlanders is a matter of history, which it is not necessary to repeat here.

The 78th Highlanders (the Ross-shire Buffs), now the Second Battalion of the Seaforth Highlanders, was raised by Francis, Earl of Seaforth. It was inspected and passed at Fort-George in July, 1793, and proceeded to Jersey and Guernsey. The following year another battalion was raised, which was inspected and passed at Fort-George in June, and received the distinctive name of the "Ross-shire Buffs." From the Channel Islands, the first battalion went on active service to Holland, while the second battalion proceeded at once to the Cape of Good Hope, and took part in the capture of the Colony from the Dutch. In 1796 it

---

serving a firm and steady authority, without which he will not be respected. Officers who are accustomed to command Highland soldiers find it easy to guide and control them when their full confidence has been obtained, but when mistrust prevails, severity ensues, with a consequent neglect of duty, and by a continuance of this unhappy misunderstanding the men become stubborn, disobedient, and in the end mutinous.—*Sketches of the Highlanders, by Major-General David Stewart of Garth.*

was joined by the first battalion, and the two battalions, incorporated into one, proceeded to India, where the regiment saw -much service before it returned home again in 1817. In 1804 another second battalion was raised. This battalion fought with great distinction at the battle of Maida, in Italy, in 1806. The next year it was in Egypt, and suffered very heavily at El Hamet. It saw some further arduous service in Holland, and was incorporated with the other battalion of the Ross-shire Buffs in 1817. The subsequent history of the Ross-shire Buffs is well known. A large number of Macraes from Kintail served in each of these three battalions.

The 72nd and the 78th (Ross-shire Buffs) were linked together in 1881 as the Seaforth Highlanders.

APPENDIX E.

KINTAIL.

THE old parish of Kintail, including Glensheil, which was made into a separate parish by the Lords Commissioners of Teinds on the 30th December, 1726, is situated in the south-west of the County of Ross. A considerable portion of its boundary runs along the sea coast, its inland boundaries being the parishes of Lochalsh, Kilmorack, Kiltarlity, Kilmonivaig, and Glenelg. The present parish of Kintail is about eighteen miles long, and varying in breadth from five to six miles. Glensheil is about twenty-six miles long, and from two to six miles in breadth. The combined area of the two parishes is rather more than two hundred square miles, a great portion of which consists of moorland and mountain. From the sea coast the country opens up in three large valleys or glens—Glenelchaig, Glenlic, and Glensheil. These glens are surrounded by steep and lofty mountains, which are frequently covered with green pasture from base almost to summit. The richness of its pastures was no doubt the reason why, in the pastoral age of the Highlands, Kintail was so noted for its cattle. It was often called Cintaille nam Bo (Kintail of the cows), and, needless to say, was one of the happy hunting grounds of the cattle lifters of Lochaber. The natural pastoral richness of the country helped also to rear a race of men who, according to all accounts, were at least as robust in mind and body, and as well favoured as any of their neighbours. The men of Kintail were usually of good physique and strong, full features.[1] They had large chests and deep voices, and in mimick-

---

[1] There are some excellent representations of Kintail faces in Benjamin West's painting of the rescue of King Alexander III. from the fury of a stag by Colin Fitzgerald, the reputed founder of the House of Kintail, the original of which is in Brahan Castle. See also page 104.

ing the speech of a Kintail man in Gaelic it is still the custom to adopt as deep a tone of voice as possible. In an old Gaelic song they are spoken of as, " Fir ghearra dhonna Chintaille " (the thick-set auburn-haired men of Kintail). They were known among their neighbours as Na Doimhich, which may mean either the bulky ones, or the barrels, while the Lochaber men were usually called —at all events in Kintail—Na Fir Chaola, which means the lean or sharp-featured men.

The earliest glimpses we get of the history of Kintail comes to us, as in the case of most Highland parishes, through legends connected with some of the early Scottish Saints, and two at least of the contemporaries of Columba, St Oran[1] and St Donan,[2] have left traces of their names in the country. Scururan, or Oran's Peak, is the highest and most prominent of the mountains of Kintail, and near the foot of it is a place called Achyuran, or Oran's field, while the small island on which the ruins of the stronghold of the Barons of Kintail still stand is called Ellandonan, or Donan's Island. So far as at present known, not even a legend has survived to explain what connections those two Saints may have had with the country, but that they were connected in some way with the places which bear their names, may be regarded as extremely probable.

About the middle of the seventh century the country was visited by an Irish Saint called Congan. He was a son of the King of Leinster, and was trained as a soldier. On succeeding to his father's dominions he ruled well, but was unfortunate in war with his enemies, and having been wounded and conquered, he

[1] Oran, a well-born Irishman, came to Iona with Columba. When Oran arrived, Columba told him that whoever willed to die first should not only go more quietly to Christ, but should confirm and ratify the right of the community to the Island by taking corporal possession of it. Oran consented, whereupon Columba not only assured him of eternal happiness, but said that none who came to pray at his own sepulchre should receive his petition till he had first prayed at Oran's. Oran was thus the first man to be buried in Iona There are many traces of Oran's name to be met with in the West Highlands. Columba came to Iona in A.D. 563.

[2] Donan was also a disciple of Columba. He founded a Monastery in the Island of Eigg, where he was put to death, together with his community of about fifty persons, by a band of pirates, probably Picts from the neighbouring mainland, on the 17th of April, A.D. 617.

was forced to flee from his native country. Taking with him his sister Kentigerna and her three sons, one of whom was the celebrated St Fillan, he sailed for Scotland, and eventually settled in Lochalsh, where he led a religious and ascetic life, and lived to an old age. He is said to have died in Lochalsh, and to have been buried in Iona. St Fillan afterwards built a Church in Lochalsh, and dedicated it to his uncle Congan. It was called in Gaelic, Kilchoan, that is, St Congan's Church, and stood very near the present site of the Parish Church.

St Fillan, whose name is associated with Kintail, flourished early in the eighth century. He was the son of an Irish nobleman called Feradach, by Kentigerna, sister of St Congan, and fled with his uncle from Ireland to Lochalsh, as already stated. The chief scene of this Saint's labour, however, was in Perthshire, but tradition says that, in addition to the church he built in Lochalsh, he built another at Kilellan (Fillan's Church), in Kintail, which, as the name implies, was called after himself. There is a burying-place still at Kilellan, and there is a local tradition that St Fillan himself was buried there. It is said that, when he felt his end was drawing near, he went to Iona, and there died, kneeling before the high altar. His body was then sent in a birlinn or galley to Kintail, and buried at Kilellan under a sod that had been brought from Iona.

The next Saint whose name enters prominently into the traditions of Kintail is St Duthac, to whom the old Parish Church at Kilduich was dedicated. He was Bishop of Ross, and flourished about the middle of the thirteenth century. His name is associated more especially with Tain, which in Gaelic is called Baille Dhuthich, that is, Duthac's Town. The Kintail tradition is that Farquhar Mac an t' Shagairt, Earl of Ross, who founded the Abbey of Fearn, and died in 1257, sent two Irish monks to Kintail to minister to the spiritual wants of the people. One of these was Duthac, who had charge of the north side of Lochduich, which has ever since been so called after him. The other monk was called Carrac, and had charge of the south side. The two monks used to meet together from time to time at the west end of the Loch. On one occasion, at the time of driving their cattle to the Sheiling, they arranged that on the way they should hold a meeting at the usual place, but when Duthac arrived there he found Carrac lying dead on the knoll where they used to meet, and which still bears Carrac's name.   Duthac was so grieved at the death of his friend that he did not care to live in Kintail any longer.   It was then he went to Tain, where, we are told, he "taught publicly with all gentleness," and became noted for his miraculous powers.   His day was celebrated on the 8th of March, and his shrine at Tain became a famous resort for pilgrims.   How far these Kintail legends may have any foundation in fact it is, of course, impossible to say.   The legend of the death and burial of St Fillan, probably refers to some other ecclesiastic who may have been connected with the old church at Kilellan, but the name of St Fillan was such an honoured one in Kintail[1] that it would not be surprising if legends of other saints gradually gathered around it.   There is no reason to believe that St Fillan was buried in Kintail.   There were other early Celtic ecclesiastics of the name Fillan, but they do not appear to have been connected with Kintail.   Some trace of another Saint survives in the place name, Killechuinard,[2] on the south side of Lochduich, where the remains of some ruins and of a disused burial-place are still to be seen, but of their history nothing appears to be known beyond a vague tradition that a monastery once stood there.

The stronghold of Ellandonan, around which most of the history of Kintail centres, is believed to have been built in the time of Alexander II.,[3] who reigned from 1214 to 1249, as a place

[1] Page 291.

[2] It is difficult to say which Saint it was whose name is here preserved. A certain Cyneheard was Bishop of Winchester from 754 to 780, and there is some record also of a Scottish Monk or Abbot called Kineard, who visited Gaul with the great British scholar, Alcuin, about the end of the eighth century, and wrote a life of Charlemagne.   It is more likely, however, that Cille-Chuinard means the Church of Donort, which in Gaelic would be Cille-Dhoinort, and would be pronounced almost exactly the same as Cille Chuinard. Donort was Abbot of the great Celtic Monastery of Murthlac, in Banffshire, from about 1056 to 1098.   According to some authorities, there was for some time a Diocese of Murthlac, of which Donort was Bishop.   It is on record that at the beginning of the twelfth century King David I. of Scotland gave to the newly-formed Bishopric of Aberdeen five churches which had been founded by the missionary zeal of the Monks of Murthlac, and which had belonged to their monastery.   It is quite possible that one of those churches, dedicated to Donort, may have stood on the spot now known as Killechuinard.

[3] See page 293 for the Kintail legend of the Building of Ellandonan Castle.

of defence against the Danes.   At that time Kintail formed part
of the Earldom of Ross, and is said to have been inhabited by
three different tribes—the Mac Beolans, who inhabited Glensheil
and the south side of Lochduich and Lochalsh, as far as Kylerea ;
the Mac Ivors, who inhabited Glenlic ; and the Mac Thearlichs,
who inhabited Glenelchaig.[1]   Sometime during the latter part of
the thirteenth century, the Earl of Ross appointed a kinsman of
his own, called Kenneth, to the government of Ellandonan Castle,
which is said to have been garrisoned by a number of Macraes and
Maclennans.   Kenneth was an able and ambitious man, and,
having quarrelled with the Earl of Ross, whom he set at defiance
during the unsettled times which followed the death of King
Alexander III., in 1286, he succeeded in establishing himself in a
position of independence as lord and ruler of Kintail.   It is said
that he ruled well, and that his influence was felt over most of the
Western Isles.   He died in 1304, and was buried in Iona.   He
was the founder of the great Clan Mackenzie, and from him they
derive their name. [2]   The Earls of Ross, however, still continued
superiors of the lands of Kintail, as part of their Earldom, and the
Mackenzies occupied the lands and the Castle as their vassals for
about two hundred years.   King Robert Bruce confirmed to the
Earl of Ross all his lands, including Borealis Ergadia, that is,
North Argyle, as the west of Ross, Lochalsh and Kintail included,
was then called.   We find many other references to the over-
lordship of the Earls of Ross until 1463, when Alexander Mackenzie, sixth of Kintail, obtains a charter direct from the Crown.

Meantime we find various contemporary references to the
circumstances and affairs of Kintail.   In 1331, Randolph, Earl of
Moray, who was then Warden of Scotland, despatched a Crown
officer to Ellandonan to prepare the Castle for his reception and
to arrest misdoers.   Fifty of these misdoers were put to death,
and their heads were exposed on the top of the Castle walls.
As Randolph sailed up towards the Castle in his barge
and saw those heads, he declared, in his zeal for the cause
of law and order, that he loved better to look upon them
then than on any garland of roses he had ever seen.[3]   In

1 Mackenzie's History of the Mackenzies, New Edition, page 45.
2 Appendix G.   3 Sir Walter Scott's Tales of a Grandfather.

1503, Alexander Gordon, Earl of Huntly, undertook to reduce Ellandonan and other castles on the west coast " for the daunting of the Isles," and to furnish or raise men to keep them when reduced, King James IV. engaging to provide a ship and artillery for the purpose.   In 1504 there was a general insurrection in the Highlands, which it took the King's forces two years to quell, and in the course of which Ellandonan Castle was occupied by the Earl of Huntly.   In 1539, Donald Gorm Macdonald of Sleat invaded the country and attempted to take the castle, but was killed during the siege by a Macrae, called Duncan Mac Gille-chriosd.[1]   Donald Gorm and his followers succeeded, however, in setting fire to the castle, for we find that in 1541 James V. granted remission to Donald's accomplices for their treasonable burning of the Castle of Ellandonan and the boats there.   The great feud which broke out between Kintail and Glengarry about 1580, and in which the Macraes took such a leading part, has been already referred to.[2]   This feud, which lasted for about twenty-five years, ended in the complete discomfiture of Glengarry, whose possessions in Lochcarron and Lochalsh were made over to Kintail by a Crown charter in 1607.   The House of Kintail had now practically reached the zenith of its greatness.

Meantime the Barons of Kintail and their people took a prominent part in the national affairs of Scotland.   John, the second Baron of Kintail, fought on the side of Bruce at Bannockburn, and is said to have had a following of five hundred men.   John of Killin, ninth Baron, who was one of the Privy Councillors of James V., fought with his followers at Flodden in 1513, and at Pinkie in 1547.   Colin, the eleventh Baron, fought as a young man at the head of his vassals on the side of Queen Mary at the battle of Langside in 1568.

In the unsettled times of the reign of Charles I., with whose cause George, second Earl of Seaforth, finally cast in his lot, the men of Kintail played an important part.   Seaforth fought at the battle of Auldearn in 1645, nominally against Montrose, but it had been arranged beforehand that his men should retire without fighting, and that Montrose should be allowed an easy victory.[3]   Shortly afterwards Seaforth publicly avowed himself a supporter of Mon-

[1] Page 25.   [2] Chapter III.   [3] Page 336.

X

trose, who was then joined by a large number of the men of
Kintail. Henceforth the people of Kintail continued to be staunch
supporters of the House of Stuart until the final defeat at Culloden
in 1745. In 1650 the Parliament placed a garrison in Ellandonan
Castle to overawe the country, but the insolence of the soldiers
becoming intolerable, they were summarily turned out by the
people, and no attempt was made to restore or to replace them.[1]
A number of Kintail men fought on the Royalist side at Worcester in 1651. In 1654, on the 26th of June, General Monk,
Cromwell's lieutenant in Scotland, visited Kintail with an army,
and remained there for two or three days. The names of the
places mentioned in the account of his visit at the time were
evidently written by men who knew no Gaelic, and are not easily
identified now. One Kintail man was killed by the soldiers,[2] the
houses and huts were burnt wherever they went, and a large
spoil of cattle was taken by them,[3] "which made some part
of amends for the hard march."[4]

A large number of Macraes took part in the rising of 1715,
and suffered heavily at the battle of Sheriffmuir. Tradition
relates that this battle made fifty-eight widows in Kintail. The
Macraes of Kintail and the Mathesons of Lochalsh were in the
centre of the second line of Mar's army, and a writer of the last
century says that they were the only part of Seaforth's men that
behaved well at Sheriffmuir, for when the rest ran away the
Macraes and Mathesons held their ground until a large number of
them was left dead on the field.[5] The same writer, who was a

<hr>

[1] Page 195.   [2] Page 31.   [3] Page 63.

[4] The events which led to Monk's visit to Kintail were as follows :—In
1653 a Stuart rising took place in the Highlands under the Earl of Glencairn,
whose place was soon taken by General Middleton. It was to quell this rising
that Monk made his march through the Highlands in 1654. Having heard
that Middleton was in Kintail, Monk led his forces there, only to find, on
arriving, that Middleton had left the day before and gone to Glenelg. Monk
did not follow Middleton to Glenelg, but plundered the people of Kintail and
then departed by way of Glenstrathfarrar. The rising shortly afterwards
collapsed. For a more detailed account of General Monk's visit to Kintail,
see a paper by Mr William Mackay in Volume xviii. (1892) of the Transactions
of the Gaelic Society of Inverness.

[5] The Highlands of Scotland in 1750, from a MS. in the British Museum,
with introduction by Andrew Lang.

bigoted Whig, and very much biased in most of his remarks on
the Jacobite clans, tells us that the common people in Kintail are
"the Macraes, who are by far the most fierce, warlike, and
strongest men under Seaforth." He then goes on to say that
until quite recently the Macraes were little better than heathen
and savages, but his only excuse for such a statement seems to have
been his Whig prejudices, and his desire to make it appear that, as a
result of Whig influences in Kintail, there was a "surprising
alteration in the people even in point of common civility, decency,
and cleanliness." As a matter of fact, there was hardly any
district in the Highlands where Whig influences made way more
slowly than in Kintail.

Early in 1719, Cardinal Alberoni, Prime Minister of Spain,
with which country we were then at war, fitted out a powerful expedition under the Duke of Ormonde[1] to support the
Jacobite cause in the Highlands of Scotland. But scarcely had
the expedition left the coast of Spain when it was overtaken by a
terrible storm in the Bay of Biscay. The storm lasted for twelve
days, and so completely dispersed the fleet that only two vessels
were able to reach Scotland. These two vessels had on board the
Earl of Seaforth, the Earl Marischal, the Marquis of Tullibardine, and about three hundred Spaniards, with arms and
ammunition for two thousand men. They landed in Kintail on
the 5th of April, and encamped on the mainland opposite to
Ellandonan. Here they lay quiet for some time in the hope that
Ormonde might still be able to effect a landing, but they were
soon joined by several Highlanders, including the famous Rob Roy
Macgregor and a party of his followers.

Shortly afterwards three ships of war—the Worcester, the
Enterprise, and the Flamborough—sailed up Lochalsh under the
command of Captain Boyle of the Worcester. On the 10th of May,
early in the morning, Captain Boyle drew up the Worcester and
the Enterprise in front of Ellandonan Castle, which was garrisoned
by forty-five Spaniards, commanded by Irish officers, and at nine

1 James Butler, Duke of Ormonde, a distinguished soldier of the reigns of
William III. and Anne. On the accession of George I. he embraced the cause
of the Stuarts, and was henceforth obliged to live abroad. Born, 1665 ; died,
1747.

o'clock sent his lieutenant with a boat under a flag of truce to demand the surrender of the Castle, which was refused.   About four in the afternoon Captain Boyle was informed by a deserter from the Jacobite side that the number of men in their camp was more than four thousand, and was daily increasing.   One thousand would probably be nearer the truth.   He therefore resolved to delay action no longer, and at eight o'clock in the evening he opened upon the Castle "a great fire," under cover of which he despatched two boats, manned and armed, under two lieutenants, to whom the Spaniards, who had mutinied against their officers, readily surrendered.   To prevent the Jacobites, whose camp lay near the Castle, from taking possession of it again, Captain Herdman of the Enterprise was sent to blow it up.   This duty he effectually performed after having first sent off the prisoners with three hundred and forty-three barrels of gunpowder, fifty-two barrels of musket shot, and some bags of meal.   At the same time he burnt several barns on the mainland near the Castle, where quantities of corn had been stored for the use of the camp. Such was the end of Ellandonan Castle.

Meantime Captain Hedesley of the Flamborough sailed up Lochduich, where a large quantity of ammunition, belonging to the Spaniards, was stored under a guard of thirty of their men, but on his first appearance within sight the Spaniards set fire to it.   This store was situated at Loch nan Corr, near the site of the Manse of Kintail, and, for many years afterwards, cannon balls and other relics of ammunition used to be found on the glebe in great abundance.   It was at the same time that the old church of Kintail was destroyed,[1] the only possible excuse for such an act of sacrilege being the fact that the incumbent of the parish was that ardent Episcopalian and Jacobite, the Rev. Donald Macrae, who was now an old man, and who died shortly afterwards.   After destroying the church, the troops landed, and, according to their custom, plundered the unfortunate, defenceless people.

On hearing of these events, the Commander-in-Chief of the Forces in Scotland ordered General Wightman, who was then stationed at Inverness, to proceed to Kintail with the troops under his command—about 1200, which included 136 Highlanders,

---

[1] Old Statistical Account.

chiefly Munros and Mackays.   The Jacobite force consisted of about 1100, which included about 200 Spaniards.[1]

The battle was fought on the 10th of June, at a place now called Eas-nan-arm (the waterfall of arms).   The fighting began at five o'clock in the afternoon, and lasted for about three hours.   The King's troops made three unsuccessful attempts to dislodge the Highlanders, but in the fourth attack Seaforth was wounded, and the heather in which the Highlanders were posted having caught fire, they began to fall into a state of confusion. Recognising the hopelessness of further resistance, the Highlanders dispersed and retired to the mountains, and next morning the Spaniards surrendered as prisoners of war.   The King's troops lost twenty-one killed, and one hundred and twenty-one wounded. The loss of the Highlanders is not known, but was probably not very heavy.   Seaforth, Marischal, and Tullibardine, with the other principal officers, succeeded in making their escape to the Continent.

Major-General Wightman spent some days in the neighbouring country, plundering and burning the houses of the guilty, and on the 28th of June he writes from Lochcarron to say he is on his way to Inverness.   The local tradition of a Dutch Colonel, who was killed in the battle, and whose ghost used to revisit the scene of the conflict, appears to have no foundation in fact.   The only officer in the Royalist side who is returned as killed in the official list of casualties is Captain Downes of Montagu's regiment, who was buried on the south side of the river, and whose grave is still pointed out.[2]

After the Rebellion of 1715, the Seaforth estates, being forfeited, were placed by Parliament under the management of the Forfeited Estates Commissioners.   The Commissioners did not find their task an easy one, for the tenants as a rule adhered loyally to their old landlords or chiefs, and refused to pay any rent to the factors whom the Commissioners appointed.   For several years the Kintail rents were regularly paid to Seaforth's Chamberlain, Donald Murchison, who continued to send them to his

[1] Tullibardine, in a letter to the Earl of Mar, gives the number as 1120, including 200 Spaniards.

[2] For a full account of the battle of Glensheil, see " The Jacobite Attempt of 1719," edited for the Scottish History Society by W. K. Dickson.

master on the Continent.   At last two Whigs of Easter Ross—
William Ross of Easter Fearn, and his brother, Robert Ross, a
Bailie of Tain—undertook to collect the rents on the estates of
Seaforth, Chisholm, and Glenmoriston, and started from Inverness
on the 13th September, 1721, with an escort of soldiers under
Lieutenant John Allardyce.   Having visited Glenmoriston, they
proceeded to Strathglass and Kintail, but a young lad, Patrick
Grant, son of Ian a Chragain, the Chief of Glenmoriston, took a
short route to Kintail, and informed Donald Murchison of the
approach of the Whig factors.   Though Murchison had been "bred
a writer," he had also some military training, and held a Lieutenant-Colonel's commission in the Jacobite army of 1715.   Part of
the funds collected from the people he used in keeping on foot a
company of armed Highlanders, whom he always held in readiness
for the protection of Seaforth's interests in Lochalsh and Kintail.
With these and several other followers, amounting in all to 300
men, Murchison set out, accompanied by Patrick Grant, to meet
the Whig factors and their military escort.   They met on the
2nd of October, at a place called Ath nam Muilach, a narrow pass
in the mountains beween Glenaffric and Kintail.   After some
skirmishing, in which several were wounded, a meeting was arranged between Easter Fearn and Murchison, with the result that
the factors retreated, leaving their commission in Murchison's
hands, and promising, it is said, not to act again in the service of
the Commissioners.   Among the wounded was Easter Fearn himself and his son Walter.   The son died on the following morning,
and his body was carried by the soldiers to Beauly Priory for burial.[1]

In the following month the Sheriff-Depute of Inverness held
Courts of Inquiry at Inverness with the view of ascertaining who
were Murchison's followers.   Among the witnesses examined was a
soldier in the Royal Regiment of North British Fusiliers, called
Donald Macrae, who was one of the escort that accompanied the
factors, and who recognised from fifty to sixty Kintail men, whose
names and patronymics are stated in his evidence.[2]   They were

[1] Fuller accounts of the affair of Ath nam Muilach are given in Mackenzie's
History of the Mackenzies (new edition), pp. 305-310; and Mackay's Urquhart
and Glenmoriston, pp. 235-236.

[2] For a full account of these inquiries see a paper on "Donald Murchison
and the Factors on the Forfeited Estates," by William Mackay, published in
the Transactions of the Gaelic Society of Inverness, Vol. xix. (1893).   See also
Appendix M.

nearly all Macraes, most of them belonging to the chief families of Kintail. Nothing appears to have come of this inquiry.

Shortly afterwards another attempt was made to obtain possession of Seaforth's estate for the Government. A company of soldiers, under Captain Macneill, formerly of the Highland Watch, proceeded from Inverness to Kintail by Dingwall, Garve, and Lochcarron. But while crossing the hills of Attadale, between Lochcarron and Lochalsh, they were met by Donald Murchison and his dauntless followers at a place called the Coille Bhan (the white wood). A skirmish ensued, in which one soldier was killed and several wounded. Captain Macneill himself was severely wounded, and, withdrawing his men, shortly afterwards made his way back to Inverness as well as he could.[1] After this the Forfeited Estates Commissioners appear to have made no further attempt to collect rents in Kintail.[2]

In 1725 General Wade,[3] in his report to the King, states that the Seaforths still pay their rents to Donald Murchison, and in the same year the Forfeited Estates Commissioners report that they had not sold the estate of William, Earl of Seaforth, as they had not been able to obtain possession of it. The constant fighting in which the men of Kintail had been engaged almost since 1640 told against their material circumstances, and General Wade states, in

[1] Mackenzie's History of the Mackenzies (new edition), p. 311.

[2] In Appendix H. will be found a list of the tenants on Seaforth's Kintail estate in 1719 and 1756, and the rents they paid. Considering the high value of money at those dates, it will be found that the difference between the rents paid in the Highlands then and now was not so great as is generally supposed.

[3] George Wade, Field Marshal of His Majesty's forces, and Privy Councillor, was a distinguished soldier whose name is still well known in the Highlands in connection with his roads and bridges. He joined the army in 1690, served in the Continental wars of his time, and eventually rose to the highest military rank. In 1724 he was appointed to a command in Scotland, and while holding that command he employed his soldiers in making roads in the Highlands. The roads gave rise to a famous couplet :—

If you had seen these roads before they were made,
You would hold up your hands and bless General Wade.

In 1745 he commanded an army in the North of England to oppose the Southward march of the Highlanders, but was too old and infirm to be of much service. He died in 1748, at the age of 80. Wade was an officer of great vigour and sound judgment, and is well entitled to a high place among the chief benefactors of the Highlands.

1725, that though they were formerly reputed the richest of any tenants in the Highlands, they had now become poor through neglecting their business and applying themselves to the use of arms. Consequently they were no longer able to pay their rents with their former readiness and regularity. In 1726 Seaforth was pardoned for his share in the Rising of 1715, and permitted to return to his native land. He received a grant of the feu-duties due to the Crown out of his forfeited estates, which were held by the Government until his death in 1741, when they were purchased from the Crown—by his mother—for the benefit of his son Kenneth, Lord Fortrose.[1]

For some time after these events, the country enjoyed peace. Law and order were more firmly established, and there was a gradual return of prosperity. Simon, Lord Lovat, then an active supporter of the Hanoverian Government, raised a company of Highlanders to keep in check the Lochaber cattle lifters, and Kintail profited to some extent from this protection. In 1722, barracks was erected in Glenelg, and a few companies of soldiers were usually stationed there until after the battle of Culloden, when the building was gradually allowed to fall into disuse. Shortly afterwards the country was opened up by one of General Wade's military roads, running from Fort-Augustus to Glenmoriston, thence down through Glensheil to the head of Lochduich, and across the hills of Ratagan to Glenelg.

In 1726, as already stated, and while the Seaforth estates were still in the hands of the Government, the south side of Kintail was formed into the separate parish of Glensheil, and shortly afterwards a Presbyterian minister — the Rev. John Beton—was settled there in spite of considerable opposition from the people, to whom Presbyterians and Whigs were equally hateful, but the

---

[1] The restored Earl did not show Donald Murchison the gratitude to which his loyal services entitled the latter. Donald shortly afterwards left the country, and died in the prime of life near Conon. A monument erected to his memory on the Lochalsh side of Kyleakin bears the following inscription:— " Tullochard.—To the memory of Donald Murchison, Colonel in the Highland Army of 1715. He successfully defended and faithfully preserved the lands of Kintail and Lochalsh from 1715 to 1722 for his Chief, William, the exiled Earl of Seaforth.—Erected by his great-grand-nephew, Sir Roderick I. Murchison, K.C.B.—1863."

Parish Church was not built until 1758.   The old Parish Church
of Kintail was at this time vacant for several years.   The Rev.
Donald Macrae, the last Episcopalian minister, died about 1721,
but his Presbyterian successor, the Rev. John Maclean, was not
appointed until 1730.

The Rising of 1745 brought fresh trouble upon Kintail.
Though Seaforth remained loyal to the House of Hanover, yet it
was well known that the sympathies of the people were on the
other side.   Sheriffmuir and Glensheil were not yet forgotten.   A
writer of the period[1] states that "some of the wild Macraes"
were out in that year, and there is a local tradition to the effect
that of those who joined in that rising not one ever again returned
to Kintail.   After the battle of Culloden, Lord George Sackville[2]
entered Kintail by Glenaffric, and with the brutal cruelty so
characteristic both of himself and of his chief, the Duke of
Cumberland, plundered the defenceless people, and drove away a
large number of cattle and other booty.[3]   In the course of his
wanderings after the defeat at Culloden, Prince Charles came to

[1] The Highlands in 1750, edited by Andrew Lang.

[2] The subsequent career of Lord George Sackville (born 1716, died 1785)
was far from creditable. He was in command of the British horse at the
battle of Minden in 1759, when his conduct was so unsatisfactory that he was
tried by Court-Martial and dismissed from the army. In 1775, under the
title of Lord Germaine, he became Secretary of State for the American
Colonies, and directed the American War, with the disastrous result that we lost
our American Colonies. The career of William, Duke of Cumberland (born
1721, died 1765), son of George II., was no less discreditable. In 1745 he was
in command of the British army which was defeated by the French in the
great battle of Fontenoy, in the Netherlands. Next year he defeated the
army of Prince Charles Edward at the battle of Culloden, after which he fixed
his headquarters at Fort-Augustus, and harried the neighbouring country with
every species of military execution. The barbarous cruelty with which he
treated the defenceless people gained for him the nickname of "The Butcher."
From Scotland he returned to the command of the army in the Netherlands,
and was again defeated in 1746 by the French, with great loss, at the battle
of Laufeldt. In the Seven Years' War he held an important command, and
suffered a great defeat at the battle of Hastenbach in 1757. Shortly afterwards he made a humiliating surrender to the French at Klosterseven, for
which he was recalled and degraded from his rank in the army. Culloden
was his only victory, and the very fates seemed to exact grim vengeance for
the cruel and cowardly use he made of it.

[3] Old Statistical Account of Kintail.

Glensheil on the 27th of July, 1746, and remained there until the following afternoon.[1]

With the defeat of Culloden it may be said of Kintail, as of the rest of the Highlands, that the old order of things came to an end, and began gradually to make way for the modern conditions of life. There arose a greater security of life and property as people learned to look to the law for protection rather than to the sword. Cattle-lifting and clan feuds came to an end, schools were established, and means of communication with the great commercial and industrial centres of the South greatly improved. But although settled peace and security thus brought many benefits, yet there came, on the other hand, many unavoidable social and economic changes which did not always prove an unmixed blessing.

In the Old Statistical Accounts of Kintail, by the Rev. Roderick Morrison, and of Glensheil, by the Rev. John Macrae, we have a fairly full description of the circumstances of the country during the fifty years following the battle of Culloden. About 1769-1774, a large number of the people emigrated to America, chiefly to Carolina. Their descendants are still numerous there and in the neighbouring States, and many of them have since been honourably associated with the affairs of their adopted country. These emigrants belonged, as a rule, to the well-to-do farmers of the country. They were not unfrequently young men to whom the idle life imposed upon them by the peace and the altered conditions which followed the battle of Culloden, was not always agreeable. Many were prompted to seek new homes, partly by love of adventure, and partly by a desire to share in the rumoured wealth of the New World. It would seem, too, that even in those days the rent question was not altogether free from difficulties, and that the more spirited of these men disliked a connection with their Chief, in which valour was no longer of any account, and of which the chief feature was the paying of rent.

We find difficulties about the rent as far back as the time of Colin, first Earl of Seaforth, who lived in far greater state than any of his predecessors, and was, therefore, obliged to raise the rents accordingly.[2] The relations set forth in Ian Mac Mhur-

---

[1] Page 210.   [2] Page 189.

achaidh's poems,[1] as existing between the people and their chief,
may reasonably be regarded as somewhat exaggerated.   The
poems containing references to such relations were evidently
composed with a view to induce as many people as possible
to emigrate with him to America, and it is but natural that
he should dwell somewhat emphatically on the disadvantages of
life in the old country, as compared with the advantages of the
promised land beyond the seas.   But the pointed and practical
advice he gives to the landlords themselves reasonably pre-
supposes some excuse for offering it, and it is interesting as
showing what the class of men to whom he belonged held to be
the landlord's wisest and most practical policy to adopt toward his
people.

> Cum na clachan steibhe
> Dh'fhag na daoine gleusda 'n coir dhut.

> Bidhe aoidheal ris a cheathairne,
> Cum taobh nan daoine matha riut,
> 'S gur mor an cliu gun chleith
> A choisininn t-athar air an t-sheol sin.

> Gur iomadh bochd 'us dinnleachdan
> Thug beannachd air do shinnscara,
> Gur maireanach an dilib sin,
> 'S gur cinntiche na 'n t-or e.[2]

On the whole, however, the relations existing between the Seaforths and the people of Kintail were usually very cordial, thanks
to the pastoral richness of the country, and the tact and sense of
justice evidently possessed by some of the Macrae Chamberlains,
who were so frequently the real rulers and administrators of the
affairs of Kintail, for during the last two hundred years of their
power the Earls of Seaforth were hardly ever resident in Kintail
themselves.   The traditions of the country have preserved fragments of songs in which the virtues of more than one Chamber-

---

[1] Appendix J.

[2] Preserve the foundation stones left to you by able and generous men. Be
courteous to the yeomanry, keep the good men on your side, great and evident
was the renown gained by your father in that way. Many a poor man and
many an orphan invoked blessings on your ancestors. Such things are an
enduring heritage, and more to be relied on than gold.

lain are set forth, and of which the lament for Ian Breac Mac Mhaighster Fearacher[1] may be taken as an example.

But the social stagnation which seemed to be setting in after the battle of Culloden was not destined to last long. A change was rapidly approaching, and scarcely had the emigration commenced when the Highlanders were called upon to fight the battles of their country in all quarters of the globe. To this appeal the men of Kintail, like the rest of their compatriots, gave a ready and willing response. A fair number of Highlanders fought in the great wars of the last century, such as the War of the Austrian Succession (1740-1748), and the Seven Years' War (1756-1763), and there were certainly a few Kintail men among them, but it was not until towards the end of the century that Highlanders were either encouraged or invited to join the army in large numbers, and that the famous Highland Regiments were enrolled. Between 1778 and 1804, four battalions of about a thousand men each were raised by the Earls of Seaforth,[2] and each battalion contained a large number of men from Kintail.

It would seem from the Old Statistical Account that the forty years following the battle of Culloden was, on the whole, a period of prosperity for Kintail. There was a steady increase of population in spite of emigration, and so well off were the people that the famine of 1782, which was felt so severely in many parts of the Highlands, was not felt at all in Kintail. In 1792 there were only fifteen poor persons in Kintail and twenty-one in Glensheil. These were supported by the weekly collections in the churches and by the charity of their neighbours. There was no confirmed drunkard in either of the two parishes, and no thieves. A baron-bailie or judge visited the country quarterly to settle such differences as might arise among the people. Those differences were usually questions connected with encroachments on marches, trespassing, and penfolding. From the beginning of June to about the middle of August the cattle were moved from the arable fields and lower pastures to the sheilings on the upper moorlands. A number of people went along with the cattle as herds and dairymaids, and huts were erected for shelter and sleeping accommodation. In fine summer weather life under such circumstances would not be un-

1 Appendix J.   2 Appendix D.

pleasant, and the season spent in the sheiling was usually regarded as a time of much enjoyment.   It was a time of mirth and love making, and the praise of nighean na h'airidh (the maid of the sheiling) forms the theme of many a Gaelic love song.   The stock consisted mainly of Highland cattle.   There were hardly any sheep, but there were about three hundred horses at this time in the parish of Kintail alone, and probably a corresponding number in Glensheil.   There was a parish school at Cro and another near the Church of Glensheil.   There was a third school in Glenelchaig supported by subscriptions from the farmers, many of whom were Roman Catholics, nearly a third of the people of Kintail at that time being of that creed.[1]   It is to the credit of Protestants and Roman Catholics alike that religious differences did not prevent them from combining to support the cause of education.   Considering all circumstances, it would appear that at the close of the last century the people of Kintail were in fairly prosperous circumstances, and quite as advanced in their views and ways as any of their neighbours.

But there was evidently a marked change for the worse during the next forty years.   The population, which was almost stationary during the period of the Napoleonic War, when so many of the men were serving in the army, began to increase rapidly after the peace of 1815, without any corresponding increase in the means of sustenance, and we learn from the New Statistical Account in 1836 that at that time there was a considerable amount of poverty in the country.   But the increase of population was not the sole cause of this change.   Francis, Earl of Seaforth, having got into debt, was obliged to sell considerable portions of his West Coast estates.   When his people came to know of the state of his affairs they offered to pay his debts if he would reside among them, but their offer was disregarded.   Lochalsh was sold under value in 1803, Kintail and a large portion of Glensheil followed in 1807, and the long connection of the Seaforth family with that country was all but ended before the death of the last Earl of Seaforth, which occurred at Warriston, near Edinburgh, on the 11th of January, 1815—the last of the direct male representatives of the House of Kintail.   The remainder of the old Kintail estate was sold by his

[1] For an account of the founding of the Roman Catholic Mission in Kintail see page 73.

grandson, Keith William Stewart-Mackenzie, in 1869, and the last connecting link between the Seaforth family and Kintail was thus finally severed.

With the severing of the old Seaforth connection, there came other changes also, changes of an unavoidable nature, which were only a part of the great social change which, during the last hundred years, has gradually transformed, either for better or worse, the circumstances and the condition of the people of the Highlands. Farms on a larger scale were let to strangers from the South; sheep took the place of cattle. The smaller tenants were gradually dispossessed of their holdings in order to make way for large sheep farms, and in many instances poverty was the result. Those who had attained to middle age in the midst of the free and primitive surroundings to which they had hitherto been accustomed, could not be expected to take kindly to a change either of abode or occupation, and when they left the country in search of a new home, as many of them did, it was only to experience failure, disappointment, and poverty.

The young and the enterprising emigrated in large numbers, chiefly to Canada, and between 1831 and 1841 there began a steady decrease of the population, which has continued ever since. The decrease of population, however, is not to be attributed solely to the formation of large farms. It was observed during the early decades of the present century that the spread of education and the increased facilities of communication with the South induced many of the more enterprising young people to seek opportunities of improving their circumstances elsewhere. This is equally true at the present time, and small though the population is, positions of honour and trust, both at home and abroad, are occupied by more than one of the sons of Kintail, who could have found no possible career in their own native parish.

It has already been mentioned that the old church in Kintail was destroyed in 1719. Another church was built some time afterwards. Part of the roof of this church fell in during divine service on Sunday, the 7th October, 1855, without injuring any one. It was then declared unsafe, and the present church built. The following is a list of the ministers of Kintail since the Reformation, with the dates of the commencement of their ministry :—

John Murchison (Reader)	-	-	-	-	- 1574
Murdoch Murchison	-	-	-	-	- 1614
Farquhar Macrae	-	-	-	-	- 1618
Donald Macrae -	-	-	-	-	- 1662
Donald Macrae -	-	-	-	-	- 1681
John Maclean	-	-	-	-	- 1730
Donald Maclean	-	-	-	-	1774
Roderick Morison	-	-	-	-	- 1781
James Morison -	-	-	-	-	- 1825
Roderick Morison	-	-	-	-	- 1877
Roderick Mackenzie -	-	-	-	-	- 1898

The Free Church principles of the Disruption of 1843 did not meet with much favour in Kintail, which is one of the very few Ross-shire parishes in which the Free Church has no place of worship. The failure of the Free Church movement in Kintail was, to a certain extent, owing to the traditional dislike of the people to the Whigs with whom they believed the movement to be in some measure associated; but the chief cause was the popularity of the two parish ministers of the time, the Rev. James Morrison of Kintail and the Rev. John Macrae of Glensheil, whose fathers, as ministers of the same two parishes, had succeeded in winning the people over to the Presbyterian Church, and who were themselves, both of them, men of ability and sound judgment, and of light and leading among the people with whom, by family and other associations, they had been so long connected.

The Roman Catholic Mission, which is still conducted in Kintail, was founded, as already mentioned,[1] by the Rev. Alexander, son of the Rev. John Macrae, last Episcopalian minister of Dingwall. For many years the mission was conducted by priests who visted the country from time to time, but towards the close of the last century a native of Kintail, the Rev. Christopher Macrae, was appointed priest in charge, and since then there has been a regular succession of priests resident at Dornie. The present priest in charge is the Rev. Archibald Chisholm. The handsome Roman Catholic premises at Dornie were built by the late Duchess of Leeds, and consist of a church, presbytery, convent, and school. The church, which is dedicated to Saint Duthac, was opened in 1861.

Although the district of Glensheil was made into a separate parish in 1726, and a minister appointed in 1730; there was no

1 Page 73.

permanent church built until 1758, when the present Church was erected. The following is a list of the ministers of Glensheil, with the dates of the commencement of their ministry :—

John Beton (or Bethune) - - - - -	1730
John Macrae - - - - - - -	1777
John Macrae - - - - - - -	1824
Farquhar Maciver - - - - - -	1840
Alexander Matheson - - - - . -	1864
Duncan Macrae - - - - - - -	1891

There is now a Free Church in the parish of Glensheil, which was built in 1865. The first minister of it was the Rev. Angus Mackay, and he was succeeded by the Rev. Kenneth Macrae, who was ordained in 1898.

Population of Kintail and Glensheil at various periods :—

	Kintail.	Glensheil.	Total.
1755 ...	693	509	1202
1790 ...	840	721	1561
1801 ...	1038	710	1748
1811 ...	1058	728	1786
1821 ...	1027	768	1795
1831 ...	1240	715	1955
1841 ...	1168	745	1913
1851 ...	1009	573	1582
1861 ...	890	485	1375
1871 ...	753	463	1216
1881 ...	688	424	1112
1891 ...	588	394	982

APPENDIX F.

I. Descent of Margaret Mackenzie, first wife of Alexander Macrae of Inverinate (page 70) :—

EDWARD I. of England had, by his second wife, Margaret, daughter of Philip III. of France, a son,

1. EDMUND PLANTAGENET, who married Margaret, daughter of John, Lord Wake, and was beheaded in 1329. He had a daughter,

2. JOAN, the "Fair Maid of Kent," who died in 1385. She married Sir Thomas Holland, Earl of Kent, and afterwards the Black Prince. By Sir Thomas Holland she had

3. THOMAS HOLLAND, Earl of Kent, who married Alice Fitzalan, and died in 1397. He had a daughter,

4. MARGARET, who married John Beaufort (died 1410), son of John of Gaunt, son of Edward III., and had a daughter,

5. JANE BEAUFORT, who married King James I. of Scotland, and, secondly, Sir James Stewart, the "Black Knight of Lorn." She died in 1445, leaving by her second marriage a son,

6. JOHN STEWART, first Earl of Atholc, who married, first, Margaret, daughter of Archibald, fifth Earl of Douglas. He married, secondly, Eleanor, daughter of William Sinclair, Earl of Orkney, and died in 1512. By his second marriage he had a son,

7. JOHN STEWART, second Earl of Athole, killed at Flodden in 1513. He married MARY, daughter of ARCHIBALD CAMPBELL, second Earl of Argyll (killed at Flodden), son of COLIN CAMPBELL, first Earl of Argyll (died 1493), son of ARCHIBALD CAMPBELL (died before his father), son of Sir Duncan Campbell (died 1453), by his wife, MARJORY STEWART, daughter of ROBERT, Duke of Albany, Regent of Scotland (died 1420), son of Robert II. (died 1390),

Y

son of Walter, Lord High Steward of Scotland, by his wife
MARJORY, daughter of ROBERT BRUCE (died 1329). By his
marriage with Mary Campbell, John, Earl of Athole, had a
daughter,

8. ELIZABETH STEWART, who married Kenneth Mackenzie,
tenth Baron of Kintail, who died in 1568, leaving a younger son,

9. RODERICK MACKENZIE, first of Redcastle, who married
Florence, daughter of Robert Munro of Fowlis, and died shortly
after 1608. He had, with other issue, Colin, of whom below, and
a son,

10. MURDOCH MACKENZIE, second of Redcastle, who, in 1599,
married Margaret, daughter of William Rose, eleventh of Kil-
ravock, and died before 1629. He had, with other issue, Finguala,
of whom below, and

11. MARGARET, who married Alexander Macrae of Inverinate.

II. Descent of Mary Mackenzie, second wife of Alexander Macrae
of Inverinate (page 70), from Jane Beaufort (No. 5 in the
first Table).

JANE BEAUFORT, as mentioned above, married, first, JAMES I.
of Scotland (died 1437), son of ROBERT III. (died 1406), son of
ROBERT II. (died 1390), son of MARJORY, daughter of ROBERT
BRUCE. By this marriage Jane Beaufort had a daughter,

6. ANNABELLA, who married George Gordon, second Earl of
Huntly (died 1502), and had a son,

7. ALEXANDER GORDON, third Earl of Huntly, who commanded
the left wing of the Scottish army at Flodden in 1513, married
Joan, daughter of John Stewart, first Earl of Athole (No. 6 in the
above Table), by his first marriage, and died in 1524. He had a
son,

8. JOHN GORDON, who married Margaret, natural daughter of
King James IV. by Margaret, daughter of John Lord Drummond,
and died before his father, leaving a son,

9. GEORGE GORDON, fourth Earl of Huntly, " the most powerful subject in Scotland," who was killed at Corrichie, near Aberdeen,
in 1562. He married Elizabeth, daughter of Robert, Lord
Keith, who was killed at Flodden, and had a daughter,

10. ELIZABETH GORDON, who married John Stewart, fourth Earl of Athole (died 1579), and had a daughter,

11. ELIZABETH STEWART, who married Hugh Fraser, Lord Lovat (died 1576), and had a daughter,

12. ANNE FRASER, who married Hector Munro of Fowlis (died 1603), and had a daughter,

13. MARGARET MUNRO, who married Alexander Mackenzie of Dochmaluag, Strathpeffer (died 1636), and had a daughter,.

14. MARY MACKENZIE, who married Alexander Macrae of Inverinate.

III. Descent of Agnes Mackenzie, first wife of the Rev. John Macrae of Dingwall (page 145), progenitor of the Conchra family, from Roderick Mackenzie of Redcastle (No. 9 in the first Table) :—

RODERICK MACKENZIE of Redcastle had, as mentioned above, a younger son,

10. COLIN MACKENZIE, first of Kincraig, who married Catherine (sasine to her, 15 Sept., 1617), daughter of the Rev. John Mackenzie of Dingwall, and had a daughter,

11. AGNES, who married, as his first wife, the Rev. John Macrae of Dingwall.

IV. Descent of Flora Gillanders, wife of John Macrae (page 179), from Murdoch Mackenzie of Redcastle (No. 10 in the first Table):—

MURDOCH MACKENZIE, second of Redcastle, had, as mentioned above, a daughter,

11. FINGUALA MACKENZIE, who married Roderick Mackenzie, first of Applecross (died 1646), and had a son,

12. JOHN MACKENZIE, second of Applecross (sasine 1663), married a daughter of Hugh Fraser, third of Belladrum, and had a son,

13. KENNETH MACKENZIE, first of Auldenny, married Isabel, daughter of John Matheson of Bennetsfield, by Mary, daughter of the Rev. Donald Macrae of Kintail (p. 162), and had a son,

14. RODERICK MACKENZIE, second of Auldenny (sasine 1709),

married Margaret (or Catherine), daughter of Simon Mackenzie of Torridon, and had a daughter,

15. JANET MACKENZIE, who married John Mackenzie, of the Dochmaluag family, and had a son,

16. KENNETH MACKENZIE, of Torrancullin, near Kinlochewe (died 1837), who married Kate Mackenzie, of the Torridon family (died 1848), and had a daughter,

17. MARGARET MACKENZIE, who was born in 1797, and died at Strathpeffer, 1888. She married Alexander Gillanders, born at Kishorn, 1792, died at Strathpeffer, 1877, and had, with other issue,

18. FLORA GILLANDERS, who married John Macrae.

APPENDIX G.

THE HOUSE OF KINTAIL.

I. KENNETH, or in Gaelic, Coinneach, who gave their name to the great Clan of Clann Choinnich or Mackenzie. He married Morbha, daughter of Alexander Macdougall of Lorn. Kenneth died in 1304, and was buried in Iona. He was succeeded by his son,

II. JOHN, the first of the race, who was called Mackenzie, led 500 of his vassals at Bannockburn in 1314. He married Margaret, daughter of David de Strathbogie, Earl of Atholl, by Joan, daughter of the Red Comyn who was killed by Robert Bruce in 1306. John died in 1328, and was succeeded by his son,

III. KENNETH, known as Coinneach na Sroine (Kenneth of the Nose), who was executed by the Earl of Ross at Inverness in 1346. He was succeeded by his son,

IV. MURDOCH, called Murachadh Dubh na' h'Uaigh (Black Murdoch of the Cave). He died in 1375, and was succeeded by his son,

V. MURDOCH, called Murachadh na Drochaid (Murdoch of the Bridge). It was in his and his son's time that Fionnla Dubh Mac Gillechriosd, the founder of the Clan Macrae of Kintail, lived. He died in 1416, and was succeeded by his son,

VI. ALEXANDER, called Alister Ionraic (Alexander the Upright) to whom, during his minority, Fionnla Dubh Mac Gillechriosd was guardian. He died in 1488, and was succeeded by his son,

VII. KENNETH, called Coinneach a Bhlair (Kenneth of the Battle). He died in 1491, and was succeeded by his son,

VIII. KENNETH, who was treacherously killed by the Laird of Buchanan, in 1497, and was succeeded by his brother,

IX. JOHN, of Killin, who fought at Flodden in 1513, and at Pinkie in 1547. He died in 1561, and was succeeded by his son,

X. KENNETH, called Coinneach na Cuirc (Kenneth of the Whittle). He died in 1568, and was succeeded by his son,

XI. COLIN, called Cailean Cam (One-eyed Colin). He died in 1594, and was succeeded by his son,

XII. KENNETH, Lord Mackenzie of Kintail. He died in 1611, and was succeeded by his son,

XIII. COLIN, first Earl of Seaforth. He died in 1633, and was succeeded by his brother,

XIV. GEORGE, second Earl of Seaforth, a leading Royalist in the Civil War, died in Holland in 1651, and was succeeded by his son,

XV. KENNETH, third Earl of Seaforth, called Coinneach Mor (Big Kenneth), also a firm Royalist. He died in 1678, and was succeeded by his son,

XVI. KENNETH, fourth Earl of Seaforth, died in Paris in 1701, and was succeeded by his son,

XVII. WILLIAM, fifth Earl of Seaforth, known as Uilleam Dubh a Chogidh (Black William of the War). For the prominent part he took in the Jacobite Rising of 1715, he was attainted, and his estates forfeited. He died in Lews in 1740, and was succeeded by his son,

XVIII. KENNETH, for whom the estates were bought from the Crown in 1741, and who was known by the courtesy title of Lord Fortrose. He was the Seaforth of the time of Prince Charles, but, notwithstanding his well-known Jacobite sympathies, he considered it more prudent to remain loyal to the House of Hanover. He died in London in 1761, and was buried in Westminster Abbey. He was succeeded by his son,

XIX. KENNETH, created Baron Ardelve and Earl Seaforth (Ireland). He died near St Helena in 1781 while on the way to India as Colonel of the old 78th Regiment, raised by him on his own estates, and now known as the 1st Battalion of the Seaforth Highlanders. He left no male issue. He was succeeded by

XX. THOMAS FREDERICK MACKENZIE-HUMBERSTON, Colonel of the Hundredth Foot, son of William, son of Alexander, son of Kenneth, third Earl of Seaforth. He was killed in India in 1783, and, leaving no issue, was succeeded by his brother,

XXI. FRANCIS HUMBERSTON MACKENZIE, created Lord Seaforth of the United Kingdom.   He sold the greater portion of the Kintail estates, died in 1815 without surviving male issue, and was succeeded.by his daughter,

XXII. MARY ELIZABETH FREDRICA, who married, first, Admiral Sir Samuel Hood, without issue.   She married, secondly, the Honourable James Alexander Stewart, with issue, and died at Brahan in 1862.   She was succeeded by her son,

XXIII. KEITH WILLIAM STEWART MACKENZIE, who sold what remained of Kintail in 1869.   He died in 1881, and was succeeded by his son,

XXIV. JAMES ALEXANDER FRANCIS HUMBERSTON STEWART-MACKENZIE, Colonel of the Ninth Lancers, and lineal representative of the Earls of Seaforth.

When Francis Humberston Mackenzie, Lord Seaforth, died without surviving male issue, in 1815, there was no known male representative left of any head of the house of Kintail since Kenneth, Lord Mackenzie of Kintail, who died in 1611.   Kenneth had seven sons, but the male issue of the first six had, so far as known, become extinct.   The seventh son was

SIMON, of Lochslin, who died in 1666, having had, with other issue—

SIMON, who died in 1664, leaving an only son,

SIMON, first of Allangrange, who died in 1730, and was succeeded by his son,

GEORGE, second of Allangrange, who died in 1773, and was succeeded by his son,

JOHN, third of Allangrange, who died in 1812, and was succeeded by his son,

(XXII.) GEORGE FALCONER, who was served heir male to the House of Kintail in 1829.   He died in 1841, and was succeeded by his son,

(XXIII.) JOHN FALCONER, fifth of Allangrange, who died unmarried, in 1849, and was succeeded by his brother,

(XXIV.) JAMES FOWLER, now of Allangrange, lineal representative of the Chiefs of the great Clan Mackenzie, and heir male to the dormant honours and ancient titles of the historic family of Kintail.

APPENDIX H.—The Forfeited Estates Commissioners collected particulars about the rental of Kintail and Lochalsh in September, 1718, and there are some lists of tenants for that and subsequent years contained in the Forfeited Estates papers in the Register House, Edinburgh. The following appears to be the most complete list as regards Kintail.

Rental of the Seaforth estate of Kintail, taken from the depositions of the tenants, as certified by Kenneth Mackenzie of Dundonel, Deputy to Edmund Burt, Esq., Receiver-General of the Rents and Profits of the unsold Forfeited Estates in North Britain, at Inverness, on the 22nd July, 172(7?) (last figure torn in original):—

Tenants' Names.	Habitations.	Muttons.	Butter.		Cheese.		Viccarage.	Rent in Scots Money.
			Stone.	Lb.	Stone.	Lb.	£ s. d.	£ s. d.
KINTAIL—BARONY OF ARDELF.								
John M'Rae ...	Achnagart of Glensheel ...	2	1	...	2	...	16 0 0	223 6 8
Donald M'Rae	Torluishich ...	2	1	...	2	...	20 0 0	266 13 4
Maurice Macra	Easter Achyuran ...	1	...	10	2	...	15 0 0	200 0 0
John M'Rae...	Wester Achyuran ...	1½	...	5	1	...	7 10 0	100 0 0
Evan M'Lennan	Ditto. ...	⅔	...	5	1	...	7 10 0	100 0 0
Murdo M'Vic Wuirich	Achnashealloch ...	1	1	10	2	...	13 0 0	173 13 4
Farquhar M'Rae ...	Mickle Ratigan ...	1	1	...	2	...	17 10 0	233 6 8
Christopher M'Rae...	Little Ratigan ...	1	1	...	2	...	17 10 0	233 6 8
Malcolm M'Rae ...	Little Achyark ...	2	1	...	2	...	15 0 0	213 6 8
Murdo M'Rae ...	} Kilcluinort ...	1	1	...	2	...	16 0 0	197 6 8
Christopher M'Rae, junr. ...								
Murdo M'Rae	Muck ...	1	...	10	2	...	7 0 0	86 11 8
Ann M'Rae ...	} Mickle Achyark ...	2	1	...	2	...	19 17 8	245 3 4
Duncan M'Rae ...								
John M'Rae, junr. ...	} Inshchroe ...	...	...	...	...	...	9 0 0	111 0 0
Duncan M'Rae ...								
John M'Ean vic Eulay ...	Linasy ...	...	...	...	...	...	...	40 0 0

Tenants' Names.	Habitations.	Muttons.	Butter Stone.	Butter Lb.	Cheese Stone.	Cheese Lb.	Viccarage £ s. d.	Rent in Scots Money £ s. d.
KINTAIL—(Continued).								
Kenneth M'Rae	Achnterd Easter	...	...	...	...	...	2 0 0	24 13 4
William Mackenzie	Achnterd Wester	...	...	...	...	...	2 10 0	30 16 8
Christopher M'Rae	Easter Druidaig	...	...	...	...	...	6 0 0	80 0 0
Finlay M'Rae	Wester Druidaig	1	...	10	1	...	6 0 0	72 16 8
Duncan M'Rae	Tollie	...	...	...	...	...	...	17 15 8
Donald M'Rae	Dale	1	1	...	2	...	10 0 0	181 6 8
Christopher M'Rae	Arieyugan	1	1	...	2	...	10 10 0	129 19 0
Mary M'Rae, widow	Camlusnagoul	...	...	...	...	...	...	80 0 0
Alexander M'Rae	} Rowrach, divided into Mickle Oxgate, Middle Oxgate, and Culmulin	...	...	...	...	...	...	40 0 0
John M'Rae-Smith		...	...	...	...	...	...	10 0 0
Domd. M'Rae		...	...	...	...	...	...	30 0 0
Angus M'Huiston		...	...	...	...	...	...	20 0 0
Domd. Bayne		...	...	...	...	...	...	60 0 0
John M'Rae		...	...	...	...	...	...	10 0 0
Donald M'Finlay Duy	} Artullich and Claehan(?)	...	...	...	...	...	...	10 0 0
Donald M'Rae		...	...	...	...	...	4 10 0	55 10 0
Farquhar M'Rae	} Morrich	2	1	10	3	...	28 9 0	351 1 4
Alexander M'Rae								
Colin Murchison	Innersheal	...	...	14	1	...	13 10 0	167 2 0
Waste	Do, one penny and half	7-10ths	...	6	...	8	5 16 0	71 12 0
John M'Crimmon	Easter Leakichan	3-10ths	...	3	...	12	1 17 6	21 15 10
Rory M'Lennan	Wester Leakichan	1	...	10	1	6	4 0 0	53 6 8
Florence Mackenzie, wifd. of Dn. M'Rae	Achidren (where the Mause is now)	...	...	...	...	...	...	84 0 0
Farquhar Finlay	} Mickle Innerinnit	2	1	...	2	...	17 0 0	226 13 4
Finlay M'Rae								
Alexander M'Rae								
John M'Rae								

KINTAIL—(Continued).

Tenants' Names	Habitations	Muttons	Butter Stone	Butter Lb.	Cheese Stone	Cheese Lb.	Viccarage £ s. d.	Rent in Scots Money £ s. d.
Donald M'Ley								
Murlo M'Coilire								
Donald M'Coilvue								
Alexander M'Rae	Keppoch Mickle	1		10		10	4 4 0	52 1 0
Duncan M'Rae	Carr	1		10	1		5 4 0	69 6 8
Donald M'Aulay	Little Keppoch	½		5	1		1 17 6	23 2 6
Rory M'Rae	Clinbow (below Carr)	2		10		10	2 12 0	34 13 4
James Mackenzie	Fadloch	1			1		9 0 0	120 0 0
Kenneth M'Ean vic Illechallum	Half Craigag (?)	1		10	1			12 12 0
John M'Conchie	Leault	1		10	1		6 14 8	88 12 0
George Mackenzie	Achyargan	1			2		17 4 0	212 2 8
Christopher MacRae								
Farquhar MacRae	Bundalloch	1	1		2		10 10 0	129 10 0
Murlo M'Crae	Biolaig	4	2		4		9 16 0	127 10 8
John M'Crae	Upper Killilan	2	1		2		12 10 0	166 13 4
Alexander M'Crae	Neather Killilan	2	1		2		13 0 0	173 6 8
Murlo Murchison	Keilliss (?)				1		6 0 0	74 6 0
Duncan M'Crae	Achig Chuirn			10	1		11 0 4	132 6 4
Finlay M'Crae	Upper Mamaig			10	1		5 0 0	59 0 0
Finlay M'Crae, above mentioned, and Kenneth M'Crae	For half of Craigag (?)			10	1		1 0 0	11 0 0
Alexander M'Crae								
Alexander M'Crae	Duyleg	1		10	2		17 4 0	212 2 8
Duncan M'Crae								
Donald M'Illichallum	Neather Mamaig			10	1		5 16 0	72 2 8
Murdoch M'Rea								
John Isane M'Ra, for half, with	Coridhoin			10	1		9 0 0	111 0 0
Murdo M'Ra								

The following Macraes were landholders in the parish of Lochalsh in 1718, and paid together, with other dues, the under-mentioned rents :—

		Scots.
Alexander M'Cra, wadset of Conchra, &c., for 4000 marks— feu-duty (Scots)		£106 13 4
Duncan M'Cra	Innerskinnaig (*near Conchra*)	73 6 8
Duncan M'Cra	Ardelve	77 6 8
Donald Macra	Ardelve	77 6 8
Hugh M'Ra	Salchy	88 18 0

Rental of Seaforth Estates—Kintail and Glensheil, 1756 :—

		Scots.
Alexander M'Rath,	Aryugan	£4710 9 4
Malcolm M'Rath / John M'Rath	Cambusnagawl Ardintowl }	1417 9 4
John M'Rath	Dall	1206 8 0
Christopher M'Rath	{ Easter and Wester Drui- daig, Glenundalan }	1919 2 0
The Widow, Alexander Mac-Challan, and Duncan M'Rath }	Wester Achintyart	705 3 4
Duncan MacMillan	Easter Achintyart	705 3 4
Rorie MacLinan	Leckichan	502 2 8
Mr John Beaton, Minister of Letterfearn {	Leckichan, Muck, Achi-gichuirn }	2309 6 8
Christopher M'Rath	Kilchuinort	1911 8 0
Kenneth M'Rath, Alexander M'Rath, John's son, and Alexander, Christopher's son }	Little Ratagan	2211 4 8
Donald M'Rath's widow, Finlay Roy M'Rath }	Meikle Ratagan	2211 4 8
Donald Oig M'Rath	Torlysich	2411 1 4
Duncan M'Rath	Achnashelach	1616 5 4
Donald M'Rath, Christopher M'Rath }	Achinagart	2012 2 8
Duncan M'Rath, Alexander Roy M'Rath }	Easter Achiguran	1818 4 0
Donald M'Rath, Farquhar M'Rath }	Wester Achiguran	1807 2 8
John M'Rath, Alexander M'Rath	Innersheall	2201 1 4
Donald Derg Maclennan, John and Donald Buy M'Lennan }	Morvich	3609 5 4
Alexander M'Lennan, Donald Maclennan, Donald M'Leod }	Little Achiyark	1913 10 8
Duncan M'Lennan, Farquhar M'Lennan, Donald M'Rath }	Meikle Achiyark	2215 3 4
Four Tenants	Inchchrow	1911 1 4
Mr John M'Lean, Minister of Crowe }	Lienassie, &c.	2908 3 4

			Scots.		
Three Tenants · · · ·	Ardhullich (?) · ·	£2501	1	4
Farquhar M'Rath · · ·	Little Inverinate · ·	2317	9	4
Alister, Farquhar's son, Alister, John's son · · · }	Meikle Inverinate · ·	2018	10	8
Duncan M'Rath · · ·	Leault · · · ·	805	6	8
John Cuthbert, Finlay Beg ·	Little Keppoch · ·	407	9	4
Three Tenants · · · ·	Karr · · · ·	1304	3	4
Five Tenants · · · ·	Dornie · · · ·	2607	9	4
Two Tenants · · ·	Bundaloch · · ·	1217	9	4
Donald M'Rath · · ·	Cambuslynie · · ·	3306	8	0
Alexander M'Rath, &c. · ·	Nether Mamaig · ·	614	4	0
Christopher M'Rath · · ·	Duilig · · · ·	1911	1	4
Duncan M'Rath · · ·	Fadoch · · · ·	1613	7	4
Duncan M'Rath · · ·	Upper Killilan · ·	2018	6	0
Three Tenants · · · ·	Nether Killilan · ·	1603	10	8
Duncan M'Rath · · ·	Corriyoine · · ·	1007	6	0

The following Macraes appear on the Rental Roll for Lochalsh :—

Alexander M'Rath · ·	Altnasou and Dronaig ·	£2912	1	4
John M'Rath · · · ·	Conchra ·. · ·	3413	4	0
Hector M'Rath · ·	Ardelve · · ·	2704	5	8

APPENDIX I.

FEADAN DUBH CHINTAILLE.

THE Feadan Dubh, or Black Chanter of Kintail, which, for several generations, was one of the heirlooms of the Mackenzies of Kintail, is now in the possession of Lieutenant Colin William MacRae[1] of the Black Watch. A full description of the chanter and the drones accompanying it appeared in the *Inverness Courier* of the 29th May, 1894, from which the following account is mainly taken.

The chanter is considered to be much older than the drones, and the note holes are very much worn. It was badly broken at some time or another, and is now held together by no less than seven silver rings. The two top rings have engraved on them the words, "A smeorach aigharach" (the merry thrush). The other rings have "Scur Orain," the slogan of the Macraes ; "Caisteal Donain," "Cinntaille," "Loch-Duich," and on the bottom ring "Tulloch Aird," the slogan of the Mackenzies. On the chanter stock is fixed a stag's head and horns in silver, the Mackenzie crest, surmounted by a baron's coronet, and underneath it the inscription, "Lord Seaforth, Baron Mackenzie, High Chief of Kintail, 1797," and below this inscription the words, "Tulloch Aird."

The stock of the blowpipe has the following inscription :— "This silver-mounted black ebony set of bagpipes, with the Feadan Dubh Chintaille, was the property of Lord Seaforth, Baron Mackenzie, High Chief of Kintail, 1797," and on the blowpipe itself is the figure of a Highlander, in silver, in full costume, with drawn claymore, surmounted by the motto, "O Thir nam Beann " (from the land of the mountains).

[1] Page 159.

The stock of the big drone has the following inscription :— "From Lord Seaforth, Baron Mackenzie, High Chief of Kintail, to Lieutenant-Colonel Sir John Macra, K.C.H., of Ardintoul, Kintail, late 79th Cameron Highlanders." The big drone has three shields, and the top shield has the following inscription :—"All Highland bagpipes, till after the Battle of Waterloo, had but two or three short or treble drones." The second shield has, "Lieut.-Colonel Sir John Macra, K.C.H., late 79th Cameron Highlanders, was the first to introduce (and it was on this set of pipes) the use of a big or bass drone;" and the third shield has, "The big or bass drone was pronounced a great improvement in the harmony and volume of sound."

The stock of the second drone has the following :—"From Lieut.-Colonel Sir John Macra, K.C.H., to his nephew, Captain Archibald Macra Chisholm, late 42nd Royal Highlanders, the Black Watch." The shield on the second drone has, "The introduction of the big or bass drone was approved, and the example was soon followed in the making of military bagpipes."

The stock of the third drone has the following inscription :— "From Captain A. M. Chisholm, late 42nd Royal Highlanders, Black Watch, Freicadan Dubh to *(present possessor)*. The shield on the third drone has "Lieut.-Col. Sir John Macra was an excellent performer on the bagpipes. He made pipes and chanters; and when military secretary to his relative, the Marquis of Hastings, Viceroy of India, he taught the natives of India to play on the Highland bagpipes."

Captain Archibald Macra Chisholm was put in possession of the Kintail bagpipes soon after the death of his uncle, Sir John Macra, in 1847. When the late Keith Stewart-Mackenzie, of Seaforth and Brahan Castle, became aware of this, in 1849, he wrote to Captain Chisholm expressing his most anxious desire to possess this old Mackenzie heirloom. He made a handsome offer for them, but Captain Chisholm declined it. Captain Chisholm was himself an excellent performer on the bagpipes, and for over thirty years acted as judge of pipe music at the Northern Meetings in Inverness. Some time before his death, which occurred on the 19th October, 1897, while this book was in the press, he presented the Kintail bagpipes to his cousin, Lieutenant Colin William MacRae, as already mentioned.

APPENDIX J.

THE following poems are given as specimens of the language and poetry of the Macraes, and as illustrations of their social, political, and religious views in olden times :—

I.

This song, composed by Fearachar Mac Ian Oig, during his exile (page 188), was given to the author in 1890 by Alexander Macmillan, Dornie.   It is given also in The Transactions of the Gaelic Society of Inverness, Leaves from My Celtic Portfolio, by Mr A. W. Mackenzie.

> Cha ne direadh na bruthaich
> Dh'fhag mo shiubhal gun treoir.
>
> Na teas ri la greine
> 'Nuair a dh' eireadh i oirnn.
>
> Laidh a' sneachd so air m' fheusaig
> 'Us cha leir dhomh mo bhrog.
>
> 'S gann is leir dhomh ni 's fhaisge,
> Ceann a bhata nam dhorn.
>
> Se mo thigh mor na creagan,
> Se mo dhaingean gach frog.
>
> Se mo thubhailte m' osan,
> Se me chopan mo bhrog.
>
> Ge do cheanaichinn am buideal
> Cha 'n fhaigh mi cuideachd 'ni ol.
>
> 'S ged a cheanaichinn a' scipein
> Cha 'n fhaigh mi creideas a' stoip.
>
> Ged a dh' fhadinn an teine,
> Chi fear foille dheth ceo.
>
> 'S i do nighean-sa Dhonnachaidh
> Chuir an iomagain so oirnn.

Te 'g am beil an cul dualach
O guallainn gu brog.

Te 'g am beil an cul bachlach
'S a dhreach mar an t'or.

Dheoin Dia cha bhi gillean
Riut a' mire 's mi beo.

Ged nach deaninn dhut fidhe
Bhiodh iasg a's sitheinn ma d'bhord.

'S truagh nach robh mi 's tu 'ghaolach
Anns an aonach 'm bi 'n ceo.

Ann am bothan beag barraich
'S gun bhi mar rium ach d' fheoil.

Agus paisdean beag leinibh
A cheileadh ar gloir.

'S mi a shnamhadh an caolas
Air son faoilteachd do bheoil.

Nuair a thigeadh am foghar
Be mo roghainn bhi falbh,

Leis a' ghunna nach diultadh
'S leis an fhudar dhu-ghorm.

Nuair a gheibhinn cead frithe
Bho 'n righ 's bho 'n iarl og,

Gum biodh fuil an daimh chabraich
Ruith le altaibh mo dhorn,

Agus fuil a bhuic bhiorich
Sior shileadh feadh feoir.

Ach 's i do nighean-sa Dhonnachaidh
'Chuir an iomagain so oirnn.

It is not the climbing of the hills that has made my walk
listless. Nor the heat of a sunny day when it rose upon us.
The snow has settled on my beard, and I cannot see my shoe.
Hardly can I see, nearer still, the head of the staff in my hand.
The rocks are my big house, and the holes are my stronghold.
My hose is my towel, my shoe is my drinking cup. If I were to
buy a bottle, I could get no company to drink it. If I were
to buy a chopin, I should not get credit for a stoup. If I were to
light a fire, some treacherous man would see the smoke. It was
your daughter, Duncan, that brought this anxiety upon us. She

who has beautiful hair from her shoulders down to her shoe.   She
who has curling hair of the hue of gold.   God forbid that young
men should make love to you while I live.   Though I cannot
weave for you, yet there would be fish and venison on your table.
Would that you were with me, my love, on the hill of the mist.
In a small brushwood hut with no one with me but you.   And a
little child that would not betray our talk.   I would (gladly)
swim the ferry for a welcome from your mouth.   When the
autumn would come, my desire would be to wander with a gun
that would not miss fire, and with dark blue gunpowder.   When I
should receive permission for the forest from the King and the
young Earl, the blood of the antlered stag would flow by the skill
of my hand, and the blood of the roe-buck would flow continually
into the grass.   But your daughter, Duncan, has brought this
anxiety upon us.

II.

The following lament on Ian Breac Mac Mhaighster Fearachar
(page 170) was taken down by Mr Alexander Macrae, farmer,
Ardelve (page 166), from the recitation of Mr Duncan Macrae,
Ardelve (page 183), and communicated to the author in 1896.
The author of this poem is unknown :—

> Gu 'm beil m' inntinn se trom,
> 'Us cha sheinnear leum fonn
> Thionndaidh disne rium lom
>   'S na clairibh.
>
> Gu 'm beil m' aigneadh fo ghruaim,
> 'S cian gur fada o'n uair
> M'an aitreabh 's an d'fhuair
>   Mi m' arach.
>
> An deigh cinneadh mo ruin
> Air an d' imich an cliu,
> 'S tric mi 'n ionad fir dhiubh
>   O'n dh' fhas mi.
>
> Cha b'e bhi 'n dubhar gun ghrein
> Fath mo mhulad gu leir,
> Thuit mi cumha luchd speis
>   Mo mhanrain.

'S ann sa chlachan od shios
Dh' fhag sinn ceannas nan cliar
'S am fear buile na 'n iarrta
    'N airidh.

Duin' uasal mo ghaoil
Chaidh a bhualladh le aog
'S ann 'n ad ghnuis a bha aoidh
    A chairdeas.

'S n' am b' fhear ealaidh mi fein
Mar mo bharail gu geur
'S ann ort a b' fhurasd dhomh ceatachd
    Aireamh.

Gu n robh geurchuis ni's leor
Ann an eudan an t' sheoid
'S bu cheann reite do ghloir
    An Gailig.

'S mor an gliocas 's an ciall
Chaidh sa chiste leat sios,
Thug sud itean a sgiath
    An alaich.

Bhun an geamhradh rinn teann
Cha robh aoibhneas dhuinn ann
'S neo shubhach an gleann
    Bhon la sin.

'S lom an snaidheadh bhon tuath
Bhi cuir Ian san uaigh
'S bochd a naigheachd do thuath
    Chintaille.

Tha do chinneadh fo ghruaim
Dol air linne leat suas,
Air an tilleadh bu chruidh leo
    D' fhagail.

Tha do dheirbhleinean broin
Mar ghair sheillein an torr
'N deigh na mel, na mar eoin
    Gun mhathair.

Nise 's turseach an eigh
Gun am furtachd ac fhein
'S mor a thuiteas dhuibh 'n deigh
    Do laithean.

'S mor an aireamh, 's a chall
Cha do thearuinn mi ann
'S cia mar thearnas mi 'n am
        A phaidhidh.

Ghillean glacibh se ciall
Tha n ur cuid air an t sheibh
'S iommadh fear bhios ag iarridh
        Fath air.

Tha na taice 's na treoir
Ann an caol chiste bhord
Anns a chlachan an Cro
        Chintaille.

Tha do cheile fo sprochd
'S i neo eibhin gun toirt,
Rinn creuchdan a lot
        Gun tearneadh.

B' fhiach a h' uidheam sa pris
Fhad 's a luighigeadh dh' i
Gus na ghuidheadh le Righ
        N an gras thu.

A Mhic Mhoire nan gras
A dhoirt d'fhuil air nar sgath
Gu 'm a duineil 'n a aite
        Phaisdean.

Heavy minded am I, nor can I raise the song (of gladness), the die has fallen for me inauspiciously as to its sides.   My mind is in sadness, and for a long time, on account of the home in which I was reared.   On account of my beloved clan, whose fame has travelled far, often have I been in the place of some of them since I grew up.   Being in a sunless shade is not the sole cause of my sadness, I have fallen into mourning for those who are the esteemed ones of my mirth.   It was down in that graveyard that we left the chief of the heroes, and the head of the township if they were being counted.   My beloved nobleman, who has been struck by death, in thy face was the expression of friendliness.   If I were a man of talent, keen as to my wit, it would be easy for me to record thy praises.   There was intelligence enough in the face of the hero, and a subject of agreement would be thy praises in Gaelic.   Great is the wisdom and the understanding that went down with thee in thy coffin, this has plucked feathers from the wing of thy tribe. The winter visited us severely, there was no pleasure for us in it, and joyless is the glen since that day. A keen bereavement for the people, putting John in the grave; sad tidings for the tenantry of Kintail. Sad were thy clansmen as they carried thee West on the water, hard for them was it to have left thee as they returned. Thy sad orphans are like the noise of bees on a mound for their honey, or like fledglings without a mother. Sad now is their cry without a time of comfort for them; many of them will fall after thy days. Great is their number, nor did I escape the loss, how can I be saved in the day of reckoning (or rent paying). Young men, be prudent, your property (cattle) is on the mountain; many a man will try to take advantage of it. Our support and strength is in a narrow wooden coffin in the graveyard in Cro of Kintail. Thy wife is downcast, joyless, listless, wounded with sores from which she had no escape. Prosperous were her surroundings and her lot as long as thou wast vouchsafed to her, until thou wast asked for by the King of Grace. Son of Mary of Grace, who shed Thy blood for our sake, may his boys be worthy of his place.

III.

The following Lament for Murdoch Macrae of Inverinate, who was killed in Glenlic (page 84), is still well known in Kintail. It is given in The Transactions of the Gaelic Society of Inverness (Vol. VIII.), Leaves from My Celtic Portfolio. by Mr William Mackenzie.[1] The author is not known :—

Si sealg geamhraidh Ghlinn-Lic
A dh' fhag greann oirn tric 'us gruaim,
'N t-og nach robh teann 's a bha glic
'S an teampull fo'n lic 's an uaigh.

A cheud Aoine de 'n geamhradh fhuar
'S daor a phaigh sinn buaidh na sealg,
An t-og bo chraobhaiche snuagh
Na aonar bhuainn 'us fhaotainn marbh.

[1] On page 383, line 8, for Mr A. W. Mackenzie read Mr William Mackenzie.

Tional na sgire gu leir
Ri siubhal sleibh 's ri falbh bheann
Fad sgios uan coig latha deug
'S am fear direach treun air chall.

Murachadh donn-gheal mo run
Bu mhin-suil 's bu leannan mnai
A ghnuis anns an robh am ball-seire
'S a bha tearc air thapadh laimh.

Chuala mise clarsach theud,
'S fiodhall do rear a co-sheinn—
Cha chuala 's cha chluinn gu brath
Ceol na b' fhearr na do bheul binn,

Bu tu marbhaich' bhalla-bhric-bhain,
Le morbh fhada dhireach gheur,
Le cuilbheir bhristeadh tu cnaimh
'S bu shilteach fo d' laimh na feidh.

Bhean uasal a thug dhut gaol
Nach bi chaoidh na h-uaigneas slan,
'S truagh le me chluasan a gaoir
Luaithead 's tha 'n snaim sgaoilt le de' bhas.

Gur tuirsach do chaomh bhean og
'S i sileadh nan deoir le gruaidh
'S a spionadh a fuilt le dorn
Sior chumha nach beo do shnuagh.

'S tursach do chinneadh mor deas
Ga d' shireadh an car 's an iar
'S an t-og a b' fhiughantaich beachd
Ri slios glinne marbh 's an t-sliabh.

Tha Crathaich nam buailtean bo
Air 'n sgaradh ro-mhor mu d'eug,
Do thoir bho bheatha cho og
A ghaisgich ghlan choir nam beus.

'S tuirseach do sheachd braithrean graidh
Am *parson* ge hard a leugh
Thug e, ge tuigseach a cheard,
Aona bharr-tuirs air cach gu leir.

Bho thus dhiubh Donnachadh nam Pios,
Gillecriosd 's an dithis de'n chleir,
Fearachar agus Ailean Donn,
Uisdean a bha trom 'n ad dheigh.

'S math am fear rannsaichidh 'n t-aog,
'S e maor e thaghas air leth,
Bheir e leis an t-og gun ghiamh
'S fagaidh e 'm fear liath ro shean.

The winter hunt in Glenlic has made us often shudder in our sadness about the youth who was not parsimonious, yet was prudent, now lying in a grave under a stone in the temple. The first Friday of the cold winter dearly did we pay for the success of our hunt—the young man of most comely appearance alone missing, and to be found dead. All the people of the parish searching on moor and mountain during the weariness of fifteen days, for the athletic brave man who was missing. The fair complexioned Murdoch of my choice, of gentle eye, the beloved of woman, of a countenance with the expression of kindness, and rare for prowess of arm. I have heard the stringed harp and the violin in harmony playing with it, I have neither heard, nor shall ever hear sweeter music than (the converse of) thy melodious mouth. Thou couldst kill speckled white trout, with long straight and sharp spear ; thou couldst break bones with the gun, and the deer bled freely at your hand. The gentle woman who gave thee her love, and who can never be well in her solitude—it pains my ears to hear her lamenting how soon the marriage knot has been undone by thy death. Sad is thy gentle young wife, with tears flowing down her cheek, plucking her hair with her hand in bitter grief that there is no longer any life in thy countenance. Sad was thy great and accomplished clan, searching for thee east and west, while the youth of most sympathetic judgment was (dead) on the moor on the side of the glen. The Macraes of the cattle folds are grievously afflicted by thy death— taken out of life so young, thou generous hero of becoming conduct. Sad are thy seven beloved brothers—the parson, though profound is his learning, though his office is one of giving comfort, yet he surpassed the others in his grief. First among them is Duncan of the silver cups, then Christopher and the two clergymen, Farquhar, Allan of the auburn hair, and Hugh, who was sad after thee. Death is an excellent searcher, a messenger who chooses in a special way, he removes the unblemished young man, and leaves the grey-haired and very old man.

IV.

The author of the following poem was Donnachadh nam Pios (page 87), writer of the Fernaig MS.   It has been transliterated from the Fernaig MS. into modern spelling by Professor Mackinnon.[1]

Aon a rimeadh leis an Sgriobhair air lath a' bhreitheanais.

Smaoineamar an la fa dheoidh
Is coir dhuin a dhol eug,
Smaoineamar peacaidh na h'òig,
Smaoineamar fòs na thig 'n a dheigh.

Smaoineamar na thig 'n a dheigh.
Gur e la na mor bhreith ;
Gach ni rinneadh leinn 's an fheoil
Cha'n fhaodar na's mo a chleith.

Cha'n fhaodar na's mo a chleith,
Maith no sath a rinneadh leinn ;
'N uair chi sinn Breitheamh nan slogh
Teachd oirnn s na neoil, tromp 'g a seirm.

'N uair sheirmear an trompaid mhor,
Cruinnicheadar na sloigh ma seach ;
Gach neach a tharlas duibh beo
Caochlaidh iad an doigh 's am beachd.

Caochlaidh muir agus tir,
Caochlaidh gach ni as nuadh,
Liobhraidh an talamh suas,
Gach neach a chaidh anns an uir.

Gach neach a chaidh anns an uir
Eiridh iadsan 'n an nuadh chorp,
Is gabhaidh gach anam seilbh
'S a choluinn cheilg an robh chlosd.

Nior chlosd an sin do na chuan,
Gluaiseadar e fa leth ;
Na bhathadh bho thoiseach tim
Liobraidh se air chionn na breith.

Breith bheir buaidh air gach breith ;
Cha Bhreitheamh leth-bhreitheach an Righ
Shuidheas air cathair na breith
'S a bheir ceart bhreith air gach ti.

Gach ti a bha cur ri olc
Tearbar a nochd air an lamh chli ;
Cairear air a laimh dheis,
Gach ti bhios deas air a chinn.

Gach ti bhios deas air a chinn
Labhraidh 'm Breitheamh riu gu ceart ;
Bho 'n is buidheann bheannaicht' sibh,
Maitheam-sa dhuibhs' 'n 'ur peac'.

Maitheam-sa dhuibhs' 'n 'ur peac' ;
Gabhaidh-s' seilbh cheart 's an rio'chd
Chomharraich m' Athair bho thos,
Dhuibhse ann an gloir gun chrich.

Oir air bhi dhomhsa fo thart,
Fo fhuachd, fo acras, chum bais,
'M priosan gun treoir gun neart,
Dh' fhuasgail sibh ceart air mo chas.

Air bhi dhomh a'm choigreach cein
'S a'm *thraveller* anns gach bail',
Fhreasdail sibh dhombsa 'n am fheum ;
Cha robh ar deagh-bheus dhomh gann.

Ach freagraidh iadsan am Breitheamh,
Cuin chunnaiceamar sibh fo thart,
Fo fhuachd, fo acras, chum bais,
'S a dh' fhuasgail sinn do chas ceart ?

Bheirim-sa dearbhadh dhuibh,—
Dh' fhuasgail 's gur ann duibh nach olc,
Mheud 's gu'n d' rinneadh leibhse dhiol,
Ri piantaibh mo bhraithre bochd-s'.

Sin labhraidh 'm breitheamh os n' aird
Riu fhuair ait' air a laimh chli,
Imichibh uamsa gu brath,
Dh' ionnsuidh cais is craidh gun chrich.

Far am bi 'n t-Abharsair am pein,
Aingle 's a chleir air fad,
Mheud 's nach d' rinneadh leibhse dhiol
Ri piantaibh mo bhraithre lag-s'.

Imichidh iad so gu truagh
Dh' Ifrinn fhuair am bi fuachd is teas,
Dhoibh-san ge duilich an cas,
Nior faigh iad bas ann am feasd.

Ach imichidh buidheann a ghraidh
A fhuair ait air an lamh dheis
Do fhlaitheanas nam flath feile ;
O ! eibhinn doibh-san an treis.

O ! eibhinn doibh-san an treis,
Eibhinn doibh-san gach ni chi,
Eibhinn bhi 'n cathair nan gras,
Eibhinn bhi lathair a Bhreithimh.

Eibhinn bhi lathair a Bhreithimh,
Eibhinn a shiochai' 's a bhuaidh ;
Cha'n fhaodar a chur an ceill
Meud eibhneis an aite bhuain.

Eibhneas e nach faca suil,
Eibhneas e nach cuala cluas,
Eibhneas e nach teid air chul,
Dhoibh-san d'an toirear mar dhuais.

Duais is mo na gach duais,
Ta shuas air neamh aig mo Righ ;
Eibhinn do gach neach a ghluais,
Air chor's gu'm buaidhaichear i.

Air chor's gu'm buadhaichear i
Smaoneamar air crich an sgeoil,
Smaoneamar ar peacaidh bath,
Smaoneamar an la fa dheoidh.

One by the writer on the Day of Judgment.

Let us meditate on the last day when it must fall to our lot to
die, let us meditate on the sins of youth, let us meditate still
further on what must come hereafter.   Let us meditate on what
must come hereafter, that is on the great Day of Judgment, when
nothing done by us in the flesh can any longer be concealed.   No
longer can be concealed the good or the evil done by us, when
we see the judge of all people coming to us in the clouds, with
the sound of the trumpet.   When the great trumpet is sounded,
all people shall assemble from every quarter ; those who happen
to be still alive shall change in manner and in mind.   Sea and
land shall change, all things shall be changed anew, the earth
shall yield up all who are buried in the dust.   All who are buried
in the dust shall rise in their new bodies, and each soul shall
take possession of the false body in which it formerly rested.

No rest then for the ocean, it shall be agitated on its own account; all who were drowned from the beginning of time it shall yield up for the judgment. A judgment that will surpass every judgment; no partial judge is the King who shall sit on the judgment seat, and give righteous judgment to all. Those who gave themselves up to evil will, on that day, be banished on the left hand; on the right hand will be placed those who are prepared for His coming. To those who are prepared for His coming the Judge will openly say : " Because you are a blessed company I will pardon your sins. I will pardon your sins; take you rightful possession of the kingdom set apart from the beginning by my Father for you in glory everlasting. For when I was thirsty and cold and hungry unto death in prison, without energy or strength, you brought true relief to my trouble. Being a stranger far away, and a sojourner in many places, you waited on me in my necessity ; your deeds of kindness towards me were not few." But they will answer the judge, " When did we see thee thirsty, cold, and hungry unto death, and brought true relief to your trouble ?" "I will give you a proof—you brought relief, nor will it be to your hurt, inasmuch as you showed compassion for the suffering of my poor brethren." Then will the judge openly speak to those placed on the left hand—"Depart from me, for ever, to everlasting trouble and torment ! Where the Adversary will continue in torment, together with his angels and ministers for ever, inasmuch as you showed no compassion for the sufferings of my feeble brethren." Miserably will they depart to dismal Hell, where there will be cold and heat ; however agonising for them may be their trouble, they can never die there. But the company of beloved ones, placed on the right, will depart to the paradise of the hospitable princes ; Oh ! joyful will it be for them the while. Oh ! joyful will it be for them the while, joyful for them all that they behold, joyful to be in the city of grace, joyful to be in the presence of the judge. Joyful to be in the presence of the judge, joyful his peace and his glory ; it is not possible to declare the greatness of the joy of the everlasting place. Joy which eye never beheld, joy which ear never heard, joy that will not cease for those to whom it will be given as a reward. Greater than all rewards is the reward up in Heaven with my King ; joyful for everyone who has so conducted him-

self as to attain to it.   That it may be deserved, let us think of
the end of the tale, let us think of our deadly sin, let us think
of the last day.

V.

The following poem, also by Donnachadh nam Pios, has been
transliterated from the Fernaig MS. into modern spelling by
George Henderson, Ph.D.[1] :—

Gne orain do rinneadh leis a sgriobhair, anno 1688.

Ta saoghal-sa carail,
Tha e daondan da 'r mealladh gu geur ;
Liuthad caochladh th' air talamh
Is daoin' air an dalladh le bhreig ;
Chreic pairt duibh-s' an anam
'S do chaochlaidh iad barail chionn seud,
Fhir chaidh ann sa chrannaig,
Dhoirt t' fhuil da ar ceannach,
O ! aoin Righ Mhoire beannuich nar creud.

O ! Athair nan gras
Na failing sinne 'nar cruas,
Ach amhraic oirnn trath
Le tlaths o d' fhlathas a nuas.
Mar thug thu le d' mhioraild
Clann Israel gun dhiobhair sa chuan,
Dionn t' eaglais da rireadh,
Ga ghuidh le luchd a mi ruin,
Bho 'sgriob-s' ta teachd mu' cuairt.

'S coir dhi-s' a bhi umhailt
Gad tha i fo dhubh ann san am ;
Gur h-iad ar peacannan dubhar
Tharruing oirnn pudhar is call ;
Ach deanmar trasg agus cumha
Ris an fhear dh' fhag an t-iubhair sa chrann,
Chon s' gu 'n ceannsuich e' bhuidheann
Chleachd an eu-coir as duibhe,
Mar tha breugan is luighean is feall.

Dhe churanta laidir
Dh' alaich muir agus tir,
Tha thu faicsinn an drasda
Mar dh' fhailing am prabar-s' an Righ ;

1 See Leabhar nan Gleann, p. 271.

Ach reir 's mar thachair do Dhaidh,
Nuair ghabh Absolon fath air go dhith,
Beir dhachaigh 'na dhail leat,
Dh' aindeoin am pairtidh,
Nar Righ chon aite le sith.

Fear eil' 's math is eol domh
Tha 'n ceart uair air fogaireadh 'na phairt,
Shliochd nan cuireannan seolta
Da thogradh 's nach obadh an spairn ;
Ga tamull leinn bhuainn thu
Cha toireamar fuath dhut gu brach ;
Sann da 'r seors bu dual sin,
Eatar mhith agus uaislean,
Bhi air do dheas-laimh an cruadal 's an cas.

Truagh nach fhaicinn thu teachd
Mar b' ait le mo chridh san am,
Far ri Seumas le buidheann
Nach geill a dh' iubhair nan Gall,
Tha 'n drasda ro bhuidheach
. Mheud s gu 'n shuidhich iad feall,
Le 'n seoladh 's le 'n uidheam
Anns na modaibh as duibhe,
Chuir fa dheoidh sibh air suibhail do'n **Fhraing**.

Ach thamar an duigh
Gu'n caochail an cursa seo fothast,
Gu'm faic mi le m' shuilibh
Bhi sgiursadh gach tnu bha 's na moid,
'S gach Baron beag cubach
'Mhealladh le caraibh 's le luban Prionns **Or** ;
Gheibh Mac Cailein air thus duibh,
Dh' aindeoin a chuirte,
'Galair bu duthchasach dho.

B'e dhuthchas bho sheanair
Bhi daondan r'a melladh gach ti,
Cha b'fhearr e 'thaobh athair
Ga b' mhor a mhathas bho' Righ ;
Ma 'se seo an treas gabhail
Thug eug bhuaith 'bhathar gu pris,
Le maighdinn sgoraidheach sgathail
Cha d' cheannsuicheadh aisith ;
Ged thuit thu cha'n athais duit i.

Iomah Tighearn is *post*
Nach eol domh-s' a nis 'chur an dan
Tha'n drasda gu moiteil
Le phrabar gu bosdail a' d' phairt ;

'S anu diubh sin Cullodar,
Granntaich is Rosaich a chail,
Nuair thionndas an rotha
Chon annsachd bho thoiseach
Gur teannta dhaibh 'chroich 'miosg chaich.

Ach fhearaibh na h' Alba
Ga dealbhach libh 'drasda 'n ur cuirt,
Gad leught' sibh bho'r leanabachd
'S bho la 'gheil sibh a dh' Fhergus air thus,
Thuit gach fine le toirmeasg
Do threig 's nach robh earbsach do'n chrun,
Ach seo t'eallach a dhearbhas
Gur h-airidh an seanchas,
Gun eirich mi-shealbhar da'n cliu.

Cha chan mi na's leir dhombh
Ri 'ur maithibh, ri'r cleir, ri'r por,
D'eis ur mionnan a Shearlas
Gu seiseamh sibh-p fhein 'n aghaidh deoin,
'S an t-oighre dligheach na dh'eis
Thuit nis go Righ Seumas r'a bheo,
Ach dh'aindeoin ur leirs'
Ga mor 'ur cuid leugh',
Ar liom-s gu'n 'reub sibh a choir.

. . . . . air coir dhirich
Le masladh na dhiobair do phairt,
Bha uair a staid iosal
S tha air direadh le uchd math an drasd;
Seann fhacla 's gur fior e
Bha riamh eadar Chriostuidhean graidh,
Gur miosa na ana-spiorad
Duine mi-thaingeil
Ghabh na's leoir dhuibh-s an aim air na chas.

Càs eile nach fas'
Dheirich mar fhasan sa ruaig' s',
Chlann feinn bhi na'n taic
Do gach neach tha cur as da mu cuairt ;
Do threig iad 's cha 'n ait daibh
'N cuigeamh faithn' bha 'chasgadh an t-sluaigh;
'N aghaidh nadur a bheart seo
Do neach 'ghabh baisteadh
Ann an ainn nan tri pearsan ta shuas.

Ach fhir 'dh'oibrich gach mioraild
Bha miosg Chlainn Israel bho thus,
Nach soilleir an giamh seo
Dh'aon neach ghabh 'Chriosdachd mar ghrund?

Bho laigh geilt agus fiamh mor
Air gach Marcus, gach Iarl 's gach Diuc,
Casg fein an iorghalt-s
Mas toil leat-s a Dhia e,
Mu tuit sinn fo fhiabhrus do ghnuis.

Is mor dh' eireas dhut a Bhreatuinn
'S nach d'fhaodadh do theagasg na am,
Cha leir dhut fath t'eagla,
Gu'n tharruing ana-creidimh ort call;
Bho'n la mhurtadh libh Searlas
Tha fhuil-san ag eigheachd gu teann,
Gabh aithri a t' eucoir,
Thoir dhachaigh Righ Seumas,
Neo thig sguirsa bho Dhe ort a nall.

Ghaidhealu gasda
Na laighidh fo mhasladh sa chuis,
Ach faighear sibh tapaidh
'S Righ Seumas na thiac air ur cul;
Ge ta Uilleam an Sasunn
Na geillibh a feasda do chrun;
Liom is cinnteach mar thachras
Thaobh innleachd a bheairtean,
Gu pilltear e dhachaigh gun chliu.

Na ma h'ioghnadh libh-p fhein seo
'S gun ghlac es' an eucoir air cheann,
Bha *manifesto* ro eitigh,
Nach faic sibh gur breugach a chainnt;
'S gach gealladh do rinn se
Do Shasunn do threig se gu teann,
Tha iad nis 'n aghaidh cheile,
Nuair thuig siad an reusan,
Ach na tha Phresbiterianich ann.

Na ma lughaid 'ur misneachd
Gu robh iad seo bristneach na curs,
Fo sgaile *religion*
B'e 'n abhaist s an gliocas bho thus;
Co dhiubh alach a nise
Nach . . . .   le mi-ruin,
Ach tha'n aite le fios dhuinn,
Ged dh'fhailing righean tric iad,
Aig gach armunn bha tiorcadh a chruin.

Gu ma h'-amhluidh seo dh' eireas
'Mhaithibh Alba s na h' Eire san am,
Tha 'coitheamh le Seumas
'S nach d' amhraic iad fein air an call;

Ach b' fheall am bathais 's an eudan
Fo gach neach bha ri eiginn 's ri feall,
Ghabh an *test* a bha eitigh,
Eadar mhaithibh is Chleire,
Thoir an anman dha 'n eucoireach mheallt.

Ach tha mi dall na mo bharail
Mar ceannsuich Dia 'charachd-sa trath,
'S mar mhealtar leis barail
'Chleamhnais fhuair alloil gun bhlath ;
Is mairg a thoisich mar ealaidh
Athair-ceile chur ealamh bho bhair,
Ach seo ordugh nam balach,
Far ri dochus nan cailleach,
San t-saoghal chruaidh charail-s' a ta.

Song composed by the writer in the year 1688.

This world is deceitful, it constantly deceives us bitterly, many
changes there are on earth and many men blinded by its falsehood.
Some have sold their souls and have changed opinion for the sake
of gain.   Thou who suffered on the Cross and spilt Thy blood for
our redemption, Oh ! Thou only King (son) of Mary, bless our creed.
Oh ! Father of Grace, do not fail us in our sore distress, but look
upon us soon with tenderness from Thy Heaven above.   As Thou
didst miraculously lead the children of Israel, without the loss of
any, through the sea, so do Thou in very deed defend Thy Church
(though her ill-wishers pray for her downfall) from the evil now
fallen upon her.   It is her duty to be humble, though she is at
this moment under a cloud.   Her sins are the cause that have
brought upon us harm and loss, but let us fast and mourn to Him
who went to the Cross without faltering, that He may subdue
them who have been practising the blackest deeds, falsehood,
sacrilege, and treachery.   O God, mighty and strong, who peopled
land and sea, Thou seest how at this juncture the rabble has disappointed the King ; but as it happened in the case of David,
when Absalom took advantage of him (to try) to ruin him, do
Thou, in Thy appointed time, lead the King home in peace to his
own place in spite of their factions.   Another man[1] I know full
well, who at this moment is in exile for his (King James's) cause—

[1] Perhaps Kenneth, fourth Earl of Seaforth, who accompanied James II.
to France after the Revolution of 1688.

of the race of the capable heroes, who would accept and never refuse the strife.   Though for a little thou art away from us, we
shall never feel indifferent towards thee.   It is in the blood of our
race, commons and nobles alike, to stand by thy right hand in the
time of difficulty and trouble.   Would that I might see thee coming as my heart at this moment would desire, along with King
James with a host that would not yield to the bows and arrows of
the Lowlanders, who are rejoicing at having planned their treachery
with the cunning and resources of their dark councils, which have
at last driven you an exile into France.   But I am in hopes that
the course of events will yet change, and that I may see with my
own eyes the discomfiture of every wretch who took part in their
councils, and of every petty, cringing baron, who, by his tricks and
wiles, deceived Prince Orange; Argyll, in spite of his rank, will, as
one of the first, be smitten with the disease that comes natural to
him.   It comes natural to him from his grandfather to deceive
everyone, nor is he better from his father, though he (the father)
received so much kindness from his King.   If this is the third
occasion on which the disease was caught from a "maiden" sharp-
toothed, clear-cutting, disgrace has not been quelled though he
were to fall by her, to him it would be no disgrace.   There are many
lords and officials whom I cannot now mention in my verse, who at
the present time, together with their rabble, boast with affected
modesty of their connection with thee (Argyll).   Among them are
Culloden, the Grants, the Rosses of the cabbage.   When the wheel
turns round to its first love they will find themselves among the
rest quite close to the gallows.   But, ye men of Scotland, though
your court (*i.e.*, your political situation) may now seem satisfactory
to you, still, if your story be read from your infancy even as far
back as the day when you first submitted to Fergus, it will be
found that every clan has fallen by appointed decree—who
deserted and proved faithless to the Crown.   But this is a forge that
will test unfailingly the truth of the saying that " a stain may fall
on their honour."   I am not going to speak about all I know, to
our nobles, our clergy, our people, after your oath to Charles that
you would stand by him, come what may, and by his legitimate
heir, who is now King James, for life ; but in spite of your sagacity,
and wide though your learning may be, you are certainly violating
the right.   (Not to speak of his) undoubted right, it is a disgrace

that so many have forsaken his cause, who were once in lowly estate, but have now climbed by good fortune upwards. There is a proverb, and a true one, which has ever been in use among loving Christians—that worse than a hostile spirit is the ungrateful man ; many such have taken advantage of him (the King) in his trouble. Another matter, not less sad, which has come into prominence in this affair—his own children supporting those who are everywhere opposing him. They have forsaken, and not to their joy, the fifth commandment given for the guidance of people. Such conduct is unnatural in anyone who has received baptism in the name of the Trinity on high. But Thou, the worker of all the wonders that were seen from the first among the children of Israel, is not this a very apparent guilt for anyone professing Christian principles ? Since a great fear and cowardice has fallen upon every Marquis, every Earl, and every Duke, do Thou thyself check their turbulence, if it be Thy will, O God, lest we fall under the wrath of Thy countenance. Much may happen to thee, O Britain, since thou didst refuse to receive warning in time. Thou dost not see the cause of thy fear, for unbelief has brought disaster upon thee. Since the day King Charles was murdered, his blood is constantly crying out. Repent of thy guilt, bring King James home, or destruction from God will surely come down upon thee. Ye worthy Gaels, don't rest under disgrace, but be of courage with King James to back you up. Though William is in England, never yield allegiance to his Crown. Certain it seems to me what will happen from the deceitfulness of his schemes, he will be driven back in disgrace. Let this not surprise you, seeing that he has seized injustice by the head (*i.e.*, has acted upon it from the outset). His manifesto was altogether perjured. Don't you see how false his words are, and how he instantly renounced every promise he made to England. They (his supporters) are now at variance among themselves since they have understood his object, except such Presbyterians as there are among them. Let not your courage be any the less that these (the Presbyterians) have always been unstable in their allegiance. Under the veil of religion it has been their custom and their policy from the first . . . . . . But we know that each hero who succoured the Crown holds his position, though Kings may often have failed them. So may it happen to the nobles of Scotland and Ireland who are

fighting for James without thinking of their loss, but treacherous
were the countenance and face of each one engaged in mischief and
deceit, who accepted the perjured "test," whether nobles or clergy,
giving up their souls to the crafty evil one.   But I am blind in my
opinion if God will not soon check this treachery, and bring to
nought the schemes of cold, unnatural, sterile blood-relationship.
Woe to him who commenced his career by suddenly making war
upon his own father-in-law ; but such is the way of clowns and the
hope of carlines in this callous and deceitful world.

VI.

Of the poets of Kintail, no one is better remembered than Ian
Mac Mhurachaidh (pp. 81-83), or has left behind him a greater
wealth of song. Though in comfortable circumstances, he disliked
the purely mercenary relations which were beginning to grow up
between landlord and people, and therefore resolved to emigrate
to Carolina. The following is one of several songs which he composed in order to induce as many as possible of his countrymen
to accompany him :—

> Thanig leitir bho Ian Beitean
> Chuir eibhneas air fear nach fhac i.
>
> Beagan do mhuinntir mo dhuthcha
> Triall an toabh am faigh iad pailteas.
>
> Far am faigh sinn deth gach seorsa
> An t-sealg is boidhche tha ri fhaicinn.
>
> Gheabh sinn fiadh is boc is moisleach
> 'S comas na dh' fhaodar thoir asda.
>
> Gheabh sinn coileach-dubh is liath chearc
> Lachan, ialtan agus glas gheoidh.
>
> Gheabh sinn bradan agus ban iasg
> 'S glas iasg ma 's e 's fhearr a thaitneas.
>
> B' fhearr na bhi fuireach fo uachd'rain
> 'S nach fuiligeadh iad tuath bhi aca.
>
> A ghabhadh an an aite 'n t' sheoid
> An t' or ged bann a spog a phartainn.
>
> A ghabhadh an an aite 'n diunloaich
> Siogaire sgugach 's e beartach.

Falbhamaid 's bitheadh beannachd Dhia leinn
Triallamaid, riadhamaid barca.

Falbhamaid uile gu leir
'S gur beag mo speis do dh' fhear gun tapadh.

Thogainn fonn, fonn, fonn,
Dh' eireadh fonn oirn ri fhaicinn.

There came a letter from John Bethune, which has given joy
to one who has not seen it.　A few of my country people about to
depart to a land of plenty, where we can find every kind of the
most delightful hunting that could be seen.　We shall find deer,
buck and doe, with permission to take as many as we want.　We
shall get the woodcock and the woodhen, teals, ducks, and wild
geese.　We shall get salmon and white fish, and grey fish if it
will please us better.　Better far than stay under landlords who
won't suffer a tenantry with them; who would take, instead of a
good man, gold, were it from the claw of a lobster; who would
take, instead of a brave man, a sulky sneak, provided he was rich.
Let us depart, and may the blessing of God be with us; let us go
and charter a ship.　Let us depart, all of us, for small is my
esteem for a man of no courage.

I would raise a chorus of delight; we should be delighted on
seeing it.

VII.

When the ship, by which Ian Mac Mhurachaidh and so many
of his countrymen were about to leave Kintail, arrived at Caileach,
where it anchored, the poet invited the captain of the ship to
dinner with him.　When the captain saw the good cheer provided,
he told the poet that he would not be able to fare so sumptuously
in America, and strongly advised him to remain at home.　The
poet's wife and some other friends who were present also urged
him to the same effect with such earnestness that his resolution
was almost overcome, but he felt that, after all he had done and
said, he could not desert the people he had induced to join him,
and who looked up to him as their leader, so he decided, at whatever sacrifice, to go along with them; and the next song, which was
probably less applicable to the poet's own circumstances than to

those of some of his fellow-emigrants, was composed to cheer and encourage them as the ship was sailing away :—

Nise bho na thachair sinn
Fo's cionn an stoip 's na creachaige,
Gu'n ol sinn air na faicinn e
'S na cairtealan san teid sinn.

Mhnathan togaidh an turrus oirbh
'Us sguiribh dheth na h-iomadan,
Cha bharail leum gun tillear mi
Bho'n sguir mi dh 'iomain spreidhe.

Mhnathan sguiribh chubarsnaich
Bho'n char sibh fo na siuil a stigh,
Cha bharail leam gu'n lubar sinn
Ri duthaich bhochd na h-eiginn.

H-uile cuis dha theannachadh,
An t' ardachdainn se ghreannaich sinn,
Lin-mhora bhi dha'n tarruin
'S iad a sailleadh na cuid eisg oirn.

Gur iomadh latha saraicht'
Bha mi deanamh dige 's garraidhnean,
An crodh a faighinn bais oirn
'Us mi paidheadh mail gu h-eigneach.

'S iomadh latha dosguineach
A bha mi giulan cosguis dhuibh,
'N uair reidheadh a chuis gu osburnaich
Bhi 'g osunaich ma deighinn.

'S beag mo speis d' an uachdaran
A chuir cho fad air cuan sinn,
Air son beagan do mhal suarach
'S cha robh buanachd aige fhein deth.

            Tha tighinn fotham, fotham, fotham,
            Tha tighinn fotham eiridh.

Now that we have met over a stoup and drinking-shell, let us drink in anticipation of seeing the quarters whither we are going. Women, take courage for the voyage, and stop your mourning; I don't think I can be induced to return, now that I have ceased to herd cattle. Women, restrain your anxiety, now that you have gone under the sails; I don't think I can be bent backwards to the poor country of destitution. Every thing is being tightened, the raising (of rents?) is what has embittered us; trawling with great nets, and salting our fish. Many a hard day was I making dykes and walls, my cattle dying, while I paid rent with difficulty. Many an unfortunate day have I borne expenses on your account, and when the matter fell into ruin, I sighed over them. Small is my esteem for the landlord who has sent us so far over the ocean, for the sake of a little wretched rent, which he did not long enjoy.

I feel inclined to go.

VIII.

Among those who accompanied Ian Mac Mhurachaidh was a certain John Macrae—a blacksmith—called Ian Mac a Ghobha (page 193). The American War of Independence began almost immediately after the arrival of the Kintail emigrants in Carolina, and they unhesitatingly cast in their lot with the Loyalists. The poet now became one of the foremost, by his songs and his example, in urging his brother Highlanders to stand up in defence of what he considered to be the just rights of their King and country, and consequently, when the Americans got him into their hands they treated him with unusual severity. Ian Mac a Ghobha lost his arm in the war, and, making his way back to Scotland, eventually succeeded, after considerable difficulty, in obtaining a pension for his services. He appears to have been a man of mark in more ways than one. He possessed an excellent voice and an excellent memory, and brought back with him to Kintail several of Ian Mac Mhurachaidh's songs, which he was never tired of singing. He died at Carndu, near Dornie, in 1839, aged ninety-three. The morning after his death an old woman, who lived by herself on the other side of the sea, opposite to Kilduich, told the first neighbour she met : " 'S mi a chuala an t-sheinn bhreagh a dol a stigh a Chlachan Duthaich an raoir, 's mar eil mi air mo mhealladh se guth binn Mhic a Ghobha a bhann."—(" What beautiful singing I heard going into Kilduich churchyard last night; if I am not mistaken, it was the sweet voice of Mac a Ghobha." Soon afterwards the news of his death arrived.[1]

The following song, perhaps Ian Mac Mhurachaidh's last, was composed by him while wandering a fugitive in the primeval forest, evidently before the close of the war, as he still looks

[1]Tradition communicated to the author by Mac a Ghobha's great-grandson, Dr Farquhar Macrae, London.

forward with hope to the arrival of Lord Cornwallis, who was
forced to surrender to the French and the Americans at Yorktown
on the 18th of October, 1781. It has been the song of many a
Kintail emigrant since the days of Ian Mac Mhurachaidh :—

'S mi air fogradh bho 'n fhoghar,
Togail thighean gun cheo unnta.

Ann am bothan beag barraich,
'S nach tig caraid dha 'm fheorach ann

Ged a tha mi s' a choille
Cha'n eil coire ri chnodach orm.

Ach 'bhi cogadh gu dileas
Leis an righ bho'n bha choir aige.

Thoir mo shoraidh le durachd,
Gus an duthaich 'm bu choir dhomh bhi.

Thoir mo shoraidh Chuitaille
Am bi manran is oranan.

A'n tric a bha mi mu'n bhuideal
Mar ri cuideachda sholasach.

Cha be 'n dram 'bha mi 'g iarraidh
Ach na b'fhiach an cuid storaidhean.

Ceud soraidh le durachd
Gu Sgur-Urain, 's math m' eolas innt'.

'S tric a bha mi mu'n cuairt di.
'G eisdeachd udlaich a cronanaich.

A bheinn ghorm tha ma coinneamh
Leum bo shoillear a neoineanan.

Sios 'us suas troimh Ghleann-Seile
'S tric a leag mi damh crocach ann.

Gheibhte bric air an linne
Fir ga 'n sireadh 'us leos aca.

Tha mi nis air mo dhiteadh
An am priosan droch bheolainteach.

Ach na 'n tigeadh Cornwallis
'S mise d' fhalbhadh ro-dheonach leis.

A thoirt sgrios air na beistean
Thug an t' eideadh 's an storas bhuam.

Tha ni sgith 'n fhogar sa
Tha mi sgith 's mi leam fhein
'S cian bho thir m' eolas mi.

I am an exile since Autumn, building houses without smoke in them. In a little hut of brushwood, where no friend will come to inquire for me. Though I am in the wood (an outlaw) no fault can be charged against me; except fighting loyally for the King because he was in the right. Take my sincere farewell to the country where I ought to be. Take my farewell to Kintail, the place of mirth and songs. Where I often sat round a bottle with a happy company. It was not the drink I desired but the worth of your stories. A hundred sincere farewells to Scur Ouran, well do I know it. Often was I in its vicinity listening to the bellowing of an old stag. The green mountain opposite to it, bright to me were its daisies. Up and down Glensheil often did I lay an antlered stag low. Trout might be found on the pool, men seeking them with a torch. I am now condemned to a prison of bad fare. But if Cornwallis came, gladly would I join him. To scourge the wretches who have robbed me of my clothes and property.

I am tired of this exile, I am tired in my loneliness,—far am I from the land of my acquaintance.

NOTE.—Several of Ian Mac Mhurachaidh's poems will be found in *The Celtic Magazine* (Inverness), April-August, 1882.

The following are some other Macrae poets whose Gaelic songs were at one time and in some instances still are known among Gaelic-speaking Highlanders :—

DUNCAN MACRAE, commonly called Donnachadh Mac Alister (page 198). Only fragments of a lament for his mother and of a song to his gun appear to be known now.

KENNETH MACRAE,[1] of the Clann Ian Charrich tribe, and a

[1] Kenneth had a son, Alexander, about whom the following paragraph appeared in *The Courier* (London) of the 28th November, 1807 :—" The oldest man now living in Scotland is supposed to be a Highlander of the name of Alexander Macrae. He was born in the parish of Kintail in the year 1687, and is now, of course, just 120 years old. In the year 1719 he fought under Lord Seaforth at the battle of Glensheil, and in 1724 he enlisted as a private in the Scots Brigade, serving in Holland, where he continued seven years, the last two of which were spent in prison in some town of France, the name of which he does not remember. In 1731 he returned to his farm and married a second wife, who died a few years after. In 1765 he fell into such low circumstances that he was forced to procure a subsistence by going about from house to house reciting Ossian's poems in Gaelic. In 1773 he married his present wife, by whom he has three children, the last when he was aged ninety-six. About

relative of Ian Mac Ian of Torlysich (foot note, page 214). He
lived at Ardelve, and was an old man at the time of the battle of
Sheriffmuir, at which he was present. On his return home he
composed a celebrated lament, or ballad, on the "Four Johns of
Scotland" (foot note, page 153), which is given in "The Transactions of the Gaelic Society of Inverness," Vol. VIII.—Leaves
from my Celtic Portfolio, by Mr William Mackenzie.

CHRISTOPHER MACRAE, Sergeant in the 78th Highlanders
(page 80). Some of his songs are still well known in Kintail and
Lochalsh.

DONALD MACRAE, a weaver in the parish of Petty in Inverness-
shire, where he was born in 1756, and died in 1837. His father
was a native of Glenclchaig in Kintail. He was the author of
several religious poems, which are spoken of very highly in *The
Literature of the Highlanders* by the Rev. Nigel Macneill.

JOHN MACRAE, schoolmaster at Sleat in Skye (page 183).

THE REV. DONALD MACRAE of Ness in Lewis (page 83) is
mentioned in Macneill's *Literature of the Highlanders* as a true
poet, though he did not produce much. His best known song is
"The Emigrant's Lament," written on the occasion of the departure of many of his congregation for Canada.

JOHN MACRAE (page 130, *c*3) composed, among other Gaelic
songs, one on the late Professor Blackie of Edinburgh.

JAMES MACRAE of Ardroil in Lews (page 193) composed several
good, and sometimes humorous, Gaelic songs.

twelve years ago, while still very stout, he was deprived of the use of his limbs
by a violent fever, and ever since has been unable to walk. He is now bed-
ridden, deaf and blind, but his memory is still very correct. His general
amusement is singing and repeating Ossian's poems in Gaelic, but he repeats
so fast that it is impossible to write them down, and, if interrupted, must
again return to the beginning of the poem. He appears to have been a stout-
made, middle-sized man, and still looks uncommonly well." The old man
lived at Ardelve, and this paragraph is believed to have been communicated to
the *London Courier* by the Rev. Lachlan Mackenzie of Lochcarron, who on one
occasion, while attending a meeting of his Presbytery at Ardelve, visited him
at his home. It is said that in the course of the conversation, Mr Lachlan
asked the old man if he was not afraid of death. "O dhuine bhoc," replied
the old man, "nam faicadh d'thu Ceither Ianan na h' Alba folbh gu Sliabh an
t' Shiorradh 's ann orra nach robh feagal roimh 'n bhas."—(Poor man, if you
had seen the four Johns of Scotland setting out for Sheriffmuir, little did they
fear death).

JOHN MACRAE of Timsgarry in Lews (page 194).

DUNCAN MACRAE[1] of Isle Ewe in Gairloch, a faithful follower of Prince Charlie, whom he accompanied throughout the Rising of 1745, and whose retreat he assisted to cover after the defeat of Culloden, composed a well-known Gaelic song called "Oran na Feannaige" (the song of the crow). It consists of an imaginary dialogue between himself and a crow which he saw in Edinburgh while there with the Prince.

---

[1] This Duncan Macrae was believed to possess the gift of the Sian. This gift was supposed to enable a man, by means of an incantation, to render an object invisible until the charm was removed, except for a short time at regular intervals usually of seven years. Shortly after the Battle of Culloden, a French ship, which put in at Poolewe, left a cask of gold for the use of the Prince. According to the traditions of Gairloch, this cask was entrusted to Duncan's care, and being unable at that time to escape the vigilance of the King's troops, and convey the gold to the Prince, he hid the cask in a place in Gairloch called the Fedan Mor, making use of the Sian to render it invisible. The cask never reached the Prince. On one occasion, about 1826, the cask suddenly became visible to a shepherd's wife who was spinning there with a spindle and distaff while herding her cattle. She stuck the spindle in the ground to mark the spot, and ran home for help to remove the treasure, but when her friends arrived at the spot neither the cask nor the distaff could be discovered.—*Dixon's Gairloch*, p. 165.

APPENDIX K.

It has already been stated, in Chapter I., that the district of Gairloch is rich in Macrae traditions. The following traditions are taken from Mr John H. Dixon's book on Gairloch, with the kind permission of the author :—

HOW THREE MACRAES FROM KINTAIL ATTEMPTED TO DRIVE THE MACBEATHS FROM GAIRLOCH AND PUT THE COUNTRY IN POSSESSION OF MACKENZIE OF KINTAIL.

Once upon a time there lived a powerful man—Ian Mac Ian Uidhir (John the son of Sallow John)—in the Carr of Kintail, and when he heard such aliens (the Macbeaths) resided in the island of Loch Tollie (in Gairloch) he thought within himself, on New Year's night, that it was a pity such mischievous strangers should be in the place, raising rents on the land which did not of right belong to them, while some of the offspring of gentlemen of the Clan Mackenzie, although a few of them possessed lands, were without possessions.

Some time after this, when the snow was melting off the mountains, he lifted his arrow bag on his back, sent word for Big Donald Macrae from Inverinate, and they walked as one together across Killelan. Old Alastair Liath (Grey Alexander) of Carr accompanied them. They walked through the mountains of Lochcarron. They came in by the mountains of Kinlochewe. They came at a late hour in sight of Loch Tollie, and they took notice of Macbeath's castle in the island, and of a place whence it would be easy for them to send their arrows to the castle. There was a rowan tree alongside the castle, which was in their way, but when the darkening of night came they moved down to the shore in such a way that the heroes got near the bank of the loch, so that they might, in the breaking of the sky, be opposite Macbeath when he came out.

When Macbeath came out in the morning, the other man said to Donald Mor, "Try how true your hand is now, if it is not tremulous after the night ; try if you can hit the seed of the beast, the hare, so that you make a carcase of him where he is, inasmuch as he has no right to be there." Donald shot his arrow by chance, but it only became flattened against one of the kind of windows in the kind of castle that was in it.

When the man from Carr saw what happened to the arrow of the man from Inverinate, he thought that his companion's arrow was only a useless one. The man from Carr got a glimpse of one of the servants of Macbeath, carrying with him a stoup of water to boil a goat buck, which he had taken from Craig Tollie the night before ; but, poor fellow! it was not he who consumed the goat buck. Old Alastair Liath of Carr threw the arrow, and it went through the kidneys of him of the water-stoup.

Macbeath suspected that a kind of something was behind him which he did not know about. He thought within himself not to wait to eat the goat buck, that it would be as well for him to go ashore—life or death to him—as long as he had the chance to cross. He lifted every arrangement he had, and he made the shore of it. Those who would not follow him he left behind him ; he walked as fast as was in his joints, but fast as Macbeath was, the arrow of the son of Big Donald fixed in him in the thickest of his flesh. He ran with the arrow fixed, and his left hand fixed in the arrow, hoping always that he would pull it out. He ran down the brae to a place which is called Boora to this day, and the reason of that name is, that when Macbeath pulled the arrow out a buradh, or bursting forth of blood, came after it.

When the Kintail men saw that the superior of the kind of fortress had flown, they walked round the head of Loch Tollie, sprawling, tired as they were ; and the very ferry-boat which took Macbeath ashore took the Macraes to the island. They used part of the goat buck which Macbeath was to have had to his meal. They looked at the man of whom they had made a corpse, while the cook went to the preparation for the morning meal. Difficulty nor distress were not apparent on the Kintail men. The fearless heroes put past the night in the castle. They feared not Macbeath ; but Macbeath was frightened enough that what he did not get he would soon get.

Although the pursuit of the aliens from Mackay's[1] country was in the minds of the Kintail men, they thought they would go and see how the lands of Gairloch lay. They went away in the morning of the next day, after making cuaranan (untanned shoes) of the skin of the goat buck by putting thongs through it, as they had worn out their own on the way coming from Kintail. They came through Gairloch; they took notice of everything as they desired. They walked step by step, as they could do, without fear or bodily dismay. They reached Mackenzie's Castle; they saluted him. They said boldly, if he had more sons, that they would find more land for him. Mackenzie invited them in and took their news. They told him about the land of Gairloch, the way in which they saw Macbeath, and the way in which they made him flee, and the time on which they lived on the flesh of the goat buck. "And Kenneth," says Donald (addressing the chief), "I shall remember the day of the foot of the goat buck as long as Donald is (my name) on me."—*Dixon's Gairloch*, pp. 21-23.

HOW IAN LIATH MACRATH (GREY JOHN MACRAE) BROUGHT JOHN ROY MACKENZIE OF GAIRLOCH INTO POSSESSION OF HIS HEREDITARY RIGHTS.

John Roy grew up a tall, brave, and handsome young Highlander. When he could carry arms and wear the belted plaid, he went to the Mackay country to visit his mother. None but his mother knew him, and neither she nor he made known who he was. In those days any stranger who came to a house was not asked who he was until he had been there a year and a day. John Roy lived in the servants' end of the house, and slept and fed with them. Mackay had two rare dogs, called Cu-dubh and Faoileag (black dog and sea gull), and they became greatly attached to John Roy, so that they would follow no one else. Near the end of the year Mackay told his wife that he suspected the stranger was a gentleman's son. Her tears revealed the truth.

---

[1] The Macbeaths were said to have come from the country of the Mackays in Sutherlandshire, probably in the thirteenth century. They had, at least, three strongholds in Gairloch, one of which was the island in Loch Tollie, as mentioned above. There are still some families of the name Macbeath both in Gairloch and in Applecross.

John Roy was then kindly received at the table of the laird, who asked him what he could do for him. John Roy begged that Mackay would give him a bodyguard, consisting of the twelve of his men whom he might choose, and the two dogs, Cu-dubh and Faoileag. He got these, and they went away to Glas Leitire in Kintail, taking with them an anker of whisky. Arriving there, John Roy placed his twelve men in concealment, and went himself to the house of Ian Liath Macrath (Grey John Macrae). It was the early morning, and the old wife was spinning on the distaff. She looked out, and saw a man there. She called to Ian Liath, who was still lying down, "There is a man out yonder sitting on a creel, and I never saw two knees in my life more like John Roy's two knees." Ian Liath got up, went to the door, and called out, "Is that you, John?" John Roy answered that it was. "Have you any with you?" "Yes, I have twelve men." "Fetch them," said Ian Liath. He killed a bull, and feasted them all. Then he told John Roy that Mackenzie of Kintail was coming that very day to hunt on the Glas Leitire hill of his (John Roy's) fathers. John Roy, with his twelve men and Ian Liath, went to the hill, taking the whisky with them. Mackenzie arrived to hunt the deer, and when he saw John Roy and his men, he sent a fair-haired lad to inquire who they were. John Roy bade the boy sit down, and gave him whisky. Whenever he rose to go, more whisky was offered, and he was nothing loath to take it. Mackenzie, thinking the lad was long in returning, sent another boy, who was treated in the same way. Mackenzie then saw that John Roy had returned, so he went back with his followers to his castle, and John Roy was not further molested by the lords of Kintail.

John Roy came back with Ian Liath to his house, when the latter told him that he had Hector Roy's chest with the title-deeds of Gairloch, and that John Roy must claim the estate. Ian Liath took all his belongings, and accompanied John Roy and his twelve men to Gairloch. They came to Beallach a Chomhla, at the side of Bathais (Bus) Bheinn. Coming down the mountain they found a good well, and there they rested and left the women and the cattle. The well is called to this day "Ian Liath's Well." They met people who informed them that Ian Dubh Mac Ruaridh Mhicleoid, or Black John the son of Rorie-

Macleod, who was governor of the old castle of the Dun, was
accustomed to walk every day across the big sand and to lie on
the top of the Crasg to spy the country. The party went to the
Crasg, and Ian Liath told Ian Dubh Mac Ruaridh Macleod,
whom they met there, that unless he left the castle before that
night he would lose his head. Macleod took the hint, and sailed
away in his birlinn, with all his valuables, except one chest containing old title-deeds, which came into John Roy's possession
along with the castle.—*Dixon's Gairloch*, pp. 39-40.

HOW THE MACRAE ARCHERS DEFEATED THE MACLEODS AT
LEAC NAN SAIGHEAD.[1]

It was after the expulsion of the Macleods that the affair of
Leac nan Saighead occurred. Many of the Macleods who had been
driven from Gairloch had settled in Skye. A number of young
men of the clan were invited by their chief to pass Hogmanay
night in his castle at Dunvegan. There was a large gathering.
In the kitchen there was an old woman, who was always occupied
in carding wool. She was known as Mor Bhan, or Fair Sarah, and
was supposed to be a witch. After dinner was over, at night the
men began to drink, and when they had passed some time thus
they sent in to the kitchen for Mor Bhan. She came and sat
down in the hall with the men. She drank one or two glasses, and
then she said it was a poor thing for the Macleods to be deprived
of their own lands in Gairloch and to live in comparative poverty
in Skye. "But," says she, addressing the whole party, "prepare
yourselves and start to-morrow for Gairloch, sail in the black birlinn, and you shall regain Gairloch. I shall be a witness of your
success when you return." The men being young and not over-
burdened with wisdom, believed her, because they thought she had
the power of divination. They set sail in the morning for Gairloch, and the black galley was full of the Macleods. It was evening when they came into the loch, and they dare not risk landing
on the mainland, for they remembered that the descendants of

[1] Leac nan Saighead is on the south coast of Gairloch, and not far from
Shieldaig.

Domhnull Greannach (a great Macrae) were still there, and they knew their powers only too well. They, therefore, turned to the south side of the loch and fastened their birlinn to Fraoch Eilean, in the shelter opposite Leac nan Saighead, between Shieldaig and Badachro. They decided to wait there till morning, then disembark and walk round the head of the loch. But all the movements of the Macleods had been well watched. Domhnull Odhar Mac Ian Liath and his brother, Ian Odhar Mac Ian Liath, the celebrated Macrae archers, sons of Ian Liath, mentioned in the last extract, knew the birlinn of the Macleods, and they determined to oppose their landing. They walked round by Shieldaig and posted themselves before daylight at the back of the Leac, a projecting rock overlooking Fraoch Eilean. The steps on which they stood at the back of the rock are still pointed out. Donald Odhar, being a short man, took the higher of the two steps, and Iain the other. Standing on these steps they crouched down in the shelter of the rock, from which they commanded a full view of the island on which the Macleods were lying here and there, while the Macrae heroes were invisible from the island. They were both celebrated shots, and had their bows and arrows with them. As soon as the day dawned they opened fire on the Macleods ; a number of them were killed before their comrades were even aware of the direction whence the fatal arrows came. The Macleods endeavoured to answer the fire, but not being able to see their foes, their arrows took no effect. In the heat of the fight one of the Macleods climbed the mast of the birlinn for a better sight of the position of the foe. Ian Odhar took his deadly aim at him when near the top of the mast. The shaft pierced his body and pinned him to the mast. " Oh," says Donald, " you have sent a pin through his broth." So the slaughter continued, and the remnant of the Macleods hurried into the birlinn. They cut the rope and turned her head seawards, and by this time only two of them were left alive. So great was their hurry to escape that they left all the bodies of their slain companions on the island. The rumour of the arrival of the Macleods had spread during the night, and other warriors such as Fionnla Dubh nan Saighead and Fear Shieldaig were soon at the scene of action ; but all they had to do was to assist at the burial of the dead Macleods. Pits were dug, into each of which a number of the dead bodies were thrown, and mounds were raised over them, which remain to this day, as anyone may see. The name Leac nan Saighead means "The flat stone of the arrows." —*Dixon's Gairloch*, pp. 45-46.

HOW FIONNLA DUBH NAN SAIGHEAD (BLACK FINLAY OF THE ARROWS) FOUGHT AND DEFEATED THE MACLEODS OF ASSYNT.

Fionnla Dubh nan Saighead was a relative of Donald Odhar and Ian Odhar, and was also of the Macraes of Kintail. Finlay usually lived at Melvaig. As a marksman, he was on a par with Donald Odhar. In his day, young Macleod, laird of Assynt, came to Gairloch in his birlinn to ask for a daughter of John Roy in marriage. He was refused, and set off northwards on his return voyage in his birlinn, which was manned with sixteen oars. They rowed quite close to the land round Rudha Reidh, the furthest out headland of the north point. Rudha Reidh was then known as Seann Rudha, a name which is still sometimes given to it. Fionnla Dubh nan Saighead sat on a rock as the birlinn passed. He called out, " Whence came the heroes ?" They replied, " We came from Gairloch." " What were you doing there ?" said Finlay. " We were asking in marriage the daughter of Mackenzie of Gairloch for this young gentleman." " Did you get her ?" said Finlay. They replied, "Oh, no." Finlay dismissed them with a contemptuous gesture and an insulting expression. They passed on their way without molesting him, because they had no arms with them. Young Macleod brooded over the insult he had received from Finlay Macrae, who was well known to him by repute. He soon returned with his sixteen-oared birlinn, manned by the choicest warriors of Assynt, to take vengeance on Finlay, who noticed the galley, and guessed who were its occupants. He called for one, Chisholm, his brother-in-arms, and the two of them proceeded to the leac, or flat stone, close to the edge of the low cliff about a mile north to Melvaig; the leac is still pointed out. They reached this place before the Macleods could effect a landing. On the way, the Chisholm said to Finlay, "You must leave all the speaking to me." As the birlinn drew near, Chisholm called out, "What do you want ?" "We want Fionnla Dubh nan Saighead." "You won't get him, or thanks," said Chisholm ; "Go away in peace."

The Macleods began to threaten them.   "If that is the way," said Chisholm, "let every man look out for himself."   The contest began.   Finlay and Chisholm were well sheltered at the back of the leac.   A number of the Macleods were killed by the arrows of the two heroes on shore, whilst they themselves remained uninjured. The Macleods, finding their losses so severe, soon thought that discretion was the better part of valour, and, turning their birlinn northwards, departed for their own country.   They never again molested Finlay.—*Dixon's Gairloch*, pp. 46-47.

NOTE.—In speaking of the Macrae archers, Mr Dixon says that the arrow fired at the serving man on the Loch Tollie Island, by Alastair Liath, must have killed its victim at a distance of fully five hundred yards.   Donald Odhar and Iain Odhar, the heroes of Leac nan Saighead, slew many Macleods with their arrows nearly four hundred yards away.   Lest any reader should doubt the authenticity of these performances on account of the marvellous range attained, Mr Dixon gives several instances of wonderful shots made by Turks, including one of four hundred and fifteen yards, against the wind, by Mahmood Effendi, the Turkish Ambassador's secretary, in a field near Bedford House, in 1794, and one of nine hundred and seventy-two yards by the Sultan himself, in 1798, in the presence of Sir Robert Ainslie, British Ambassador to the Sublime Porte.—*Dixon's Gairloch*, p. 20.

APPENDIX L.

THE MACRA BURSARIES.

THE following information has been kindly supplied by Mr P. J. Anderson, librarian of the University of Aberdeen, from the old Minute Books of the Macra foundation :—

Alexander Macra, ironmonger in Bristol, who died on 24th August, 1780, sets forth in his quaintly-worded last will and testament (dated at Edinburgh, 8th November, 1763), his desire "that a considerable portion of such share of worldly substance as I shall at the time of my death be entrusted with .by the providence and bounty of Almighty God, my gracious Creator and Supporter, may be employed in perpetuity for the mantenance, education, and instruction of indigent children, with preference to male children or boys, of the Sirname of Macra, natives of that part of Great Britain called Scotland." For this purpose he appoints as his executors the President of the Court of Session, the Dean of the Faculty of Advocates, the Senior Baillie of Edinburgh, the Senior Manager of the Orphan Asylum in Edinburgh, the Principal of King's College in Aberdon, the Professor of Divinity, the senior Professor of Philosophy, and the Professor of Humanity there, the Senior Minister, the Senior Baillie, the Dean of Guild, and the Deacon Convener of Aberdeen: directing them to allow his estate to accumulate until of the value of £20,000 Scots. Subject to an annuity of £150 Scots payable to each of his sisters (Margaret, spouse to John Matheson in Duiriness, and Mary, spouse to John Matheson in Rairaig), and to a perpetual payment of the interest on 7300 merks Scots to John Macra, son of the testator's late uncle Mr Roderick, and his heirs male, whom failing, the interest on 2000 merks Scots to the heir male of the testator's great grandfather, Alexander Macra of

Inverinet: the yearly produce of the said £20,000 Scots is to be spent "on the decent cloathing, mantenance, education, and instruction of as many indigent boys or male children of the Sirname of Macra, and all natives of Scotland, as the said nett yearly produce can sufficiently support."

The boys are to be above the age of nine, and under the age of twelve ; and preference is to be given to descendants of the testator's said great grandfather. On attaining the age of thirteen, each boy, if "he is found to have an extraordinary genius for Letters," is to come to Aberdeen to attend one of the burgh schools, "until he be fit for the Humanity class in the King's College in Aberdon . . . . and for as long thereafter as is usually allowed there, for being instructed in the Latin, Greek, and Hebrew Languages, Mathematics, Philosophy, and Divinity, if he so inclines." If not found "quite acute for Letters," a boy may be bound apprentice to some handicraft.

"And I hereby ordain that any boy's father's or other of his predecessors' using to add the letter e, h, w, or y to his surname of Macra . . . . shall not be sustained an objection to the admission of such boy, but the addition of any of these four letters to the proper surname of Macra is to be construed an inattentive complyance with the pronunciation of the word Macra, which is as various as the accent of the language is different in the several countrys wherein the father and other predecessors of such boy resided."

An action in the Court of Session for reduction of the will was unsuccessful, and the duties of the Trust were undertaken by the eight last named executors, the others declining to act.

In 1794, by which time the required sum of £20,000 Scots (£1666 13s 4d sterling) has been realised, "in consequence of information sent to Ross-shire, where the relations of the mortifier reside, sundry applications from them, supported by the clergymen of these parishes, are transmitted to the agent at Aberdeen, along with certificates of the propinquity of several familys who had children qualified in terms of the mortification to be admitted to the benefit of it."

Kenneth, son of Duncan Macra, in Linasee, Kintail, late lieutenant in the 78th Foot, and Alexander, son of Farquhar Macra, at Fadoch, Kintail, are admitted as "nearest in degree to Alex-

ander Macra of Inverinet," and come to Aberdeen, being entrusted
to the care of Professor Macleod.   Alexander, another son of
Lieut. Duncan, accompanies his brother.

In 1796 the testator's sisters and his cousin John are reported
dead, and in 1798 "Captain" Duncan, who visits Aberdeen, is
recognised as heir male of the mortifier's great grandfather, "which
is proved by the genealogys transmitted by the ministers of the
parishes where the several branches of the family reside."

1799. Alexander, son of Farquhar, enters bajan class at King's
College: graduates M.A. in 1803.   (*Officers and Graduates of
King's Coll.*, 1893, p. 268.)   A fourth boy, Duncan, son of John,
in Morvich, is admitted.

1800. Kenneth, son of Duncan, enters bajan class at King's
Coll.: in 1803 goes to London "to be placed in a mercantile
house."

1804. Alexander, son of Duncan, enters semi-class at King's
Coll.

1805. Duncan, son of John, in Morvich, "has not much
genius," and is bound apprentice for five years to Mr Littlejohn,
wright in Aberdeen.

1806. Admitted, and comes to Aberdeen to attend Grammar
School: Alexander, son of John, son of Duncan, son of Donald,
son of Christopher, lawful son of Alexander of Inverinet.   Enters
bajan class 1809; M.A. 1813.

1813. Admitted: Duncan, son by a second marriage of Captain
Duncan.   Enters bajan class in 1820, and attends four sessions,
but does not graduate.

1816. Admitted: Farquhar, son of Farquhar in Camuslunie.
Enters bajan class in 1819; M.A. 1823; appointed schoolmaster
at Lochcarron; student of divinty 1823-27; minister of Free
Church, Knockbain.

1824. Admitted: Christopher, whose propinquity is certified
by Archibald Macra of Ardintoul and many respectable persons
of the clan, "the boy being in a state of absolute nakedness and
starvation"; proved to be over age.

1826. Admitted: Farquhar, son of Alexander; proved to be
over age.   Duncan, son of Murdoch, in Stornoway; proved to be
over age.   John, son of Duncan, in Camuslunie.   Donald, son of
John, in Conchra.

1831. A. Mitchell, Headmaster of the Grammar School, Old Aberdeen, reports, 1st September, that John and Donald "have attended the Grammar School of Old Aberdeen for the space of three years and ten months. Their attendance has upon the whole been sufficiently regular; but their application has by no means been such as to ensure success in the study of the Latin language; consequently they are both very deficient. I cannot say that there is much difference between them, but on the whole I think Donald the better scholar. Neither the one nor the other appears to have any 'extraordinary genius for letters.'" To be sent home to their parents.

1832. John and Donald wish to follow some liberal profession, but this is not sanctioned. The former is apprenticed to Mr Rennie, shipbuilder; the latter to Mr Simpson, wright.

Mr Alexander Macrae, only surviving son of late Captain Duncan, authorises payment of the annuity to his mother (?stepmother).

1833. Admitted: Alexander, son of Finlay, Auchtertyre. Dies of smallpox; has not been vaccinated; this to be a *sine qua non* in future.

1834. Applications from John, son of Christopher, Drudaig; Donald, son of Finlay, Auchtertyre; Kenneth, son of John, Camuslunie; James, son of Donald, Kintail; the first is admitted, and is subsequently apprenticed to Mr William Henderson, builder.

1839. Applications from Colin, son of Christopher, Inchroe; Donald, son of Farquhar, Glenshiel; Donald, son of Finlay, Lochalsh; Donald, son of Farquhar, Glenshiel: the second is admitted, subsequently apprenticed to Messrs Blaikie & Son.

1843. Finlay Macrae admitted, subsequently apprenticed to Mr Cook, tailor.

1847. In this year the trustees authorised their agent, Mr James Nicol, advocate, to uplift the funds from the Northern Investment Company, in whose hands they then lay, and to lend them on heritable security, which he reported had been found. The money, however, Mr Nicol retained in his own hands unsecured, and in 1850 his firm, Nicol & Munro, became bankrupt.

Mr Alexander Anderson, advocate, who was appointed judicial factor on the Macra Trust, was able to recover £419 14s 3d from the sequestrated estate, and £1246 19s 1d from the Macra Trustees, who were held to have been guilty of gross negligence. In 1862 he reported that the fund had now been restored to its original amount of £1666 13s 4d; and a body of trustees was constituted *de novo :* those accepting office being the Principal, the Professor of Divinity, the Senior Minister, the Senior Baillie, the Dean of Guild, and the Deacon Convener.

During the succeeding twenty-six years a considerable number of applications were received by the Macra Trustees, accompanied usually by proofs of descent from Alexander Macra of Inverinet ; but of those admitted to the benefits of the Fund, no one seems to have proved himself worthy of a University education. Under the scheme of administration of the Aberdeen Educational Trust, dated 17th November, 1888, two bursaries at the Grammar School "shall be known by the name of the Macra bursaries, and these two bursaries shall be awarded to any candidates properly qualified in the opinion of the Governors to avail themselves of the education given at the Grammar School of Aberdeen, who shall satisfy the Governors that they are of the lineal descendants of Alexander Macra of Inverinet, the great grandfather of the said Alexander Macra, ironmonger, Bristol."

On the death of Mr Alexander Macra, Demerara, son of Captain Duncan, the right to the perpetual annuity seems to have passed to Dr John Macrae, H.E.I.C.S.,[1] son of Dr John Macrae, younger brother of Captain Duncan ; but no payments were ever made to him. On his death in 1864, a claim was put forward by John Anthony Macrae, W.S., son of Colin, younger brother of Dr John, senior. On 31st March, 1865, the Trustees having considered the proofs advanced by him, find that he "is now the heir male lineally descended from the testator's said great grandfather." On 1st October, 1868, Colin George Macrae, W.S., was served heir to his father, John Anthony ; and he now represents the family.

[1] Page 103.

APPENDIX M.

INVERNESS, 20th November, 1721.   In presence of Master Robert Gordon of Haughs, Sheriff-Depute of Inverness,

Compeared Donald McRae, soldier in the Royal Regiment of North British Fusiliers, who, being solemnly sworn in a precognition, maketh oath that he was of the detachment of His Majesty's Forces, appointed to attend the Factors on the Forfeited Estates, when the insult and murder was committed on the saide Forces and Factors at Loch Affrick, upon the Second day of October last by several Bodies of Highlanders, and that he knew and seed the persons following amongst the saide Bodies of Highlanders, viz. :—

Donald Murchison, Chamberland to the late Earl of Seaforth.

Donald Murchison of Auchtertyre.

John McRae of Inverinat.

John Dow McAlister Vic Gilchrist, in Achyark.

Christopher, Ferquhar and Murdo McRaes, sons to Christopher McRae, in Arivugan.

Don McRae in Glensheil, nephew to the said Christopher.

John McUrchie Vic Alister Vic Vinister, in Killelan.

John McFinlay Vic Ean, in Killelan.

Duncan McEan Vic Conchie, in Killelan.

Alexander McEan Vic Conchy, in Killelan.

John McEan Vic Conchy, in Killelan.

John McEan Vic Conchy Vic Alister, in Glenelchak.

John Dow McAlister Vic Gilchrist, in Achayouran of Glensheall.

Donald McAlister Vic Gilchrist, in Achyouran-begg.

[1] Page 358.   See also paper on "Donald Murchison and the Factors on the Forfeited Estates," by Mr William Mackay, published in "The Transactions of the Gaelic Society of Inverness," Vol. XIX.

Alexander McConchy Vic Gilchrist, in Rategan of Glensheal.

Alexander McRae, son to Master Donald McRae, minister of Kintail.

John McRae, son to Alexander McFerquhar Vic Rae, in Morvich.

John McKenzie, in Inverinat, son to Kenneth Roy, brother to the late Aplecross.

Ferquhar Oig McFerquhar Vic Alister, in Inversheile.

Murdo McFerquhar Vic Alister, in Croe of Kintail.

Alexander McFerquhar Vic Alister, in Morvich, in Croe of Kintail.

John McRae Vic Vinister, in Letterfearn.

John McRae, eldest son to Donald McRae of Driudaig, living in Letterfearn.

Murdo McAlister Vic Vinister, in Camboslynie.

Alexander McAlister Vic Vinister, in Glenelchak.

Alexander McHuistan Vic Rae, in Meikle Salachy of Lochalsh, nephew to Aryvogan.

Donald Oig McLennan, in Achnafearn of Lochalsh.

Murdo McRae, in Coriloyne of Glenloyne.

John McRae, son to the said Murdoch McRae, in Coriloyne of Glenloyne.

Ferquhar McConchy Voir Nakaime, in Glenloyne.

Alexander McHutchan Vic Rae, in Sallachy More.

Duncan McHutchan Vic Rae, in Sallachy More.

John Dow McLennan, in Achnaguiran.

Colline McEan Vic Iver, in Inversheal.

Murdo McEan Vic Iver, in Inversheal.

Duncan McConchy Vic Gilchrist, in Islandonanbeg.

Evander Murchison, son to John Murchison McEan Vic Conil, in Achnabein.

Donald Roy, son to the ground officer of Glenmoriston.

John McAlister Vic Rae, in Cambouslyne of Glenelchak, one of the baggage men to the Rebells.

Donald McRae further maketh oath that the said John McAlister Vic Rae, baggage man, and others of the party who conducted the troops and factors back through the wood, informed him that the persons following were amongst the committers of the said insult and murder, viz.:—

John Dow McAlister Vic Gilchrist, in Achyark.

Duncan McConchy Vic Charlich, in Sallachy More.

Alexander McFinlay Vic Ean, in Achnabein.

Duncan McAlister Vic Conchy Matheson, in Achrachen of Lochalsh.

Murdo McConchy Vic Ean, in Killelan.

Alexander McConchy Vic Vinister, in Aglachan of Lochalsh.

Christopher McFerquhar Oig, in Letterfearn.

Alexander McAlister Vic Gillichrist Vic Ferquhar Oig, in Mamaig
of Glenelchaig.

Alister McAlister Vic Gilchrist, in Kilaric.

John McEan Vic Conchy, in Ratigan.

Donald McAlister Vic Gilliechrist, in Achyark of Glensheal.

Donald Murchison, in Achachoraran, brother to the deceast
Achtertoir.

Murdo Murchison, brother to the deceast Achtertoir.

Alexander Murchison, brother to the deceast Achtertoir.

John McGilchrist McRae, in Comer of Strathglesh.

Christopher McEan Vic Conil Vic Vinister, in Conchraig of Cambouslyne.

Christopher McUrchie Vic Vinister, in Glenelchack.

Alexander and Mylies Murchison, sons to John Murchison McEan
Vic Conil, in Achnabein.

John McDonald Reach Vic Conchy Oig, in Meikle Salachie.

John Dow McEuan Gou, in Meikle Salachy.

John McLennan Vic Conchy Voi, in Mid Ausgett of Kintail.

Donald McEan Doi Brebater, in Mid Ausgett of Kintail.

Finlay McEan Doi Brebater, in Mid Ausgett of Kintail.

Duncan Mac Ean Glas, in Achnasou of Lochalsh.

Donald Matheson, in Conchra of Lochalsh.

Duncan Matheson, in Achnashew.

Donald McDonald Oig, in Ardinar.

Finlay McCoil Reach Vic Conchie Oig, in Letterwhile of Kintail.

Donald McRae furthur maketh oath that he seed Patrick Grant,
son to the late Glenmoriston, with the saids companies of Highlanders; all which he declares to be truth, as he shall answer to
God, and declares he cannot write; and further maketh oath that
he seed Kenneth McConchy Vic Alister, in Ratigan of Glensheall,
in company with the saids Highlanders.

ADDENDUM I.

——:o:——

The following version of the Gaelic poem given on page 388 was sent to the author by Mr William Mackay, Craigmonie, Inverness, but it was too late to be included in Appendix J. It was written down in 1877 by a well-known Gaelic scholar and poet, the late Mr Farquhar Macdonell, of Plockton, Lochalsh, and sent by him to the Rev. Alexander Stewart, LL.D., of Nether-Lochaber, by whom it was afterwards sent to Mr Mackay. According to Mr Macdonell, it was composed immediately after the burial of Murdoch Macrae in Kilduich. The author considers this the best, as it is also the most complete, of several versions of the same poem that he has come across :—

Deanam na marbhrainn s' as ur
Air miann suilean Chloinn 'ic Rath,
Air Murachadh donna-ghcal mo ruin
A bha lan do chliu gun chleith.

A dheagh mhic Alasdair uir,
Togamaid do chliu an tos,
Sud an laoch fo'n robh a' mhuirn,
'Shliochd Fhearachair nan cuirt 's nan corn.

Si sealg geamhraidh Ghlinne-lic
Chuir greann oirn gu tric 'us gruaim,
M' an og nach robh teann 's a bha glic,
Bhi 's an teampull fo'n lic 's an uaigh.

Chiad aoine de 'n gheamhradh fhuar,
'S daor a phaigh sinn duais na scalg,
An t-og bo chraobhaiche snuagh
Na aonar bhuainn 'us fhaotainn marbh.

Tional na sgire gu leir
A suibhal sleibh 's a falbh bheann,
Fad sgios nan coig latha deug,
'S am fear dilcas, treun air chall.

'S turseach do chinneadh mor deas,
Ga d' shireadh an ear 's an iar,
'S an t-og a b' ionmholta beachd
Ri slios glinne marbh 's an t-sliabh.

Clann 'ic Rath nam builtean bo
Air an siarradh gu mor mu d'eug,
Mu d' thoirt as a bheatha so oirn,
Mhic athair nan corn 's nan teud.

'S turseach do dheas bhraithrean graidh
'S am *parson* ge h-ard a leugh,
Thug e, ge tuigseach a cheaird,
Barr tuirse air cach gu leir.

Air thus dhiubh Donnachadh nam Pios,
Gillecriosd 'us dithis na chleir,
Fearachar agus Ailean Donn
'S Uisdean a tha trom do dheigh.

Bu tusa an t-ochd shlat ghraidh
Dh'ios nam braithrean glana coir,
A' nochd gur dosgach an cradh,
Gu 'n fhroiseadh am blath dhiubh og.

Gur tursach do cheud bhean og,
'S fliuch frasach na deoir le gruaidh,
I 'spionadh a fuilt d' a deoin,
Sior chumha nach beo do shnuagh.

Bhean uasal a thug dhut gaol,
Nach bi chaoidh na h-uigneas slan,
'S truagh le mo chluasan a gaoir,
Luaithead 's a sgaoil an t-aog a snaim.

Bu tu 'n t-slat eibhinn, aluinn, ur,
Bu mhiann suil 's bu leanan mna,
A ghnuis an robh am breac seirc,
Bha cho deas air thapadh lamh.

Bu tu marbhaich' a bhalla-bhric bhain,
Le mordha 's le lan chrann geur,
'S le cuilbheir bhristeadh tu cnaimh,
'S bu shilteach 'o d' laimh na feidh.

Do chul buidh' fainneach ri lic,
Bha ruthaidh, 's e gle gheal, dearg,
'Ghnuis an robh 'n gliocas gun cheilg,
Air nach d'fhiosraicheadh riamh fearg.

Chuala mise clarsach theud,
Fiodhall 'us beus a cu-sheinn,

'S cha chuala, 's cha chluinn gu brath,
Ceol a b'fhearr na do bheul binn.

'S math am fear rannsachaidh 'n t-aog,
Gur maor e dh'iarras gu mean,
Bheir e leis an t-og gun ghiamh,
'S fagaidh e fear liath bhios sean.

Bha thu fearail anns gach ceum,
Bu bharant thu 'n deirce bhochd,
'S tha thu air deas laimh do Righ,
Le lughad 's chuir thu 'm pris an t-olc.

Tha sluagh taght' aig deagh Mhac Dhe,
Gun easbhuidh, gun fheum air ni,
'S tha thus' a nis 'an aoibhneas mor,
'An cathair cheoil aig Righ nam righ.

ADDENDUM II.

——:o:——

Page 109.—Surgeon-General Sir William Alexander Mackinnon died in London on the 28th of October, 1897.

Page 141.—Captain Archibald Macra Chisholm of Glassburn died on the 19th of October, 1897.

Page 158.—Colin Macrae, Camden, South Carolina, lineal representative of the Macraes of Conchra, died on the 20th of September, 1898. He was succeeded as representative of that family by his brother,

Duncan Macrae of Kames Castle, who died on the 14th of December, 1898, and was buried on the 21st at Kilduich, his clansmen in Kintail making his funeral the occasion for a remarkable display of clan sentiment and loyalty. His eldest son,

Stewart Macrae (page 158), of Newark-on-Trent, is now lineal representative of the Macraes of Conchra.

Page 281.—In addition to the marriage of Alexander Macrae and Agnes Gordon, there appears also to be some record of a marriage, about the same time, between a William Macrae and a Thomasine Gordon of Carleton. It is not impossible, however, that a confusion of names may have occurred with regard to one and the same marriage.

ERRATA.

——:o:——

Page	67	-	line	2	-	-	Comma after property.
„	67	-	„	22	-	-	Read has.
„	69	-	„	1	-	-	„ VIII.
„	84	-	„	17	-	-	„ untimely.
„	87	-	„	25 (last)	-		„ farther.
„	193	-	„	1 of footnote 2			„ Ghobha.
„	269	-	„	2	„	2	„ Loudon.
„	282	-	„	8	„	2	„ Herdman.
„	283	-	„	7	-	-	„ Dunnay.
„	284	-	„	19	-	-	„ Georgiana.
„	335	-	„	12	-	-	„ Mantuanus.
„	383	-	„	8	-	-	„ Mr William Mackenzie.

Map.—Achyark, inadvertently left out in preparation of block for map, is at the foot of Glenlic.

MAP OF THE

MACRAE COUNTRY

Statute Miles

G. Philip & Son, 32 Fleet St. London.

INDEX.

——:o:——

MS. NOTES AND ADDITIONS.

www.ingramcontent.com/pod-product-compliance
Lightning Source LLC
Chambersburg PA
CBHW052332110726
47901CB00005B/1217